D1111657

The Dark Sword series

"Grant creates a vivid picture of Britain centuries after the Celts and Druids tried to expel the Romans, deftly merging magic and history. The result is a wonderfully dark, delightfully well-written [series]. Readers will eagerly await the next Dark Sword book."　　　　*—RT Book Reviews*

"Another fantastic series that melds the paranormal with the historical life of the Scottish highlander in this arousing and exciting adventure."　　　　*—Bitten By Books*

"These are some of the hottest brothers around in paranormal fiction."　　　　*—Nocturne Romance Reads*

"Will keep readers spellbound."　　　*—Romance Reviews Today*

IGNITE

DONNA GRANT

St. Martin's Paperbacks

This is a work of fiction. All of the characters, organizations, and events portrayed in this novel are either products of the author's imagination or are used fictitiously.

IGNITE

Copyright © 2019 by Donna Grant.

For information address St. Martin's Press, 175 Fifth Avenue, New York, NY 10010.

ISBN: 978-1-250-18289-0

Our books may be purchased in bulk for promotional, educational, or business use. Please contact the Macmillan Corporate and Premium Sales Department at 1-800-221-7945, ext. 5442, or by email at MacmillanSpecialMarkets@macmillan.com.

Printed in the United States of America

St. Martin's Paperbacks edition / April 2019

St. Martin's Paperbacks are published by St. Martin's Press, 175 Fifth Avenue, New York, NY 10010.

10 9 8 7 6 5 4 3 2 1

To Jillian S

There's always laughter and fun
whenever you're around.
Can't wait to see what kind of
trouble we get into next.

ACKNOWLEDGMENTS

A special shout out to everyone at SMP for getting this book ready, including the amazing art department for such a stunning cover that matches the character to perfection. Much thanks and appreciation goes to my exceptional editor, Monique Patterson, as well as her assistant, Mara.

To my amazing agent, Natanya Wheeler who is on this dragon train with me.

A special thanks to my children, Gillian and Connor, as well as my family for the never-ending support. And to G. You know why.

Hats off to my incredible readers and those in the DG Groupies Facebook group for keeping the love of the Dragon Kings alive. Words can't say how much I adore y'all.

(MIS)ADVENTURES OF A DATING FAILURE BLOG

My Options Suck

Dating sucks.

Being alone sucks.

What is a woman to do when all options . . . well, suck the big one? That's what I've been asking myself for some time now. I don't think I can handle even one more horrid date.

Just when I think they can't get any worse, Fate is standing behind me, waiting to prove how wrong I am. Which happens to be every time I go out lately.

Let me break it down for you, my readers.

I'm on five dating sites. (Honestly, I think I lost my mind for an hour or two because, FIVE? Really?)

Out of those five, two are what I consider real sites that try to match you with someone other than just a hookup.

Now, I can hear all of you asking, "Then why are you on the others? Do you want a hookup?"

The answer to that question is a resounding NO. I'm on those other sites because I have friends who have actually found their current

significant others on them. They weren't looking
for hookups, and neither were the people they went
out with.

I think there are just so many instant gratification
factors out there. Not to mention, people want to
find someone they're compatible with. So, they'll
try anything.

Hence my being on five ::shaking my head::
dating sites.

Not to sound conceited, but I don't have an issue
getting noticed by men. Let's be frank, if you're on
these sites, you have to know how to work a picture.
And use filters. We all want to put our best foot
forward, especially when the people we're trying
to attract are basing their interest on pictures first.
If you can't get them to notice you there, then
you're in big trouble.

I despise taking selfies (I even hate saying the
word). ::insert massive eye roll here:: But I do have
a few of them. Mostly, I get my BFF to snap pictures
of me so they don't look posed. And then I filter
the hell out of them.

I used to think getting all the attention was what
I needed from men. It's only taken me three years
to figure out that I was dead wrong.

For those who have been on these sites, we've
all gotten the unsolicited dick pic. (Seriously, guys.
WTF?) I've even received them from men I would
have bet money wouldn't do such a thing. So,
pictures and bios can be deceiving. As I discovered
the hard way.

Needless to say, I used to consider the number
of men asking me out from these sites as a success.
I admit, I was so desperate to find The One that I

went out with just about anyone who could type a text with proper punctuation and spelling.

The fact this blog does so well tells you how abysmal those dates were. Are.

::sigh::

Yes. <u>Are</u>.

I thought I had finally developed an approach to weed out men who weren't my match—despite what the dating site algorithms might say.

I'm going to stop for a second to tell you that I'm really good at my day job. Really good. And I love it. Why I can't take the same energy and use it for dating is beyond me, but that's the rub of it.

So, here I am, moving from the initial wink, smile, wave or whatever it is that a particular site uses for potential couples to greet each other, to having a conversation with a man through the site. Then, one of us, after a day or two, gives our phone number so the communication can move to our mobile devices.

It's the next step. During all of this, we're asking each other questions, seeing if we have anything in common, and just making sure the other person isn't a complete psycho.

(It's happened. So, all of you who just chuckled at that comment, just wait. It'll happen to you, too. Be prepared!)

If we've moved on to exchanging numbers, then obviously we each believe there's a potential connection possible—at least we hope there is. By this time, we've talked about wanting to meet the other. I usually ask for an actual phone call at this point, but I've recently moved beyond that to FaceTiming.

I truly believed that this would be my way of sorting through those that might look good through text and in pictures but just not live up to that in real life. Because, let's be honest, IRL matters, people.

A lot.

Out of the five sites, along with my new approach, I had six dates over the last two weeks.

Hold on, all of you who are freaking out at that number. Understand that if I had clicked with any of these men, I would have cancelled any other date. I'm a one-man woman. My mother taught me to share, but not when it comes to my men. :D

My expectations for these dates have severely diminished over the years. (Gah! Years. Years!!!)

::headdesk::

However, I do get excited because if I don't have any enthusiasm to meet a man, then why in the world would I agree to a date in the first place?

Because I've been at this for so long, I like to keep track of what has worked and what hasn't. The entire point is that I don't want to spend my life alone. It just makes good sense to take notes.

I won't tell you how many dates I've been on in the last year because even I am shocked by the number. When I counted, it was a good thing I was sitting down and had already drunk half a glass of wine. Otherwise, I might have fainted.

What I will tell you is that out of those dates, less than half resulted in second dates. And less than a third of those became third dates.

And there were no fourth dates.

::loud sigh::

I'm constantly meeting new men, so I'm begin-

ning to think that I need to write a book on how to put nerves aside the first time you meet up with someone. Not sure anyone would buy it since I've obviously failed at securing a boyfriend.

Then again, it's not all my fault. There are two people on a date, so I'll only take half the responsibility.

The thing is, seeing the actual numbers for the last year was . . . disheartening. In this day and age, it seems the only way to meet someone is through the dating sites. However, I'm beginning to believe that it's just not going to work for me.

I think I'm going to be that spinster cat lady who all the kids play pranks on. And while that used to terrify me, my pathetic and ineffectual hunt for The One has shown me something.

I'm okay on my own. It's not what I'd like or even what I'd hoped for, but there are worse things. I like my own company. I'm not one of those who can't survive without having a significant other (and I've run across plenty of men like that, so it isn't just women). I can go to the movies on my own. I can even go out to eat on my own.

To all those out there searching—or maybe just waiting and hoping—to meet your One, keep your heart open. As for me, I'm going to go on one last date tonight before I shut down all the dating sites and give myself a little break.

Never fear, I've got a ton more stories that I've not written about, so I won't disappear anytime soon.

Until next time!

CHAPTER ONE

Dreagan
April

Things weren't going well, and they didn't look to be improving anytime soon.

V wearily ran a hand down his face. All he wanted was to go to his mountain and figure out why his sword wouldn't work. But he couldn't. If he did, every Dragon King at Dreagan would know that something was wrong.

Eons after having his sword stolen and then hidden from him, it was now back in his possession. But it did no good. And every King was counting on him to use it in order to check on the dragons.

He paced his room inside the manor, wondering if it was somehow his fault that his weapon wouldn't respond to him anymore. Had he done something to . . . ? That couldn't be it. The blade was his, part of him. All Dragon Kings had a sword that only they could use.

So, if it wasn't him, then what was it? What kept him from being able to use his blade to check on the dragons? Ever since the Kings forced the dragons to leave during the war with the humans, they'd had no idea if their clans were alive or not. The Kings didn't even know where the dragons were.

The dragon bridge was a manifestation of the combined magic of all the Kings, and it was the one and only time they had ever used such a thing.

V couldn't stay in his chamber any longer. He stalked from his room and made his way downstairs. As he walked across the vast expanse of Dreagan—staying far from the Visitor's Center at the distillery where people lined up to take tours—he was glad he didn't run into any of his brethren.

Only Cináed knew about his conundrum. If this continued, V would have no choice but to tell the rest of the Kings. After everything he and Roman had gone through in Iceland just to find his stolen sword, it wasn't right that he couldn't make it work properly.

V kept walking. He didn't care where he went. He just needed to burn off some of the anger and anxiety that churned within him like a raging storm. His first choice would be shifting into his true form and taking to the skies, but that wasn't something they could do during the day. The fact that they were hiding from the humans prevented it.

V could use his power. Every Dragon King was granted a special type of magic. For him, it was disguising his dragon form when he shifted. He was so tempted to do that, but he didn't. It wouldn't be fair for him to take to the skies while the others could not.

He had no idea how much time had passed before he found himself walking along a paved road. V paused and looked up to get his bearings. He was no longer on Dreagan, and with their land encompassing sixty thousand acres, that meant he had walked quite a ways.

V heard the roar of an approaching engine. He grimaced when he recognized the unmistakable sound of the Maserati GranTurismo MC Stradale that belonged to none other than Constantine, King of Dragon Kings.

V watched as the bright blue sports car came into view. And just as expected, Con slowed when he spotted V. The Dragon Kings were the most powerful beings of the realm, but even they had someone to answer to. That someone for V was Constantine.

Con rolled down his window, his black eyes locking on V's face. He was attired in his usual—a suit, starched shirt, gold dragon head cufflinks, and no tie. "Everything all right?" he asked.

V nodded. "Just walking."

A blond brow shot up on Con's forehead. "Toward the village?"

"I needed to stretch my legs."

"And you couldn't do that on Dreagan? Or was it that you didn't want to run into any Kings?"

V blew out a breath and looked over the top of the car to the opposite side of the road where some sheep grazed on the steep hill.

"I see," Con said after a moment. "You know you can talk to me about whatever is troubling you."

"I know." V met Con's black gaze. "I just need some time. Finally having my sword back after so many millions of years without it is taking some getting used to."

Con blinked, his expression devoid of any emotion, but V knew him well enough to know that Con was trying to discover what V hid. It was one of the many reasons Con was King of Kings.

"You know where to find me," Con replied.

V gave a nod. Con stared at him a moment longer before he drove off. The last thing anyone at Dreagan needed was the knowledge that something was wrong with V's sword. With all he and Roman had discovered in the mountain on Iceland regarding the Others, there was much the Kings had to do.

The Others.

The mere thought of them made V want to retaliate. The mysterious group was a mix of good and evil Druids, as well as Dark and Light Fae. Why such an alliance would form still confused the Kings.

Worse, the Others seemed to be after the Dragon Kings. And they had waited thousands of years before taking action. Though no one knew why the Others had been so patient.

Or what they were after.

V waited until he saw the taillights of Con's car disappear over a hill before he turned and resumed his walk. He couldn't think about the Others right now. He had to focus on his sword. Yet, the two were connected.

It was the Others who initially tried to get his sword. Fortunately, a group of humans that V had once protected discovered the Others' plan and used their skills to steal the weapon from V and hide it before the Others could lay claim to it.

V wished the gypsies would have shared their plan, but he knew he wouldn't have listened to them even if they had tried. He would've told them that he could take care of things himself. The truth, however, was that he would've underestimated the Others. The gypsies had not.

The Others spelled V so he lost his memories about when and how his sword had been stolen. But he remembered now. His memories gave him little insight into the group, however. What they did show him was the lengths that some mortals would go to in order to help the Dragon Kings.

That was in direct opposition to what the majority of humans had done to the Kings in the past, the transgressions which began the war between them. V still couldn't believe that the Dragon Kings—the strongest, greatest beings in the realm—had given up *everything*.

That was a road V didn't need to wander down. His mind returned to the Others. Despite the gypsies' attempt, the Others found the man who had taken V's sword. The gypsies made sure that the Others couldn't touch it, but the nefarious group put other traps in place throughout the mountain in Iceland to hinder anyone's attempts to retrieve the weapon.

It was with great difficulty and the help of friends that V and Roman were able to escape the mountain, not only with their lives but also with the sword.

This wasn't the first time the Others had set traps and deceptions for the Kings. Perhaps it was because of the tricks the Others used that V was apprehensive. First, it had been the wooden dragon carved as a replica of Con. One touch, and the figurine caused chaos to erupt.

Then there was the incident in New York with the black dagger and a fellow King, Dorian.

And now this.

At least, those were the only ones V knew of. There could be more. That in itself made his worry double.

It had taken all of V's considerable magic and strength to bust through the spells woven through his memories from the Others. For millions of years, V hadn't known that anyone touched his mind. But now, he knew what to look for.

His mind was clean of any enchantment from the Others, but he hadn't checked his sword yet. In fact, he hadn't held it since attempting to use it after returning to Dreagan.

For eons, he'd lived with the knowledge that he'd failed as a King because mortals had stolen his sword. While he now knew the truth, it didn't help him feel any better.

He was a Dragon King. No one should have been able to get to him through magic. No one. But they did.

With tragic results.

If he'd kept a hold of his sword, he could have checked on the dragons several times. And called them home.

V looked up and found himself standing in front of the medical clinic. Sophie, who was mated to another King, Darius, ran it. Many of the Kings hadn't been sure how Sophie could continue to work as a doctor and keep the secrets of Dreagan, but so far, she'd done admirably.

She wouldn't be able to do that forever, though. As a mate, she was given the gift of immortality. Sophie had a few more years before others started to notice that she didn't age. Then, she would have to close the practice for a few generations before she could open it up once more.

V's gaze swung to the parking lot as he heard the squeal of tires and a white Mini with black racing stripes pulled to a stop. He sidestepped to conceal himself behind a tree and watched as Claire got out of her car. V couldn't understand how she drove so fast and didn't worry about getting killed. He gave her credit for being an expert driver, but mortals only had one life. He really wished she would slow down.

Her blond locks were haphazardly pulled back into what he had heard Sophie call a messy bun—whatever that was. He didn't care what it was called. He just knew that he liked it on Claire. He liked it more when she left her locks free to fall down her back.

She was always changing her look. Some days, she had on vivid makeup with her long hair styled in various ways. Other days, she wore very little makeup and had a messy bun.

He liked it all.

The few times he'd happened to be near when Claire

arrived at the clinic, she made her way into the office singing whatever had been blaring on her car radio. But today, she was subdued. Her oval face was pensive as if she were deep in thought.

She adjusted the big, black bag she carried on her shoulder before she pulled out her mobile. The moment she looked at the screen, she stopped. A second later, a smile broke out over her face.

V found himself grinning in response because her smile—even when not directed at him—was infectious. He didn't know what it was about the blond beauty that had first captured his attention, but it hadn't let go since.

His vantage point gave him a perfect view of her face. Whatever was on the phone lit up her expression. He'd seen the mated Kings do that to their women. V wondered if he would ever cause someone to smile like that.

The majority of his life after the war with the humans had been spent sleeping in his mountain. He hadn't had time to think about anything more than reclaiming his stolen sword. Now . . . now, those who had something to occupy their time with regards to Dreagan were all around him.

Then there were those who had found love.

It was difficult to be around so many who were happy. Those like Vaughn, a solicitor for Dreagan, who had found his place in the human world. Then there were the pairs who were always together, always sharing secret words and looks. And touches.

The weight of eons of time spent alone crushed V. He'd thought sex would help. And it had. For a short while. Then, that haunting ache filled his chest again.

He wasn't stupid. He knew exactly what it was. Loneliness. He was surrounded by his brethren but felt utterly, completely alone.

V drew in a deep breath and watched Claire's pace quicken as she hurried into the clinic. He shifted around the tree to continue observing her, catching one last look before she walked through the door and disappeared into the building.

He'd spent a lot of time at the clinic lately, helping out when it was needed. Most of the Kings did from time to time. Sophie was part of the family, and as such, they were always there for whatever she needed.

Not that Darius couldn't handle things himself, but sometimes, it was just an excuse for them to be together. Just as everyone not only went to Laith's pub but also helped out there. The Dragon King had owned the pub for hundreds of years, legally passing it down to himself after disappearing for decades at a time.

Who knew how long such things would work. The people of the village near Dreagan seemed happy. Then again, so had the mortals before the war.

"She's pretty, is she no'?"

V closed his eyes at the sound of Darius's voice. He should've heard the King approach, and he would have, had he not been so engrossed in Claire.

He opened his eyes and turned to face his friend. He could try to lie, but there was no point. "Aye. She certainly is."

"Sophie and Claire are verra close," Darius stated.

V quirked a brow. "I'm aware of that."

"I know you've picked up Rhys's habits of a different woman every night—"

V was affronted by the charge. "It's no' every night."

"Somehow, despite everything that happened to her and Sophie in Edinburgh, Claire doesna know about us."

V crossed his arms over his chest. He didn't know the entire story about how Claire and Sophie had been taken by the Dark Fae, but he knew that it had been a close call for both women. "Are you sure she doesna?"

Darius glanced at the building. "She would've said something to Sophie if she did. You're welcome at the clinic anytime, but Claire is like a sister to Sophie."

"You want me to keep away from her." Somehow, that hurt V more than he'd expected.

"If you think she could be your mate, then I'll no' stand in your way."

"I didna say that."

Darius nodded slowly. "I just doona want Claire hurt."

V squared his shoulders. "I'm well aware that she is off-limits."

Darius gave a nod of appreciation. "Thank you. Since you're here, I could really use your help moving some more boxes. I never knew so much was needed to run a medical clinic."

V was slow to follow Darius. While he understood his friend's caution, he was nonetheless hurt by it. More than that, he wondered about the lie he'd told regarding Claire. And the consequences of not admitting what he'd known in his heart for some time now.

CHAPTER TWO

"I don't like him."

Claire grinned at Sophie's statement. The two had been friends for many years and had been through a lot together, which is why she wasn't taken aback by Sophie's blunt statement. "I know."

"He didn't text you at all yesterday. Not once."

Claire looked into Sophie's olive eyes and nodded. "I know. I'm the one who told you."

Sophie blew out a breath as she jammed a file into the hanging folder and shoved the cabinet drawer closed. She came to Claire's desk and stood before it, her golden hair in a loose braid. "I'm sorry. I don't mean to sound so harsh. I just want better for you."

"I like Calvin. He just . . . he's busy."

Sophie gave her a flat look. "You're making excuses for him. Did he even tell you why he didn't reply to your text yesterday?"

"No."

"Are you going to ask him?"

Claire threw up her hands. "We haven't been seeing

each other that long. Honestly, I don't even know what we are."

"Because you won't ask him."

"I . . ." Claire stopped and shook her head, hating that her friend was right. "No, I won't ask him. It's not easy."

"Sure, it is. You send a text that says, 'Hey, Calvin. We've been talking for a bit, and while neither of us has said anything, I was wondering if we're exclusive or not.' Easy."

"Not for me."

"Want me to send it?" Sophie volunteered, holding out her hand for the mobile phone.

It was on the tip of Claire's tongue to take her friend up on the offer. But she was an adult. She'd had relationships. She was also a take-charge kind of woman, so why, *why*, did she get insecure and neurotic when it came to men?

Because she didn't want to do anything to upset them.

And how fucking wrong was that?

"You're doing that internal dialogue thing again," Sophie said with a twist of her lips. "Care to share?"

"So you can hear for yourself that you're right? Like always? No thanks."

"That reminds me. Did you read the last entry on the *(Mis)Adventures of a Dating Failure* blog? She has some great advice. You should read it."

Claire nodded. "I meant to read it last night, but I forgot."

When Claire tried to walk away, Sophie stepped in front of her. "I want you to have what I have. I want you to find someone who will move the very earth itself to be with you."

"I want that, too. But I hate to tell you this, I think you

got one of the last of those. I don't think men like that really exist. At least not the ones I meet."

"Claire—"

"Don't feel sorry for me. You're right about Calvin. We've been texting for a month now and saw each other three times. Both of our profiles said that we only dated exclusively, which is why I never actually asked him. But he didn't ask me either."

Claire paused and swallowed. "I hate that when I didn't hear from him last night, I lay in bed crying, wondering what *I* had done wrong."

"You?" Sophie gasped in outrage.

"I know, I know," Claire hurriedly said, lifting her hands to calm her friend. "It's stupid. He could have been doing any number of things. I'm not saying he was out with someone else, but the simple truth is, he could have taken two seconds out of his day to reply to my text. The fact he didn't. . . . Well, it kinda says it all, doesn't it?"

Sophie shrugged. "Maybe he's in the hospital. Maybe he got sick. Maybe his day was just so busy that he. . . . Nope. That one doesn't work. You've told me yourself how much he's on his phone."

"Yeah." As if Claire needed another reason to believe that Calvin hadn't texted because he simply didn't want to. That's what it boiled down to.

And it hurt.

Then men wonder why women are so anxious and irrational during dating. They're trying to figure out every move a man makes so they don't misstep, but inevitably, it happens.

"Just ask him why he didn't text," Sophie suggested.

Claire jerked back. "And sound like some clingy woman needing to know where he is every minute? No thanks."

"He's hours away from you. The two of you don't even

see each other once a week. It's not irrational to want to know why he didn't respond."

"Maybe to you, but not from where I'm sitting."

Sophie rolled her eyes as she shook her head. "You told me he has no problem asking you direct questions like that."

"That's different."

"How so?"

"Because I'm not the one doing the asking."

"Dear lord, Claire," Sophie said tightly, her irritation evident. "You'd clear up so much if you just asked."

Claire cocked out her hip and raised a brow at Sophie. "Oh, really? That's how you feel? Perhaps we should go back to when you and Darius first started seeing each other."

"That was different."

"The hell it is. Would you have come out and asked Darius these questions?"

Sophie parted her lips to reply, then shook her head. "Okay, okay. I see your point. It's not so easy when the shoe is on the other foot."

Despite her argument, Claire was upset that she hadn't come up with a viable solution to her problem. Her eyes still burned from the tears she'd shed the night before. And she hated herself for it.

"What did his text say this morning?" Sophie asked.

Claire almost hated to tell her. Mostly because she knew how her friend would react. "It just said 'good morning.'"

"That's it?" Sophie asked, her indignation evident in her voice and the shocked expression on her face. Then she smiled tightly. "Sorry. I meant to say that it was good you heard from him. Did you reply?"

"Of course. I told him the same."

"And?"

"Nothing."

"How long has it been?"

The sad part about it was that Claire knew the exact time Calvin had texted. She looked at her watch and said, "Twenty-four minutes."

"Give me your phone," Sophie demanded with her hand out.

Claire barked a laugh. "Why?"

"So you don't text him today."

Claire held up her wrist, showing Sophie her smartwatch. "I can still do it on this."

"Dammit," Sophie mumbled.

"Besides," Claire said, shifting her feet, "it's not during the day that's the hardest. It's at night. When I'm alone and thinking up all the different scenarios for why I haven't heard from him."

Sophie's lips flattened. "And you wonder why I don't like him."

"If I don't hear from him today, that's it. It's over."

"It's better to be alone than to have someone treat you like that."

Claire watched her friend walk away. "That's easy for you to say when you have someone who loves you," she whispered.

She turned when she heard the back door open. A moment later, the sound of Darius's voice reached her. She didn't want to be envious of her friend's love or the happiness Sophie had found, but it was hard not to be. Especially when it was the very thing Claire coveted with all her heart and soul.

So many freely gave advice for her to stop looking and let love find her. That was a load of horseshit. She had stopped, and nothing had happened. Nothing happened when she did look either. So what was the answer?

If there was one at all.

She was beginning to believe that the old saying that there was someone for everyone wasn't true. Maybe she was destined to live out her life alone. Sophie was right. It was better to be on her own than have someone twist her feelings as Calvin continued to do time and again.

Because this wasn't the first time he'd done this to her. There had been three in all. Sophie only knew about two of the events. The other, Claire would keep to herself, simply because it would just feed more wood to the fire her friend tended for Claire to get rid of Calvin.

She shook her head. She had to stop thinking about him. Otherwise, she wouldn't get anything done, and every appointment spot was filled at the clinic again today. As it had been from the first week Sophie had opened it.

Claire went to the back room to restock some supplies before the doors opened. Two steps in, she came to a halt when she spotted wide shoulders encased in a burgundy shirt. She didn't need to see the face to know it was V.

He was mysterious and quiet with a look that smoldered, but she liked that about him. V had a way about him that instantly put her at ease. He didn't come to the clinic as often as some of the others, but she was always glad to see him when he did.

He yanked open a box, his back muscles moving under his tight shirt. Claire's mouth went dry as she stared at the perfectly formed V his body made from his shoulders to his narrow waist. She wondered if that's why his name was V.

His dark locks were long and swept back into a queue. Claire imagined running her fingers through his hair as he kissed her. Would he be a wild and fierce lover? One who dominated, but with a gentle side. The exact kind of man that made her knees week?

Suddenly, he stilled and turned his head to the side. "Claire?"

His voice was deep and rich. Seductive. She cleared her throat, thankful when her voice worked. "It's me."

He turned and faced her. Her gaze was instantly drawn to his unfathomable light blue eyes. His look was direct, but he obviously held a part of himself back. Almost as if he refused to allow anyone to know all of him.

"Are you all right?" he asked, a slight frown marring his gorgeous features.

She wanted to rub away the lines of concern on his forehead and then let her fingers run along his strong jawline before moving close to his wide lips. Then she'd sink her hands into his thick, dark locks.

Claire blinked and took a half-step back. What was wrong with her? She knew everyone at Dreagan was gorgeous, and she freely looked her fill at all of them—furtively, of course. Maybe it was her yo-yo emotions over the past several days that had her in such a state.

Or . . . Claire inwardly frowned as she realized that this was the first time she had been alone with V. There was no one else there to talk to or look at. No one else to distract her as she fell into his intense gaze.

Dimly, she remembered that he'd asked a question. What was it again? Oh. He wanted to know if she was okay. A few minutes ago, she would've said no, but now, she felt much better.

"Yes," she replied, her voice sounding hoarse. She cleared her throat again and spoke louder. "Yes, I'm good."

His look said he didn't believe her. "If anyone is bothering you, you do realize that those at Dreagan will take care of them."

Claire laughed softly, his words mending her tattered

feelings. "Thank you. I really needed to hear that this morning."

He nodded and rubbed a hand down his arm, bringing her attention to the hard muscle there. Unable to look away, she followed his hand from his arm as it moved to glide over the deep brown tresses of his hair, removing the strip of leather that held the strands in place.

Her lips parted as the silky tendrils slipped through his fingers. He'd cut the thick length. No longer did it fall down his back. The ends now brushed his shoulders.

The quiet suddenly reached her, and she realized he was watching her stare at him. Feeling like an utter fool, Claire grinned. "Sorry. I was just thinking about your hair. It looks good, but I liked it long."

"Did you? Everyone else said I needed to cut it."

"Do you always listen to them?"

He chuckled, the corners of his eyes crinkling charmingly. "Actually, no."

"But you did this time."

"Surprising, is it no'?" he asked with a grin.

"Not really. I usually always listen to Sophie."

V's smile widened. "She gives good advice?"

"Always, dammit," Claire said with a roll of her eyes and a chuckle. She loved listening to his accent. "Just don't tell her that."

"Your secret is safe with me."

And, oddly enough, she believed him. "How did they rope you into helping today?"

"I was nearby."

"With as much work as so many from Dreagan do here, we should add you all to the payroll."

He shook his head, still holding her gaze. "We're family. We help each other when it's needed."

"Sophie is lucky."

"You're part of that family, too," V told her.

The smile that wrought made Claire feel as if she were walking on clouds.

CHAPTER THREE

The time he spent at the clinic was refreshing. V declined Darius's offer to drive him back to Dreagan. Instead, he chose to walk once more.

His mind had been filled with other things for a short time. Beautiful things like golden hair, soft brown eyes, and a laugh that made him yearn to hear more.

But as soon as V was alone again, his thoughts returned to his sword and the problems he faced.

A growing fear filled him that his brethren would need his sword, and he wouldn't be able to help them. They needed to be prepared for such an event. V hated that he had to share such news with Con and the others, but keeping silent was putting everyone in jeopardy.

When V reached Dreagan, he made straight for the manor and his chamber. He grabbed his sword and started toward Con's office. Then he had another thought. V walked out of the mansion and headed for the Dragonwood. When he was within the confines of the forest, he opened the mental link that all dragons had and told Con to meet him.

V looked up at the sky, recalling a time when it had

been filled with dragons. A time when none of the Kings had to wait until dark or for a storm to fly among the clouds. When they could look down upon their domain while feeling the sunlight or moonlight anytime they wished.

The rays of the sun filtered through the dense foliage to fall upon V's face. It was nothing compared to the feel of the beams upon his scales. Of being free.

He lowered his head and let old memories come to the surface. Despite the passage of time, he still knew every peak and valley of his domain, the Carpathian Mountains. He knew where every cave was. And he knew the perfect summit to sit upon to watch the sunrise.

As good as those memories were, they were also dangerous. The Kings had worked tirelessly for countless millennia to remain hidden. If any of them—even just one—gave in to the memories and the need for the freedom they all dreamed of, it could unravel everything that had been put into place.

V tucked his memories away and opened his eyes. Only to find Constantine before him. The King of Kings stood as though he didn't have a care in the world, but one look into Con's black eyes showed his shrewdness, his intelligence, and the cunning many humans underestimated.

A soft breeze rushed by them, ruffling Con's wavy, blond hair. A lock fell into his eyes, but he didn't so much as move it away.

V gripped his sword tighter. "You were right earlier."

"Oh?" Con asked softly.

"I didna want to run into any Kings. Particularly you."

Con's gaze briefly lowered to the sword. "What did you no' want to tell me?"

"I can no' use it," V stated flatly.

There was a long stretch of silence. Then Con said, "Explain."

"There isna much to tell. I can no' see where our dragons are, which means, I couldna call them home even if I wanted."

A muscle ticked in Con's jaw, the only sign that he wasn't pleased. "Did the Others do something to your weapon?"

"No' that I can tell."

"And none of us can use your sword, so we can no' attempt to see if it's you or the weapon."

V twisted his lips. "Precisely."

"You've been grappling with this since your return from Iceland? Alone?"

V gave a nod of his head.

"We're here for each other. Did you no' realize that?"

"Do you share your concerns or worries with us?"

"No' all of them."

"Then doona expect the rest of us to," V snapped. He drew in a breath to gain control of his anger. "I doona know what the fuck is going on. I doona know if it's me, the sword, or something the Others did. All I know is that Roman and Sabina risked their lives to help me retrieve my weapon. And for nothing."

Con shook his head slowly. "It wasna for nothing. We discovered a lot of information about the Others."

V thought about the cave in Iceland and how his friends had come to help. Eilish had been able to read part of the Druid script. Then there was Rhi. The Light Fae was a true friend to the Kings. Because of her, they had been able to determine some of the Fae markings they found.

"Maybe we did get some knowledge that could be of use," V said. "I also reclaimed my sword, but was it worth it?"

A small frown furrowed Con's brow. "Do you finally have peace now that you know how your sword was stolen and why?"

"Aye."

"Then it was worth it. The Others knew how powerful your weapon was to us. Now that you have it in your possession again, you'll figure it out."

V looked down at the blade. He didn't know how to get the next part out. Mostly because he couldn't decipher the feelings within himself. All he knew was that he didn't belong there.

"There's more you want to say," Con said.

V raised his gaze. "I've spent more of my life asleep in my mountain than awake. I know why you made me sleep. I doona hold that against you. Things happened to the humans when I went looking for my sword, and you didna want to bring attention to us."

"I should have tried harder to help you find your blade."

"I doona think we would have found it even had we tried. The only reason we did this time was because of Sabina and her brother. Without them, we would still be searching."

Con put one hand in the pocket of his pants. "I took the easy road by forcing you to sleep."

"Forcing?" V repeated with a quirked brow. "I slept because I wanted to, no' because you told me to. Each time I woke, I truly believed it would be the time I found my sword. I thought having it returned would make everything better."

"But it hasna."

V swallowed and then shook his head. "I've been awake for months now. The longest since before we sent the dragons away. I doona like this world, Con. I doona belong here."

"You just need time."

"The ache within," V said, touching his chest, "will

only intensify. I thought it was the sword that was missing from my life. But I have it now, and the ache remains."

Con looked away while taking a deep breath. "You're going back to your mountain."

"I am."

"When?"

V wanted to head there immediately, but he couldn't. Not yet. "I'll wait until after Ulrik and Eilish's mating ceremony."

"Three weeks," Con said, his gaze sliding back to V.

"I doona want anyone else to know yet. I'll tell everyone when it's time."

Con bowed his head in agreement. "Of course. How many times have you tried to use the sword?"

"You think I lie?" V asked, affronted.

"No' at all. I'm merely asking."

Con never did anything without a reason. He always planned out every move. Well, except for one time in his life. Then Con had been reckless and uncontrolled—all because of love. The complete opposite of what he was now. But it hadn't lasted.

V lifted the tip of the sword until it was pointed at the sky. His dragon magic warmed his palm and heated the hilt of the weapon. To his surprise, there was a tingle of something that he hadn't felt in ages. It was so fleeting, he wondered if he'd imagined it.

He tried again, urging the sword to find the dragons. But whatever he'd felt or imagined, the sword didn't respond this time.

"Nothing," he said and lowered the weapon.

Con looked at the ground a moment. "You realize this may have nothing to do with you. Your sword may no' work because the dragons are no' there for you to find, much less call home."

"Nay," V stated vehemently. "I refuse to believe that."

"You know it, though. You've thought it. It's part of what troubles you."

Damn Con for being so perceptive. V hadn't allowed himself to think about that, but it was a driving force in him wanting to return to his mountain.

"We sent our clans away to save them from the humans." V shoved the blade of his sword into the ground. "We all hoped that they would find a place to live and thrive. The thought that. . . ."

"Do you know why I doona sleep?"

V's brows snapped together at the interruption. Con never volunteered information freely. "Why?"

"There are three things I relive each time I do. Watching the dragons cross the bridge to another realm, and banishing Ulrik."

V didn't need to ask what the third thing was. He knew who it involved and why. The fact that Con had even mentioned it was such a rarity that V decided it was best not to act as if he'd heard it.

"Ulrik is back now," V said.

Con lifted one shoulder. "My decision changed us and Ulrik. Aye, he's back, but I doona want to test my dreams to see if I'll be relieved of one torment. What I'm trying to tell you is that we all dream about the time before the humans came. We all have nightmares of sending the dragons away. And we all wish we could change the decisions we made. But looking to the past willna do us any good."

"The Others came at me sideways, Con."

"You can no' hold yourself responsible for any of that. You didna even know of them. None of us did." Con's eyes narrowed, and his lips lifted slightly at the corners as he took a step toward V. "But we do now."

V snorted. "Because they want us to."

"That's their mistake. They think to frighten us, but they doona know who they're messing with. We're Dragon Kings, V. We might have allowed the mortals their victory, but we willna do the same with the Others."

"I have no doubt we will win."

"It's going to take all of us."

V looked out over the forest. "You know I'll always fight with you against any enemy." He swung his eyes back to Con. "But you'll have to wake me to do it."

"There is nothing I can say to change your mind?"

V shook his head then pulled his sword from the earth and started back to the manor.

"Well, damn," Ulrik said as he walked into the clearing toward Con.

Con looked askance at him. "What are you doing here?"

"I was strolling through the forest."

"You don't stroll," Con said with an eye roll.

Ulrik continued as if he hadn't been interrupted. "Walking the Dragonwood was something I dreamt about when I was banished. I didna mean to eavesdrop."

Con snorted. "Aye, you did."

Ulrik chuckled softly. "You know me so well, old friend." But the smile died quickly. "I started to leave when I heard V say he wanted to return to his mountain."

"He's another mistake I made. If I hadna sent him to his mountain to sleep all those eons, he might no' feel as he does now."

"You did that because every time V woke, a catastrophe struck the humans. The Great Fire of Rome and the Black Plague, just to name a few. He gave you no choice."

Con sighed loudly. "I believed, just as he did, that all

he needed was his sword to heal whatever was missing in his life."

Ulrik shrugged. "It made sense to believe the weapon was the answer. It was stolen from him, and his memories wiped. I was in that cave in Iceland. The Others wanted to ensure the weapon could never be claimed by him again."

"He has it back. We won. It was simply a skirmish, but it's something."

Ulrik looked in the direction that V had taken to the house. "He's floundering. V needs something to focus on."

"He has his sword. He has us."

"You can be dense at times," Ulrik stated dryly.

Con raised a brow, staring at him silently for a few moments. "You want to throw a woman at him?"

"He's lonely. I know no' even you could fucking miss that when he was talking."

There was a beat of silence. Then Con said, "We're all lonely."

"You can change that anytime."

"The hell I can. And *you* know that."

Ulrik watched as Con spun on his heel and strode away, then he whispered, "Keep running from it, old friend. It's going to find you soon. Verra soon."

CHAPTER FOUR

Claire unlocked the back door of the clinic and walked inside, her eyes feeling as if sandpaper had been used on them. She made sure to lock up behind herself as she walked with one eye closed to her desk.

She sank onto her chair and dropped her head into her hands. The cup of coffee she'd drunk at her house had been enough to get her eyes open and her body moving, but it was going to take gallons of the caffeinated beverage to get her through the day.

Her fingers wrapped around the largest cup she could get at the café and brought it to her lips. She wasn't looking forward to the day for many reasons, most of all because she knew exactly how the conversation with Sophie would go.

It had been two days since Claire had made the decision to end it with Calvin. Partly because of everything Sophie had said, but also because she knew it was the right decision. Claire liked him, but not enough to continue on the roller coaster ride of emotions he put her through.

Actually, she knew it was her fault. She just wanted so much to find someone to spend her life with, that when she finally ran across someone who wasn't a total tosser, she gravitated toward them. Which is what she'd done with Calvin.

Two days ago, Calvin had texted her repeatedly. And he was the one making the conversation instead of the other way around. It was almost as if he knew she was about to end it. And just like usual, she'd let that sway her decision.

Then, yesterday she woke up to his morning text. Claire happily replied back, and they exchanged another few emails. It wasn't until she returned home and faced the silence of her house that she found herself reaching for her phone. She didn't want to spend the weekend alone. Before she could overthink it, she'd sent him a text, offering to come to the city for an extra-long weekend.

Claire kept herself busy with takeaway for dinner and some online shopping as she waited for his reply. The hours ticked by with no response.

To her chagrin, she ended up in tears again, wondering what it was about her that made it so she couldn't find a decent guy. She must have messed up really badly in a past life to get screwed in such a royal fashion in this one.

The tears, along with no sleep, had her barely able to keep her eyes open this morning. She probably should have taken the day off, but the thought of spending another minute alone in her house was too much. She would rather face whatever comments Sophie gave.

After several sips of coffee, Claire was able to sit back in her chair. She even cracked open her eyes. That's when she saw the note stuck to her monitor.

Don't forget I have the meeting in Inverness today.

Claire dropped her head back on her chair. She'd completely forgotten about the appointment. Sophie had even told her to take the day off. Claire had actually considered it for all of two seconds, but she'd decided she would rather be at the clinic catching up on the never-ending paperwork than at home.

At least she wouldn't have to put on a fake smile and pretend that everything was all right around patients. Claire didn't move from her reclining position as she finished her coffee.

Only after she'd drained the last drop did she sit up and turn on some music. She opted for something a little upbeat since she was still depressed. Love songs or anything slow would have her crying again, and she wanted to avoid that.

Claire searched through the large music library on her phone and decided on "When Will I Be Loved." The Linda Ronstadt song was just what she needed.

As soon as the first strings sounded, Claire started moving. She turned up the volume so it blared over the office speakers and began singing along. The song was the anthem of her love life.

She danced her way to the stack of files and picked up a handful before spinning over to the correct cabinet and pulling open a drawer.

Music had always been a way for Claire to express what she was feeling in the moment. Songs could pull her out of a bad mood or drop her into old memories. Today, she was counting on the playlist she'd selected making her forget all about Calvin and her wasted tears.

She was singing "Queen of Hearts" by Juice Newton at the top of her lungs when she turned and spotted V standing in the doorway, watching her. Claire froze as her eyes locked with ice blue ones. She didn't have a particularly good voice, so she didn't sing in front of others. Or dance.

And yet, the enigmatic man with the searing eyes had caught her doing both. There was no laughter upon his lips, making fun of her. If there had been, she might have sunk to the floor.

"I didna mean to interrupt," V said over the music.

Claire turned down the volume from her watch, her eyes sweeping over his mouthwatering form as she did. "I'm sorry you had to witness that."

"You were enjoying the music. There is something beautiful about getting lost in a song, regardless of what it is. And you were utterly lost in it."

Claire didn't have a response to that. Others enjoyed music, but no one seemed to understand her connection to it. She loved all music genres, preferring to take it all in instead of focusing on one kind.

V's brows drew together as he pushed from the wall and walked toward her. "Are you feeling all right?"

"Fine," she hastily replied.

"The redness of your eyes says otherwise."

She looked away, embarrassed that he saw the evidence of her bad night. A lie came to her. One that would explain away the redness, but that's not what she told him. Instead, she found herself speaking the truth.

"I didn't sleep last night."

He studied her a moment longer. "You were crying. Did someone hurt you?"

She actually found her lips softening at the anger in his voice. The knowledge that he was upset on her behalf did wonders to soothe her wounded pride. "It's nothing, really. Just a guy I've been casually seeing."

"Did he hurt you?" V asked again.

"Only by not returning my text. It's not the first time, and Sophie has told me to end it. I should've taken her advice a few days ago."

V raised a dark brow in confusion. "You decided to remain with him?"

"I don't even know if I am with him." She rolled her eyes and sighed. "It's just so damn complicated. Finding someone to spend the rest of your life with shouldn't be so hard."

"Nay," he said softly.

Claire cleared her throat as an idea came to her. "You know what? I'm going to do it now."

She felt his gaze on her as she went to her desk, found her purse, and dug out her mobile. When she looked up, V still watched her.

Claire opened the text string with Calvin. She spoke aloud as she typed. "I've enjoyed our time. . . . No. Delete that." She bit her lip and lifted her gaze to V.

"What do you really want to say to him?" he asked.

"To go bugger himself." She laughed as soon as she said it.

V smiled. "Tell him."

"I think I will."

"What else?"

She didn't have to think long to come up with an answer. "That if you're seeing someone, it's common damn courtesy to reply to their texts. Even if it's just to say that you can't answer because you're busy."

"Then do it," V urged.

Feeling more courageous and inspired, Claire did just that. Then she hit send before she could change her mind. She was smiling until she realized that a crucial part of the message hadn't been added. "Also, I don't think we should see each other anymore," she said as she typed.

Once that message was gone, she set her phone down and sighed.

"Feel better?" V asked.

"Much. Thank you for that."

"I didna do anything, lass."

She grinned as heat rushed over her. As a Scot herself, Claire had always hated when others called her lass. Or she had until V said it. Now, she wanted him to say it to her again and again and again.

Because in his deep and sexy voice, it was an endearment.

"You did," she insisted with a swallow.

V glanced to the side. "Darius said there were boxes that needed to be moved."

"There are?" she asked with a frown. "I thought they were all taken care of."

She turned and made her way to the back, all the while aware that he was behind her. She wondered if he was looking at her ass. Then she pondered how it looked. Sophie didn't require her to don scrubs, so Claire took full advantage of wearing jeans to work.

If only she'd worn the pair that everyone told her made her butt look really good. Then her thoughts shifted to the exercises she'd stopped doing to tone said derriere. Now, she wished she'd kept at them.

She inwardly sighed with relief when they finally reached the back, because she could focus her thoughts and not fall down a rabbit hole of stupidity about a man who probably didn't look twice at her.

"Oh," she said as she came to a stop in front of some boxes. "Where did these come from?"

V walked around her, inspecting the packages. "I doona know. I'm just here to move them."

"They don't look heavy. Normally, I move things like that."

"I doona mind doing it. Go back to your music. I'll take care of this."

She hesitated. "I don't even know what's in the boxes or where they should go."

"I do," V told her. "Darius left me detailed instructions. Apparently, I'm to rearrange this entire storeroom."

"Okay." She backed up a step. Claire wanted to stay with him, but she couldn't think of a reason to linger. But she didn't want to go. She wanted to remain right there with V, listening to him talk and enjoying how he made her feel. Though everything she felt was probably nothing more than a response to what Calvin had done to her. Or was it?

She'd never reacted to V like this before.

You've never been alone with him before a few days ago.

That was true. Normally, there were others around, and she and V had said very little to each other. But still . . . she had noticed him. Hell, she noticed every man from Dreagan. It was hard not to when they all looked good enough to lick.

But V stood out from the rest. She thought it was because of his eyes, but she was beginning to realize that it was more than that. It was the whole bloody package.

And it was a damn fine one. Great hair, a jawline she wanted to touch, muscles for days, and a voice that could melt the Arctic.

"I promise I willna screw anything up," V told her with a grin.

Claire could have kicked herself. She'd been caught staring again. She quickly smiled. "I apologize. I was lost in thought." *About you.*

"You can turn up your music as loud as you want."

"Is there a certain kind you don't like so I don't play it?"

He shrugged one shoulder. "I'll listen to anything."

She turned to leave when she recalled what he'd said

earlier. The fact that it just now registered told her how wrapped up in him she was. "You're rearranging this room?"

"Aye. Sophie ordered more shelves that'll be delivered later today. I'm making room for those."

"Um . . . okay." She was thoroughly confused. Sophie never did any of the ordering. Claire did. And Sophie had said nothing about new shelves.

V leaned an arm atop a stack of boxes. "If it will ease your mind, call Sophie."

"No need," she hurried to say. "I've been out of it for the last couple of days. Maybe she took pity on me and ordered them herself." Claire lifted her hands and backed up. "I'll just be in the other room filing that mountain of paper if you need anything."

She rolled her eyes at herself once she had her back to him. Stupid things seemed to just fall from her mouth whenever she wanted to say something witty. It was like her brain and mouth were wired wrong.

And all she could do was inwardly cringe at the outcome.

CHAPTER FIVE

Dreagan

"You sure it was a good idea?" Keltan asked as he walked into the room.

Ulrik kept his gaze directed out the window in the direction of the village. "How many times have we heard Sophie and Darius tell us how lonely Claire is? And we've both seen V lately."

"Aye, but. . . . I'm no' sure about this."

Ulrik looked over his shoulder at Keltan. "You were all for setting them up last night."

"Then I started thinking about how I'd feel if someone did that to me."

"You would mind?" Ulrik faced him.

Keltan narrowed his amber eyes. "Damn right, I would. I can get my own women."

"And so can V. I've seen that for myself. But there is a difference between having a woman in your bed and having one in your heart."

Keltan shook his head. "I doona understand all of you falling in love like you were bitten by some bug."

Ulrik chuckled. "Keep saying things like that, and you'll be next."

"The hell I will. I quite like things the way they are. I answer only to myself. And Con, when he needs me."

"You think love will pull you down?"

"Without a doubt."

Ulrik considered that for a moment as his gaze swung back to the window. "I disagree, and one day when you do find love, you'll see for yourself."

"Bite your fucking tongue," Keltan stated angrily. "Take it back. Right now."

Ulrik threw up his hands and chuckled at Keltan's tone. "I take it back."

"Good. Now, let's return the talk to V."

"V needs something to focus on."

Keltan crossed his arms over his chest and raised a blond brow. "Besides his sword, the Others, and whatever else might be coming our way? Do you no' think he has enough already? Why throw a woman into the mix?"

"A hunch."

"I can no' believe I'm helping you play matchmaker."

"Would you rather help Hal and Guy with the sheep?"

Keltan shot him a dry look. "I merely want to point out, that as someone who doesna want a woman, I'm betting this willna work."

"Have some faith."

"Oh, I do. That it willna work, and that this foray into matchmaking will be your one and only."

Ulrik grinned, eager to take the bet. "And if my plan does work?"

Keltan dropped his arms to his sides. "Shite. I doona want to even consider it. No' to mention, Con willna be happy. You know he doesna want any Kings to mate."

"That's no' true. Con wants everyone to be happy. He also bears the weight of looking at every outcome and preparing for the worst."

Keltan released a loud snort. "You were no' here when the first of the Kings fell in love. Con wasna at all happy. In fact, I thought he might step in and try to break it up."

"Con would never do that. I know him well enough to know that he might let what he really feels slip out sometimes, but he will always keep his focus on the wellbeing and happiness of the Kings."

Keltan slowly ran a hand along his dark blond beard-covered jaw. "And V? Have you thought about what you'll tell him if this works?"

"I doona plan to tell him anything whether it works or no'. I willna hide it from him, but I also willna hand him the information without first being asked. He's been through enough."

"Aye." Keltan drew in a deep breath. "He's changed so much from before the war to now. Hard to imagine that when he's spent so much time sleeping."

"You slept, but you've spent large chunks of time awake. You adapted to your surroundings, subtly changing like the landscape around you. V is the same man he was when he first went into his cave. He's no' the one who changed. We are."

Keltan flattened his lips and nodded. "What do you need from me?"

"Nothing for now. V and Claire will spend the day together, which is what I wanted."

"You believe that one day will be enough to jumpstart something between them?"

Ulrik bit back a grin. "When there's something there, it doesna take long. And if there isna anything between Claire and V, then we've lost nothing but a wee bit of time."

"That we have in spades," Keltan grumbled as he walked from the room.

Ulrik's head turned to the side when the hidden door

opened, and Eilish walked in. He held out his hand for her. The moment their fingers touched, he pulled her against him.

"You're taking a chance," she said after she kissed him.

"I always take chances."

She eyed him. "Oh, please. We both know that isn't true. You plot, you manipulate, you maneuver. You rarely take chances."

"I did with you." He rubbed his nose against hers. "Look how well that turned out."

"Hmm. That it did."

"Because you couldna resist me."

She pulled back and barked with laughter. "More like you couldn't resist me."

"You're right," he admitted as he tugged her against him again. "I couldna. I still can no'."

Eilish lifted her face to his, their lips meeting. The desire inside Ulrik flared to life, as it always did when it came to her. Soon, they would be joined, their hearts and souls united for eternity.

He ended the kiss and wrapped his arms around her as she rested her cheek on his chest. They stood in silence for a long time, each of them lost in thought.

"You're happy here, aren't you?" Eilish asked.

Ulrik smiled. "Aye, love. I am. Are you?"

"I'm happy anywhere I'm with you."

He kissed the top of her head. "But you're worried about the Others."

"As are you."

"I have a feeling that we'll discover something else they've made sure we'll find. But how long until we come face-to-face with them?"

Eilish leaned back to look at him. "The Druids involved are long dead. There's even a possibility that the Fae are, as well. This could be nothing. At least it was nothing until Dorian and Alexandra in New York."

Ulrik's lips twisted as he thought of the Queen of the Light Fae's involvement in what had happened there. "Aye."

Eilish sighed and shook her head. "I keep thinking about Iceland. That cave seemed so familiar."

"You said you've never been to Iceland."

"I haven't. I can't explain it. Then there were the huge stones with the writing on them. You didn't see Rhi's face. It drained of color when she looked at the one with the Fae writing."

Ulrik nodded since they'd had this conversation before. "I asked Rhi about it. She said she's still working out the meaning. She has no reason to keep anything from us. She's a friend to the Dragon Kings."

"But what if she *is* keeping something from us? What if she read something that impacts her or the Fae? She's the only one of us who can read the Fae writing."

That bit still frustrated Ulrik. A Dragon King's magic allowed them to read and write any language, but the Others had used their combined magic to make it so the Kings couldn't decipher anything on the stones in Iceland. As if the Others only wanted a Druid and a Fae to find and read what was there.

"I wish you had been able to read more of the Druid stone," Ulrik said.

Eilish returned her head to his chest. "Me, too. I know there was something important there."

Isle of Skye

Rhi stared out over the dark water. She didn't care that the rain soaked her. She felt none of it.

Ever since helping the Dragon Kings on Iceland, she'd been acting as if everything were fine. Actually, she'd been doing that for far longer. All because she'd read the Fae writing on the wall. Literally.

She still wasn't sure how she had been able to decipher it. The languages were from the ancient times of the first thirty Fae families. The only record left that she knew of was in the hands of the Reapers.

The fact that the writing had moved from Light to Dark and back again was confounding enough, but Rhi hadn't even had to pause to understand it. It was like the words were already in her head.

And that terrified her.

It was one of the reasons she'd stayed away from Dreagan. She feared that one of the Kings would bring up the writing and ask her once more how much she'd read.

Worse, she suspected that Eilish knew that she was hiding something. And if the Druid knew, then that meant Ulrik did, as well. No doubt Con would soon, too.

Rhi lifted her face to the rain and closed her eyes. She was supposed to be continuing her search of the Druid archives on Skye to look for anything out of the ordinary that might point to the Others.

Instead, she was lost in her thoughts.

Perhaps it was a good thing. With Rhi's stomach in knots at what she'd read in the cave, it cleared her mind of her plot for revenge against Usaeil.

The Queen of the Light's days were numbered. Rhi had promised Con that she would wait so the two of them could attack together, but she was growing impatient. Usaeil had banished her from the Light.

And that was only a fraction of what the queen had done to her. For weeks, Rhi had allowed Con to talk her into waiting. A lot had to do with Ulrik and defeating Mikkel, but now that Mikkel was out of the way, there was no reason to delay.

An image of the giant stone wall flashed in Rhi's mind.

She squeezed her eyes closed. She didn't want to think about Iceland. She didn't want to think about the writing. And she didn't want to think about the knowledge that she now held in her head. It was better if she forgot all about the stone. Besides, there was something more important at the moment—defeating Usaeil.

With just a thought, Rhi teleported to her private island where the sun shone so brightly that it blinded her. She didn't get into her bikini and lay on the white sand.

Instead, she walked into the open-walled hut and sat at the small table. She spread her hands from the center out, using her magic to craft a map of upper Ireland where the Light Castle sat.

She marked each place where she knew Fae guards patrolled in case any mortals or Dark Fae tried to approach. Rhi knew that Usaeil would leave those patrols but also add new ones to try and thwart her. The queen's mistake was underestimating Rhi because no one knew the territory like she did.

Rhi marked additional Xs for the new patrols at the most optimal places. She could teleport to the castle, but no doubt Usaeil had put spells in place that would alert her of such an action. That meant Rhi would have to go about gaining entrance and assassinating the queen another way.

While Usaeil enjoyed the limelight of pretending to be a famous American actress, she would put that on hold and wait at the castle for Rhi to attack.

Because they both knew she would.

Usaeil had pushed her too far. The queen wanted the attack, it's what she planned for.

But she wasn't going to be prepared for this Rhi.

CHAPTER SIX

She was adorable.

V had a hard time focusing on moving everything in the storage room around since he couldn't stop trying to catch a glimpse of Claire.

He'd hated the pain he saw in her eyes when he first arrived. The knowledge that some man had been stupid enough not to hold onto her boggled V's mind. He also didn't understand why she was still single. Claire was . . . perfect.

She was beautiful of spirit and face. She was compassionate, generous with her time and advice, and always had a kind word for everyone. And she had a body that drew his gaze again and again as he imagined what she would feel like in his arms.

V would be lying if he said he wasn't happy about it being just the two of them at the clinic. He could be done with the storage room quickly, but he didn't want to leave. So, he took his time shifting boxes, emptying shelving, and moving everything to the center of the room.

The hours passed far too quickly for once. V enjoyed the songs she played. They were a truly eclectic mix from every era of music. And with each song, he learned a little about her. His favorites just might be the blues songs.

The soulful, poignant melodies struck a chord within him. Probably because they were very deep and personal, something that everyone could relate to on some level. Even a Dragon King.

Or maybe especially a Dragon King.

V was so attuned to Claire, he knew the moment she stuck her head around the corner of the doorway. His gaze snapped to her. No longer were her eyes red and full of sadness. While she still looked a little tired, her smile came easier and filled her entire face.

He couldn't take credit for that, but he wanted to think that he'd had a hand in it. He'd never been in such a situation before, but he liked it. Really, it came down to the fact that he enjoyed Claire. Everything about her was fascinating.

But the best part was the little thread of excitement that had been there from the moment he realized that she was in the clinic.

"How is everything coming?" Claire asked.

V looked at the bare walls and then everything piled in the center of the room. "Pretty good."

"Want some help?" she offered.

He was about to tell her that he could handle it, but then he realized that if she were in the room with him, he could talk to her instead of maneuvering himself to try and catch just a few glimpses. "If you'd like."

Claire walked to him and put her hands on her hips as she looked at the organized mess behind him. "Where do we begin?"

V motioned to the far wall and described what Darius had mapped out for him. By the time he'd finished, Claire was smiling.

"This will actually work out much more efficiently. Sophie is not exactly organized, and I did the best I could when we initially set up. I moved some things, but others I couldn't do myself, and didn't want to ask for help."

"You doona like help?"

She laughed, her deep brown eyes meeting his. "Not at all. I'm mostly the one who deals with everything in this room, and it wasn't that big of a deal."

"Obviously Darius and Sophie didna think so."

Claire's gaze slid away from him as her arms dropped to her sides. "Sophie has been my best friend for a long time. We've been through a lot, and I'm so happy that she and Darius found each other. I've gotten so used to believing that they don't see anyone but each other."

That made V frown. "You doona think they see you?"

"Oh, they know I'm here, but when they look at each other, the rest of the world disappears. It's just the two of them."

"Aye. There are others like that at Dreagan."

She smiled wryly. "I've seen that the few times I've gone."

Now that surprised him. "You've been?"

"Was I not supposed to go?" she asked cautiously.

"That's no' what I meant. The fact you were invited says a lot about your relationship with Sophie."

Claire grinned. "I have no doubt it was Sophie urging Darius that allowed me to go. I've only been twice, but both times were spectacular. That place is. . . . Well, I have no words," she finished with a laugh.

"Did you walk the grounds?"

"The first time I visited during the day. Sophie and Cassie brought me behind the scenes of the distillery. And I got to have lunch. The second time, I went at night to a small gathering of the wives and girlfriends. I think Sophie invited me because she felt sorry for me, but I didn't care. I had a great time."

V couldn't take his eyes from her. Her expressions held him transfixed. But he also noticed that she was careful with her words, as if she chose each one judiciously. Whether that was to keep something secret or not, he wasn't sure.

But he wanted to find out.

She looked around at the room. "I didn't say anything about wanting to reorganize this area. How did Darius know?"

"Observation, I assume. He's here often. Even I noted the last time I helped bring in an order that things could be shifted to make it easier."

Claire swallowed loudly. "I consider Sophie my family. She's like a sister, and Darius a brother."

"They are family."

"Yes," she said, looking at him.

"Darius comes with a rather large family."

Her lips curved into a smile. "I've noticed."

"That means we're your family now, too."

His statement was meant to soothe her, and yet he realized that it had done the opposite if the way her forehead creased in a frown was any indication.

"Did I say something wrong?" he asked worriedly.

Her smile was a little forced as she shook her head. "No, I'm the one who should apologize. It made me think of my actual family. Mom and Dad are still happily married and living just outside of Edinburgh in the same house I grew up in. They have a small group of friends that they do everything with. My parents are utterly devoted to each other."

V drew in a breath, her words making him think about his own. "I doona have any blood family anymore."

"That must be hard. Though you have everyone at Dreagan, it isn't the same, is it?"

"Nay. Do you see your parents much?"

She gave a small shake of her head. "Sadly, no. I'm a bad daughter. But we talk at least once a week, and text constantly."

"Family should be treasured."

"Yes, they should. I've missed the past several holidays with my parents. Though that was by choice. You don't have that option. It must be hard during the holidays."

V shrugged. He wasn't sure how he felt about the image of him and Claire together that flashed in his head. It left him in such turmoil, he wasn't able to reply to her comment.

"I bet everyone at Dreagan makes up for it."

He cleared his throat, determined to answer this time while doing his best not to think about what his mind had conjured. "They do. When you doona go home, you stay here?"

He really hoped she did, because maybe then he could see her. As soon as that thought went through his head, he thought about returning to sleep. But he would much rather be with Claire. Maybe he could put off going to his mountain for a few more months.

She twisted her lips. "I should point out that when I moved out on my own, my parents started a tradition of traveling for Christmas. They always invite me, but sometimes, I don't want to go or I can't. So, I end up staying wherever I am."

"I know Sophie and Darius will include you." And if they didn't, V certainly would. A woman like Claire should never be alone.

"Being a third wheel isn't very nice," she stated with a laugh.

V flashed her a grin. "I doona think that will be the case this year."

"Okay," Claire said and rubbed her hands together. "Where do we begin?"

He pointed to the wall before him. "This one."

"Shelves?" she asked.

"Shelves."

He waited as she went to her side of the shelving unit. V could easily lift it himself, but he quite liked that she was with him. Together, they moved two of the six storage stacks side by side.

Then they sorted through all the contents that he had moved and figured out what should go on the shelves. When he started to put something down, Claire stopped him.

"Set it in front of it for now," she urged him. "That way, I can see what all is going on the shelving and figure out the best way to organize it."

In no time, both units had several boxes and other things set in front of them. When he turned to Claire, she was grinning at him.

"What?" he asked, hoping he hadn't done something stupid. He was still finding his footing in this world, but he hadn't felt off-balance once with Claire.

"We've gotten a lot done thanks to you."

He shrugged, but he liked her praise. "Glad I could help."

"It's noon. You hungry? We could break for lunch."

"Of course. Where would you like to go?"

No sooner were the words out of his mouth than he realized he had no way to pay for food. If he'd thought about that before, he would have suggested going to The Fox & The Hound since another Dragon King, Laith, owned the pub.

"I love the fish and chips at the pub. How about that?"

V nearly sighed in relief. At least he knew that he didn't have to worry about payment now. "Sounds good to me."

While Claire turned off the music and gathered her purse, V opened a link to Laith and said his name. In moments, the King of Blacks answered him.

"Everything all right?" Laith asked.

"Aye. I'm coming to the pub with Claire."

"Okay." There was a pause, then Laith said, *"Ohhh. I got it. Doona worry, brother. I'll take care of everything. There's a booth in the back that I'll keep open for you. Sit with your back toward the kitchen. You'll find some money tucked between the booth and the wall."*

"Thank you."

"We've all been where you are. Remember that, V. We've got your back. Always," Laith said.

"I know."

V severed the link and stood with Claire outside the clinic as she locked the door. She dropped her keys into her purse and said, "Let's walk."

V fell into step beside her. He searched his mind for something to say, but the longer the silence went on, the harder it was for him to come up with anything.

Then he looked over at her. Claire was smiling, her eyes taking in the various flowers planted all over the village. She didn't care that they weren't talking. She was simply enjoying their stroll. Something he should do, as well.

V relaxed then. Now that he didn't worry about coming up with something to talk about, he realized how nice it was to just walk with her and enjoy her company.

They continued another few minutes before she asked, "What does V stand for?"

He glanced at her. "Vlad."

"Vlad?" she repeated. "As in . . . Vlad?"

He laughed, nodding. "Aye."

"And you go by V because you don't like the name?"

He tried to remember how everyone began calling him V, but it was too long ago. "There are nicknames for a few of us. We call Warrick, War. Constantine is Con. Haldor is Hal. And somehow, I became V."

"It's better than Claire," she said with distaste.

His head snapped to her. "There is nothing wrong with your name."

"It's an old woman's name."

That made him smile. "I like it."

"Thank you," she replied. "Does anyone call you Vlad anymore?"

"No' really. I've been . . . away . . . from Dreagan for a long time."

"Doing what?"

He hesitated, trying to come up with a reason that she would believe. "I had some things to sort out on my own."

"But you came back."

"I'll always return to Dreagan."

She turned her head to him. There was something in her deep brown eyes that he couldn't quite place. He almost thought it was as if she knew his secret. But surely that couldn't be true. Darius would have alerted everyone at Dreagan if that were the case.

And yet. . . .

"What about you?" V asked. "You're from Edinburgh. Will you go back?"

She shrugged and looked forward. "There's Sophie. We work well together, which helped cement our friendship."

"And you followed her here."

Claire laughed. "You make me sound like a dog or a stalker."

V's lips parted as he tried to think of a way to reword

his statement. But by then, Claire was already talking again.

"When Sophie asked me to come with her, I didn't need to think about it. The hospital wouldn't have been the same without her. Plus, I liked the idea of working in a clinic rather than the vastness of a hospital with all the trappings that go along with it."

"So, you're happy here?"

"Most definitely," she replied. "The village is perfect. And it's not that far from Inverness, which allows me to actually find men to date."

V took offense at that. Dreagan had any number of un-mated Kings available.

"I mean, take a look around," she said. "The men here are either old enough to be my father or young enough to be my son."

"There are others."

She looked sideways at him, her gaze briefly meeting his. "A few, yes."

It's not like he could blame her for her thinking. It wasn't as if anyone at Dreagan were asking her out, though that was more because of Darius than anything. And V couldn't tell Claire that.

Bloody hell, he really wanted to ask her out now and forget about the promise he'd made to Darius.

CHAPTER SEVEN

Once in the booth at The Fox & The Hound, Claire was very aware that she was with a Dragon King. No one—not even Sophie—realized that Claire knew their secret.

But after what had happened in Edinburgh with the Dark Fae and the Kings coming to her rescue, how could she forget? She'd made everyone believe she had no memory of the encounter simply because she feared that the Kings would try and take those memories away. And she refused to allow that to happen.

All her life, nothing had ever happened to her. Until that night.

She had been terrified of how the Dark Fae could make her lose control of her body in such a way. Claire had wanted them, but it had been an empty need. Hollow and meaningless. Though she knew that, she couldn't stop herself.

While she'd begged the Dark to take her body, inside her mind, she had been screaming for someone to help. It had been the worst feeling in the world to be so helpless.

And then, the Dragon Kings were there. Claire knew that she had gotten caught up in the fight because she was

Sophie's friend. She liked to believe that the Kings would've helped her regardless, but she knew that being with Sophie had a lot to do with it.

It also helped that Sophie was right there, begging Darius and the others to help.

The moment Sophie had mentioned opening a practice near Dreagan, Claire hadn't hesitated. It gave her the opportunity to remain with her best friend and maybe get another chance to see the Kings.

And now she was sitting down to lunch with one.

Not just any Dragon King. V.

Vlad. Who happened to be the sexiest of them all. She didn't care that she'd spent the past few hours working nonstop. Sure, a lot had gotten done at the clinic, but she wasn't thinking about that. Her mind was on the hunky Scot sitting across from her. The one with the ice blue eyes and the ability to make her knees go weak with just a smile.

"You're quiet," V said.

She laughed nervously, thankful that he couldn't read her mind. Once she looked into his eyes, it was difficult to look away. They sucked her in, taking hold and refusing to let go. Not that she minded being seized in such a way.

Claire blinked, reminding herself that there was much she had to keep to herself. "I was thinking about how long Sophie and I have been friends."

"Oh?"

"She's a workaholic. She never used to take time for herself."

V quirked a dark brow. "Some would say you work just as hard."

Claire had to giggle at that. "I work long hours, but I'm all about self-love. I take a spa day as often as I can."

"Sophie didna?"

"Never," she said with a shake of her head. "She never did anything for herself. And dating? Pfft. That didn't happen at all."

V cocked his head to the side. "While you did?"

"I'm a glutton for punishment, obviously."

"Why do you say that?"

Claire shrugged, wishing she hadn't said anything. Now that she had, there was no getting out of it. "I'm a poster child for the perpetual dater who is never in a relationship."

V's brows snapped together, confusion filling his ice blue eyes. "Why is that?"

Luckily, before she could answer, they were interrupted by Iona, who was mated to Laith. The woman smiled, looking between Claire and V. Her gaze was probing, but she didn't pry. "Hi," she said, her Scottish accent heard even in that one word.

V nodded in acknowledgment.

Claire returned the woman's smile. "Hello."

"Do you want your usual?" Iona asked Claire.

"Please," Claire said.

Iona swung her brown eyes to V. "What would you like to eat?"

"Have Laith surprise me," V said.

"Oh, goodness," Iona said with a laugh. "This should be interesting."

Claire watched Iona walk away. Then she looked at V. For a moment, she couldn't remember why he looked at her so expectantly. Suddenly, she recalled his question. "I'm a serial dater because I can't seem to find a man who wants to be with me."

"I doona believe that."

"That's kind of you, but it's the truth. Well, there is also the fact that some of them aren't datable. I learned that pretty quickly. Just wish I could figure that out before I agree to a date and waste both of our time."

V studied her a silent moment. "Perhaps you're seeing the wrong men."

"Without a doubt," she agreed with a laugh. "It's something Sophie and Darius point out often. All the algorithms in all the dating sites in all the world just can't help me find who I'm supposed to be with."

"Maybe he isna on the sites."

She twisted her lips, chuckling. "I've thought of that. With my luck, he's already married."

"Or hasna found you yet."

Claire looked down at the table. She hated talking about her love life—or lack thereof. Mostly because it reminded her of the emptiness in her life. It was even more difficult at this moment because she was talking about it with V. All she could hope for was that she didn't sound desperate.

Even though she was.

"Maybe."

"I'm sorry."

Her gaze jerked to V's face. "Why are you apologizing?"

"Because it's obviously a sore subject, and I've made you talk about it."

"It's fine," she said with a shake of her head. "Seeing Sophie and Darius happy makes it hard sometimes. I don't begrudge them, but when I want what they have, it makes it difficult."

"Aye," V murmured. "I know the feeling."

Iona returned then with their drinks. She set them down with a smile and then left once more.

V rested his arms on the table. "Where is it you meet these men?"

"Dating sites. It's pretty much the only way people date anymore."

Was it her imagination, or did he look confused? She might know that V and the other men at Dreagan were Dragon Kings, but that's about all she knew. She was insanely curious, but it wasn't as if she could come out and ask him why he didn't know about the sites. So, she played along.

"You should give the sites a try. There are a few I recommend if you're actually interested in a relationship and not just sex."

V's head jerked back. "They have one of these sites for sex?"

"Oh, yeah," she said and nodded emphatically. "Several, in fact."

"I doona understand. Why can people no' just talk to each other?"

She laughed. "I ask myself that all the time. I wish I had an answer."

He lifted the glass of ale to his lips and took a drink. "Interesting. Have you found companionship on these sites?"

If it had been anyone else asking, Claire would've taken offense, but she could tell that he was really interested. "I admit, I was on one or two of those sites. I even talked to a guy and considered meeting him, but when it came right down to it, I couldn't. Meaningless sex isn't for me. I need a connection."

V nodded slowly. "Aye."

"What about you?" she asked. "Are you out in the dating world?"

"I doona have anyone."

"I can't imagine you'd have a hard time finding a woman. That is if you want one," she quickly added.

V's head swung to the side as a tall man with long, dark blond hair and gunmetal eyes walked up and placed a plate of fish and chips before each of them.

Claire grinned up at Laith. "I've been craving these for days."

"Eat your fill," he replied with a wink.

"Thanks."

Claire didn't wait to dive into the food. But after she'd put a bite into her mouth, she happened to glance up and see Laith and V exchanging a look. When Laith walked away, V's gaze slid to her.

She grinned around her mouthful of food and tried to pretend like she hadn't caught that exchange. She failed miserably.

It was no wonder she was perpetually single. She should be pretty suave at sneaking peeks, but she had yet to master that skill. Clearly, she needed to take a class in it.

They continued eating, but the silence that she'd enjoyed so much on the way to the pub was now uncomfortable. Perhaps it was all the dating talk and becoming aware of how alone she was.

"How are you involved with Dreagan?" she asked.

V swallowed his bite. "I'm no' as involved with the running of the distillery as others are. I've learned a little bit, but my attention has been on locating something that was stolen from me."

"I hope you were able to find it."

"Finally. After many, many years."

She wiped her fingers on her napkin. "Now that you have it, what will you do?"

"I'm still trying to figure that out."

"No doubt those at Dreagan are happy to have you home."

A peculiar look passed over his face. "I suppose."

"They're your family. Of course, they are."

He looked down at his plate. "I'm contemplating going away again."

Now that shocked her. "Why? Don't you like it here?"

"Aye, I do," he said as he met her gaze.

There was something in his eyes, a look that she didn't quite understand. She also saw longing there, which she didn't comprehend. He was part of a large family, who seemed very tight and loving. What could he long for?

Love. Companionship. The same things she yearned for? She wanted to reach across the table and touch his hand. Actually, she'd wanted to do that all day, but now that she had the opportunity, she was afraid. Frightened of what she might feel.

And terrified that she was so attracted to him that she was seeing something that wasn't there. "Then why do you want to leave?"

His lips flattened. "It's . . . difficult to explain."

"Oh." She was kind of hurt that he didn't want to share with her, but then again, they barely knew each other. It wasn't as if she were spilling her secrets. How could she expect him to?

"Have you ever been somewhere that you love, but doona think it's where you belong?"

She nodded slowly. Claire knew that feeling all too well. It was something she experienced daily. "I have."

"What did you do about it?"

"Nothing," she confessed. "I'm still here."

He moved aside his plate, his food clearly forgotten as he leaned his forearms on the table. "What would you like to do about it?"

"I don't know. Is there a way to fix it? Because I think I'll feel like this anywhere I go."

"Why do you think that?"

She licked her lips, suddenly no longer hungry. Her gaze lowered to her plate, not seeing the food as she searched for the words to explain.

Claire took a deep breath and looked up at V. They had been honest with each other, and she found it incredibly easy to talk to him about things that would embarrass her with others. "I can't seem to stop looking for The One."

"The One?" he repeated, a frown marring his brow.

She shrugged one shoulder. "Some women call it Mr. Right, The One, or their other half. Soulmate, even."

"I think most everyone is looking for their One."

"I agree, but that doesn't make it any easier."

V glanced at the others in the pub. "I've seen those who have been lucky enough to find love, like Darius and Laith. I've seen others find it and lose it." V paused for a moment as if considering saying a name. Then he said, "The pain they live with every day is something I can only imagine."

"What's worse? Never knowing love? Or having it and losing it?"

He shrugged. "For those of us who have no' found it, we'd say no' having it. For the ones who have lost it, they might say the opposite."

"I have a good life, a great job, terrific friends, and my health. Why isn't that enough?" Claire couldn't believe she was confessing so much to V.

But it was nice to know that someone else felt as she did.

"You feel incomplete because your destiny has yet to be fulfilled. And that willna happen until you find The One."

She grinned at his use of her term, but it quickly faded. "Unfortunately, that doesn't make me feel any better. The odds are stacked against me."

"They've always been stacked against me."

Claire understood how he felt. Without thinking, she reached across the table and put her hand atop his. The instant their skin met, something electric sparked between them, causing her stomach to quiver in surprise.

And excitement.

CHAPTER EIGHT

Usaeil stared at her reflection in the mirror. No one was more beautiful than she was. She was the perfect match for Constantine in every way. Who better to be the King of Dragon King's mate than the Queen of the Fae?

She smiled at the thought of ruling the entire Fae race. The Dark and Light had been divided for too long, but she was about to change that.

It had come to her while she was attempting to stop the letters from moving on the page of the book she'd found in the hidden chamber of the library. The tome was several million years old and written in a dialect she couldn't read. But there was no misinterpreting the mention of the Dragon Kings.

She'd made the mistake of touching the page to turn it. As soon as she had, the letters started to jumble and shift. And they had yet to stop.

Whatever she might have found was now lost. But she wasn't giving up. There was a way to stop it. She had tried all kinds of spells, and she would continue. So far, nothing had worked, but she wasn't giving up.

It would only be a matter of time before she discovered the magic needed to stop the letters and put them back in the right order. As for reading the book, well, there had to be someone among the Fae who could decipher the content. Because if there were mention of the Dragon Kings, she wanted to know what it was about.

Con had rebuffed her, and that simply wouldn't do. She would get his attention one way or another. Once he figured out that the Fae could give the Kings children, they would forget about the humans and flock to the Fae.

Her destiny was to rule not just the Fae but also the Dragon Kings.

Usaeil turned away from the mirror to look over her chamber. Returning to the Light Castle had been a necessity, but one she wasn't pleased about. She quite liked living among the humans. The love they showered her with while she pretended to be an American actress was glorious. They knew how to treat a queen.

It was different than the attention the Light Fae gave her. But it was also what made her realize that she wasn't living up to her full potential. All these eons of time, she'd allowed herself to be content ruling the Light. She should have gone after the Dark long ago.

Once she ruled the Fae and had Con as her husband, there wasn't a realm in the universe she wouldn't be able to conquer. And the first person she was going after was Death.

Just the thought of the bitch made Usaeil grind her teeth. Death had had the nerve to enter Usaeil's castle, her chambers, and threaten her. No one did that without retaliation.

Usaeil couldn't believe that she had feared the Reapers all these years. They'd come for her but hadn't followed when she ran. Because they knew they were no match for her. If only she had confronted them. If only she had forced them to bow to her.

Then she could control them, too.

And that's exactly what she intended.

One step at a time, though. First, her gaze was directed closer to home. Precisely on Rhi. The plan was brilliant, and the meddling Rhi would never know what happened until it was too late.

Usaeil could hardly wait. The first of many moves to acquire all she desired was about to start. It had been a long time coming. She'd waited, hoping all Con needed was time to see that he loved her.

That was her mistake. She always went after what she wanted. She'd done the same with Con. Only she had backed off, letting him be in control. That wasn't going to happen again.

The fact that she could no longer teleport into Dreagan was infuriating, but not something she couldn't overcome. Eventually. She was furious with Constantine right now, and it was Rhi's fault. The meddling Fae had managed to turn Con's heart and mind from Usaeil.

It was Rhi's retaliation for Usaeil doing the same thing to her all those eons ago, but the difference was that Usaeil was queen. She was stronger and more determined. And unlike Rhi, she wouldn't just accept what was before her. She was going to change the outcome to suit her.

Because that's what queens did.

Usaeil flicked her long, black locks over her shoulder. She missed the throngs of people on the movie sets fawning over her. Mortals were so easily swayed by beauty. And their minds were weak. They were the inferior race. And yet the Dragon Kings had lost a war to them. It was inconceivable.

Yet, Usaeil could fix that problem for the Kings. All she had to do was unleash the Fae upon the humans. In no time, the mortals would be decimated. And then annihilated.

The Kings could rule once more. Well, with the Fae beside them.

Usaeil smiled again. There was no one to share her excitement with because she didn't trust anyone. She didn't mind that, though. Soon enough, Con would be beside her to share everything with her.

The touch of Claire's hand on V's was electrifying. He was unprepared for it. His heart skipped a beat. There was nothing sexual about it, but nevertheless, it made his balls tighten and need burn through him.

She looked at him with confusion and sympathy in her eyes. And for a few precious seconds, there was only the two of them sharing a private moment that few others could understand.

When Claire pulled her hand away, he wanted to grab hold of it and stop her. Instead, he did nothing.

"Look around you," she said.

He hesitated but did as she asked. With one sweep of his gaze around the pub, he noticed the full tables, the laughter, the food, and the noise.

"What about it?" he asked when he turned his attention back to her.

She chuckled softly. "Didn't you notice the women staring at you?"

He frowned, shrugging.

"None of them interest you?"

How could he tell her that she was the one that drew his notice?

"Hmm," she murmured. "Maybe give the dating sites

a try. It doesn't take much to set up a profile. You'll be beating the women off with a stick."

He grinned at her excitement for him, but he didn't feel the same. In fact, he didn't want to talk about himself. He wanted to talk about her. "I'm sure you have your choice of men."

"I guess," she said with a little shrug. "I have men show interest, but few are what I'm looking for. Call me picky, but when you have others lined up by their pictures, it's like having a menu in front of you. You can weed out those too tall or too short, those too skinny or too large, those who make too little money. But no one skips those who make too much." She laughed. "The point is, not everyone takes good photos. I can't take a picture of myself for anything. I've spent hours trying. I've watched all kinds of tutorials. I make Sophie take my pictures. Yet, there are some who take their own and don't do a good job."

V leaned back slowly as he took in everything she was telling him. "Bad pictures?"

"Oh, yeah. The worst was the one profile I saw of this guy. He was in the same pose in front of a mirror for all twelve shots. The only thing different was his clothes. Oh, or the nose pictures."

"What?" V asked, confused. By her description, he imagined someone taking a picture of their nose.

Claire laughed out loud. "Oh, you should see your face. It's when people—guys mostly—take a selfie with their phone down low like this."

He leaned forward to see her holding her hands in her lap pretending that she had her mobile.

"That causes the angle to go right up your nose," she continued. "Therefore, nose pics. Let me show you."

V waited as she pulled out her phone and found what she was looking for. As soon as she turned the device around and he saw the angle of the picture that went straight up the man's nose, he couldn't help but laugh.

"Exactly," she said and set her phone aside. She licked her lips and shrugged. "I've known several friends who found their significant others through online dating, so it does work."

"You doona sound convinced."

She took a long drink of her water. "I think anyone who has been on the sites for over a year should acknowledge that something is wrong. I've been on multiple sites for that long or longer. It's time for me to admit that it isn't working. I can get a man's attention, but I can't keep it. Which means, there is something wrong with me."

"It means there is something wrong with them."

"I'd like to think that, but when you look at my dating history as a whole, I'm the common denominator."

V wasn't buying it. Claire was beautiful, charming, and witty. He couldn't understand why someone hadn't snatched her up yet. It was good for him because she was free for him to. . . .

To what? Hadn't he told Darius that he'd keep away? The problem was, he didn't want to. Nor did he think he could. Being with Claire made things better. The outside world didn't look so harsh or uninviting with her near. She softened everything. Or maybe she just shifted his focus. Whatever the reason, he didn't want it to stop.

He glanced down at his hand. Even now, he could feel her skin on his, the warmth, the softness. He wanted more of it. He *needed* it.

The ache that had been his constant companion for eons was significantly diminished. And that was because of Claire. He knew it with the same certainty that he knew his sword could give him the answers he sought about the dragons.

But did he forget his promise to Darius? Did he throw caution to the wind and follow the desire that thundered through him for the beautiful mortal across from him?

V stared into her brown eyes. He wished he knew what she was thinking. It was enough that they were together.

"You two didn't eat much," Iona said as she walked up. "Everything taste okay?"

Claire hurried to say, "It was great. We got to talking."

V met Iona's gaze. He didn't need to look toward the bar to know that Laith was watching. His friend had been observing them from the moment he and Claire walked into the pub.

Iona shot them a smile. "Let me know if you need anything else."

Once she was gone, Claire twisted her lips ruefully. "I feel like I'm turning you off the dating sites. I don't mean to."

"I like hearing your stories."

She grinned, looking at him askance. "I could write a book about all my exploits. It wouldn't be a fun read."

"Perhaps you need someone to show you what a proper date is."

"A proper date, huh?" she replied with a teasing grin. "Are you offering?"

"I am. Let me take you to dinner." He knew he was taking a chance, but he couldn't let the opportunity pass him by.

Her eyes widened. "I was joking."

"I'm no'."

She blinked at him several times before she drew in a deep breath. "I wasn't looking for a pity date."

"That isna what this is."

"V . . . I don't know."

Now that he'd offered, he needed this to happen. He

wanted to take Claire out, show her that not all men were like the ones she went out with. It was suddenly very important for him to show her every aspect of who he was.

And the thought of being alone with her was too good to pass up.

"Why no'? What's holding you back?"

"Many things."

"Like what?" he urged.

She pressed her lips together, frowning. "For one, you're Darius's friend."

"So?"

"That's . . . it's just not a good idea."

Dread took root that she would refuse. But V hadn't become a Dragon King because he gave up easily. "Are you afraid you'll enjoy the evening?"

Her lips parted to respond, but she paused. Then finally, she said, "Yes."

"What's the worst that can happen?"

Claire raised a brow and gave him a flat look. "Really? You know the answer to that."

She was close to giving in, he was sure of it. "I'm leaving soon. If it goes badly, you willna have to see me for much longer."

"What if the night goes well?"

"Then we have fun."

She blew out a breath. "You make it sound so simple."

"Because it is. Why are you making it so difficult?"

"I don't know."

"Say yes, lass," he urged.

She was wavering. He could see that she wanted to agree, but something held her back.

He shot her a grin. "What do you have to lose?"

She held his gaze for a long minute. "Nothing. And everything."

"Then there's no reason no' to say yes."

Finally, her lips turned up at the corners. "You have your date."

V's smile widened in anticipation. "How does tonight sound?"

CHAPTER NINE

Claire couldn't believe that she'd agreed to the date. With a Dragon King! She must have lost her mind.

But V was so bloody perfect. She'd wanted to say yes from the very beginning, but it was the knowledge that she knew his secret that held her back. Not to mention the fact that the night could go horribly.

Then how would she ever look at him again?

It didn't make her feel any better that he was leaving soon. She didn't know the real reason behind him wanting to go away, but she knew it must be important.

After lunch, she and V returned to the clinic and continued working, but she looked at him differently. She saw him as a man who might be interested in her. He'd said it wasn't a pity date, and she was going to believe that. Because to think otherwise was just too much.

Now, she stood in front of her closet and stared at the clothes before her. Thankfully, she had gotten waxed a few days before. Not that she expected anything to happen, but she'd learned the hard way what happened when she wasn't prepared for any eventuality.

Her stomach went weak when she thought about having

sex with V. Claire put a hand on her chest and took a deep breath to calm herself. The excitement mixed with trepidation was a combination that had her stomach in knots.

"What the hell, Claire?" she asked herself. "He's taking you to dinner. That's it. Stop thinking there's going to be sex or kissing or, well . . . *anything*."

But no matter how many times she told herself that, a little kernel of hope whispered in the back of her mind, "*you never know.*"

Claire still hadn't figured out how the smallest speck of hope could make a person cling to it with all their might. It was what she had done for years waiting for her One. Through disillusionment, hurt, pain, tears, and depression. Hope remained.

It tantalized her with possibilities. It made her dream— both awake and asleep—of a life that could be hers. One that was just out of reach.

Even when the sting of loneliness was too much to bear, and she couldn't hold back her tears, through it all, she clung to hope.

Her eyes blurred as she recalled the horrible nights where she silently screamed into her pillow, wondering what she had ever done to Karma that she was made to suffer so. She'd had her heart broken so many times, but she had never broken any hearts. She had never cheated or wronged anyone.

So why did it feel as if she were being punished? What did she need to do to find the happiness and love she craved more than air itself?

Claire looked at the ceiling as the tears rolled down her face. In front of Sophie and everyone else, she put on a brave face. It was easy to pretend that everything was fine, especially when others were so deliriously happy.

Maybe V had the right idea. Perhaps she should consider leaving. The idyllic Scottish village next to Dreagan and the Dragon Kings was amazing, but she would eventually let something slip about what she knew of them.

As much as Claire was looking forward to the night with V, she was also aware that nothing could come of it. She wouldn't allow it. It was simply a night of fun to help her forget about her diminishing options.

She chose a sleeveless gold shirt that dipped low in the front to show plenty of cleavage. Since she had nice breasts, there was no reason not to show them off. Claire paired the slinky shirt with white pants and her favorite white heels.

With her clothing picked, she turned to her vanity and sat before the bright lights. She pulled back her length of hair with a clip to get it out of her face. After dabbing at the tear streaks, she prepped her face with moisturizer and primer. Then she put on her base and concealer along with powder to set it.

Her next step was the eyes. Claire looked over the many palettes she had and opted for a bronze metallic look for the night. With her eyes primed, she set about creating the nighttime smoky eye look. She took her time, wanting it to be perfect.

With the shadow done, she donned eyeliner and mascara before working on her eyebrows. Once those were finished, she contoured her face with a little bronzer and blush.

Claire turned her head this way and that to make sure everything looked good. She removed the clip and slid her fingers through the strands of blond hair, deciding to leave it down and free. Her hair was thick and straight, so she didn't have to worry about it frizzing or doing much of anything for that matter.

All Claire had to do now was get dressed. There was

no mistaking the ball of nerves in her stomach. Which was silly. It wasn't like this was a real date.

You don't know that.

"I do actually," she argued with her conscience.

Do you? Why else would he ask you out?

"I don't know. But he's not shown any interest in me before."

That you know of.

"Oh, God. We could do this all night."

Take a chance, Claire. What's the worst that can happen?

She refused to say it aloud because to give voice to it meant that it might very well happen. And she'd had her heart broken too many times already.

"I'm so bloody pathetic," she whispered.

Because her conscience was right. She didn't know why V had asked her out. It could be because he felt sorry for her. Or . . . it could be because he was attracted to her.

She rose from the chair and walked back to her closet where she removed her robe and dressed. Then she put on a pair of long, gold, dangle earrings and a bracelet on each wrist. She slipped a thin gold ring onto her left thumb and a butterfly ring on her right middle finger.

Then she returned to the vanity and pulled out the drawer that held her lipstick and lip gloss. Her gaze moved to the section of nude colors, and she chose her favorite. With a slow, steady hand, she primed her lips, lined them, and then put on the color.

Claire turned off the lights of the vanity and rose to stand before her full-length mirror. She looked good, if she did say so herself.

Now, all she had to do was wait for V to arr—

Her thought was interrupted by a knock on her front

door. Claire's stomach dropped to her feet. Her hands shook as she reached for the small, white envelope purse in her closet. With every step to the door, her nerves jumbled, tangling with each other until she was nearly hyperventilating.

She had to fist her hand to get it to steady before she reached to open the door. It swung open to reveal V. He looked utterly magnificent in black slacks and a dress shirt that came close to matching his ice blue eyes. His long hair was pulled back at the base of his neck, giving her a perfect view of his jaw.

"You look beautiful," he said as his eyes ran over her.

She couldn't help but smile at the compliment. "You look pretty amazing yourself. Come in." As he stepped inside, she walked to her every-day purse on the kitchen counter. "I'm nearly ready. I just need a moment."

"Take your time," he said.

Claire put some money, a credit card, her ID, mobile, and house keys in the clutch before she turned to him.

"Ready?" he asked.

She nodded. "I am."

He held out his arm toward the door. Claire walked to it, and he fell in step behind her. When the door closed softly behind her, some of her nervousness dissipated.

She spotted the dark silver hypercar parked behind hers and glanced at him over her shoulder. "Nice car."

"Thanks. I can no' take credit for it. It's one of the vehicles owned by Dreagan."

"Dreagan has that many?"

"A few," he said with a grin as they approached the vehicle. "It's a Rimac C."

Before she could reach for her door, he had the butterfly door open and waiting for her. She climbed inside the vehicle, marveling at it. He closed the door and proceeded to walk around the back. Claire hurriedly reached over and opened the door for him.

When V folded his large frame to get inside, he shot her a smile. He pushed the button to start the engine, but nothing revved. That's when she realized that it was an electric car. He then pulled out of the driveway. It wasn't until they were driving down the road that she realized she had no idea where he was taking her.

If it had been anyone other than V, she would've demanded to know. But it was V, and while she didn't know him well, Darius did. Claire trusted Darius, and if he trusted V, then so would she. And all of that had to do with the Kings saving her and Sophie from the Dark in Edinburgh.

The car sped down the road. Claire wracked her brain, trying to think of something to talk about, but she kept coming up empty. Her. The woman who could speak to anyone about anything couldn't find a single topic to start a conversation.

"If you want some music, feel free to find some," V told her while motioning to the radio. "Con told me it has something called satellite radio."

Finally! Something she could discuss. "Really? The options are endless with satellite."

Claire turned on the stereo. The first station it came to was some 90s station. She began pushing the right arrow button, letting it scroll to the next available station. She glanced at V occasionally to see if there was something he might like. So far, nothing.

Then she landed on the perfect station. They were playing Frank Sinatra. She leaned back, content in her finding.

"Happy?" V asked.

She nodded as she looked at him. "Who wouldn't be

happy listening to Frank? It's the Rat Pack station, which means they'll play Dean Martin and Sammy Davis Jr., along with others like Bing Crosby."

"It's nice. I like it."

"You make it sound as if you haven't heard it before."

He lifted his shoulders in a half shrug. "I have no'."

"Oh, you've been missing out. I have so much to teach you."

To her surprise, he smiled as he briefly met her gaze before returning his eyes to the road. "I'm looking forward to that."

"Since we've now driven from the village and in the opposite direction of Dreagan, I'm guessing we're going somewhere else?"

"Did you want to go to Dreagan?"

"No," she hurriedly said. "I like the idea of being alone with you."

He nodded. "Good."

She waited for him to continue. When he didn't, she said, "So, will you tell me where we're going?"

"Do you no' like surprises?"

"Most people say they do, but I don't. The few times I've been surprised, it wasn't nice."

V glanced at her. "I'm taking you to Inverness."

That meant a thirty-minute car ride. In close proximity to a very virile, very handsome man that she'd been thinking about kissing and touching for hours. "That sounds nice."

"I can turn around," he offered, slowing the car.

She jerked her head to him. "Please don't. I want to do this."

"You didna sound so sure."

"I still hold concerns about being out with you since you're Darius's friend."

"Forget Darius and everyone else. Let this night be about us."

It was a good suggestion, one she probably should've thought of herself. How irrational she must seem, continuing to bring up Darius.

"I like that idea," she said.

The headlights of an oncoming car showed V smiling as he pressed the accelerator.

DATING ADVICE

If there is any advice I can give, it's to ask questions. Lots and lots of questions. Oddly enough, I hear from both men and women that they're afraid to ask someone they're interested in questions.

WHY?!?!

How are you ever going to learn anything if you don't ask? I always imagine the worst thing that could happen to prepare myself. No matter what the outcome is, I know how to react if it's as bad as I think it could be.

SIDE NOTE: It's never as bad as I imagine it will be. So take that into account.

There are three things you need to ask the other person you're dating. When and how you ask is up to you, but these are the top three. However, I think the earlier the better to prevent some of the disasters we've all encountered.

Now, some people will be fine asking these questions to someone's face. They are quite personal, so some might feel better posing the questions via text or email. It allows the other person—and yourself—time to think and craft a response rather than being put on the spot.

Question #1: What are you looking for in a woman/ man?

This is pretty important, folks. You'll be able to tell right from the get-go if the two of you mesh. And the guy better turn around and ask what you're looking for. Be brutally honest. You're just getting to know each other, and if you put it all out there at the beginning, then he'll feel like he can, as well. It sets the stage for a relationship.

Question #2: What do you like as far as sex goes?

In some ways, this is more important than Question 1. For starters, if you're wild in bed and he isn't, one of you is going to be disappointed the first time you're together. Both of you may play it off as nerves, but the second time you have sex, it'll be the same. Then it gets awkward because one of you has to bring up that something isn't working. And one of you will have to make a change. Sometimes, that works out. Sometimes, it doesn't. It's better to know going in if you'll be compatible than to be surprised.

Question #3: What do you want/need in a relationship?

If you've made it past the other two questions with honesty, this one should be a breeze. This is where you lay it all out. It doesn't matter if you're in your early 20s or in your 60s. No one has time for games, and quite frankly, I don't know anyone who enjoys playing them. So, put all the good and bad out there. If you're someone who needs your man around all the time, you better tell him. If you need to talk and/or text with your man every day, let him know. If you like more space or don't like to constantly have his arm around you, tell him. Whatever you need him to do, you need to make sure that you return the favor when he tells you.

I know from your messages that you all believe I have all the answers for dating. Trust me, if I did, I wouldn't be single.

BUT . . . I have learned a few things along the way, and if I can pass them on to help someone navigate the minefield of dating life, I'm happy to do it.

Besides, you can never do enough good Karma, right?

Something else I learned was to be confident. Yes, we're all nervous the first time we meet up—even the guy. He may not show it, and that's fine. You'll see it in other ways. Women want men to be confident, and in turn, men want the same from women.

We are naturally drawn to self-assured and poised individuals. It's a great first in-person impression. So even if you spill your drink all over yourself (yes, I did that) or trip on the way to the bathroom (sadly, I've done that, as well), it'll be embarrassing, but it'll give both of you a reason to laugh.

In turn, he'll get to see another side of you. Hopefully, you won't burst into tears or run away if something bad happens. Just laugh it off, clean *yourself up, and tell him that you were too focused on his eyes/face/voice to concentrate properly. He'll eat that up.*

Yes, ladies, men LOVE being complimented. Everyone does. So, if you want him to dole out praise, make sure you do the same.

Oh. One last thing. We all have baggage we carry around from our childhood and/or relationships. There will come a time when both of you share such stories, but keep the start of this blossoming relationship positive and upbeat. Let him see you for the beautiful, vibrant, intelligent, and funny woman that you are.

In other words, when you're asking and answering those questions I mentioned above, I suggest being honest. But that doesn't mean you should go into detail of what you hated about your ex-lover or husband or whatever. Generalities work best here.

Now, I'm taking my Advice Hat off to finish getting ready for a date. Keep your fingers crossed I have something good to report.

Until next time!

CHAPTER TEN

V let his gaze move over Claire's nicely shaped backside as they walked into the restaurant. It had been nearly impossible to keep his eyes from her chest. The shirt allowed him a great view of her breasts.

He lightly placed his hand on the small of her back when they entered the establishment and saw the men look at her. Claire was beautiful every day. But tonight, she was breathtaking. The gold and white outfit complimented her blond hair and brown eyes.

V made sure to meet the gaze of every man who stared at her. Claire might not be his, but she was tonight. And he wanted everyone to know it.

Once they were seated, Claire reached for the menu and shot him a smile. "I had no idea we were coming here. I've heard so many rave things about this restaurant."

"Asher talked about it last week. Some of the others have been here as well, so I thought we'd give it a try."

"Thank you," Claire said, her eyes flashing with glee.

He'd had no idea his choice of restaurant would make her so happy. V liked the dim lighting and the soft music

playing. It was, he admitted, a romantic atmosphere. Not
that he knew anything about being romantic.

His attention was pulled from the menu to Claire once
more. He couldn't stop staring at her. Her skin looked as
if it glowed, and he had the overwhelming urge to reach
across the small table and run his finger from her neck
down to her breasts.

His cock hardened just thinking about it. Would she like
his touch? Would she lean toward him, seeking more? He
looked at her lips. He couldn't wait to taste her, and he was
definitely going to kiss her.

V made his fingers relax on the menu. The night was
still young. They had hours alone together. No one from
Dreagan was there watching, observing his every move.
It was just him and Claire.

She looked at him over her menu and smiled. That's all
he needed. She was content and relaxed. And while desire pounded through him as it had since that morning, he
found that the ache he'd realized was gone at lunch still
hadn't resurfaced.

They placed their orders. With the waiter gone, they
looked at each other over the single candle on the table. V
didn't usually spend a lot of time conversing with the women
he was with. But he wanted to know more about Claire.

Before he could ask her anything, she said, "Tell me a
secret."

V blinked. "A secret?"

She grinned. "Everyone has them. Tell me one."

"I expect the same in return."

"Deal," she stated with a grin.

V thought about it for a moment. She was right. He had
many secrets. Nearly all of them he couldn't share. But
there was one he could. "I doona particularly like people."

"I can see that. There are days when others are especially rude that I can't stand to be around them."

"I've spent so much time by myself that being with others is sometimes painfully difficult."

"Is it now? With me?" she asked hesitantly, a small frown forming.

He shot her a grin. "No' in the least. I promise you. Your turn."

"Hmm," she said, tapping her chin. "I hate clothes shopping."

"Now that does surprise me."

She leaned forward conspiratorially. "That's because I get a box delivered every month with clothes. Essentially, I have my own stylist. She knows what I like and what I don't. She knows my sizes, and we talk about what I'm looking for or need, and then she gets it to me."

"I had no idea anything like that was even available."

"It's not just for women, either. They have a men's division. And a kids'."

"Interesting. I suppose with all the shopping the women at Dreagan do, I assumed all of you enjoyed it."

Claire shrugged one shoulder. "I like clothes. I just hate trying to weed through racks of them looking for something. Shopping online is even worse. There is just so much to choose from. With my stylist, it's her problem to find things."

"I can see how that would be nice."

"Makeup on the other hand," Claire said with a laugh. "I shop for that way too much. I have quite a bit of it."

"It's something you love."

"It is. Some might think too much."

He considered that a moment. "Can you love something too much?"

"If we're talking about things like makeup, a job, a way of life, or where you live, no. People? Maybe."

"Have you ever been in love?" Since he hadn't, he was curious to know about her.

She looked down at her hands that were linked on the table. "There was a guy in school I thought I loved. Then I met one at University and realized what I felt for the first one was nothing. I got my heart broken a dozen times after that. All the while, I believed that I knew exactly what love was." Her eyes slowly lifted to meet his. "Then I watched Sophie fall in love. I saw the way Darius treated her, how devoted he was. And I knew I was seeing true love from someone other than my parents, who I'd believed all this time were a rarity. Sophie and Darius give me hope."

V nodded, understanding exactly what she meant.

"People bandy the word love around a lot," Claire continued. "I'm not sure most people know what it means. Now that I do, I refuse to settle for anything less than what Sophie and Darius have."

"You shouldna settle. No one should."

"It's the fear of being alone. That's why so many mistake what they're feeling for love. Or perhaps they want it so badly that they grab hold of the first person who likes them back."

V cocked his head at her. "You have no' done that."

"I can see why so many do, though. Everywhere you look, there're couples. It's hard not to want that, dream about it, wish to experience it. What about you? Have you ever been in love?"

V shook his head slowly. "Never."

"Do you believe in it?"

"It's hard not to when I'm surrounded by so many at Dreagan who are in love."

"Do you want to fall in love?"

He swallowed. "Yes."

Thankfully, the food arrived, so the conversation ended as they dug into their meals.

CHAPTER ELEVEN

"You've surprised me."

Claire smiled at V's admission. She lifted the glass of whisky to her lips and drank. "You didn't think women liked Scotch?"

"I knew they did, I just didna expect you to be one of them. You doona have the look."

"There's a look?" Claire asked with a chuckle. "Should I be offended by that?"

He quickly shook his head. "Please, doona be. I didna mean it that way. If you'd seen the women I have while drinking whisky, you'd understand."

Claire held up the glass and looked at the amber liquid. "I drank my first whisky at University. It was horrid. I hated it. But one of my friend's boyfriends came from money, and he told me that not all Scotch is the same."

"It isna."

She grinned. Of course, V would say that. He was part of the most famous distillery in the world. "I didn't believe him until he brought a bag full of the tiny bottles to our room. That night, he taught me and my friend all about whisky."

"All?" V asked, brow raised.

"All that he knew," she admitted. "I discovered that I preferred single malt and that the more expensive the brand, the more I enjoyed it. I got away from it for a long time, but being so close to Dreagan, I started drinking it again. It's an expensive habit that I only indulge on special occasions."

V leaned back in his chair, watching her with a half-smile that made her all too aware of how sexy he was. "That's shite, lass. You have a direct connection to Dreagan. Surely, Sophie or Darius has been giving you all the bottles you want."

"I wouldn't dream of asking for that."

"You shouldna have to. I'll bring a bottle tomorrow."

She set down her glass. "I wasn't fishing for that."

"I know."

"Well, thank you."

Claire couldn't believe the evening was flying by so quickly. The conversation had gotten deep before dinner, but once the food arrived, it was as if they silently agreed to move to lighter subjects. He'd asked her about University, and before she knew it, she was telling him all her crazy stories while they ate.

"I've dominated the conversation," she said after their plates had been removed.

He licked his lips after taking a drink of whisky. "Your exploits are quite entertaining. I could listen all night."

"It's your fault. You kept asking questions. Now, it's my turn."

His smile faltered a fraction. "Ask away."

Though he said the words, she didn't feel as if he really meant them. Claire took another sip of the whisky. "The dinner was delicious. This place is fantastic. Thank you for bringing me."

"It was my pleasure. Truly. And, Claire?"

"Yes?"

"Ask your questions."

She crossed her arms on the table. "I get the impression that you'd rather I didn't."

"We're getting to know each other. If I doona want to answer something, I'll tell you."

"Okay," she hedged. Damn. Now she had to come up with something that she hoped V would answer. "Who are you closest to at Dreagan?"

V drew in a breath as he contemplated her question. "I interacted with Con more than the others while I was away. However, Roman and I are pretty close. He helped me locate what was stolen."

"I've seen Roman. That is to say, Sophie pointed him out to me when I was at Dreagan, but I've never met him."

"What do you think of Con?"

"He's intimidating," she confessed with a laugh.

V grinned. "He would enjoy hearing that."

"No doubt. Actually, he was very polite."

Claire finished off her drink. As she set it down, she realized that V's was also empty.

"Do you want dessert?" he asked.

She grimaced at the thought of more food. "I don't think I could take another bite of anything."

Their gazes met and held. Claire's thoughts were no longer on food but on V. The way his blue eyes looked at her, she thought he might be thinking the same thing.

She licked her lips, tasting the remnants of the Scotch, and to her surprise, his gaze lowered to her mouth. Her heart raced as her blood heated. She didn't want to desire him, but it had been out of her hands from the moment she looked into his eyes. There was something special about

V that she connected with. As if they were two pieces of a puzzle that fit together.

"Is there anything else you want?" he asked.

It was on the tip of her tongue to say, "you," but she managed to hold back. Then she wondered why she didn't say it. The only way to know if something might happen was to take chances.

He smiled slowly, causing her stomach to quiver at the intense look in his eyes. She didn't want the moment to end, but it did with the arrival of the waiter.

In no time, the check was paid, and they were walking back to the car. Claire didn't want the night to end. She was thoroughly enjoying herself. Maybe it was because it wasn't a real date. She knew V most likely wasn't interested in her, so she didn't feel like she had to put her date face on and try to say and do all the right things to impress the guy.

In the car, V started the engine, but he didn't put it in drive. His head swung to her. "Are you ready to go home?"

"Not if you aren't. I'm up for anything."

"Is that so?"

She shot him a flirty look. It was time to take a chance. "Oh, yes."

"Then I know the perfect place."

"You going to tell me?" she asked as he pulled out of the parking lot.

V's gaze was locked on the road. "You'll have to wait until we get there. I hope you're adventurous."

"I hope so, too." Claire wasn't at all daring. Or spontaneous.

And yet, tonight, she'd been both.

Her gaze was directed out the passenger door window. The moon was nearly full, but the stars still shone brightly.

"As a child, I used to lie on the ground at night and just stare up at the sky."

"Were you looking for something?"

"I just loved the stars."

"Do you still look up at them?" he asked.

She glanced at him. "Sadly, no. Every once in a while, like tonight, I'll take notice of the moon and stars. I remember how much joy I used to get out of simply looking at them, wondering if there was life out there other than us. I'd dream up all these different places and imagine the people there."

"You were no' part of the stories?"

"No." She frowned and looked at him. "I wasn't, actually. When people make up fantasies like that, it usually includes them, doesn't it?"

"I doona think there is a right or a wrong way for something like that."

Claire folded her hands in her lap, her mood dimmed by the realization that her daydreams had been anything but normal.

Then V spoke. "When I was a lad, all I wanted was to explore. My mum died soon after I was . . . um . . . born. It was just my da and me for many years after that. He knew I stayed because of him, so he urged me to find my way in the world."

"That was good of him."

"While I explored, he stepped in to help out someone of our clan. In the process, he was killed by a rival clan."

Claire knew that the clans had to be dragons. At least, she assumed. If only she could ask. "I'm so sorry."

"It was a verra long time ago," V said.

She touched his arm, wanting him to know that she understood his pain. "That kind of pain never goes away."

His gaze briefly met hers. "Aye."

Her hand fell away as he slowed and pulled off the road. She had no idea where they were headed. They had driven back toward Dreagan, but the road took them deeper into the forest.

"If you doona like where we stop, tell me. I'll take you wherever you want to go," V stated.

She smiled, nodding. Claire enjoyed being with him. And she liked how she felt when she was with V. The last thing she wanted was to go home. The simple fact that he hadn't ended their *date* after dinner made her very happy.

It wasn't long before she saw the loch through the trees. She sat up straighter, trying to get a better look at it. There were lochs all over Scotland, but this was one she hadn't seen before.

V pulled to a stop on the side of the road and turned off the engine. Her head swung to him. For long moments, he was silent, simply holding her gaze. Then he unbuckled his seatbelt and got out of the car. By his silence, he was leaving the decision of whether to get out up to her.

Claire followed and came to stand next to him at the front of the car, looking out over the water. "It's spectacular."

"Do you trust me?"

She'd said she wanted to take chances. Well, here was one right in front of her. She looked down at V's outstretched hand. There was only the briefest of hesitations before she put her palm against his. "Yes."

He smiled and pulled her after him as he walked to the edge of the loch. The water lapped gently against the rocks lining the shore.

"I don't see any houses," she said.

"This is part of Dreagan."

"Oh."

He leaned toward her and pointed to a peak toward the left. "That's my mountain."

"Yours?"

"Aye. Each of us at Dreagan has our own."

Of course. Where else could a dragon go but inside a mountain? Why hadn't Claire thought of that before? "It's lovely."

He straightened. And for the next five minutes, they stood in silence. Claire was lost in thought about the Dragon Kings and what they might do if they learned she knew their secret. But that quickly shifted to the realization that V hadn't said anything.

Maybe he was waiting for her to talk. The longer she remained silent, the more he might think she didn't want to be there. And the more she thought about that, the more she was cognizant of his body next to hers. They still held hands, their shoulders brushing against each other.

"Want to go for a swim?"

His question startled her. Claire blinked up at him. "Are you serious?"

"Aye."

"But . . . I don't have a swimsuit."

His grin was slow curving his lips. "Neither do I."

This wasn't something Claire would do. It was rare for her to sleep with a guy on the first date, but this wasn't even that. This was V seeing her naked to swim.

And why the hell shouldn't she?

Life was too short. Not to mention, she was an adult. She didn't have to answer to anyone but herself. It was time she did something just for her. Something that made her happy. Something fun.

"Yes."

V didn't hesitate in removing his shoes and unbuttoning his shirt. Claire couldn't believe what she had agreed to. It was so out of the norm for her, but it felt right. And she felt safe with V.

She bent to unbuckle the straps around her ankles. Then she removed her heels. Next, she took off her jewelry and set it all inside her shoes. Her pants were next.

It wasn't until she had one leg out that she realized she wasn't taking advantage of watching V. Her gaze shot to him, and her heart skipped a beat. His shirt was gone, giving her a wonderful view of his amazing chest and all the hard muscle there from his shoulders down to his washboard stomach.

He looked up then and smiled at her as he unfastened his pants. Claire swallowed heavily and finished removing her own pants. She turned to the side and folded them before grabbing the waist of her shirt and pulling it over her head.

She let it drop atop her pants. Then, with a deep breath, she faced V. He stood beneath the moon in all his glory. And was he magnificent. Every inch of him looked molded from granite. From his wide chest to his narrow hips and long legs.

Her gaze snagged on his hard cock, and her blood ran like fire through her veins. She snapped her eyes back to his face, but it was in shadow. She couldn't see his expression to know what he thought of her looking at him. Then she realized that if he didn't want her to look, he would already be in the water.

"You can change your mind," he said.

Claire shook her head. "I don't want that."

He turned and walked to wade into the water. She thought she saw a tattoo on his back, but the shadows made it difficult to see. When he got waist-deep, he dove beneath the surface. Claire watched, mesmerized. She had to shake herself to remember that she was supposed to be in the loch with him.

But she wasn't going to do it with her bra and panties on.

She unhooked her bra, letting it fall from her fingers when V's head surfaced. He stilled then, watching her. Claire slowly tugged her panties down until they puddled at her ankles.

With more confidence than she'd ever had before, she made her way toward the water. As soon as she stepped in, V stood. The water rushed down his chest to fall back into the loch at his waist.

Once more, he held out his hand. Claire reached for him as she walked deeper into the cool water—and into something unknown.

And totally exciting.

CHAPTER TWELVE

The water swirling around V's body did nothing to calm the desire that had been roused. It had simmered all day by being close to Claire.

Dinner had been a special kind of exquisite torture. To be so near her—and yet doing his best to keep his hands to himself.

V might have kept from touching her, but his thoughts had undressed her a million different times. Yet nothing had prepared him for seeing her shed each piece of clothing. The uncertainty in her gaze had disappeared quickly enough, replaced by anticipation and exhilaration.

When the last layer was gone, and he got to see her gorgeous body, he was awestruck. Claire was simply perfection in his eyes. From the full globes of her breasts to the depression of her waist—and the sexy flare of her hips.

To his utter shock and delight, her sex was bare of any hair. He never would have expected it of her. It showed that there was much more to Claire than anyone knew.

He held out his hand, waiting for her fingers to latch on to his. There was a hint of vulnerability in her gentle brown eyes. Despite the many times she had been hurt, she kept putting herself out there, waiting and hoping to find the man who matched her heart.

There was much he could learn from her. No wonder he had been drawn to her. For many weeks, he'd kept his distance. All that time wasted when he could have gotten to know her and enjoyed countless hours with her.

Hearing her laugh, watching her lips turn up in a smile, seeing her eyes look at things with wonder and intrigue. And joy.

When he had a hold of her, V slowly pulled her toward him. He wanted her body against his, but he stopped himself. Because once she touched him, he wouldn't be able to hold back. It was taking all of his willpower as it was to be on his best gentlemanly behavior.

"You're beautiful in the moonlight," he told her.

Her gaze lifted to him. "What is it about you that makes me do things I normally wouldn't?"

"Maybe it has been inside you the entire time, and you didna know it. Perhaps you needed someone to show you that you can."

"Or maybe it's just you."

V's eyes lowered to the water. The dark made it hard for mortals to see, but for a dragon, it didn't hinder him any more than the light did. And when he saw the water lapping against Claire's hard nipples, all the blood rushed to his already aching cock.

His gaze jerked back to her face when she stepped closer. Inches separated them now. He couldn't stop himself from putting his hands on her waist.

"Why the water?" she asked.

He shrugged. "It's a beautiful, warm night. Why no' enjoy it?"

"Do you do this often with women?"

"I've never done this before."

Her lips curved into a small smile.

His statement pleased her, and in turn, that made him happy. He saw her shiver. "Is it too cold?"

"It's not the water that made me shudder." Her gaze held his as she paused. "You did."

Did she have any idea how deeply her simple confession touched him? The idea that being with him in the loch, drenched in moonlight made her shiver only made her more attractive.

When he pulled her toward him, she didn't resist. Instead, she placed her hands on his chest. The heat of her palms on his skin was like a brand marking him.

V wasn't sure if he was the cause or if it was Claire, but suddenly, their bodies were pressed against each other. Her face was lifted to him, and her lips slightly parted.

There was no use in him attempting to claim even a modicum of control. He'd lost it the moment Claire agreed to swim with him. He just hadn't realized it. And it didn't matter. He'd known exactly what he was doing by getting her naked and in the water.

He wanted her. In every way possible.

V lowered his head. When Claire's eyes drifted shut the same time she tilted her face, there was no going back. He pressed his lips to hers and felt their softness.

A soft moan escaped Claire as she slid her arms up and around his neck. He moved his to her back the same time he grazed his tongue against the seam of her lips. They opened instantly.

Their tongues brushed against each other. The hotter the fire between them grew, the deeper they kissed. In moments, their breathing was ragged as they clutched desperately at each other, seeking to get closer, to become one.

V reached down and grasped Claire's thigh, pulling her leg up so he could grind his arousal against her. She tore her lips from his and moaned loudly. He caught sight of her neck and began licking and kissing it as he continued to rock his hips.

She dug her nails into his shoulders and leaned her head back to give him better access. The more he saw of her passion, the more he wanted.

But this wasn't an ordinary woman. This was Claire. V liked her. A lot. He also respected her.

She was in his arms, willing and ready for whatever he wanted. The taste of her kisses was delicious. Her touch . . . mind-blowing. Holding her was everything he'd thought it would be. And more.

So fucking much more.

It would take nothing to lift her higher and sink his cock inside her. He craved it so much that he shook with it. And yet, V released her leg. Before he changed his mind, he spun her around so that her back was pressed against his chest.

He briefly closed his eyes and drew in a deep breath of her hair that smelled like fresh summer rain. Then he cupped her breasts in his hands, massaging them.

"Yes," she murmured.

Her husky tone made his balls tighten. V kissed along the top of her shoulder. Her head tilted to the side so he could continue his path up to her ear. He lightly scraped his tongue along the lobe of her ear and felt her shiver in response.

The sound of her breath sucking in through her lips when he squeezed her nipples made him clench his jaw as longing rushed through him.

He moved one hand down the side of her body to learn every hill and valley. At her hips, he slowed his advance and shifted toward the juncture of her thighs. Smooth skin met his fingers. Her legs parted, granting him access.

V moved his hand lower and felt her. "You're so damn wet," he murmured.

"You do it to me."

If she kept talking like that, his willpower would crumble. But he didn't stop touching her. His finger found her clit and circled it, slowly at first and then gradually faster.

"V," Claire cried out as her head rolled back against his chest.

He kept kissing her ear and neck while teasing her nipple and stroking her clit. Her body undulated against him, and every time her ass came in contact with his cock, he had to bite back a groan.

She reached back an arm and sank her fingers into his hair. Then she turned her head toward him. Without hesitation, he took her lips, drinking in her cries as he worked her body faster and faster.

Claire climaxed moments later. The sight of her mouth open on a silent scream as her body convulsed with rapture was the most beautiful thing he had ever seen. V pushed her to the point where pleasure became pain. Right as he reached it, he spread his hands over her body and simply held her.

It was long minutes later before her breathing returned to normal, but neither of them moved. V didn't want to shatter whatever peace they had found together. But he knew it couldn't last forever.

The longer they remained, the more he realized that he had discovered something he'd been searching for his entire life.

And he'd found it in the arms of a mortal.

Without a word, Claire turned in his hold. He looked down into her face and caressed her cheek. There was no turning back now. He'd crossed a line, one that he'd never thought he would find.

"Why did you stop?" she asked.

He frowned. But before he could think of a reply, she wrapped her fingers around his arousal.

She gave him a slight squeeze. "Why did you stop when you aren't finished?"

"I wanted to give you pleasure."

"Then let me give it in return."

V was helpless to refuse as she kept a hold of him and drew him into shallow water. He could only watch, enthralled, as she dropped to her knees. She hadn't taken her hand from his cock the entire time. Now, both her hands grasped his length as she looked up at him.

She kept his gaze as she leaned forward and wrapped her lips around the head of his rod. It was the sexiest thing he had ever seen. He watched as her hands moved up and down while her tongue swirled around his tip. Then she cupped his ball sack, and he was lost.

V's head dropped back, and he looked up at the stars while being given such delicious pleasure. Claire's mouth and hands had him on the edge faster than he'd ever been before.

She worked him effortlessly until he was flung toward an orgasm that he couldn't control. He pulled out of her mouth right before he came. V fisted his hand as his seed shot from him and landed on Claire's bare breasts.

"Bloody hell," he murmured when he could finally speak again.

There was a smile on her face as she sat back on her heels. "I wanted to return the favor."

"You did. Nicely, I might add."

She licked her lips and looked down at the mess he'd made on her. "No one has ever brought me to orgasm as quickly or easily as you."

He could, in fact, say the same to her. But he chose to

keep that to himself. He was already treading dangerous ground as it was. If he wavered too much, he might. . . . Hell, he didn't know what might happen, but he wanted to find out.

Then he thought about his promise to Darius and the issues with his sword. He'd decided to take to his mountain because he didn't feel as if he fit in. Now, he wasn't so sure. He was confused.

It was best if he kept things as they were between him and Claire. Right? It wasn't what his body wanted, though. There, he'd royally fucked things up already. But he hadn't been able to help himself. Claire was too . . . well, she was too *everything*. Too pretty, too kind, too sexy, too desirable.

Too perfect.

How could he stand against that?

He kneeled down beside her and cupped his hands in the water before bringing them up to her breasts to wash away his seed. She said nothing, just watched him.

When he finished, he said, "I know the others wouldna have wanted me to bring you here. I probably shouldna have."

"I'm glad you did," she interrupted him.

"I wanted to show you that no' every man is like the ones you've dated."

She nodded slowly. "I know."

"You're verra beautiful."

"Then why do I feel as if you're trying to tell me good-bye?"

He paused, frowning. Was that what he was doing? What could he offer Claire when he didn't know his own path? "I suppose I am."

"I have to say that this night has been the best of my life."

V had never been anyone's best of anything. He could only watch as she stood and wrung out the ends of her hair that had gotten wet. Then she turned and walked back to her clothes. She said nothing while getting dressed. And he had no choice but to follow her lead.

Once they were back inside the car, he realized that the night was coming to an end, and that saddened him greatly. The day had been amazing. And once it was over—it was over. He wouldn't let himself get near Claire again.

Because if he did, he might never leave her.

CHAPTER THIRTEEN

The moment Claire opened her eyes the next morning, the sun seemed brighter, the sky bluer. She wasn't sure if it was the lack of sleep the previous night or the powerful climax she'd received at V's hand, but she'd slept like the dead.

Though, if she had to guess, she would say her deep slumber had everything to do with V. The man was so damn yummy.

But Claire knew better than to let herself fall for him. Not only was he a Dragon King, and she happened to know his secret, but he was also leaving soon.

It saddened her that he was going away. While she got on well with the other Kings, V was different. She was comfortable around him. The only other person who could get her to open up so easily was Sophie, yet around V, Claire was an open book. More like she word-vomited everything, but she couldn't seem to help it.

Was it because he was a Dragon King?

Claire threw off the covers and rose from the bed. If it were because he was a King, then Darius and the others should have the same effect on her. And they didn't. So, that wasn't it.

She stopped in front of the bathroom mirror and propped her foot against the other ankle. The entire episode in the loch replayed in her head, causing her to smile. V had the best hands. And mouth. And he'd only touched her.

Desire pooled in her belly at the thought of him thrusting inside her. She'd held his arousal. She knew just how impressive he was. Oh, to have him inside her.

Claire cleared her throat and inwardly shook herself. If she went down that road, she'd find herself pulling out her chest of sex toys. And while that might give her brief satisfaction, it wasn't what she wanted.

She wanted V.

"Vlad."

For years, she'd been content to know the kernel of truth about those at Dreagan. Now, she wanted to know everything. Every last detail and secret.

No way would that happen, however. At least, that's what she assumed. She could go to V and tell him that she knew what he was. There was a chance he would fill in the massive blanks about the Kings.

Or, he could take her to Dreagan and wipe her memories and make her forget all about them.

That, she simply couldn't chance. While it killed her to guess who the Kings were and why they were hiding their magic, she liked the knowledge she carried. Then there was the previous night with V. She didn't want those memories taken from her for anything.

When she was an old woman and dying, she would be able to think of a loch and remember how special she'd felt in Vlad's arms.

She glared at herself in the mirror. "Curiosity be damned, Claire. You'll never know anything more than you already do about them." She wouldn't even say Dragon Kings aloud for fear someone might be listening. "Deal with it."

With her declaration delivered, she began getting ready for the day. When she sat down at her vanity and looked at all the makeup, she decided that she didn't want to wear much that day. She opted for an illuminating primer that brought out the highlights in her skin.

Despite the multitude of eye creams she'd bought, not a single one helped diminish the dark circles under her eyes that still lingered, so she had no choice but to put on a little concealer. Then she added light brown eyeliner to the top of her lid, extending it just a tad.

She looked at herself in the mirror and decided that the bottom of her eyes didn't need any liner. Then she pulled out her mascara and got to work on her lashes. A quick comb through of her eyebrows, and her favorite pale pink lip gloss, and she was ready.

Claire went to take her hair down but paused. It boggled her mind how she could throw up her hair just to put on her makeup, and it turned out fabulously. But when she tried to recreate it for a night out, it never worked. Since it looked so good, she opted to leave it up.

She popped on her large, pink faux diamond stud earrings, her smartwatch, and thumb ring. Just as she was about to leave, she spotted a necklace and put it on. It was a small gold compass, but she always felt good when she wore it.

Then she went to the door. She nearly tripped over the bottle of Dreagan sitting in her path. Claire smiled as she grabbed it to bring inside. V had said he'd bring her a bottle, and he hadn't lied.

There was a spring in her step as she headed to her car. It wasn't until she was backing out that she realized she hadn't drunk her usual cup of coffee while getting ready.

Claire drove toward the clinic, smiling at how a great

night could change everything. The day before, she'd seriously contemplated everything that was wrong with her because, obviously, it was her fault that none of the men she dated seemed to work out. As she told others, she was the common denominator. Who else's fault could it be?

Now, she could not care less about her failed dates and relationships. V had helped her get her head on straight. Well, he'd given her a mind-blowing orgasm, but that'd helped her prioritize things.

Claire chuckled at herself. Yet the memory of the pleasure swimming through her made her squeeze her legs together, her sex pulsing. Her breathing grew labored, and her palms started sweating.

She was so wrapped up in thinking about her reaction that she passed the café. But she didn't turn around. She was still too freaked to attempt to navigate anything other than a straight line for the moment.

With only two turns to traverse, she managed to pull up next to the clinic. Claire turned off the engine and put her forehead on the steering wheel.

"It was just a night of sex. Not even sex," she corrected herself. "We pleasured each other. It can't be considered sex if he wasn't inside me. Right?"

She rolled her eyes at herself because there was no one there to answer. But she knew one thing, no matter how many times she'd had sex with other men, none of them had made her have such a drastic reaction the next day.

"Shit. Shit, shit, shitshitshitshitshit," Claire mumbled and squeezed her eyes closed.

This was bad. Really bad. She wasn't supposed to do anything but have a good time with V.

"Oh, I had that, all right."

Claire straightened and opened her eyes. Maybe it was

all in her head. There was a chance that it had just been such a good date that it eclipsed everyone else. Yes. That's all it was.

Because to think it might be something more was playing with fire. And she didn't want to get burned. If she dared to play with such a flame, she knew she wouldn't survive it. She wouldn't just get singed. She would come away so scorched that the scars would never fade.

"Hey!" Sophie said as she knocked on the window.

Claire screamed and jumped. "Sophie!"

Her friend laughed and opened the car door. "I got you good."

"Yeah. That you did," Claire replied sarcastically to hide her anger. She hated being startled like that.

She grabbed her purse and got out of the vehicle. After she shut the door, she turned and found Darius beside Sophie. The couple stared at her.

Sophie blinked, her gaze intensifying.

Darius frowned and said, "There's something different about you this morning, Claire."

"I haven't had any coffee," she replied.

Sophie shook her head as a smile tugged at her lips. "I know that look. Claire had sex last night, and whoever he was, he must have been really good to give her that glow."

In the time that Sophie and Darius had gotten together, he'd learned early on that there wasn't anything she and Claire didn't share. Which was why Claire wasn't the least bit embarrassed by Sophie's statement.

"It's true." Sophie clapped and glanced at her husband.

Claire swallowed and walked away. It wasn't like she could tell them anything, even if she did want to talk about it. Which she didn't.

"Hold up there," Darius said from behind her. "When did you become a fast-walker?"

"She does that when she's trying to get away," Sophie answered.

Claire sighed. This is what happened when her best friend shared everything with her husband. There wasn't anything about Claire that Darius didn't know. And in situations like this, it was like being ganged-up on. Though Claire loved them both dearly and wouldn't change anything for the world.

"Claire."

She came to a stop at the sound of Sophie's voice. Claire pivoted and faced the couple. "What? I just want to get inside."

"You always tell me about your dates," Sophie said, her brow puckered in concern.

Darius put an arm around his wife. "The fact she doesna wish to talk about him suggests that it went verra well."

"What makes you think it was a man?" Claire said with a lift of her chin. Then after shocking them both, she turned and unlocked the door to get inside the clinic.

Her trick didn't last long. Sophie was on her in an instant. "Don't try to fool me. I know you only have the hots for men, despite you being hit on by that pretty female nurse in Edinburgh."

When Claire looked at Sophie, Darius was gone. The man had a knack for knowing when she needed Sophie all to herself. The problem was, it didn't matter if he was around or not. She wouldn't tell either of them about V.

That was her secret. One she would treasure for the rest of her life.

"Why aren't you telling me?"

The worry and sadness in Sophie's voice pulled at Claire's heartstrings. She took her friend's hands in hers and smiled. "I love you like my sister. Why else would I follow you to the middle of nowhere to help with your practice?"

"But?" Sophie pressed.

"I can't tell you about this one."

Sophie's olive gaze narrowed in thought. "You either like this man that much, or . . . you're worried we'll find out who he is. Or both."

Damn Sophie for being so smart. She always did manage to work things out like that. Claire released her and let her hands drop to her sides. "Please don't ask any more. Know that I had a wonderful time. Know that no one has ever treated me so special before. And know that I need to keep this one to myself."

"Are you seeing him again?"

Sophie shook her head. "I don't believe so."

"If you had such a great time, why in heavens not? Tell him how you feel."

"He knows."

"Then, I don't understand. Surely, he had a good time, as well."

Claire forced a smile that she didn't feel. "I believe he did."

"After all the wankers you've gone out with, you finally found a good one. Claire, help me understand why you won't hold onto this with everything you have."

She couldn't come up with a reason that wouldn't cast either her or V in a bad light, so Claire decided not to say anything at all.

Sophie shook her head in confusion. "You're glowing. Actually glowing. Whoever this man is, I could kiss him for taking such good care of you. Then I could hit him for letting a woman like you slip through his fingers."

Claire hugged her friend before walking to her desk.

She sat down and looked at the day's schedule. While she appeared as if she were reading the list of patients coming in, she saw nothing because, out of the corner of her eye, she spotted Sophie staring at her.

It wasn't until her friend left that Claire was able to take a deep breath and focus. She put the first three patients' names to memory and rose to get their files. When she turned around, Darius was in the doorway, watching her.

Claire froze, wondering about the curious look in his eyes. But Darius walked away before she could ask him.

CHAPTER FOURTEEN

When was the last time he had become so lost in thoughts of a woman? V honestly couldn't remember. Surely, there was someone, but no matter how hard he searched his memories, he found nothing.

He'd been obsessed with getting back his sword for so many eons that nothing else mattered. Whenever he woke and left his mountain, he sated his body with willing women. But none of them meant anything.

He couldn't say the same about Claire.

V rubbed his forehead and turned away from the library window. He looked down and saw a book in his hand. When had he pulled it from the shelf?

"Fourth shelf up. Halfway to the right."

V froze at the sound of Roman's voice. He took a breath and returned the book to where he had gotten it from. Then he turned to his friend.

Roman stood with his feet braced apart, his arms crossed over his chest while his sea green eyes scrutinized V. "You seem distracted."

V shrugged in reply. There was no need for words.

Because he couldn't—and wouldn't—tell Roman the truth. And his friend didn't deserve a lie.

"I heard you took a car last night."

V wasn't surprised by the question. He'd expected someone to ask. "Aye."

"I also heard you were dressed up."

"Aye," V said with a sigh. "Spying on me now, are you?"

Roman glanced at the floor and dropped his arms to his sides. "We're worried. I was in that cave with you in Iceland. I know what happened, remember?"

"The fucking Others happened." V hated to even think about the group who seemingly made it their mission to screw with the Kings every chance they got.

Roman took a couple of steps toward him. "It's good that you got out last night. Did you meet someone?"

There was something about Roman's tone that told V his friend knew exactly who he had been with the night before. When V put that with Darius's request that he move around the entire storage room by himself, V realized what had happened. His friends had set him up.

Well, they'd put him in a position to spend time with a beautiful woman.

He'd done the rest.

"You know I was," V stated.

Roman didn't deny it. He flashed a quick smile. "Did you have fun?"

Fun? V had experienced a great many things while he'd been with Claire. Fun was only one of them. "I did."

Roman nodded slowly. "That's good. Are you seeing her again?"

V had seen her in his thoughts and memories every second since he walked her to her door and gave her one last kiss, something that had nearly brought him to his knees.

As much as V yearned to see Claire again, he wouldn't.

His world was too chaotic and dangerous to bring someone like her into it. Roman and the others might not think
twice about it, but V wouldn't do that to someone. He liked
Claire too much.

Which is why it hurt so bloody much to let her go. V
had finally found someone he connected with, someone he
couldn't get enough of. Someone who made him feel as if
he'd found a place in the world.

And he had to let her go.

"V?" Roman urged, his brow furrowed. "Are you going
to see her again?"

"No."

He walked past Roman and left the library. V stopped
when he came to the stairs. He looked up, thinking about
his chamber. But the bed made his thoughts turn to Claire.
Hell, everything made him think of her.

V squeezed his eyes closed and turned toward the side
door. The only place he could go now where no one would
bother him was his mountain. Maybe there he could find
some peace.

But he knew the truth. Only more memories of Claire
would be waiting for him.

"Well?" Roman asked as he walked to the doorway of the
library.

Ulrik stepped from behind one of the large columns and
said, "Something happened between V and Claire last
night."

"That's obvious. It's rattled him."

"It certainly has. Maybe that's a good thing."

Roman's brow quirked at the statement. "He's still
messed-up from Iceland. Are you sure about this?"

"From what Darius told me, Claire has had V's attention

for some time. By the way he's acting this morning, I'd say he's smitten."

Roman leaned a shoulder against the doorway. "I want him to use the sword as much as you do, but I doona know about this. With what little we know of the Others and their apparent vendetta against us, and the weapon going missing from Con's mountain, this seems like something we shouldna be focusing on."

Ulrik walked into the library and stopped before one of the large windows. Roman followed him and spotted V on his way toward his mountain.

"This is exactly what we should be focusing on," Ulrik said. "The weapon . . . will be found."

Roman frowned as he turned his head toward the King of Silvers. "You say that as if you are no' worried about it falling into enemy hands."

"At this point, it doesna matter."

"What is it exactly that you and Con know about the weapon that you willna tell us? It could no' have gotten free of Con's magic on its own. It had help."

Ulrik's chest expanded as he drew in a breath. "Aye, it did. And we will find it."

"You're awfully calm about something that has the ability to destroy us," Roman said and returned his gaze to V.

"I trust that we will win," Ulrik stated. "Just as with the Others. Whatever their endgame, we will triumph. I'm no' saying there willna be costs, but I do know one thing. The Others went after V's sword. I think it's because it holds more significance than even V knows."

Roman got it now. "And if V can get his head right, he might be able to figure out what that is."

"Precisely."

Still, Roman wasn't totally convinced. He watched V

disappear over a rise before he shifted toward Ulrik. "You're playing with his heart."

Ulrik faced him. "I'm opening V's mind. He's closed off to everything. He doesna know this world. Nor does he know where he fits in. Con and I are the only ones who have no' slept since we sent our dragons away. We watched everything change around us, bit by bit. V was driven half-mad by the Others when they took his sword and messed with his memories. He needs a reason to be here. And then, somewhere along the way, he'll figure out what's wrong with his sword."

"Are his brethren no' enough?"

"Step into his shoes, Roman. No one helped him for millions of years. He slept more than any of us. Each time he woke and left, Con would bring him back."

Roman rubbed the back of his neck. "You know as well as I do that even had we tried to aid V back then, nothing would've come of it."

"I do know that. So does he. But he needs to rectify that in his head, along with finding his footing here. He's good with women. Verra good. Yet they mean little more to him than a moment's pleasure."

Roman snorted loudly. "And you thought Claire would be a good distraction? I can no' believe Sophie agreed to this."

"She did, but only because we doona believe Claire is a distraction. Darius told me how he found V watching her the other morning. Something happened between V and Claire last night, but I doona believe it was just sex."

"He was distracted like he was deep in thought," Roman admitted.

"Or thinking about someone."

The grin Roman wore quickly faded. "What if Claire

doesna feel the same? She's been around many of us, and no' once has she done more than casual flirting. I doona believe she's interested in anyone at Dreagan."

"I'm taking Sophie's word on this. She said it was just what Claire needed."

"What if Claire remembers what happened in Edinburgh?"

Ulrik's lips thinned. "I've no' figured that part out yet."

"Have you figured out how you'll tell Con about this?"

"He's no' blind. That's the first thing all of you should remember. Con sees and knows more than any of you believe."

Roman jerked his head back. "I doona believe that. He isna the Keeper of History like Kellan. Besides, Con can no' read minds."

Ulrik just smiled. "Remember something for me. It takes more than just an incredible amount of magic and strength to become King of Dragon Kings. There is a mental aspect to it, as well. Con hides more than he'll ever show anyone. And he knows more than he'll ever admit."

"I'm really glad you're back. You understand Con as none of us ever have."

"Doona get me wrong. He keeps much from me, but I know him better than most of you. It's how I know when he's . . . well, when he needs time alone."

Roman was suddenly overcome with sadness. "So many of us have found love. We're even plotting to help V have a good time. And Con sits alone in his office."

"He made his decision because of the rest of us."

"It wasna right. None of us thought so. No' then. No' now."

Ulrik slapped Roman on the arm. "If you think I'm no' going to interfere in Con's life to put him on the right course, you'd be wrong. He once had the kind of love we have. I want to make sure he has it again."

"That's no' going to be easy."

"Nothing with Con ever is," Ulrik said with a grin.

Roman looked around the library. "Sabina just came into my life. I'm no' ready for any of this to end by the weapon or the Others."

"We're fucking Dragon Kings," Ulrik said and spread his arms wide, a smile on his face. The expression dropped, replaced by a look of reckoning and vengeance in his gold eyes. "Our magic is the strongest, and we're the most powerful beings on this realm. Whatever comes our way, we *will* stop it."

The moment V was in his mountain, he released a sigh. This was the only place he felt comfortable. Well, that wasn't entirely true. He also felt that way anytime he was with Claire.

Claire.

He walked deeper into his mountain, following the narrow passageway into the large cavern. He didn't stop until he came to the place where he'd hidden his sword. It was shrouded with magic now so that no one—not even a Dragon King—but he could touch it.

V wrapped his fingers around the hilt and lifted it. A long, deep sizzle ran through his fingers and into the sword. The weapon vibrated in his palm.

He was so shocked by the long-lost feeling that he froze. V released the sword and tried it again, but the same sensation didn't repeat itself. Yet, he had hope. His sword had accepted his magic. It had been brief, but it had happened.

And that meant there was a chance he could call the dragons home once more.

First, he had to figure out what he'd done to make the

sword work. Until he sorted that out, he wouldn't tell Con or the others what had happened. He didn't want to let his brethren down.

He sat against a large boulder and kept hold of the blade. With a sigh, he closed his eyes and allowed his mind to drift to thoughts of Claire. He sank deeper into reliving the moments of the previous night. Every sound, every touch, every sensation. He was surrounded by Claire.

And each time, his weapon reacted, sending volleys of magic through him. Without a doubt, there was some kind of connection between him being able to use his sword again and Claire. Now, he just had to figure out what it was.

HOW IT ALL CAME TO BE

For those who are regulars to the site (Thank you. Thank you very much!) you know the drill. However, some newbies have asked some questions. So, here it goes.

I never post about my dates—good or bad— until weeks (sometimes months or even years) after. It's to protect myself. I don't want the douche . . . I mean, guy . . . reading about himself the next day.

Because there are quite a few men who read these posts. And even more who email me asking if they were the man I wrote about. (I kid you not! You'd be shocked at how many of those emails I get.)

::add in massive eye roll::

Anyway. This blog began as a way for me to vent. I had a little pity-party one night that involved ice cream, too much wine, romantic movies, and sad songs. I watched the sun come up the next morning, and I needed to talk. To just . . . get all the pain and heartache and fear that was inside me out.

I didn't want to talk to my best friend again. I mean, she's awesome. But they can only hear the same thing so many times, right? I knew she'd never complain to me, but I didn't want to become a burden. And what was inside me HAD to come out. I couldn't leave it because it festered like a wound. And I really wanted to heal.

I still don't know why I posted that first message for all the world to see. There are private diary apps that I could've used. But maybe, deep down, I knew (or hoped!) that I wasn't the only one suffering. I wanted to find others like me.

Mostly so I didn't feel like I was an outcast who somehow didn't know the secret to dating. Obviously, I was doing something wrong, and I hoped that by putting my pain and embarrassment out to the rest of you, that someone would be willing to point out what I could or needed to change.

Instead, I discovered that there were countless others in a similar agonizing void of dating failure.

It saddens me that there are so many of us in the same boat. But at the same time, it makes me feel less like a catastrophe. That's why I kept the blog going. I had (sadly) many horrible dates to choose from to post about.

Some are really old while others are more recent. If you're new to the site and feeling depressed about your dating disasters and disappointments, all you need to do is read the comment section on any post to see that you aren't alone.

Life is hard. And then we date.

Which, in some cases, feels like we're traversing Dante's nine circles of Hell.

Sure, we'll all meet the assholes (men and women). The ones who cheat and lie and leave us feeling . . . less than. But every once in a while, we meet a true gem.

The ones who make us smile days after the date. The ones who give us butterflies before the first kiss—and even after when we think about it. The ones we find a connection with.

Sometimes, they last for just a day. Sometimes, longer. And if we're really, really lucky, they last forever.

I'm very picky about what I want in a man. I'm a strong woman, so I need a guy who is strong, as well. One of my friends labeled them alphas. Which, I have to be honest, is a pretty good description. They're always the guys I go for in movies, TV, and books.

Being alpha doesn't mean being an asshole. That's where so many men get it wrong. And some men are alphas without even realizing it. THOSE are the ones who get me Every. Time.

Hmmmmmmmmm.

Sorry. Got lost in a fantasy for a moment. My point is that it's not wrong to know what you're looking for in an individual. If you are aware, then that means you've looked at yourself closely, and you realize what will make you happy.

I think that's why online dating works so well. We list out what we're looking for in a potential match. My favorite sites are the ones that tell you how well you match up with someone. I tend to get solid 83%-88% with most men.

Occasionally, I'll get a 95%.

That's cause for celebration, right?

No. Because, inevitably, anyone with a 90% rating or higher is exactly what I'm not attracted to. I keep thinking that Karma must be a woman who loves to give me those kinds of things, all while laughing her ass off.

At least I like to think of Karma as a practical joker. Otherwise, I might start to get a little paranoid.

So, my lovely readers, I tell you all of my humiliations and shame so you'll know you aren't alone. Because you aren't. Just keep the hope alive that there's someone out there for you. They are out there. They may just need a little help to find you.

Until my next failure!

CHAPTER FIFTEEN

The tele was on, but Claire didn't see or hear it. It just filled the silence of her small house.

She couldn't remember a day that had passed so quickly before. Thankfully, she didn't have many chances to look up and hope to see V. The few times that did happen though, it had been a disappointment *not* to see him.

Even though she knew she wouldn't.

But she still hoped. And it was hope that ruined everything for once in her life.

She curled her toes to stretch them. Claire had come home, changed into lounge clothes, and immediately laid out on the couch. She didn't attempt to cook, instead ordering food to be delivered. The half-touched cartons of Chinese takeaway spoke of where her mind was. But the wine sure did taste good.

She lifted the glass to her lips and took another drink of the pinot noir. No matter what Claire had told herself, no matter what truth she knew, she'd still looked for Vlad when she left the clinic that evening.

Her gaze had searched for some sign of him. And when he hadn't been there, the disappointment that filled her had been debilitating. It was so bad that it had nearly threatened to ruin the happiness of the night before.

That's when she got herself under control. The date with V had been incredible, and she didn't want anything destroying that. She allowed herself to feel a little sad, but she also remembered that he'd told her he planned to leave.

He also hadn't said anything about seeing her again. What he had done was tell her that he wanted to give her a nice night. And he'd done that and more. It was a night she would never forget.

Claire rose from her reclining position and set aside her wine on the coffee table. She walked into the bathroom and wound her hair atop her head. Then she washed her face, removing the little bit of makeup that she had put on that morning.

She straightened as she patted her skin with the towel. She gazed at the tub. A nice long soak might be just what she needed, but when she thought of the water, she thought of V.

And her body hungered for more of him.

All day, the desire had struck her at inopportune moments. She'd held his length in her hand, tasted him on her tongue. But she hadn't felt him inside her.

Her eyes closed. She gripped the sink as an intense need flooded her, so powerful the room spun. When she was able to open her eyes again, she hurried to her bedroom and kneeled next to her bedside table to reach for the decorative box.

She opened the lid and looked inside at the various sex toys. Her sex drive was something she'd embraced early on in life. And while she did indulge in the rare one-night stand, she found that to really enjoy sex, she had to have an emotional connection.

How she managed to have that connection with Vlad after only one date, she'd never know. But that was the only explanation she had for orgasming at all. It was a fact of her life that she never climaxed the first time she slept with a man.

Actually, it was rare even during the second time. And she blamed herself for not being upfront and honest with the men in telling them what she wanted and needed.

But she hadn't had to do that with V. He'd known. Somehow, he'd known exactly where and how to touch her to bring about such exquisite pleasure that she still craved it.

Claire reached for one of the toys, but just before her fingers closed around it, she changed her mind. She discarded one after another until there was nothing left to choose. And yet she needed to relieve the ache V had woken.

She squeezed her legs together. If she were brave or forward or whatever it was people called it, she would get dressed and go see him. If they let her into Dreagan.

It wasn't like she knew his number. He didn't even know hers, so she couldn't contact him that way. And she certainly wasn't going to ask Sophie or Darius for it. That would just be embarrassing.

That meant she could either sit here with need thrumming through her, or she could make use of a toy. Since she'd suffered all day, she knew she had to do something, or she wouldn't sleep at all.

Claire closed her eyes and reached inside the box. Her fingers closed around one of the many satin bags that individually held each toy and pulled it out.

She laid it on the mattress and quickly stripped out of her clothes. Then she opened the bag and pulled out the vibrator. She got into bed and let her mind drift to V as she turned on the toy.

V made himself walk past Claire's house. If he stopped like he wanted to and looked inside for some glimpse of her, he was nothing more than a stalker. But he couldn't go to the door and knock.

He couldn't see her. Because if he did, he would kiss her. And if he kissed her, then he would make love to her. So far, he'd managed to hold himself back, but it was getting harder and harder.

Was it because he couldn't have her that he wanted Claire so desperately? Or was it something else? Something . . . more? The very thing he craved.

V wasn't sure, and it didn't matter. All he knew was that the hunger to taste her lips again was crushing. And that wasn't all he wanted to sample on her body.

He'd gone for a walk earlier after his time in the mountain. He'd told himself it was to stretch his legs and think, but he had thousands of acres on Dreagan to do that. Instead, he'd walked to the village—and straight to the clinic.

Because he couldn't stop thinking about Claire.

When he saw her making her way alone from the building to her car, he'd almost called out. But at the last minute, he'd ducked behind a tree. It was just a second later that she had looked around as if searching for someone. Was it him? Had she wanted to see him?

V had tried to go back to Dreagan after that, but instead, he'd ended up at the pub. Laith attempted to talk to him. Even Guy and Tristan sat with him, but he'd had no interest in conversing with anyone.

Not when all he wanted was Claire.

After a couple of ales and twice as many fingers of

whisky, he'd started back to Dreagan. Except he ended up near Claire's house, walking back and forth while trying to tell himself to leave her—and the attraction between them—alone.

He stopped and stared at her door, but when he actually thought about what he would say to her, V realized he didn't know where to start. And that's where he should leave it.

With her, he'd found something special. She'd helped him find the missing connection to his sword, which he would be forever grateful for. But he still hadn't gotten the weapon to respond to him properly. He needed to focus on that for his brethren.

"Good-bye, Claire," he said and turned on his heel.

It was better if he never saw her again. In fact, he was going to make sure of it.

CHAPTER SIXTEEN

Deep inside Dreagan Mountain

Henry rubbed his eyes with his thumb and forefinger. He'd stared at the map for so long that his vision was blurring. He walked around the room, moving his neck from side to side to help stretch out the kinks that had knotted his shoulders.

He stopped and leaned against a wall, dropping his head back against it. He would have never thought in a million years that he would be sitting in a manor in Scotland with a race of immortal, magical beings.

Then again, he hadn't expected to ever just be himself. Not a spy for MI5. But he'd left his position to give himself and all his contacts to the Dragon Kings so he could help them in any way possible.

Not that they needed it. While they didn't use their magic for such things, the Kings were highly intelligent and resourceful individuals. Constantine even more so.

Yet Henry had wanted to help. Ryder was a mastermind with computers and anything electronic. Vaughn handled all of Dreagan's legal issues, and he wasn't a solicitor any-one in the world wanted to tangle with. He never lost.

Each Dragon King brought something different and unique to the mix. And that wasn't even counting their magic. So, why had they asked him for help? Was it pity?

Henry shook his head. His friendship with Banan had begun his introduction to the world of the Dragon Kings, Fae, Druids, Warriors, and even Reapers. But if Henry had learned one thing about those at Dreagan, it was that they kept to themselves. He wasn't there because someone felt sorry for him. Because anyone associated with the Kings could be compromised, and their secret revealed. The Dragon Kings had worked too hard to hide their true selves.

Henry wanted to believe that he brought something unique to the table, but he was no fool. There wasn't a sin-gle thing that he did that one of the Kings couldn't do better.

"I know that look."

Henry's head swung toward the open door as his sister walked in. Esther had become entangled with the wrong people while working for MI5. That had brought her to the Kings, where they discovered that her mind was controlled by a Druid.

And yet, somehow, Esther hadn't just been freed of the magic, she had found love in the arms of a King. Now, she was mated to Nikolai. Henry couldn't be happier for her, but that didn't mean he didn't feel sorry for himself. Espe-cially since the one he wanted wouldn't even look at him.

The moment he thought of Rhi, Henry slammed the door on such thoughts. One kiss from the Light Fae and he'd fallen hard for her. Everyone said it was only because she was Fae, that he didn't really love her.

Frankly, he was tired of talking about it.

"Henry?" Esther asked as she walked closer. She wore a frown that warned that this wasn't a casual visit. She was here for something.

He forced a smile. "I'm good, sis."

"You don't look it."

"I'm tired."

"That I can see." She put her hands on her hips and looked him over in a stern British way. "You need sleep."

Henry ran a hand over his jaw, feeling the scrape of whiskers. A reminder that he hadn't shaved in days. Or was it weeks? He couldn't remember. "I sleep. And eat," he said before she could make a comment about that.

"When was the last time you got out?"

"Of this room?" he asked.

She rolled her eyes in frustration. "The bloody house, wanker."

"I have."

"When?" she demanded, lifting a dark brow.

Henry started to answer, then realized he couldn't recall where he'd gone.

Esther blew out a breath and dropped her arms to her sides as she walked to stand before him. "Henry, I'm worried about you. All you do is stare at that bloody map," she stated, pointing at the massive backlit chart that encompassed the wall opposite him.

"First, it was the Dark Fae," she continued before he had time to reply. "Now, it's the weapon."

"I still have my eye on the Dark."

Esther turned her head away for a brief moment. When her brown gaze slid back to him, there was resolve there. "You have to stop this."

"And do what?" he demanded. "If I don't do this, there

is nothing for me here. Do you want me to go back to England? Rejoin MI5?"

She gaped at him. "Of course not."

"Then what?" He pushed away from the wall and towered over her, glaring. "What do you want from me?"

"I want you to be happy."

"I am."

"The hell you are," Esther replied angrily. She narrowed her brown eyes at him. "You focus on anything you believe will benefit the Kings, all so you can remain here in the hopes of catching a glimpse of Rhi."

Henry didn't deny it. What good would that do? Now that he'd seen the inner workings of the Dragon Kings and knew just how much they fought not only for themselves but also for Earth, he couldn't imagine doing anything else.

Even if he was very aware of everything he lacked compared to the Kings.

"This isn't about Rhi," Henry said.

Esther snorted loudly. "I wish I could believe that."

"Tell me, sis," he said, catching her gaze. "After you discovered the Kings, and before you fell in love with Nikolai, could you have walked away?"

"Y—"

"Who's the liar now," Henry interrupted before she could finish the word.

Esther blew out a long breath. "Perhaps, you're right. Maybe I wouldn't have been able to leave."

"You didn't."

"I stayed because of you."

Henry raised a brow, daring her to continue in that vein.

Esther rolled her eyes again. "All right. Fine. Maybe it was because I was intrigued and terrified of all I'd learned."

"And you want me to walk away?"

"Not away from the Kings or even Dreagan. But away from this," she said, her voice rising with her conviction as she motioned to the map. "You haven't felt the sun on your face in weeks. You eat, but do you taste anything? And I know you don't sleep more than a few hours at a time."

He looked away, not wanting to hear her. But there was no getting away from this. "Who sent you? Banan? Con?"

"I sent myself when none of them would say anything to you," she replied in a soft tone.

Henry walked around her to stand before the map. "When you look at this, what do you see?"

She moved beside him and crossed her arms over her chest. Esther issued a half-shrug. "I see countries with different colored pins stuck in them."

"I see so much more. Each colored pin means something different. The red ones are for the Dark Fae. See how they're still clustered in the lower half of Ireland? But you can also see that they've begun to spread out around the world again," he explained, motioning with his hand. "Then there is the black pin. That is where the weapon was last seen. Right here on Dreagan. I use the yellow ones for any mention of something out of the ordinary that might pertain to the weapon or magic."

"Stop," Esther interrupted him.

Henry swung his head to her. "You wanted to know. I'm telling you."

"You are, but you're not talking about the real issue."

"What's that?" he insisted. "Rhi? Or that I'm not getting a daily dose of sunlight?"

"You haven't mentioned any more about what we are."

Henry barked out a laugh, but he felt no joy. "You mean how our parents lied to us? How we're really adopted and part of some Druid policing society?"

"I'm the TruthSeeker. You're the JusticeBringer. Neither of us can run from our destiny."

"Destiny?" His lips twisted in a sneer at the thought. "Just because we found out we're adopted doesn't mean anything."

Her head cocked to the side as anger flashed in her expression. "You are compelled to beget righteousness. It's what you're doing even now, though you may not want to admit it. You want to right the wrongs done to the Kings, and find the weapon."

Henry looked back at the map. He didn't want to have this conversation. Not now. Not ever.

"We spent weeks on the Isle of Eigg searching for the woman who helped to hide our real identities. You agreed then that we were part of something more."

"I don't want it."

"You can't just turn it off and on like a switch. Ignore it all you want, but the truth is in every action you take. Why do you think you went to work for the highest agency in England? Not because you wanted to be a spy. Because you wanted to right the wrongs. You wanted to be able to go after those the authorities couldn't touch. And MI5 gave you that opportunity."

Henry had told himself those same things, and they didn't sound any better coming from his sister.

Esther sighed loudly. "You wanted a reason to be useful to those at Dreagan. You are. More than ever before. Why isn't that enough?"

"I don't know," he whispered.

"I can't help you if I don't know what's causing all of this. Tell me if you know. And if you don't, then maybe you need to step away from this map and take a look at yourself."

Henry swallowed and looked her way. "We still know

so little about our past. We don't know why we were given new identities and adopted."

"And we may never know. Don't get me wrong, I desire the truth. But it doesn't change what I know in here," Esther said and placed her hand on his chest over his heart. "We were born for so much more than normal lives. I thought my fate lay with MI5, but now I realize I hadn't uncovered my true self yet."

Henry took her hand and held it between his. "Being Nikolai's mate? Or being the TruthSeeker?"

"Both. No one said it had to be one or the other."

"And what if we discover things about our past that are . . . undesirable?"

Esther shrugged. "So? No one is perfect, and lest you forget, we had no control over those who came before us. But our ancestors paved this road we're on. I'm ready to walk it. But I can't do it alone. We work as a pair. That's how it's meant to be."

Henry swung his gaze back to the map. "I know what my role is in this room. If I walk out of it, if I embrace being the JusticeBringer, I don't know what awaits me."

"Neither do I."

"But you have Nikolai."

"I also have you." She tugged at his hand, gaining his attention. Then she smiled. "And you have me."

He knew she was right, though it still didn't make everything better. But he knew he couldn't run from things anymore. Once Esther had learned of their heritage and told him, dreams of finding justice for those who sought it against Druids had plagued him.

Esther's fingers tightened on his. "It's going to be okay, you know. But you have to leave this room every once in a while."

It was his sister's way of telling him that he wasn't

needed to track down the weapon. How could he be? He didn't have magic that could find it. The Kings did.

Henry frowned then. If anyone could find it, Con could. Why then wasn't the King of Dragon Kings using his magic to locate whoever had stolen the weapon?

"What is it?" Esther asked, a frown marring her brow. "You've thought of something. I can see it in your face."

Henry pulled her against him and hugged her tightly before walking around her. "Thank you for the talk. You helped me see something I didn't before."

"And that is?" she called as he strode to the door.

Henry opened it and walked out to find Con. He'd tell Esther later.

CHAPTER SEVENTEEN

Con didn't look up from his desk as he signed one of a dozen documents for the day. Henry's glare didn't bother him. Con was used to the mortal wearing a constant frown over the past few months.

But the moment Henry closed the office door, Con set aside his Montblanc pen and lifted his gaze. By the tightness of Henry's face, there was something important the man wished to discuss.

Henry had done much for the Dragon Kings. So even if Con didn't want to take the time to talk to the mortal, he would. He owed Henry at least that much.

Con pushed back his chair and walked to the sideboard where he poured two glasses of whisky. His enhanced hearing caught the sound of Henry's light steps on the rug as he walked toward him. Con added more to each of their tumblers before he put the top back in the decanter.

"What's on your mind?" Con turned and offered the human a glass.

Henry took it without answering, draining it in one swallow. He didn't look at Con when he set the tumbler down on the sideboard and made his way to a chair.

Once Henry lowered himself into the seat, Con hesitated. Henry's jaw was set in a way that alerted Con to the fact that whatever he was about to learn wouldn't please him. Then again, not much discussed in his office did.

He blew out a breath and returned to his desk, forgetting about the tumbler of whisky waiting for him. Con sank back in his chair and crossed an ankle over his knee. The list of problems and Dreagan's enemies continued to grow, and it weighed heavily upon him.

It was a burden he'd readily accepted the moment he became King of Dragon Kings. And while sometimes—*most* times—he struggled under the weight of it all, he wouldn't change a thing.

"It's better to just say it," Con said. "Sitting there trying to find the words to voice whatever is on your mind will only make it harder."

Henry swallowed, and for the first time since entering the office, his gaze met Con's. For a long minute, Con stared into Henry's hazel eyes. It was easy to see why the mortal had been such a valued spy for MI5. Henry kept his secrets close and his emotions guarded. But Con had come to know him well over the last several months.

Henry never gave up. Once he had the bit in his mouth about something, he didn't let go until he got whatever he was after. Be it man, Fae, or anything else.

"You know where the weapon is," Henry stated.

Con set the tumbler on his desk, noting Henry's refined British accent. But it was also the carefully worded statement and even tone that got his notice. "Nay, I doona."

"But you could find it."

"There are many answers I could give to such a statement."

Henry raised a brow. "How about the truth?"

"Why should I give it to you?" Con demanded.

"Because I've been working closely with everyone here. First, keeping track of the Dark Fae. But why?"

It was Con's turn to raise a brow. "Why did I want you looking for the Dark?"

"Why did you take my help when I offered it? The truth, if you please."

"I'm offended you'd believe I give you anything but honesty."

Henry issued a small snort. "We both know how carefully you word things."

"Just as you did when you made your claim just now."

"I'm not blaming you," Henry continued. "I know you have to tread cautiously with all the threads that you hold."

Con lowered his foot to the floor. "I like you, Henry. I didna want to. Banan told me how valuable an asset you were, and I didna believe him. At first. But it quickly became apparent to everyone that day you aided us with Jane, and then again with Kellan and Denae, that we could use your help."

"Because of my contacts with MI5."

"Because you know mortals. We've spent so long hiding and shying away from them that we forgot to learn about your kind."

Henry glanced to the side. "Ulrik knows us humans better than I do."

"That's debatable. But, he's a Dragon King."

"There's also the fact that you have several women here who could do my job. Especially my sister."

So that's what this was about. Con should've recognized the issue. "Everyone at Dreagan brings something different to the table, be they Dragon Kings, Fae, or mortal. You are a valued member. If we have no' made that clear, then I'll rectify that immediately."

"I admit, I often wonder why I'm here. I'm no fool. I know I bring very little in the way of help."

"That isna true."

Henry gave Con a flat look. "You're not only immortal, you also have magic. And money. There isn't anything you can't get if you want it."

"If we wanted to act like that, then we would. But we doona. We have more finesse."

"I realized that. Then I thought perhaps you wanted me because of Rhi. Or, should I say, my infatuation with her."

Con watched the mortal carefully. He wasn't fooled by Henry's calm tone. While he might call it an infatuation, Con knew from experience how susceptible humans were to the Fae. Especially one like Rhi.

But Con didn't call Henry out on the lie. Instead, he folded his hands in his lap and waited.

It didn't take long.

Henry looked around the office. "I didn't come here to talk about Rhi."

"Good." It was a topic Con didn't want to discuss.

Henry's gaze swung back to him. "I came to talk about the weapon."

"What about it?"

"Why you have allowed me to believe that you wanted me to track it. Ryder could do it in his sleep."

Con briefly looked at his hands. "That isna exactly true. Ryder could find the weapon in a heartbeat if I gave him the information he needed to locate it."

"Why haven't you?"

"Every person who has ever taken a position of power accepts the secrets that go along with it. The weapon is one of them. Just because it's gone doesna mean that I'm able to tell the other Kings what kind of weapon it is."

Henry shook his head, his face lined with confusion. "Why not?"

"Many reasons."

"Is that why you came to me?"

Con nodded once. "I knew I could give you what little information I had, and you would take it and make it work. Which, I might add, you have."

"Ryder could have done the same."

"Aye. And in the process, discovered what the weapon is."

Henry shifted his head slightly. "And I'm not smart enough to figure out what it is?"

"Oh, you most definitely could. And you no doubt will."

Henry's face clouded with confusion. "I don't understand."

Con looked at the whisky decanter on the sideboard. "It's my job to know anyone associated with Dreagan. Be they Dragon Kings, mates, or friends. I know you, Henry. You're a good man. One of the best of your species. I knew there was something more to you than met the eye, and now that we know you're the JusticeBringer, it makes sense."

"So, you want me here because of my Druid association? You realize I have no magic, right?"

Con shot him a quick grin. "If I valued magic so highly, do you no' think the Kings would use it more than we do? I believe our magic is so great because we doona turn to it for everything."

"I came here to tell you that I knew you could find the weapon yourself. How did we get on this conversation?"

"It's needed to be said for some time. I wanted to give you space after your visit to Eigg. Esther has embraced her new role. You, however, are still having difficulty with yours."

Henry ran a hand down his face wearily. "It's a lot to take in."

"I can only imagine."

"Do you want me to find the weapon?"

Con knew this was his chance to put an end to things before they went too far. Every time he started to, something stopped him. And, somehow, it was because of Henry.

When Henry first helped the Kings, Con hadn't known how deeply the mortal would become involved with Dreagan. And now, years later, he knew that Henry wasn't there by accident. The mortal was destined to play an important role—and somehow Con didn't think it was only because the man was the JusticeBringer.

"I've tasked you with a critical mission," Con told him.

Henry gave him a flat look. "That isn't an answer."

"It is. When you locate it, because you will, come to me. And only me. Doona tell anyone else."

"Of course." Henry slowly rose to his feet and walked toward the door.

"And, Henry," Con called. "You are part of this family."

The mortal shot him a smile over his shoulder. When Henry opened the door and left, his steps were lighter. It was too bad Con couldn't say the same about his own.

Everywhere she looked, everything she did made Claire think about sex.

Actually, sex with V.

What was wrong with her? She enjoyed pleasure as much as the next woman, but it was as if she were suddenly addicted to one man.

She dropped her head on her desk, her lunch forgotten. No matter how many of her toys she'd used the night before, none of them had given her the fulfillment V had. And while her orgasm had been nice, it was lacking.

"You feeling all right?" Sophie asked as she walked past.

Claire jerked upright. "Yep. I'm good."

"You sure?" Sophie looked at her over her shoulder after putting away a file. "You look a little tired."

"I didn't get much sleep last night." That seemed to be a recurring theme of late.

"Calvin?" Sophie faced her and put her hand on her hip. "Is that pig still texting you?"

Claire shook her head. "No, no. As I told you when you came back from the meeting, Calvin is history."

"I think that was a smart move."

"Yeah." The real question was had it been smart to go out with V? Or to get into the water naked with him? Or to let him touch her and kiss her? Or to—

"Claire?"

She jerked at her name being shouted. When she blinked, Sophie was leaning on her desk, her face inches away.

Sophie's eyes narrowed. "You're thinking about someone. I'm betting it's who you went out with the night before. The one you don't want to share with me."

"Maybe," Claire said and leaned back in her chair. She heard the hint of hurt in her friend's voice, and she didn't want to make it worse by saying that she was definitely thinking about the man from her date. Because then Sophie would start hounding her about who it was.

Sophie sat on the corner of the desk and laughed. "For many years, I lived vicariously through you."

"And look at you now." Claire tried not to sound jealous or bitter, but she thought that maybe a little of it seeped into her voice.

Sophie's face crumbled. "Claire, I—"

"Please, don't," Claire hurried to tell Sophie. "I'm just feeling depressed right now. I didn't mean to take it out on you. Forget about it. I'll be right as rain tomorrow."

"Will you?"

"Yes." Believing something was half the battle. Wasn't it? At least Claire hoped it was.

Sophie smiled. "We have a light afternoon. Why don't you take the rest of it off?"

"We can barely run the clinic with the two of us. It'll be insane for you to do it by yourself."

"No' if I'm here," Darius stated as he walked into the room. "Sophie's right. Take the afternoon off. You deserve it."

Claire almost argued with them, but she had yet to win when they both stood against her. She gathered her purse and got to her feet. "I guess I'll see you in the morning."

"Bye," Sophie called cheerfully. "Get some rest and do something just for you! Oh, and make sure and read the new post from the *(Mis)Adventures of a Dating Failure* so we can talk about it later."

"Will do!" Claire shouted as she left.

After Claire had gotten into her car and backed out of the parking lot, she knew she didn't want to go home. Maybe it was time she pampered herself a little. Just as Sophie had suggested. It had been a while, and self-care always made her feel better.

Not that she expected it to work miracles this time, but every little bit helped.

CHAPTER EIGHTEEN

A spa day. That's exactly what she needed. Claire didn't mind driving the twenty minutes to reach the spa that she and Sophie had found a few months earlier. She pulled into the parking lot and hurriedly made her way into the building.

As soon as she walked in, the calming music instantly put her at ease. The woman behind the desk smiled in welcome. Within minutes, Claire was directed to a separate room where the lights were dimmed. She had barely sat down before another woman came to get her.

The facial was nice, and Claire enjoyed the hour of someone pampering her skin. But it was the ninety-minute massage that was really what she needed. Her mind wandered as the masseuse worked her magic unknotting muscles and easing aches Claire hadn't known she had.

Unfortunately, it came to an end all too soon. She reluctantly dressed, all the while wondering if she could get another hour. But she ended up walking from the room to the last part of her self-care—a manicure and pedicure.

Claire was directed by yet another woman to a station where there were hundreds of colors of polish to choose from. She looked at them, trying to figure out which color called to her the most.

"You can pick more than one."

The sound of the Irish brogue caught her attention. Claire turned her head to see the woman beside her. She was utterly breathtaking. Black hair, silver eyes, and a perfectly shaped body in an outfit that would make anyone envious.

Claire realized she was staring and promptly put a smile on her face. Then she couldn't remember what the woman had said. "I'm sorry?"

The woman laughed and jerked her chin to the rows of polish. "You can have them put more than one color on your nails. It doesn't cost more."

"Oh." Claire nodded. "I didn't know that. I always have the hardest time picking a color."

"Really?" The woman's full lips—in a perfect shade of light pink that Claire couldn't ever seem to find—lifted in a grin. "I love choosing colors."

Claire made herself look away before the poor woman thought she was coming on to her. "Perhaps you should pick mine."

Before Claire could blink, three colors were plunked into her hand. She looked askance at the woman. "Um . . . that was easy for you."

"Hi. I'm Rhi, by the way."

She faced the Irish woman and said, "I'm Claire."

"You look as though you've had a day of pampering," Rhi said.

Claire chuckled. "I had a facial, which is why I'm without makeup. Then a massage. Now, I'm about to get my nails done."

"That's why I'm here," Rhi said.

One of the nail techs ushered both Claire and Rhi to

the pedicure chairs where warm water already waited for them to dunk their feet. Claire settled in her chair while Rhi took one next to her.

In seconds, a woman brought up a rolling stool and set about working on Claire's feet. In the next heartbeat, another came up beside her with two small bowls that Claire put her hands in.

"Multitasking at its finest," Rhi said with a laugh.

Claire grinned. "I really needed these past couple of hours."

"Bad day?"

"Not exactly." She turned her head toward Rhi. "Weird, really."

Rhi rolled her large, silver eyes. "I've had the year from Hell. No matter how much I try, none of this pampering helps for too long."

"I'm sorry," Claire said.

Rhi shrugged a shoulder. "It's all about to get sorted."

"That's good, at least." Claire looked down at her lap and the bottles of polish. She wouldn't have picked the colors herself, but she liked them. Perhaps it was time for a change—and not just in her nail color choices.

"You have a guy on your brain."

Claire jerked her head to Rhi. "What?"

Rhi shot her a knowing grin. "I know that look well. You're thinking about a guy."

"Well, yeah, I was." No matter what Claire did, V was always there. Awake or asleep, she couldn't stop thinking about him. Of the way his hands had held her, of how his blue eyes seemed to pierce her very soul. Of how his lips felt against hers.

Or how he made her feel coveted and yet strong at the same time.

"You like him."

Claire swallowed and looked at the water where her feet were. It brought her back to the loch, the moonlight, and V—and the heart-stopping pleasure she'd discovered. "It's . . . complicated."

"It always is."

"That's the bloody truth." Claire sighed loudly.

Rhi then said, "Tell me about this guy. Does he treat you right?"

"Like a queen," Claire answered instantly.

The women doing their nails looked up at Claire, a spark of jealousy in their eyes.

"I had someone like that once," Rhi said.

Claire looked over to find Rhi gazing off to the left, her eyes distant. Claire had an epiphany that she would have that same look on her face a year from now—or ten years or forty.

Every time she thought of V, she would yearn for him. For the way he made her feel. For the things he made her crave.

Suddenly, Rhi plastered a wide smile on her face as she looked at Claire, but it didn't reach her eyes. "Why aren't you with this man?"

"It's—"

"Complicated," Rhi said over her, nodding.

Claire hesitated a moment, wondering if she should ask Rhi about her man. Sometimes, people didn't want to talk about such things. But, sometimes, they *needed* to. With strangers.

"What about you and your man?"

Rhi's smile was sad, her eyes holding a pain so deep that Claire felt as *she* were kicked in the stomach. Maybe she shouldn't have asked.

"I lost him," Rhi replied. "I've gone over everything I did, everything I said, but I still can't figure out why he ended it."

"Did you talk to him?"

Rhi shook her head of long, midnight locks. "That wasn't an option."

"You gave up?" Somehow, that surprised Claire. She didn't know Rhi that well, but she didn't seem to be the type who accepted things so readily.

"I . . . well, I didn't handle it well," Rhi admitted. "By the time I pulled myself together, it was too late."

"It sounds like you really loved him."

Rhi looked away, but not before Claire saw something intense spark in her eyes. "Yes."

"It's never too late, you know. Go after him."

The smile Rhi gave Claire was full. "Oh, I plan to. What about you? You obviously have strong feelings for your guy. You going after him?"

"He's leaving."

"Long-distance relationships work for some."

Claire bit her lip. "I've not had the best of luck with men. I wasn't even expecting this one. It just kinda . . . happened."

"You've got it bad for him," Rhi said with a chuckle.

"I've never met anyone like him. He . . . well, he's. . . ." Claire couldn't find the right words. Everything that kept coming to mind to accurately describe V was lacking.

Rhi grinned. "I know exactly what you mean."

Claire blew out a breath. "I used to think I was someone who wouldn't let anything stop me from going after what I wanted. Actually, I used to be like that. After so many failed relationships, I realize I've changed."

"So, find the woman you used to be."

"That's easier said than done."

"I'll help," Rhi offered. "I need something to take my mind off things for a bit anyway."

Claire blinked, unsure if she'd heard Rhi correctly. "Really?"

Rhi laughed softly as she pulled her hand away from her nail tech and pointed to the bottles in Claire's lap. Then she told the women working on Claire's nails, "Put the darkest one on the first and third fingers. The second lightest on the thumb and middle. The palest goes on the pinky."

The women didn't hesitate to do as Rhi instructed. Claire glanced over to see Rhi's choice of polish.

"The dusky mauve is called Reykjavik Has All the Hot Spots. My accent color is the dove beige named Icelanded a Bottle of OPI," she said.

Claire laughed. "The names are great."

"I was in Iceland recently. Beautiful country, though it was harsh. These colors are from the Iceland collection of OPI."

Claire nodded. "Iceland. Wow. That's amazing. I've only ever been around the British Isles."

"Do you want to know the name of your colors?" Rhi asked with a teasing glint in her eyes.

"You know them?"

"I know all of them," she claimed.

Claire held up the lightest bottle. "Give it a shot."

Rhi raised a black brow. "The shade that's about the color of milk is called Don't Cry Over Spilled Milkshakes."

Claire turned the bottle over and read the label, shocked that Rhi had gotten it correct. "Lucky guess," she said.

"You have two more. I bet I can get all three."

"Okay," Claire said. "I'll take you up on that."

"And if I win?" Rhi asked, brows raised.

Claire shrugged. "I'll talk to my guy."

"Deal."

"And if *I* win?"

Rhi tilted her head to the side. "I'll contact the one I let get away."

Claire really didn't think Rhi would win all three, so she quickly held up the second bottle, the darkest shade of the three.

"That's an easy one," Rhi said with a grin. "Teal Me More, Teal Me More."

Claire turned the teal blue bottle over and gasped when she read the name of it. "Two out of three."

"It's about to be three out of three. Hope you know what you're going to say to your man."

Claire held up the turquoise bottle. "Well?"

By this time, all four nail techs working on them had stopped. They were looking at Rhi, waiting to see who would win.

Suddenly, Rhi grinned. "You don't think I'll get it, do you?"

"No," Claire said with a smile.

"All three came from the Grease collection, and the final bottle is called Was It All Just a Dream."

Claire looked at the bottom, and her stomach dipped. Oh, no! Now she had to contact V.

Rhi put her hand on her arm. "Claire, you don't have to do anything you don't want to do."

"We made a deal," she said woodenly. Though she felt something odd go through her. Not exactly painful, but not pleasant either. It must just be her nerves.

"Let's talk about the girl you used to be. What did you like about her?"

Claire eagerly grasped another topic. The thought of going to see V left her hyperventilating and the world swimming. This new topic was something safe. "I was confident. The future didn't scare me."

"And it does now? Why?"

"I don't want to be alone."

Rhi smiled sadly. "I don't think you're meant to be alone."

"How can you say that?"

"I look at you and see someone who embraces the world. The good, the bad, and the strange. I see someone with hope still shining in her eyes. I see someone who has an open heart, waiting for the right man to find her."

Claire looked away as her eyes filled with tears. "You see all of that?"

"And so much more. The woman you think you lost is still in there. She's buried under the insecurities that the world and useless people have heaped upon her. Let her come out and shine. I think you might be amazed at what happens."

"You've cleared away years of fog in my mind in a matter of minutes. You could charge people for this."

Rhi chuckled. "I save it for those I like, and I like you, Claire."

By the time she left the spa, Claire had exchanged numbers with Rhi. There was something about the woman that drew Claire. Maybe it was Rhi's open and giving personality, which was rare to encounter. Whatever the reason, Claire was thrilled to have found a new friend.

And a new outlook on things.

CHAPTER NINETEEN

Something was going on. It wasn't just the whispering between Darius and Ulrik, it was the looks exchanged between Laith and Roman that V noticed.

"What's wrong with your drink?" Iona asked.

V looked up at Laith's mate, who stood behind the bar. He now regretted taking Darius's suggestion to go with them to The Fox & The Hound for a drink.

"Nothing," V answered.

"You're not drinking it," Iona replied.

He drew in a breath and grasped the glass of ale before bringing it to his lips and taking a long drink. He set it down and licked his lips. "Happy now?"

She gave him a hard look. "I'll be happy when you are. Sort of like you were the other day when you brought Claire in here."

V had been waiting for someone to bring that up. Out of the corner of his eye, he saw his four friends watching him. The bastards had known he wouldn't answer them had they asked the question. So, they had gotten Iona to do it.

It was smart of them, but he wasn't going to give in that easily.

"Claire and I were working, and it was lunch. There was no reason I couldna treat her to a meal," V answered.

Iona braced her hands on the bar and grinned. "Just a meal, huh? All right. I believe you."

V turned his head to look at the others. Darius wouldn't meet his gaze. Neither would Roman. Laith walked away to tend to other customers. The only one who returned his stare was Ulrik.

"Care to tell me what's going on?" V demanded.

Ulrik lifted a shoulder. "We're just having a drink."

"Something we could do at Dreagan."

"Aye, but it's good to get out."

V pushed away his ale. "Is this because none of you believe I'm acclimating to this . . . to things?"

"Nay," Roman stated quickly.

Darius twisted his lips. "We know something is bothering you. We just want to help."

"I'm fine," V told them.

Ulrik got down from the bar stool and came to stand on V's other side. He put an arm around V's shoulders as he leaned close. "I saw you when you came back the other night. Find that woman again. She put a smile on your face."

"Nay." And that's all V was going to say about it.

If any of them knew how desperately, how badly he wanted even a glimpse of Claire, they would ensure that he found her. The pleasure he'd experienced revealed just how great things could be with her.

He'd be lying if he said he hadn't considered it. But he would only be thinking of himself if he went to Claire. She would give herself to a man, not knowing that he was a Dragon King mixed up in a war with faceless enemies out to destroy them.

Claire was happy and carefree. She didn't know about

or carry the worries that the other mates at Dreagan did. And V didn't want that for her. She deserved so much more.

V straightened, knocking Ulrik's arm away. He turned to stand when the door of the pub opened. As if his thoughts had conjured her from thin air, Claire walked in.

For a second, V forgot to breathe. She was even more beautiful than the last time he'd seen her. Her long, blond hair was down, framing her beautiful face. She wore a thin, white shirt beneath a black blazer with the sleeves shoved up to her elbows. Black skinny pants that outlined every curve of her hips and bum covered her legs. And on her feet were the sexiest black stilettos he'd ever seen.

He caught a glimpse of color on her toenails and fingernails, but his gaze was drawn to her face. She scanned the pub, seemingly unaware of how the men stared at her with such longing—just as when he had taken her to dinner.

Then her deep brown eyes landed on him. She made her way to him. While he couldn't pinpoint what it was, something had changed about Claire.

She drew closer, and he spotted the red lipstick and black winged eyeliner. She had no color on her lids, which somehow made the look even sexier.

V was vaguely aware of Roman, Ulrik, and Darius moving out of the way. But he only had eyes for Claire. He thought she would sit on the stool next to him. Instead, she gave him a smile that speared him all the way to his balls as she walked past.

He turned on the stool, watching her. She didn't speak to anyone as she took the same booth they'd used during their lunch.

V was struck senseless. Why hadn't she stopped by him? Why hadn't she talked to him? By the look in her eyes when she caught his gaze, he'd thought for sure she was there for him.

With the way she was dressed, she was definitely there for someone. A woman didn't dress like that for nothing.

His hand fisted when he saw a man stand and make his way toward her. Without another thought, V got to his feet and blocked the mortal's way.

"Excuse me," the man said.

V stared him down. He didn't have to say a word. After a few tense moments, the human returned to his table. V then looked around the pub, daring anyone else to approach Claire.

When his gaze landed on his friends, V held their stares. He didn't want them coming over and interrupting. And he sure as hell didn't want them watching.

Ulrik was the first to turn his head away. Roman and Darius soon did the same. Only then did V face Claire.

She smiled in thanks as Iona set down two glasses of whisky on the table. V didn't need to ask if it was Dreagan. Somehow, he knew that's exactly what Claire had ordered.

Then her eyes lifted to him. He forgot to breathe again. She was the type of woman that could wreak all kinds of havoc—namely things involving his foolish heart. And no amount of caution would stop him from falling.

The problem was that he feared he'd already done just that.

He stopped fighting the longing to see Claire. V's feet ate up the short distance between them, and he sat across from her. She said nothing. Simply lifted her tumbler and took a sip of whisky. Then she licked her lips.

V barely held back the groan. If they were alone, he'd grab her and lay her on the table so he could ravage her lips and leisurely kiss and touch her body.

But they weren't alone.

"You look verra beautiful," he said to break the silence.

There was a small smile about her red lips. "Thank you."

By the stars! Her husky voice reminded him of her mouth on his cock, stroking him. His balls tightened as more blood rushed to his rod.

"Are you meeting someone?"

She glanced coyly at her hands wrapped around the glass. "You."

He was so fucked. He knew it and didn't care. It didn't matter all the reasons he had—and good ones at that—to leave Claire alone. They faded away like smoke on the wind.

"What did you do to me beneath the moonshine?" she asked. "I can't stop thinking about you."

She had to stop. V tried to get the words past his lips, but his heart and mind were warring with each other. His brain knew what needed to happen. But his heart knew how wonderful it felt to have Claire against him, to taste her kiss.

And hear her cries of pleasure.

"I simply touched you," he said.

She shook her head slowly. "Oh, you did so much more."

V clenched his teeth in an effort to hold back the words he wanted to say. And once more, his heart won. "I think of you often."

"Then why didn't you come to me?"

"I was thinking of you."

She leaned closer, making her shirt gape to give him a view of her breasts. "I'm a big girl, Vlad. I can take it."

By the stars, he loved his name on her lips. He wanted to hear it again. "What if I can no'?"

She paused, her gaze searching his face. "Then that's a different conversation."

"This isna a good idea, Claire."

"Whisky?" she asked, quirking a brow. "Conversation? Or admitting that we want to finish what we started at the loch?"

"All of it."

She moved her hair off her shoulder and sat back. "That's a pity. I wanted to experience more with the man who could bring me to the brink with one touch."

"Keep talking like that, and I'll have you over that table and in my lap in a heartbeat," he said in a low voice raw with a desire that he didn't bother to hide.

Claire's lips curved into a sensual smile. "Promise?"

"Woman, you doona know what you're doing to me."

"I think I do," she said in a whisper. "The same thing you've been doing to me since you dropped me off at home the other night."

V swallowed, the sound loud even in the noisy pub.

Claire took another drink of whisky. "Not even the toys I have for my own pleasure can ease me. I fear, Vlad, that only you can."

Shite. She just had to say his name again. The sound of it falling from her lips was more erotic than anything he could've imagined. He wished he had the wherewithal to stand and walk out of the pub and forget her. But he knew it for the fantasy that it was.

"I warned you about what you said," V told her.

"I'm not keeping us in this place. You are."

He fisted his hands. "You doona understand how close I am to the edge."

"The edge of what?" she asked innocently.

This time, he didn't hold back his groan. It was a mix of pleasure and pain. She was driving him wild. His blood boiled with hunger, and there was only one woman on the menu.

She slowly ran her finger around the rim of the tumbler. "I want you. I came to tell you exactly that. I'm going to get up and walk out the door now. If you don't come outside, then I'll never bother you again." She leaned forward once more and lowered her voice. "But don't forget that I know the pleasure you felt at the loch. I felt your need. Your . . . craving. I'm yours for the taking."

The words had barely penetrated his mind before she was on her feet. He watched her walk to the door. She didn't look back at him before she took the final step out, and the door closed behind her.

V told himself to stay. He begged himself to remain. But it was a losing battle. She anchored him to this chaotic world in a way he couldn't explain. Then there was the uncontrollable longing, the raging desire he had for her.

He stopped fighting it. V slid from the booth and strode to the door, ignoring everyone else.

Once outside, he looked around for her, but not even his dragon eyesight could find a trace of Claire or her car. The disappointment that filled him was immense.

"I knew you'd come."

His head jerked to the side to find her leaning against the pub. She pushed away from the building and smiled. V walked to her and slid his arms around her body. He bent her backwards. She didn't protest, simply leaned her head back to expose her long neck.

"You should've stayed away from me," he murmured as he brushed his lips along her skin.

Her fingers tightened on his shoulders. "I couldn't. I burn for you."

"This is your last chance, lass. You doona want to get tangled up in my life."

Her head lifted to meet his gaze. Then her fingers slid into his long hair and against his scalp. "I want to be tangled in your arms and in your life. I want all that your lips and body promised me beneath the moon."

"Claire," he begged.

She put a finger to his lips to quiet him. "You came out here for me. Any argument you might have had ended the moment you did that."

As much as he hated to admit it, she was right.

And, somehow, in that second, all the fight went out of V. Or maybe his desire won. All he knew was that the woman he wanted was in his arms and willing.

"Where's your car?" he asked.

COULD HE BE . . . THE ONE?

Who doesn't love falling in love?

For anyone who doesn't enjoy the rush of it, I have to wonder if you're human. There are those who are in love with the idea of being in love.

And who can blame them?

The quiver in your stomach when the one who holds your affection is near. The anticipation of the first kiss. The desire that explodes with newly kindled attraction. The yearning to be close to them all the time.

There is nothing that can match falling in love.

We all seek it. Some are more aware of it than others. There's no getting around love. It's in books and magazines. It's shown in the things we watch from ads to shows.

Romance is everywhere.

It's ingrained in us from birth to seek out love, to find the other half of ourselves. Whether you call it soulmates, kindred spirits, or your true love, everyone is looking, searching . . . hoping.

Sometimes, we get hurt so many times by

potential soulmates that we shut off our feelings. I've done it. It's a way to protect ourselves and our fragile hearts. After all, there is only so much pain we can endure before we need to go off and lick our wounds.

And every once in a while, someone comes along that makes us think that all our hunting and seeking has paid off. Everything aligns perfectly.

He says all the right things.

He likes all the right things.

He does all the right things.

He has the looks and voice that send your heart skidding erratically.

He is, in fact, your perfect man.

At least, you think he is at the beginning. It isn't long before he does or says something that makes you pause. It could be as simple as the sound of his laugh—not horrible, but not something that makes you want to join in.

Or it could be worse. He could treat a waiter or someone he perceives as lower than him badly.

If it's the former, it's something minor that you can get past. After all, there are things you'll do that get on his nerves, as well. That's called a relationship.

If it's the latter—run like hell! He's giving you a glimpse of a part of himself that he's kept carefully hidden from you to pull you in. But people like that will always show their true colors eventually.

So. You found The One. You've been anxiously waiting and hoping for this day. You know all there is to know about dating and how to attract a guy's attention, but you soon realize that you might not know all there is to know about being in a committed relationship.

I wish I had answers for you. The fact is, I don't have a clue either. People call me a serial dater. I suppose I am, but it isn't by choice.

When someone is set on a course like mine, you become an expert, of sorts. Since the goal is to find my person, I must be doing something wrong if my dates aren't working out, right? I own a library— both physical and electronic—of articles, books, and audio on self-help topics, what a woman needs to do to find her significant other.

Do you know what I found? Every damn one of those books, articles, and recordings contradicts each other. It showed me that no one has the answer, because if they did, it would work! Everyone in the world would find their perfect match and be happy.

My one piece of advice, trust yourself. Ask friends who are in a happy relationship. And, more importantly, talk to your soulmate. Communication is everything, folks.

Be honest. Be open.

And for the rest of us still on the hunt, we will be happy for you while also being slightly jealous. But our turn is coming.

CHAPTER TWENTY

Claire couldn't catch her breath. The anticipation of having V's hands on her naked flesh kept her shaking from need.

It must have been apparent because V took her keys and put her in the passenger seat. He looked unruffled by their exchange. At least he did until his gaze met hers.

In the oncoming lights of a car, she saw the truth blazing in his ice blue eyes.

Her stomach clenched, and need rushed through her so intensely that she had to squeeze her legs together. She'd never wanted anyone like she did V. He was addictive. His voice, his body, his hands, and that mouth.

Oh, God, his mouth.

She closed her eyes and tried to swallow. Neither said a word. She kept her hands locked together in her lap while she imagined all the things V would do to her, which only made her hotter.

Claire hadn't known if V would be at the pub tonight. She'd gotten dressed while thinking of him, of wanting to see him. If he hadn't been at the bar, she'd intended to go to Dreagan.

She still wasn't sure what had prompted her to visit the pub first. But the moment she saw V sitting at the bar, calm overtook her. She knew she was supposed to be there. That she was meant to show him what he could have, what was his if he wanted it.

When he blocked the man from coming to her, Claire had wanted to run to V and throw her arms around him. Instead, she'd remained at the table, waiting for him to come to her.

And he had!

She still couldn't believe it'd worked. Or that he was going back to the house with her. Her thoughts came to a halt as he turned into her drive. Then the car was parked and the engine off.

V didn't look her way as he got out of the car. She had to try twice before she could get her door open. He waited for her at the front of her vehicle, and when she reached him, he took her hand as they walked to the door together.

Her hands shook as she struggled to get the keys in the lock, but it wasn't from nervousness. It was from anticipation.

Finally, she got it open. Then they were inside the house. She hadn't taken two steps before V whirled her around and yanked her roughly against him. The kiss he gave her was . . . everything.

A current ran along her skin from the savagery of his kiss. In it, she felt the hunger that fought to break free. She sensed the passion that ran deeper than she could fathom. She recognized and welcomed the longing he kept hidden from others.

When he pulled back, she moaned and tried to kiss him once more, but he tangled his fingers in her hair and held her head in place as he searched her eyes.

"I doona want you regretting this later."

She wanted to scream in frustration. Didn't he realize that she wanted him so desperately that she had gone to extremes to get him? "I won't."

"Remember that."

Claire frowned. It was on the tip of her tongue to tell him that she knew his secret, but she held back. She didn't want anything to ruin this night. "I will."

He stared at her for another silent minute. Then his fingers loosened their hold on her hair. This time when she leaned in to put her lips on his, he didn't stop her. V didn't allow her control for long, however. In a heartbeat, he had her against the wall, his hard body pressed to hers while his fiery kiss took her breath and made her knees weak.

She ran her hands over his back, feeling the muscles she'd put to memory the other night. Her blood heated in her veins when his chest rubbed against hers, causing her nipples to harden.

It was so easy to sink into the passion that surrounded her and V. The pleasure consumed her. It sank into her skin, becoming a part of her. Every breath she took, every moan she made, the passion grew until she couldn't tell where it started and she ended.

"I need you," V whispered in her ear.

Chills raced over her skin, and her heart beat double-time from his breath that fanned her neck. And because of the raw need she heard in his raspy voice.

She opened her eyes to find him staring at her. "Don't stop. Please, don't ever stop."

"Tell me what you want me to do."

She swallowed, her mind going blank. He couldn't be serious, surely.

His fingers caressed the side of her face. For some reason, he had put the brakes on, slowing them down considerably, and Claire wasn't sure she liked it.

But he was allowing her to tell him what she needed. No one had ever asked her to do that before. She licked her lips. With someone else, she might not have had the courage to speak the words. But with V, she was different. That, combined with finding the woman she used to be, gave her the daring she wouldn't otherwise have.

"I want you to dominate me."

V's smile was slow, approval shining in his eyes. "You set the limits, lass. Tell me when it's too much."

She nodded, but Claire knew that with V, it would never be too much.

He moved his hands to her waist beneath her blazer. Then, slowly, he ran them up her sides to her chest. He paused there, letting his thumbs brush against the undersides of her breasts.

The movement had scarcely registered before his fingers were on her arms under her jacket. With just a little shove, he had the blazer off her shoulders. Claire let her arms drop and arched her back, allowing the garment to fall to the floor.

"So sexy," V murmured as he lightly ran his fingers up and down her arms.

Claire closed her eyes and leaned her head back against the wall. All her senses were overloaded—and it was the most amazing experience.

"Take your clothes off," V ordered. "Slowly."

Claire's eyes snapped open. And when she saw that he was dead-serious, desire tightened low in her belly. This was exactly what she wanted, what she needed.

Claire slid from between V and the wall. She removed one shoe and then the other, never taking her eyes from him. Then she turned her back to him and walked to her bedroom.

She stopped when she reached the doorway and put her arms on the frame before looking over her shoulder at him. The desire that filled his gaze made her knees weak with longing.

CHAPTER TWENTY-ONE

She was so bloody sexy. V wasn't sure how much longer he could stand watching Claire before he buried himself inside her. Every movement she made caused his blood to heat hotter and hotter until he felt as if he were burning from the inside out.

But he would sustain all manner of torture—both good and bad—for her.

Now that he had given in to his need, V couldn't fathom what had kept him away. He knew the reasons, but they didn't seem important anymore.

Nothing was more important than Claire.

Than having Claire.

The moment he'd given her the command, he saw the flash of delight in her eyes. She hesitated only a heartbeat before she moved away from him and slowly removed her heels. The soft thud as each shoe hit the floor was like the sound of the last of the walls he'd tried to put up crumbling to dust.

He watched Claire walk to her doorway. The look she shot him over her shoulder made his cock jump. Because on her face was hunger so stark and visceral, so genuine that it almost brought him to his knees.

"Remove your pants," he told her.

Claire turned around in the doorway. She bit her lip and unbuttoned her pants before gradually sliding the zipper down. With both hands on the waist of the pants, she shimmied her hips until the material was down to her thighs.

He'd never seen someone remove a pair of pants so erotically before. She moved slowly, sensuously, and he waited with bated breath until first one lean leg and then the other was revealed.

It was a good thing he wasn't beside her, or he wouldn't be able to keep his hands from that gorgeous body of hers. When he caught sight of the nude lace panties, he swallowed thickly.

When she stood, waiting, V said, "Now your shirt."

Claire crossed her arms and grabbed the hem of her shirt before slowly pulling it over her head. The way her arms lifted caused her torso to stretch and show off more of the curves he craved.

She shook out her hair and then dropped the shirt as she stood in her nude bra and panties for him to look his fill. And did he ever take his time.

"Turn around," he ordered.

She did as he instructed. The moment his gaze caught on the back of her panties that had a section cut out with thin strips of material crisscrossing her ass, he took two steps toward her before he got control of himself again.

He called her name. When she looked at him, he crooked a finger at her, beckoning her to him. Once she stood before him, he knew he was a glutton for punishment. Why else would he put himself so close to her in the state he was in?

"Remove my clothes."

Her eyes lit up. "With pleasure," she all but purred.

The moment her hands touched his chest, V knew it would be the ultimate test if he could keep himself from reaching for her, from claiming her body as he'd done in his dreams so many times.

One button at a time, she opened his shirt. Only when the last fastener was undone did she place her palms on his chest and push outward, moving the material over his shoulders and down his arms until the garment landed on the floor.

He could remove the rest of his clothes with magic, but he liked watching her face as she undressed him. He wasn't sure who enjoyed it more. Not that it mattered. Both of them were getting pleasure from the action.

V bit back a groan when she dropped to her knees and looked up at him, waiting for him to give her his foot. When he did, she wasted no time removing one boot and then the other. She got to her feet again and met his gaze before her fingers slid into the waistband of his jeans.

He sucked in a breath when her fingers brushed the tip of his arousal. Her eyes widened, and her lips parted as her breaths came faster.

They stared at each other, lost in the passion for a moment. Then Claire opened his pants. The moment air hit his aching rod, it was over. V yanked off his pants and then grabbed her.

He held her against him as he walked into her bedroom. V stopped beside the bed and kissed her. Her hands moved over his back and down to his hips.

V pushed her down onto the bed. Then he grabbed her ankles and pulled her bum to the edge. Her chest heaved, and her eyes were heavy-lidded as he kneeled on the floor in front of her. His hands smoothed up her legs and then back down again.

The next time he caressed upward, he ran his hands along the inside of her thighs, stopping just short of touching her sex before he removed her bra and panties. He leaned forward and softly blew on her bare skin.

She groaned breathlessly and scraped her nails on the covers as she wound them in her palms. But V was just getting started with her. He continued to lightly run his hands along her thighs before moving to the seams of her legs. The closer he got to her sex, the louder her breathing became.

"P-please," she begged as she tried to shift her hips so his fingers could meet her aching flesh.

V took pity on her and flicked his tongue over her swollen clit. Her back arched, thrusting her breasts upward. He dipped a finger just inside her to feel her wetness. Then it was his turn to groan.

"Vlad," she cried out softly in need.

He slid his finger deeper as his tongue began to leisurely swirl around her clit. If he thought he could tease her for just a moment, he underestimated his control. One taste of her and he was lost.

V added a second finger and began to softly thrust his digits in and out of her as he licked her. Her cries grew louder. He didn't stop until her body tensed before contracting around his fingers as she climaxed.

When he lifted his head, she was panting, her body flushed with pleasure. He flipped her onto her stomach and kneeled on the bed. His hands grasped her hips and raised her to her hands and knees.

He kneaded the globes of her ass. Then she turned her

head and looked at him. They made eye contact before she leaned back and rubbed her bum against his cock.

Pleasure vibrated through her from her orgasm as if it had a life of its own as she waited for V to fill her. She couldn't stand the anticipation any longer. Then she glanced at him. The way he stared at her as if she were something prized, something that was precious, made her heart skip a beat.

She wasn't given long to think about that as he guided his arousal to her entrance. Claire bit her lip when he pushed inside her. Inch by inch, her body opened for him until he was fully seated.

"Oh, yes," she murmured.

He felt better than she had imagined. She sucked in a breath when he ran a hand up her spine and grasped a handful of hair. V pulled back until she had no choice but to straighten. When she realized what he wanted, she eagerly complied.

With her back against his chest, his hands found her breasts and fondled her nipples as his hips moved, shifting his cock just enough that she felt him inside her.

"You have a beautiful body," he said as he kissed along the side of her neck.

"Th—"

The word died on her lips when he pinched her nipple, sending pleasure rippling through her. She didn't have time to recover from that before his finger was on her clit again.

"You will come for me again," he ordered.

She nodded, unable to form words.

Claire didn't know how long they remained like that with his hands roaming her body, teasing her until she was shaking with need, all while gently moving inside her. A reminder of what was to come.

She sank deeper into the desire, into the promise of more pleasure that he tempted her with. Her body was no longer her own. He commanded it with a simple touch. And she willingly gave herself to him and all that he offered.

His teeth scraped along her ear before gently biting down on her lobe. "You're mine now."

"Yes," Claire replied breathlessly. "Always."

She found herself on her back in the next second with V leaning over her. She reached for him, needing his weight on top of her. And she missed the feeling of him inside her.

Claire sighed when he ran his hard rod against her sensitive sex. He did that twice more before he thrust once and filled her completely.

"Yes!" she cried and lifted her legs to wrap around him.

He kissed her then, deeply. Passionately. Thoroughly. All while pumping his hips so that his length slid in and out of her.

She held onto him as if he were the only thing between her and oblivion.

"Let go," he urged her. "I'll catch you, lass."

Claire opened her eyes and looked at him. A Dragon King was making love to her. He was right. She hadn't known what she was getting into, not really. But now that she did, she didn't regret her decision at all.

She sank her nails into him and felt the sweat on his skin. The same perspiration that covered her. He moved with slow, deep thrusts.

"Faster," she urged.

He immediately complied, pumping his hips quicker while going deeper and deeper.

She felt the orgasm building. "I'm coming," she told him.

V didn't relent. He kept the pace she asked for until she cried out from her climax. While the pleasure rippled through her like waves upon the ocean, she heard V shout her name before he buried himself deep and stilled.

They remained tangled with each other, content to bask in the afterglow of their lovemaking.

"That was incredible," she murmured while stroking his back.

V rose up on his hands and looked down at her. "Aye. It certainly was."

He pulled out of her, and Claire immediately missed him. But no sooner was he on his back than he pulled her against him. She settled comfortably with her head on his chest. Though she tried to stay awake, her eyes drifted closed.

"You're dangerous for me."

It took a second for his words to penetrate her pleasure-filled brain. She shifted her face to look at him. "Why?"

He was silent for a long time as he stared at the ceiling. "Because I doona care about consequences or anything else when it comes to being with you."

She rose up on her elbow and waited until his ice blue eyes met hers. Claire reached up with her free hand and moved a lock of his dark hair from his face. "I can take care of myself."

"Nay, Claire. You doona understand."

"I do," she insisted. The thought that V might pull away from her was just too much. Despite the caution her mind was screaming she said, "I've already been through an encounter with a Dark Fae."

The way V's body tensed made her wish she could take back the words. She'd known better than to let that bit of her secret out, but she hadn't been able to think of anything else to say to keep him with her.

Desperation was a tool of fools, and that's exactly what she was proving to be.

"Explain," he demanded.

Claire swallowed and scooted to the opposite end of the bed. Then she rose and reached for her black floral robe. V watched her, never moving.

Finally, she looked at him. "I've kept a secret for years now. One I feared would be taken from me if anyone at Dreagan discovered it. I remember everything from that night in Edinburgh when the Dark Fae and Ulrik took Sophie and me to use against Darius. I recall every touch of the Dark, every way my body wasn't my own, and how it wasn't men but dragons that saved me. I lied to Darius, Sophie, and anyone else who asked when I said that I didn't remember any of it. I lied . . . because I knew it was important."

CHAPTER TWENTY-TWO

For a moment, V could do nothing but stare at Claire as he slowly sat up. Surely, he hadn't heard right. Because the implications were vast and far-reaching.

"You know about us?" he asked softly, hesitantly.

She swallowed nervously and nodded her head. "I don't know a lot. I know you can shift into a dragon."

"You kept this secret for how long?"

"Years."

"Without telling even Sophie that you knew?"

She lifted one shoulder in a shrug. "Yes."

V wasn't sure what to make of Claire or her confession. He had been drawn to her, but never did he imagine that she knew what he was. "And you were no' afraid? You didna caution Sophie against Darius?"

"Afraid?" she repeated wide-eyed. She snorted loudly and shook her head as she glanced away. "I was terrified. But of the Dark Fae. It was Darius and the Dragon Kings who saved me."

"We're no' human."

"I know," Claire replied softly.

The more he talked to her, the more confused V became. "You no' only kept what you knew to yourself, but you followed Sophie to the village, aware that you would be around us?"

"Dragons saved me from some horrible beings who made me do things I didn't want to do. I may not know all there is to know about the Dragon Kings or why you're on this planet, but of course, I came here. In my opinion, there's no safer place in the world than near Dreagan."

V ran a hand through his hair and swung his legs over the side of the bed as he tried to sort through what he'd just learned. He'd thought he would spend an hour or more with her against him before he made love to her again. Now, all he could think about was her confession.

"Oh, my," she murmured.

V jerked his head around and saw that she was staring at his back. He then realized she was seeing his tattoo for the first time.

Despite it being on his back, V knew exactly what it looked like. The black and red ink mixed together to create a dragon spread across his skin. The wings of the dragon followed the backs of his arms so it looked as if the dragon moved each time V did. The head of the dragon was turned to the right while the long tail curled inward.

"The tattoo is stunning."

He nodded. "Thanks."

She licked her lips and swallowed. "Your reaction to my secret is why I never said anything. Not even to Sophie."

He turned his head to Claire, taking in her arms crossed over her chest, the anxious way she studied him, and the frown that hadn't left her brow.

V sighed and got to his feet to face her. "You've proven you can be trusted. You had ample opportunity to no' only dig up more information on us, but to leak that information to the world."

"I would never do that."

"Why?" V wanted to know.

She blinked as if taken aback by his question. "I don't know. Maybe it's because I keep an open mind about things. I'm one who believes that there are other beings out in the vast universe. If they're out there, why can't they be on this Earth, as well? But there are those who don't understand. Who would never accept you."

"That's truer than you could possibly know."

"I don't want you because you're a Dragon King. I want you because of the way you make me feel. Man or dragon. My body doesn't care. I desire *you*."

There was sincerity in her voice and in her eyes. V didn't know details about Edinburgh, and he wasn't going to make her relive it. But he was going to find out the truth.

And if the Dark who touched her were still alive, he would find them and engulf them in dragon fire.

He walked to her and took her hands in his, pulling her arms away from her body. "What do you want to know about us? I'll tell you."

"Really?" she asked in a shocked tone.

V couldn't help but grin. "I think you've earned that."

"What will the others say?"

"I doona need to ask their opinion."

Her gentle brown eyes looked up at him excitedly. "Tell me all you can. I want to know everything."

"Then we better get comfortable. It's a verra long story."

She tugged him after her into the living area. They dropped hands so he could pull on his jeans and then join her on the sofa. Claire sat on one side, facing him, and he mimicked her on the other.

V had never told this story before. He knew many of the other Kings had to their women, but he'd never thought to ask how they had begun it. Or what they had said. With no other option, V started at the beginning.

"This realm was ours," V told Claire. "The dragons ruled all."

"Were there many of you?"

He nodded. "Millions. So many clans called this planet home."

"Clans," she said. "Like Scottish clans?"

"Something like that. There were dragons of all sizes, and each clan was designated by a color. We had territories that we controlled, disputes that had to be managed, and even wars."

She pulled an accent pillow to her chest and held it. "And your clan was?"

"Copper."

"Copper," she repeated with a smile. "Was your clan large?"

"Verra. Our territory was what you now know as the Carpathian Mountains."

Her eyes widened. "Romania. Yeah, I can see that."

V drew in a breath. "Each clan had a ruler, a King."

"Chosen? Or was it hereditary like most monarchies?"

"Chosen," he replied. "But no' by anyone."

Claire cocked her head to the side. "I don't understand."

"The Kings are chosen by the magic of this realm. The strongest dragon with the most powerful magic of that clan is chosen to lead. Sometimes, it happened after a King was killed. Other times, a dragon had to fight for the position."

"Whoa," Claire said. "I have so many questions. First, if the Kings were strong, how did they get killed?"

"Only another Dragon King can kill a King."

"That's pretty important information." She licked her

lips. "But it makes sense. Was it often that someone over-threw a King?"

V nodded. "It happened. Sometimes, the present King lost his way and forgot why he earned that position. Sometimes, another dragon was born stronger."

"People lose their way all the time, so I can see how that could happen, even with a dragon."

V rested his arm along the back of the sofa. "It was rare. The magic knows a dragon's true heart. If it senses any kind of evil, that dragon, no matter how strong or the power of his magic, isna chosen to be a King."

"But couldn't he still fight for the right?"

"Aye. And some fools did, only to lose their lives."

Claire's brows lifted. "Oh. I see. I do have to point out that you're only talking about males. Were females not considered?"

"It didna happen, though I doona believe it was because the females were deemed incapable. Male dragons are much bigger and stronger. I knew many females who would have made excellent Queens, but they wouldna have lasted long in their roles because other Kings would've attacked, killing them. A clan is only as strong as its leader."

Claire looked down briefly and twisted her lips. "That makes sense. So, the ones who think they should be King, they just tell the current one?"

"A challenge is issued."

"How does a dragon know they're meant to be a King?"

V allowed himself to drift back through memories of that long-ago time. "They feel it."

"You mean you felt it," Claire replied in a soft voice.

He nodded. "Aye. I did. Our King was good to us. He protected our clan and our lands for many hundreds of years." When V saw her shock, he grinned. "Dragons can live for a verra long time. A King is immortal."

"Wow," Claire murmured.

"When I first felt the call to challenge my King, I didna heed it. As a result, our King was ambushed and killed by a clan we had a shaky truce with."

Claire held up her hand. "Wait. You just said the magic never picked a dragon who was evil. How is ambushing and killing another King not evil?"

"It was our life. The larger the clan, the bigger the territory. Much as you humans have. How many civilizations tried to conquer the world?"

She flattened her lips. "Touché."

"And the other King didna murder mine. It was an ambush, aye, but the fight was just between the two Kings. And mine lost."

"What happened?"

V shifted his leg to stretch it out on the cushions. "The warring clan attacked. We were without a King, and they believed they could take a chunk of land before a new King took over. They also thought they could easily kill the next King."

"You talk as if you know that for a fact."

"Because I do. The moment my King was killed, I became a Dragon King. I was too busy taking over and trying to find where the previous King had been killed that I didna sense the attack. The other clan underestimated the Coppers and me. I called the largest of my clan to head off the attack with me. We got there in time to save several families, but no' all of them. When I made myself known, the opposing King came straight for me."

"You had just taken over, and you were already in a fight to the death?" Claire's face was filled with awe and surprise.

V shrugged. "The battle was long and bloody. He got the upper hand a few times, but ultimately, I came out on top. I had him at my mercy. I could've killed him, but I let him go on the condition that the truce made before was enforced, or we would take the matter to Constantine."

"Why Con?"

"He's the King of Dragon Kings."

Claire laughed, nodding. "Of course, he is. It makes sense now."

"Each King is powerful, but none of us can best Con. He didna just have to earn his position within his clan of Golds, he also had to battle to be King of Kings."

"I admit, I'm impressed."

V rubbed a hand along his jaw. "Con was born to be King of Kings."

"That's how you became King of your clan?"

"King of Coppers," he corrected. "I wasna a King verra long when the first mortals appeared. Each King shifted into our human form and was given a sword and a tattoo unique to each of us."

"So, every King has a tattoo?"

V nodded. "Aye. Each is different, but they are all made up of the same red and black ink." After she nodded, he continued, "Con gathered us, and we approached the mortals. It was immediately apparent that the arrivals had no magic. No' only that, but they could barely defend themselves. We agreed and made a vow to protect this small band of people.

V laughed dryly. "If only we'd known what that action would bring. Each King gave up a small portion of land and allowed the humans to choose where they wished to live. We helped them build shelters and forge weapons so they could hunt for food. At first, things were good. But we soon discovered that humans procreated at a surprising rate.

"The small group soon turned into a village and kept

multiplying. We gave up more and more land. Yet we still managed to get along. Some Kings took humans as lovers. Though we learned quickly that if a mortal became pregnant by our seed, the women soon lost the child. On the verra rare occasions that a woman managed to carry the bairn to term, it was stillborn."

Claire's face crumpled. "That's so sad."

V drew in a deep breath. "It wasna long before the mortals began hunting the smallest dragons for food. They were about the size of a cat. We didna know what was going on until it had gone too far. Con stepped in, and we tried to work out a truce, but the occasional dragon would snatch up a human for food. It took a while, but we got it sorted. However, the easy peace between our two species was gone. There was a chance at solidifying it when Ulrik set to marry a human."

Claire's eyes bugged out. "Whaaaaaat?"

"His uncle, angry that he hadna become King, turned the woman against Ulrik and convinced her to murder Ulrik. Con discovered her treachery and sent Ulrik away on a mission. Then he called to the rest of the Kings and told us what had happened. We all agreed to go after the mortal. And we killed her so Ulrik wouldna have to."

"I'm gathering things didn't turn out well after that?" Claire said.

V shook his head. "When Ulrik discovered what had happened, he was furious. But he didna blame us."

"He blamed the humans," Claire guessed.

"Aye. And Ulrik and his Silvers began attacking the mortals."

CHAPTER TWENTY-THREE

Claire wanted to reach across the short expanse and take V's hand. He kept his voice even, but she could still pick up hints that he hadn't completely let go of his past.

Not that she blamed him. It wasn't something she or anyone else would easily get past either.

She didn't state the obvious: that the Kings didn't wipe out the mortals. Though she was dying to know why the Kings hadn't made that decision, she waited for V. She'd bombarded him with questions early. While he didn't seem to mind, she also sensed that the next part of the story was even more difficult to tell.

His chest expanded as he inhaled deeply. "The war was a bloodbath. On both sides."

"How?" Then Claire cringed and shook her head. "Sorry. I didn't mean to interrupt."

"Doona hesitate to ask questions. Ever."

She smiled and untucked one of her legs so their feet brushed against each other. Their eyes locked, and for a moment, V's gaze cleared of memories, and he gave her a heart-stopping grin.

But it was gone quickly.

"The mortals were no' without means to harm us. Or, specifically, the smaller dragons. They hunted and trapped them. And within weeks of Ulrik's first attack, the humans had annihilated two clans. It only incensed Ulrik and the Silvers. Several Kings had already joined Ulrik, but after this, more came to him."

Claire knew the answer, but she still asked. "You sided with Ulrik, didn't you?"

"Aye. I doona regret it. I'm sorry if that offends you."

She blinked, taken aback. "It doesn't offend me at all. Those people might have been humans, but not only was that a long time ago, they also brought it upon themselves. Or, at least some of them did."

V looked away. "So many innocents died on both sides. Dragons that Kings stationed around villages to protect the mortals with express instructions no' to harm them were slaughtered. All because they were told no' to fight back."

Claire's eyes stung as emotion clogged her throat. She hastily blinked away the tears, but the pain and sorrow were there for anyone to see. And that made her heart ache for V all the more.

"With every dragon that was murdered, more and more Kings joined Ulrik," V continued. "Con proved how capable he was to be King of Kings because he worked tirelessly to move every one of us back to his side. And he did it."

"Even you?"

V nodded. "Even me. Ulrik never wavered. He continued his attacks on the humans. I wanted to be there with him. I wanted every human gone from this realm." He stared at her intently. "Does that bother you?"

"No. Even if it did, it wouldn't change what happened. Or how you feel."

He looked away for a few moments. "Even Con wanted to help Ulrik, though he only recently admitted that. This was our world, invaded by another species who wanted us gone. Instead of co-existing peacefully, the mortals intended to take over."

"You were the stronger species," Claire argued.

"But we'd made a vow to protect your kind. It's why Con and many other Kings didn't go to war alongside Ulrik. Doona mistake their honor for cowardice. Every one of us regretted the day we welcomed the humans."

Claire nodded in understanding. "I don't know anyone who wouldn't feel the same way if their world were invaded."

"Aye," V whispered. Then he shrugged. "Con had no choice but to force a confrontation with Ulrik since he wouldna stop killing. That day . . . changed all of us."

"How?"

"None of us were sure if Ulrik would heed Con's call. Even if Ulrik did, there was no guarantee that a truce could be brokered with the humans."

Claire gaped at him. "Why would you want to? One of them betrayed you. They killed."

"So did we. By the thousands."

Just when she thought she understood him, V surprised her. "You just talked about how much you hated mortals. Now you sound like you're defending us."

"Perhaps," he said with a slight shrug. "I was angry. All of us were. Did it mean we should have killed so many? Nay. Nor should the humans. We were both at fault. Con saw all of it clearly while the rest of us were wrapped in our emotions. Con attempted to talk to the leaders of the mortals, but they refused. That left us two options."

Claire wasn't sure she wanted to hear what they were.

"Wipe the realm clean of every mortal and any evidence they even existed. Or send our dragons away and go into hiding."

Claire squeezed her eyes shut and shook her head. When she lifted her lids again, she wasn't sure what to say.

"We are no' murderers, Claire. As much as we wanted to take back our planet, it isna who we are. We each called our dragons to us and used our magic to open a bridge to another realm. We had no idea if the dragons would find somewhere safe, but they had a better chance elsewhere than they did with us."

She wiped at a stray tear that fell down her cheek and tried to swallow.

A sad smile played upon V's lips. "I'll never forget looking up that day and watching all the dragons flying toward the bridge. It was a colorful rainbow of our kind. Until they disappeared."

Claire leaned forward and put her hand on his foot. "I'm so sorry."

"We did what had to be done. It wasna what we wanted, but none of us could stand to have another of our kin killed."

"The only dragons left here are the Kings?" she asked.

V slowly shook his head. "Ulrik ignored Con, but as King of Kings, Con can make any dragon—even one no' of his clan—answer to him. That's what he did with Ulrik's Silvers. And all but four answered Con's call."

"I can tell by the sorrow in your eyes that the next part wasn't good."

He gave a snort. "Nay, it wasna. In fact, I could argue that it was worse than sending our dragons away."

The breath rushed from Claire. The anguish she heard in V's voice and saw on his face was almost too much. And he was just relating the story. Though, she had a suspicion that he held a lot back.

She wanted to tell him to stop, that she could hear the rest of it later, but she wasn't sure that she could. For so long, she'd hungered for any type of information about the Dragon Kings—and she was finally getting it.

"The four largest Silvers remained with their King," V continued. "Ulrik didna care that the others had left or that none of the other Kings stood with him. He had one goal, and he intended to see it through. Unfortunately, that left Con with only one option. Though to truly understand the situation, you should know that Con and Ulrik were closer than brothers. No one stood a chance when the two of them were together."

Claire licked her lips as she imagined the stoic, silent Con preparing himself to face his friend at such a trying time. There were times Claire wondered if Con felt anything since he kept his emotions hidden, but perhaps that's what made him such a good leader. He put his own feelings, wants, and wishes aside for what was best for all Dragon Kings.

She'd seen Ulrik when he had his mind set on something. The fury in his gold eyes in Edinburgh had told her that he would do whatever he must to achieve the victory he wanted.

Two such powerful Kings and friends. Claire didn't envy Con the decision he'd had to make that day.

V ran a hand through his hair as his blue eyes slid away from her. "I've been over that day in my head so many times, wondering if there had been another way to handle things. The only one who could have challenged Con to be King of Kings was Ulrik, and all of us knew it. If Ulrik had no' been so consumed by his need for revenge, he might have challenged Con that day. Both of them are level-headed and calm in situations. That was the first—

and only—time any of us saw Ulrik lose his infamous composure."

V paused and drew in a deep breath. "All the Kings stood with Con as we caught the four Silvers. Our magic put them into a deep sleep, and then we caged them within a mountain on Dreagan."

"Oh my God. They're still there?" Claire asked, dumbfounded. And a little excited.

V nodded as he glanced at her. "With his Silvers gone, Ulrik grew even more furious. He was . . . is . . . a brilliant strategist, but that day, fury clouded his mind. When he faced off against Con, he never saw that Con would bind his magic, preventing Ulrik from being in his true form."

Claire covered her mouth with her hand, her eyes wide as she waited for the story to continue.

"The binding made Ulrik shift into a mortal. The sight of him trying to change back into a dragon nearly broke me. Ulrik had always been there for everyone, and now we stood against him."

"Because it was the only way you could think of to help him," Claire said after she dropped her hand to her lap.

V shrugged. "Having his magic bound enraged Ulrik, as it would any of us. Then Con banished Ulrik from Dreagan."

"What?" she asked in such a high-pitched voice that it came out more like some sound a strangled cat would make.

"Con realized that Ulrik couldna remain with us. It was a kindness, really. With his magic bound, he wouldna be able to shift as we could. That would make things worse for him."

Claire had her doubts, but V knew Ulrik and Con better than she did.

V rubbed a hand over his mouth, his gaze on the floor. "We waited until Ulrik walked from Dreagan, and then each of us found our mountains. We slept for thousands of years, waiting for a time when humans would forget about us."

"But we never have," Claire said. "Every culture in the world has a dragon myth."

"But most believe that it was a mistake in the recordings of ancient peoples who happened to stumble upon dinosaur bones and believed they were from dragons."

Claire raised a brow and gave him a flat look. "Not everyone."

"Enough of them."

"So, you slept. All of you? How did you know when it was time to wake?"

V's nostrils flared as he drew in a breath. "Two of us remained awake the entire time. Ulrik. And Con."

"I've seen Ulrik. I've talked to him. He's back at Dreagan, so I'm guessing that all worked out."

"Only recently. It wasna an easy road, but Ulrik is back where he belongs. His journey was . . . difficult. He intended to do us harm, and to be honest, I might have felt the same in his shoes."

Claire flexed her toes before rubbing her foot along V's leg. "So both of them were awake but essentially alone since Ulrik wasn't at Dreagan."

"Aye. I'm no' sure how Con did it. It must have been terribly lonely."

It explained a lot about the mysterious King of Dragon Kings. Claire no longer thought of Con as harsh. Not when she knew more of his story. But she knew there had to be so much more that no one knew.

"What about you?" she asked. "How long did you sleep?"

V stared at her a long time in silence before he said,

"Dreagan has a magical barrier around it that makes mortals no' want to pass through it. Once we began distilling whisky, we had to alter the barrier to allow humans in to work, as well as those who visit. Every Dragon King at Dreagan has worked tirelessly to forge a path for us to live among the mortals. Everyone, that is, except me."

Claire was so taken aback by his words that she could only stare at him for a moment. "That can't be true."

"Before the war with the humans began, before we sent the dragons away, and before we hid in the mountains, I ruled the Carpathian Mountain region. Unlike the others, a part of me—my blood specifically—is within the blade of my sword."

"How do you know that?"

V shrugged and gave a small shake of his head. "My magic told me. Just as it told me that my weapon was different than the others. I knew the moment the dragons left that I could not only check on them, I could also call them home with my sword."

"That's a neat ability. And very important. I imagine you wanted to do that many times."

"I couldna." He paused and swallowed. "Because my sword was stolen."

CHAPTER TWENTY-FOUR

Saying the words aloud to someone else brought all the eons of pain and frustration rushing back to V once more. He started to tamp down the emotions, but then he stopped himself.

That part was over. He had his sword returned. The question of why it wasn't working was another matter entirely.

"Stolen?" Claire repeated, shock causing her eyes to bulge. "How? Why? I mean . . . you're a Dragon King."

V slowly let out a breath. "I asked myself those same questions for countless centuries, and I never got an answer. Until recently."

"Please don't stop there," Claire begged him, her brows furrowed in worry.

"It's a long story, and I doona actually shine in a good light."

She gave him a hard stare. "I highly doubt that's possible. But even if you're right, you had something of yours taken. That has to be considered, as well."

V wished he knew what it was about Claire that made her know how to handle any situation. "I slept, like the other Kings. I doona know how long I was in my mountain before I woke. I should've gone straight to Con, but I didna. All I could think about was finding my sword. Things . . . happened."

"What things?"

Every time Claire looked at him, her clear brown eyes held nothing but interest and desire. He didn't want that to change, and he feared once he told her the truth, it would.

"V?" she urged. "You can tell me."

"I didna stay awake long. Con would find me every time and return me to Dreagan where he ordered me back to my mountain to sleep some more."

Claire's brow was furrowed. "If you ruled the Carpathians, then you went there. I'm not a history buff, but surely, if it was something terrible, it would've been mentioned. Now I'm getting irritated for you. Why wouldn't Con or any of the others take you to your mountain so you could look for whoever stole your sword? Surely, your magic would've helped you find it."

V swallowed, feeling hollow inside. "I couldna remember where I ruled."

She blinked slowly. "I don't understand."

"Neither did the others."

"Okay," she said and twisted her lips. "But why didn't they just tell you?"

"Because each time I woke, really terrible things happened. Like the Great Fire of Rome and the Black Plague, just to name a few."

Her lips went slack. "Bloody hell," she whispered.

"I didna hurt anyone on purpose. I merely wanted to find my sword."

"I don't blame you," she said angrily. "I blame Con and the others. They could've helped."

V shook his head. "Nay, lass. They couldna."

"I don't buy that. You told me the Dragon Kings have magic. Why didn't any of them help you?"

V rose from the sofa and paced before it, raking his hands through his hair. "I woke this last time and left once again. I was intent on finding my sword once and for all. Ulrik found me first, and then I came back to Dreagan. That's where Roman offered to go with me to sort out the answers that I couldna find. He's the one who told me my domain was in Romania."

"The others could've told you that at any time."

He paused and looked at her, smiling softly. "Aye, but it wouldna have done any good. You see, when Roman and I searched, we ran across two gypsies, siblings. It was only after I touched the brother, Camlo, and fell unconscious that I was able to access the memories that had been blocked."

Claire shifted on the couch until both of her feet were on the ground. "Con took your memories?"

"Actually, it's Guy who has that ability."

"I knew it," Claire mumbled and glanced away. Then she jerked her gaze back to V.

He wanted to press her on that statement, but he let it go. For now. "It turns out that Sabina and Camlo are descended from the mortals I protected in my territory. Most gypsies can see the future, but Sabina is able to see the past, which is how she was able to discern a critical piece of the puzzle to my history."

"Which was?"

"A group called the Others. Dark and Light Fae combined with *mie* and *drough* Druids."

Claire rubbed her hands on her thighs. "Dark and Light. And I'm guessing the others are good and bad?"

V nodded.

"Yikes," Claire said.

"Dragons have the most magic of any species on this realm, but somehow, the Others realized that combining their magic gave them an edge. And they used it on me. They hid my memories so I wouldna know that the gypsies took my sword to keep it from them."

Claire nodded slowly in understanding. "The gypsies were helping, but they must have realized that you never would have listened to them."

"I wouldna have. They took the sword and managed to reach Iceland, where they hid it deep inside a mountain. The Others couldna take the sword because the gypsies had ensured that there was only one person who could—Sabina."

Claire jerked back as if it hit. "Sabina? The Sabina that you and Roman just met?"

"Aye. Her gift allowed her to travel back in time. She is actually the one who took the sword from me and gave it to the gypsies."

"Bloody hell."

"So, it was Sabina who had to get the sword back and give it to me. And she did, though no' everything went as planned. The Others want to hurt us, and we've yet to figure out why."

Claire's brows snapped together. "How do you know they want to hurt you?"

"They trapped a white dragon on Fair Isle, and didna let it use the dragon bridge with the others. Then they tortured and finally killed it. No' that long ago, Faith Reynolds discovered the dragon bones in a cave on one of the isles. It was Dmitri's territory, so Con sent him to keep an eye on things. As he helped Faith uncover the bones, he learned what had happened. Worse, they found a small wooden dragon carved in the image of Con. When a mortal touches it, they want to kill us."

"And when a King touches it?"

"We want to kill humans."

"I was going to say bloody hell, but I think that calls for something a bit harsher. I just can't think of anything at the moment."

V saw how Claire struggled to take it all in. Her mind was likely racing with the information dump he'd just thrown at her, and yet she hadn't run from him or demanded that he leave.

"Do you know who makes up these Others?" she asked.

"Sadly, no' yet. We do know one person involved, Usaeil, the Queen of the Light Fae."

Claire's eyes bugged out. "What? The queen? Have you confronted her? Why hasn't anyone done anything?"

"It's just a matter of time before we figure out the others. The Druids would be long dead, but there is a chance that we could find the rest of the Fae involved. As for why Usaeil hasna been dealt with yet, that's another long story."

Claire pressed her fingertips to her temples. "Wait. So the Fae and Druids have been around since our war?"

"Druids, aye. We assumed that the magic on this realm eventually made its way to some mortals, but perhaps that assumption is wrong. The Fae came later."

"Then how did they kill a dragon?"

V returned to the couch and sat beside Claire. "It's one of the things we have to figure out. There is a lot that doesna make sense, but we know the Others are no' finished with us. Everything they've done has been calculated and planned down to the last detail, millennia before we would ever stumble upon any of it."

"They wanted your sword," Claire said, her head jerking to him.

"Aye."

"Why?"

"Because they knew it could return the dragons."

She rolled her eyes. "You have the sword now, right? Then use it and call the dragons home."

V took her hand in his and smiled. "What do you think the rest of the world would do if they suddenly saw dragons in the sky? And where would the dragons live?"

"I'll admit, you have valid points, but if the Others didn't want the dragons here, there has to be a reason for that."

"Aye. I've come to that same conclusion."

"What are you going to do?"

V ran his thumb along the back of her hand. "I doona know. Ever since I got my sword back, I can no' use it."

"Did the gypsies or the Others do something to it?"

"I can no' be sure."

She scooted closer to him. "How can you have this hanging over you and yet walk around as if nothing is wrong?"

"Will worrying about it help?"

She wrinkled her nose. "No."

"Exactly. Look how long I twisted myself in knots about finding my sword. I couldna claim it until it was time. I believe the same will happen with battling the Others."

"Aren't you worried about them? They seem like a formidable enemy."

V smiled then. "They have no' faced the might of the Dragon Kings as one."

"Surely, something like that would bring the Kings out of hiding and pronounce you to the world."

"This is our home. We will always protect this realm and its occupants. If that means our secret is revealed, then we will deal with the consequences."

Claire suddenly grinned at him.

V frowned. "What?"

"Your confidence is damn hot."

One side of his lips lifted in a smile. "Is that right?"

"Oh, yes. Very, very hot."

"Then what are we doing still talking?"

"I was asking myself the same question."

V removed their clothes with just a thought. When Claire looked down and saw that they were naked, her lips turned up in a huge grin.

"Now that could really come in handy," she told him.

"Why are you still talking?"

She straddled his lap and wound her arms about his neck. "You're the one talking now."

His hands splayed on her sides and then slid up her back as she lowered her lips to his.

TO MATCH OR NOT TO MATCH

Hello, lovelies!

You know how there are matchmakers out there that will help you find the right person? I'm actually tempted to hire one. The only problem is that the good ones cost a bit of money.

Hmm. Maybe we should have Date Analysts instead. Someone who could evaluate every step of a date from the initial meeting through to the end and then give a report. I wonder if that would help.

Sadly, I've considered this very thing for . . . well, awhile now. Every time I think I have one issue figured out, another pops up. This could be why there is no such thing on the market to help us date-disasters.

That brings me back to the matchmakers. Which—I hate to admit—are exactly what online dating is. They've just taken out an actual person and plugged in some algorithm to help sort through the thousands of people to find us proper candidates.

Why then isn't it working?

And that *brings me to me.*

Perhaps I'm too picky. Maybe I want too much from the men I go out on dates with. Perhaps the faceless man I see in my dreams doesn't exist, and I should accept that.

Or . . . maybe I shouldn't even consider lowering my standards and being anything but deliriously happy with a man with off-the-charts chemistry that they always show in movies.

A lifetime of loneliness while waiting for The One, or settling.

I don't know about you, but I'd rather be lonely than settle.

And yet I accepted another date yesterday. Hope that the next one might be IT keeps me going, I guess. After the last date where his pictures were at least ten years old so he looked nothing as I expected, I'm a little leery now. It's my own fault.

I used to make sure that my date and I shared a selfie before we actually met. I didn't with this guy, and I paid the price.

I was put off by his lie—because that was exactly what it was. In his pictures, he was fit. Very fit. Wide shoulders, muscular arms. So, imagine my surprise when a man with no muscles and a potbelly walked up at our meeting place.

Now, everyone knows with online dating that first impressions are the photos. That's why people like, smile, wink, or whatever at you. So, if you don't have recent pictures, you're duping others.

That really upset me, but I didn't want to be rude and end the date based on looks. I'd like to say I'm not that shallow, but if we're honest, we have to be attracted to our mates, right?

And there was no attraction.

None. Nothing. Zip. Zero.

I made the decision to stay on the date. He immediately took my hand. Which, I still don't know how I feel about. I'm affectionate, but we'd just met in person despite texting for over a week. Still . . . work up to that.

And he kissed me. Now I really fought about what to do regarding the date. I had driven some distance to see him and had a hotel to go back to, but I'm just not a mean person. So, I stayed.

Surprisingly, we had a good time. He was very easy to talk to, and we laughed a lot. But I kept going back to two very important things.

1. His older pictures making me believe he was something he wasn't.
2. I felt no physical attraction to him.

What made it worse was that he really liked me. And he let me know it. He wanted not just another date, but a relationship. While I also want a relationship, it's not something you jump into willy-nilly.

Especially not after just one date.

I have a policy for being honest with others. As hard as it is sometimes, I keep to that with the men I date. So, I told him the truth. He wasn't happy and tried to make up excuses and reasons for his older pictures. But it still came down to the attraction.

If it isn't there, it isn't there. No one can force it.

So, what did I come away with after this meeting? I definitely need to get back to sharing current selfies with potential dates if I haven't met them in person.

I also need to follow my instincts and let someone know if I'm uncomfortable with what they're doing or saying instead of always worrying about hurting someone's feelings.

While this date wasn't a complete failure—I did have a good meal and conversation—it was still a dud.

I'm ready to hear about your dating failures in the comments so I don't feel so alone.

CHAPTER TWENTY-FIVE

Isle of Skye

Rhi blew out a breath and looked at the pile of scrolls and books that the Skye Druids had given her access to, but no matter how many she looked through, there was nothing about any Fae being on the realm when the Dragon Kings and humans were at war. Or before.

Yet she knew Usaeil must have been here. Because, without a doubt, the queen was part of the Others. Rhi just hadn't been able to actually connect Usaeil—or rather, Ubitch—to anything.

Rhi had spent the majority of her time searching for any kind of clue, and yet she had found nothing. It was the excuse she needed to put her hunt aside and focus on a bigger issue—Usaeil.

Con had even said it was time they went after the Queen of the Light. Why then was Rhi hesitating?

She shoved back her chair and stood. The small room was filled with yellow light that she had created with her magic, illumination that wouldn't harm the ancient texts in the chamber. She longed to leave and go to her island to sink her toes into the sand and let the turquoise water lap at her ankles.

The island called to her so loudly that she closed her eyes. With very little effort, she could hear the waves rolling onto the shore and feel the grains of white sand rubbing her skin.

"There is nothing holding you here."

Her eyes snapped open. She knew that voice. Slowly, she turned to look into the lavender eyes of the very being that could wipe her from existence with merely a snap of her fingers. "Death."

Otherwise known as the Mistress of War or Erith to a select few, Death was one of the most powerful beings Rhi had ever encountered. It didn't matter that she was petite in stature or so beautiful that it seemed incomprehensible, she controlled the destinies of all Fae. Once Death judged you, she sent her Reapers to be the executioners.

Erith's lips curved into a grin. "You don't seem happy to see me."

"On the contrary, I'm delighted that everything worked out for you and that you defeated Bran." Rhi looked over the long, inky hair that hung freely down Death's back.

"Is that approval of my attire I see in your eyes?"

This time, Rhi smiled. "It is. The gowns were gorgeous, but this," she said, motioning to the black pants and form-fitting black top with her hand, "is definitely you. And while I can sit and talk fashion all day, I don't think that's what brought you here."

"No, it isn't."

"Do I have to ask what is?"

Erith moved away from the doorway and entered the small chamber. She walked around the table and let her fingers brush over the books and scrolls. "You seek something that you won't find here."

"How do you know?"

"Because you know it. You just won't accept it."

Anger quickly rose up in Rhi. "You have no idea what goes on in my mind."

Erith paused in her walk and met Rhi's gaze. "I could read your mind, but I don't need to. Because I know how you think."

"Why do you say that?" There was something in Death's tone that made Rhi very wary.

"Because I walked a similar path long, long ago. The difference is, I was very much alone. You have others who care greatly for you. The Warriors and Druids at MacLeod Castle, the Dragon Kings and their mates at Dreagan, your nail tech, Jesse, and yes, even Balladyn. The King of the Dark loves you deeply."

"I can't give him what he needs."

A black brow rose. "Are you sure of that?"

"Yes." Then Rhi frowned. "Why do you ask?"

"You fight it and hide it well, but I can see the darkness within you. It's been there since Balladyn put the Chains of Mordare on you. And there was a time that you welcomed it."

Rhi didn't bother to refute any of what Death said. "Is it that obvious?"

"No. As long as you keep fighting it, your light will continue to shine."

"But if I give in, I'm lost. Is that it?"

Erith nodded. She placed her hands on the table and leaned her weight upon her palms. "You've long wanted to know why I sent Daire to watch you."

"Will you finally tell me?"

"Are you sure you want to know? Sometimes, it's the truth we can't handle."

Rhi lifted her chin. "I'm a Light. I come from a noble family of Light who has sacrificed much for the Fae. I can handle whatever it is you have to tell me."

"Can you? Is that why you didn't tell Con or anyone at Dreagan about the name you saw written upon that stone in the cavern on Iceland?"

It took everything Rhi had to hold Erith's gaze. "How do you know about that?"

"How do I know which Fae need to be judged? It's my power." Death pressed her lips together and glanced down. "Rhi, I don't think you realize what a formidable Fae you are. Usaeil knows it. She's known for some time. It was why she befriended you, why she made you feel as if the two of you were as close as sisters. It's why she seemed to push you to do great things, but why you never quite reached whatever it was you sought."

"Keep your friends close, but your enemies closer," Rhi said.

"Precisely."

"How did I not see who Usaeil really was? Why did I miss what was right in front of my face?"

Erith blew out a breath and straightened. "Because she's very good at fooling others. Usaeil wasn't the only one who saw your potential. I did, as well. I kept an eye on you through the centuries, but the queen's recent actions caused me to become concerned. It's why I sent Daire to you. I couldn't watch you all the time, but he could."

"Why not just ask me what you wanted to know?" Rhi demanded.

"I wanted to see how you handled the darkness within you. I needed to see that the Fae I know you can be is still in there, waiting to show herself."

Despite her better judgment, Rhi asked, "And?"

Death's smile was slow as it filled her face. "You have the power to defeat Usaeil. But you have to be careful. One wrong step, one wrong decision, and you will lose the very thing you covet."

"My light," Rhi mumbled.

"I cannot interfere, but know that if I could, I would join you to fight Usaeil."

Rhi let her anger show in her eyes. "You could judge her now. You, more than anyone, know the crimes she has committed. If anyone deserves to be taken by the Reapers, it's her."

"Yes. I could do that. But I won't."

"Why?" Rhi demanded angrily.

Erith came to stand before her. "Because she is yours to take. A future you can't even see yet lies before you. It's up to you to decide what you will do. But know this, Usaeil has caused enough havoc. I will not stand by much longer while you make your decision. Take her. Or I will."

Rhi nodded. In the next instant, Death was gone, leaving Rhi with a lot to think over.

CHAPTER TWENTY-SIX

The morning came too soon. V hadn't slept, but he had enjoyed holding Claire in his arms. It had been a wonderful experience. From her cuddling against him after hours of making love, to her lips parting and her breathing deepening, to her twitching in her sleep.

He'd loved every second of it.

And he wanted another night. The problem was, he feared that all the nights for eternity wouldn't be enough for him.

He didn't pretend to sleep when Claire's alarm went off, and she grunted in response before rolling over to turn it off. She sat up, swinging her legs off the bed. There, she paused. She looked over her shoulder and cracked open one eye.

"It wasn't a dream," she mumbled.

He grinned as he came up on one elbow and smoothed her hair from her face. "Nay, lass. It wasna a dream. It was verra verra real."

"I love your voice," she said with a smile, her eye shutting again. "It's verra sexy."

V laughed at her imitation of a brogue. He wanted to

stop her when she stood and shuffled into the bathroom. He didn't take his eyes from her as she moved about, turning on the shower and getting a towel.

He bit back another laugh when she looked confused about being naked. Then a smile came over her face, causing her to flush slightly as she glanced his way.

She was so damn adorable.

When she got into the shower, he was tempted to join her, but if he did, he wouldn't be content with just touching and looking. He'd want her again.

V fell back onto the mattress and threw an arm over his eyes. If he'd had the power to make the night longer, he would have. The precious few hours he'd had with Claire had not been enough.

He'd shared his past—and the pain that went with it. Each time he saw her anger on behalf of him and the dragons, a little of his heart had healed. It was almost as if the time spent with her had made him into a new man.

A push against his mind alerted him that another King was trying to communicate telepathically. He opened the link, only to cringe when he heard Ulrik's voice.

"Morning, Sleeping Beauty. Did you faint again? Or could you have found comfort in the bed of a pretty nurse we all know."

"You can stop calling me that anytime," V replied.

Ulrik chuckled. *"Sorry. The name has stuck."*

"Did you just want to annoy me this morning?"

"Actually, I wanted to let you know that Con is looking for you," Ulrik said, all teasing gone from his voice.

V could not care less who knew where he had spent the night. What he did with a woman was his business. *"So?"*

"He's on his way to Claire's."

"Thanks," V said before severing the link and jumping out of bed.

As he walked from the bedroom, he called his clothes to him. They were back in place in two steps. He ran his hands through his hair and stopped before the door. He didn't want Claire uncomfortable, and Con had a way of doing that to humans. Part of it was intentional, but another part was just Constantine himself.

V opened the door, but before he could step outside, his gaze landed on Con leaning against the side of Claire's car. He didn't even turn his face to the house.

With a sigh, V walked outside and closed the door behind him. As he made his way to Con, he spotted the immaculate black suit. The closer V got, the more he realized that the material of the suit was a black on black plaid print. Along with the white dress shirt—unbuttoned at the top and without a tie—Con had on the gold dragon head cufflinks he always wore.

Everyone had armor of some kind. For Con, it was his suits.

At least while in mortal form.

No human wanted to see Con when he was riled in his true form. It wasn't a sight for the faint of heart.

V came to stand beside Con, leaning back on the car, as well. They stood in silence for several minutes. V knew that when Con was ready to talk, he would.

Finally, Con asked, "Was it Ulrik who told you I was here?"

"Aye."

"Good."

V frowned and turned his head to Con. "Good?"

"I didna want to surprise either you or Claire. I happen to like her."

A brow quirked in V's forehead. "You like her? You doona like anyone."

"That's no' entirely true." Con's lips flattened when he met V's gaze. "All right. It's true sometimes."

V grinned as he chuckled. "Is this where you tell me I should stay away from her?"

"I've stopped trying to warn any of you against entanglements with humans. No one can ignore what their heart wants."

"I'm no' in love with her."

It was Con's turn to raise a brow. "I didna say anything about love."

"You said the heart."

"Aye. Everyone has needs and wants. That includes desire and love, but I wasna referring to that."

V swallowed and looked away. He couldn't figure out why he was arguing the point. He liked Claire. A lot. "Just so you know."

"I wanted to let you know that if being with Claire is what you need, then do it. See the world, if you want."

V lowered his eyes to the ground. This was Con's way of trying to push him to do something other than returning to his mountain to sleep.

A few silent moments went by before V looked out over the neighbors' yard and their perfectly trimmed hedges. "There are worse things than me going to my mountain."

"No harm has befallen the mortals since you woke this time."

V felt Con's gaze on him, but V couldn't look at his King. "The Others targeted me. Was it just because of my sword? Or was it because of something else? Did I cause all those horrible things to happen when I woke before or was that something else the Others did? I doona know anymore."

"Nothing is going to happen to Claire."

V pushed away from the car and faced Con. "You can no' know that."

"I know it because I know you willna let it happen. Just as you had Roman's back in Iceland. Each of us became a Dragon King because we're protectors, V. You always had a big heart when it came to anyone who needed help. You never turned anyone away. Why do you think the mortals you sheltered—the gypsies—went to such lengths to protect no' just you but all the Dragon Kings?"

"I've made my decision."

Con dropped his chin to his chest for a heartbeat. Then he straightened from the vehicle. His black eyes met V's, intense and demanding. "You look . . . rested. Relaxed, even. Whatever Claire is doing to you, let her continue. It's doing you good."

V watched Con walk to his car before driving away. Then he went back into the house. Claire was just getting out of the shower.

"Do you eat breakfast?" he called.

"Um . . . not usually. Mostly it's because I don't have time."

"No' a morning person, huh?" V asked with a grin.

She leaned out of the bathroom with her robe on and her blond hair wet and freshly combed. "Mornings suck. I actually have breakfast food. Every week I tell myself I'm going to get up fifteen minutes early and cook. And every week, I don't."

"Then I will," he offered.

Her eyes closed as she moaned. "Keep this up, and I might never let you leave."

She ducked back into the bathroom before he could reply, but it made him smile nonetheless. The sound of a blow-dryer reached him a second later.

V searched the pantry and fridge to find the items he

needed. He was just learning to cook, and he wasn't very good, but he wanted to do something for her. The one thing he could make was fried eggs.

Next on his list to learn was an omelet. He loved them.

Why are you learning to cook if you're returning to your mountain?

V had the skillet in his hand over the stove when the thought went through his mind. He paused before slowly setting down the pan and lighting the gas.

He put the question out of his mind and concentrated on frying the eggs while putting some bread in the toaster. Once the skillet was hot enough, he cracked the eggs and laid in a couple of links of sausage to cook together.

It was just a few minutes later that Claire shouted, "That smells so good!"

V looked at the coffee maker and frowned. Then he spotted the little pods and remembered how Cassie had shown him what to do. With that going, he checked on the eggs and sausage before getting the butter out of the fridge and putting it on the table.

Next, he went searching for plates and utensils. By the time he returned to the stove, the eggs were about to burn. He dished them onto the plates and checked the sausage before adding them, as well. No sooner had he set the plates down than the bread popped out of the toaster.

He grabbed the slices, putting two on each plate. V stepped back, looking over the table. Something was missing. He looked around the kitchen, his gaze landing on the coffee. After getting it on the table, he brewed a mug of his own.

The blow-dryer clicked off, and then Claire walked into the kitchen. She stopped dead in her tracks when she saw the table. Her gaze lifted to his, her face giving nothing away.

"Where have you been my whole life?" she asked.

V shrugged. "Sleeping."

"You're spoiling me."

He held out her chair. "There's nothing wrong with that."

A wide smile split her face. "I could get used to this."

The thing was, so could he.

They sat down. V was about to dig into the food when he realized that it might not taste good. V started to warn Claire, but she already had a bite in her mouth.

His balls tightened when she moaned, a look of ecstasy coming over her face.

"This is delicious," she said and took another bite.

V couldn't move. Blood drummed in his ears as he watched her enjoying the meal that he'd made. He'd missed so many things like this while he slept.

And he wouldn't be a part of them now if he returned to his mountain.

"V?"

He blinked as he realized that Claire was frowning at him. "What is it? Does it taste bad?"

"It's great," she said. "It's you I'm worried about. You looked a million miles away just then. Are you all right?"

"Aye, lass."

She shook her head and pointed her fork at him. "You can't do that."

"What?" he asked in confusion.

"Say *lass* like that. After dinner and the visit to the loch, and then last night and breakfast this morning. . . . A girl can only take so much before your charm gets to her."

Was that what he was doing? Charming her? Wooing her? Damn. It was.

"I like being with you."

She looked up from her plate and smiled. "I like being with you."

"I like how you make me feel when we're together."

Claire set down her fork and put her hand atop his. "I can honestly say the same."

"I've spent so much time away from others that I doona always remember the right things to do and say."

"That was definitely the right thing," Claire said with a smile.

He jerked his chin to her food. "Eat before it gets cold."

In between bites, she filled the silence with talk of some of her favorite patients that were regulars at Sophie's practice.

He was enamored with everything she had to say. All the stories and thoughts. When she laughed before telling a story, he found himself smiling, waiting to join in on the mirth with her.

Just like the night, breakfast was over too soon. She tried to clean up, but he stopped her, urging her to finish getting ready. She gave him a kiss on the cheek and relented her grip on the plates.

V took his time cleaning the kitchen as she dressed. When she came out of her bedroom thirty minutes later, she was dressed in jeans and a black shirt with her makeup on.

She walked to him and put her arms around his waist. "This was the best morning."

"When can I see you again?"

Her grin widened. "Whenever you want."

"Tonight then."

"I can't wait."

CHAPTER TWENTY-SEVEN

"Well?" Ulrik asked after Con had pulled into the garage and got out of his car.

Con looked at his friend after he'd closed the vehicle door. "Your plan could have backfired."

"Since you say that, it means it didna," he replied with a grin.

"You're a matchmaker now?"

Ulrik twisted his lips and shrugged. "V was floundering. I saw the push he needed. Are you going to tell me what he said? Or do I have to pull every word from you?"

Con walked past Ulrik into the manor and started up the stairs. He spotted Roman and Darius nearby, but he didn't stop. While he'd never tell any of them—especially Ulrik—that what they did to V was exactly what was needed, he was glad they did it.

Mostly because he would never have done such a thing himself. His position included many things but messing in the love lives of the Kings wasn't one of them. After all, who was he to give relationship advice?

Con was halfway up the stairs to his office before he realized that Ulrik hadn't said anything more. He heard his friend's footsteps behind him, so Ulrik hadn't given up on finding out more about V and Claire. Ulrik's silence could only mean one thing—he knew what was on Con's mind.

Or rather *who* Con was thinking about.

Once inside his office, Con walked behind his desk, but he didn't sit. He leaned his forearms on the back of his chair and met Ulrik's gold eyes.

"You were right about V and Claire. He's different."

Ulrik's brows rose as he slowly sat in one of the chairs. "After just one night? I didna expect that."

"Yes, you did."

Ulrik laughed and bent his leg to place his ankle over his knee. "Based on the way Darius said V was looking at Claire, I thought things might go well."

"V seems more . . . stable. If that's the right word." Con frowned and shook his head. "I can no' explain the difference exactly, but it is visible."

"Then what's the problem? Because there obviously is one."

Con drew in a breath and pulled his chair out to sink into it. "When all those atrocities happened throughout the ages, did you know it was V?"

"No' at first. Later, I did. I tried to get to him, but I was never quick enough." Ulrik pressed his lips together as he frowned. "You're afraid that something like that might happen again? Why? He has his sword now."

"We doona know what the Others did to him. We doona even know if he was responsible for those acts. What if it was the Others? What if it happens again?"

Ulrik made a face. "Con. This is V we're talking about."

"That's right. And I doona need to remind you that he joined you against the mortals."

"That was long ago," Ulrik bit out.

Con closed his eyes briefly, fighting to keep control of the emotions and worries that raged inside him. "You're right. And he's been fine for weeks until he and Roman went looking for his sword."

"And he's been fine since." Ulrik dropped his foot to the ground and leaned forward. "What's really bothering you?"

"I doona want V to go to his mountain. I've sent him there so many times. He needs to live. Even if it's just a half-life as a human."

Ulrik lowered his eyes to the floor for a heartbeat. Then he looked at Con. "Brother, you're the only one living a half-life."

"Am I?" Con questioned. "I think every Dragon King is since we can no' be in our true forms without hiding."

"I went eons without being able to shift. During that time, I recalled every moment of my life before being banished. I could tell you in detail how it felt to be a dragon, to fly and roar and breathe fire." Ulrik released a breath. "I thought once I had my magic restored that I would be myself again. It didna happen. In fact, I did no' begin living until Eilish."

Con gave Ulrik a hard look. "I'm going to stop you right there. You're treading on dangerous ground. I doona care if you're my best friend or no'. I willna discuss this."

"Because you know I'm right? Because you ache for it more than any other King?"

Con shoved back his chair so hard that it slid across the floor and slammed into the wall behind him, causing a picture to bang.

Ulrik slowly got to his feet, a tight smile on his lips. "Just as I thought. You know, one of these days, you're going to have to face the past you try so hard to forget."

"I have *never* forgotten it."

Ulrik studied Con for a long, silent moment. "Nay, perhaps you have no'."

Con inhaled and slowly released the breath he'd been holding as he once more let calm overtake him. Few things could set him off so, but Ulrik knew just what to say to send him over the edge.

There was a shimmer in the air a moment before Rhi appeared. She looked a little dazed, but the moment she saw Ulrik, she hid it.

"I really am going to have to remember to start teleporting into the hallway and knocking," she said.

Con and Ulrik exchanged a look. That wasn't something Rhi would say. She took great joy in interrupting Con.

"Everything all right?" Ulrik asked her.

Rhi licked her lips and nodded once. "I can wait outside."

This made Con's frown deepen. Something was wrong. And it wasn't the same shock that Rhi had worn when she discovered that Usaeil had banished her or the Light Queen's involvement in Rhi's past.

"We were discussing V." Con didn't know why he told Rhi. Perhaps to let her know that she wasn't interrupting anything dire.

Rhi nodded absently. "Really?"

Con slid his gaze to Ulrik for a heartbeat. "Ulrik is playing matchmaker."

"I thought it might be a good idea," Ulrik said with a shrug.

Rhi's silver eyes widened as she asked excitedly, "Did it work?"

"Perfectly," Ulrik replied with a smile.

Con looked at the two of them and saw just how far those at Dreagan—and their friends—would go to make someone happy. How many countless years had he worried that the Kings wouldn't form the family that he knew they needed to be to survive without their dragons?

Somehow, despite his mistakes, it seemed to have happened.

But he couldn't take the credit. If it hadn't been for Erith's friendship at crucial times, he might have made different decisions that led the Kings down a much rockier path.

Not that the one they were currently on was smooth. Yet Con knew that whatever came at them, the Kings would be able to face it. They were that close as a species and a family. And while he hadn't wanted any of them to fall for humans, even he had to admit that the love the Kings found made them stronger.

For now.

It might not always be so since no one really knew what would happen even a few hundred years from now when the humans who were never supposed to live that long did.

He blinked and saw Rhi shoot him a glance. Con focused on the conversation to hear Ulrik tell the Light Fae that V had spent the night with Claire.

"I'm happy for them," Rhi said.

Con saw her sad smile.

Ulrik must have as well because he cleared his throat. "I'll leave the two of you to talk."

As soon as the door shut behind Ulrik, Con turned to Rhi. "What happened?"

"I don't want you to think that every time I come that something happened or that I've come running to you for help. Because that isn't what this is."

When she became irked, her Irish brogue deepened. Con would have smiled, but he suspected that she was putting on a brave face.

"We both know you're more than capable of handling any situation alone," Con told Rhi.

She turned her face away and looked at a map of Dreagan that hung on the opposite wall. She remained silent for several minutes, and Con didn't push her to talk. Whatever had happened, Rhi would get to it in her own time.

"*Con.*"

Ulrik's voice in his mind wasn't a surprise. Con opened the mental link. "*Aye?*"

"*Is she all right?*"

Con knew that he was asking about Rhi. "*I'm no' sure yet. Keep everyone away from my office.*"

"*Of course. I'll be close.*"

Con disconnected from the link and focused solely on the Light Fae who suddenly couldn't stop staring at the map. Rhi was a great many things, but the two things she was above all else was loyal and true. She had developed close friendships with many Kings to such extents that she had put her own life in jeopardy several times over the centuries for them.

Con's disastrous affair with Usaeil was what had him and Rhi working together now. Usaeil was smart enough to expect him and Rhi to team up to go against her. Which is one reason he'd been cautious about attacking the queen. They needed to be smart if they were going to win.

And he always won.

Con was prepared to do whatever it took to bring down the queen. Rhi was of the same mind about things, but she had been impatient to go after Usaeil. Con had kept putting her off. Not because he feared what might happen, but because he wanted to concentrate solely on the queen and not the other myriad enemies the Kings had.

But that wasn't going to happen, it seemed.

He'd recently told Rhi that it was time for them to go

after Usaeil. And he suspected that's why the Light was there now.

"My thoughts are filled with only a few things now," Rhi finally said into the silence. "Usaeil, Balladyn, my banishment, and the Fae involved with the Others. I miss the days where I had no such worries. But I fear they're gone. Possibly for good."

"They're only gone if you allow them to be," Con told her.

She nodded, her long waves of jet black hair moving against her back. "Such wants seem so frivolous now." Rhi turned to face him then. "I don't think I ever truly realized the weight you bear daily."

"I've never asked anyone to grasp what this position holds."

"I know." She walked closer. "I've been on Skye continuing my search for any mention of Fae in the time before and during your war with the mortals."

Con tamped down the hope that sprang up. "Did you find anything?"

"Unfortunately, no. However, I had a visitor."

He raised a brow, waiting for her to tell him who it was. "Death."

The few times Con had interacted with Erith, it had been because she saw a need for it. Whether she saw the future or something else, Con still didn't know. But Death didn't pay visits lightly.

Rhi snorted softly. "I can see by your expression that you realize how important such a visit is."

"What did she say?" When Rhi hesitated, Con said her name.

Rhi wrapped her arms around herself. "She said she had Daire follow me because she wanted to make sure I could handle the darkness growing inside me."

For a moment, Con couldn't think. He kept hearing Rhi's words in his head and tried to remember if he had seen anything dark inside her.

"It was the Chains of Mordare that began it," Rhi explained.

Con wished he had Balladyn before him right now because it would feel much better to punch the wanker than to hold it all in. "You broke them. Something that was impossible."

"Apparently, that didn't stop the darkness from taking root inside me." Rhi shot him a look, shame filling her silver eyes. "I've known it was there. And I ignored it, but there are times that its call is . . . seductive."

"It's that way for everyone. We all have light and dark inside us. You know that. It's a battle everyone fights. Some give in. Others never do."

Rhi lifted one shoulder in a shrug. "Erith said she hasn't judged Usaeil because the queen is mine to take out."

"Good."

"Death also said that she wouldn't wait much longer."

Con walked to stand before Rhi. "Then neither shall we. I think it's time we begin our plans to go after Usaeil."

Rhi's face lit up as she smiled. "I'm ready."

CHAPTER TWENTY-EIGHT

No matter how many times Claire tried to tell herself not to be too excited and not think about V every second of the day, she couldn't help herself.

There were a few times over the years that she had met someone she really liked. Some had turned into brief relationships, but some hadn't. What was exciting—and rather terrifying—was that she couldn't remember ever feeling so at peace in all her life.

She thought it might be because V wasn't a normal man. He was a dragon, which surely made a difference. Because it certainly had changed things while making love to him.

The man was an expert when it came to knowing how and when and where to touch her. His hands, his mouth, and, oh God, his tongue did such delightful, *carnal* things to her.

All before he'd even filled her with his impressive cock.

Claire's mouth went dry, and she inwardly shook herself. It was only a little after two in the afternoon, but her entire day had been spent thinking the same thoughts again and again. And it left her body aching and so needy that she thought she might need to change her panties.

She couldn't focus on anything properly. Thank goodness she was no longer at the hospital, but even so, she needed to get her head on straight and finish for the day.

But it was so hard when all she wanted to do was relive the night before—and dream about the night to come.

Claire found herself smiling as she stared down at the file in her hand. She then saw another hand grasping it and looked up to find Sophie staring at her with a knowing grin.

"I don't need to ask what that smile is about," her friend said. "Everyone in town knows you and V left together last night."

Claire opened her mouth to say something, but she realized she didn't have a clue how to respond.

Sophie laughed and tugged the file out of her hands. "Since I've never seen you so at a loss for words, I take it he was . . . adequate?"

Claire glanced around to make sure no one could hear. "Oh, more than adequate."

"Ohhhh. Nice."

Claire couldn't stop smiling. She wanted to tell Sophie that she knew the story of the Dragon Kings, but something stopped her. The only thing she'd ever kept from her best friend was the Dragon Kings. And Claire hated that. She missed sharing everything with Sophie.

Even if Sophie now considered Darius her best friend. Claire wasn't upset about that. Maybe it was because they still worked together, and she got to spend so much time with Sophie, but even she knew that couldn't last forever.

"Was it just a one-time thing?" Sophie asked.

Claire licked her lips nervously. "Actually, last night was the second time."

"Is that so?"

She narrowed her eyes at Sophie. While her friend tried

to act shocked at the statement, it was obvious that she'd known. And Sophie hadn't said anything to her.

"What?" Sophie asked the longer Claire stared at her.

"You knew about the first time."

Sophie didn't try to lie. Remorse filled her face. "Okay, but don't be mad."

"At what?" Claire asked, suddenly worried.

"Well, I knew the thing with Calvin was really messing with you, so we thought it might be nice to put someone near you to take your mind off him."

Claire crossed her arms over her chest. It was a good thing all the patients were in the waiting room and not in the back to hear them.

"You're mad." Sophie's face fell.

"Did you find the first available guy at Dreagan who didn't turn up his nose at me?"

"It wasn't like that."

A retort filled her mind, but Claire didn't say it. She realized she wasn't upset. If it hadn't been for Sophie and Darius, she might never have been able to experience being in V's arms.

"Claire, I'm sorry," Sophie began.

She held up a hand, stopping Sophie from talking further. "I know I should probably be upset, but I also know that you did it because you're my friend. If I had been able to do something similar for you, I would have."

"Really?" Sophie asked skeptically.

Claire then held out her arms, and they embraced. "Really."

"I've been dying to tell you. I hate keeping things from you."

Claire felt even worse since she had kept an important secret from Sophie for months. When Sophie pulled away,

Claire knew she wouldn't be able to look her in the eyes and not spill everything.

Sure enough, Sophie caught her gaze, a frown forming.

Claire looked to the ceiling and turned away. "Don't ask. Please, don't ask."

"Well, of course I'm going to ask now."

Claire walked to her desk, trying to ignore Sophie. "We have patients."

"One more for the day. It's Mr. Brown, who I'm just checking to see how the medicine I gave him is working, and he's not even here yet. Stop stalling, Claire, and tell me whatever it is you don't want me to know," Sophie urged.

Claire put her hands on the edge of her desk and hung her head. "I lied to you and Darius in Edinburgh."

There was a beat of silence. "About?"

"What I remembered when I was taken." Claire straightened and faced Sophie. "I can recall every detail. How I lost control of my body around the Dark Fae, and how Darius and the others saved us. I knew about the Dragon Kings, Sophie. And I thought if I told you what I remembered that those at Dreagan would take the memories away."

Sophie reached behind her, searching for something to grab to steady herself. She swayed before finally finding a file cabinet. "All this time, you remembered? You never said anything about the Fae and what they did?"

"What was there to say? It wasn't painful. Quite the opposite, but I've never been so scared in my life. I didn't want them to touch me."

"Some would liken that to rape."

"They didn't have sex with me," Claire stated more firmly. "That's why I was able to get past it. I also knew that the closer I stayed to Dreagan, the safer I would be from the Dark."

"You aren't wrong there."

Claire swallowed. "I'm sorry for lying to you and Darius. The Dragon Kings saved both of us, and I owe them so much for that. I would never tell anyone about them, but I wasn't sure if anyone would believe me."

"I would have."

"I know," Claire said with a smile. "I told V last night that I knew."

Sophie's olive eyes widened. "Oh?"

"He filled in the blanks that I've been wondering about for some time."

"So you know everything?"

Claire shrugged. "I don't know about *everything*, but he did tell me some things."

"And then?" Sophie asked while smiling.

Claire tried to look nonchalant but ruined it with a big smile. "He wanted to know when he could see me again."

"Don't make me ask," Sophie demanded with a laugh.

"I'll be seeing him when I leave tonight."

"I'm ridiculously excited for you," Sophie said as she rushed to her and enfolded her in another hug.

Claire held her tightly. "You're the sister I've always wanted. It killed me to keep things from you."

"Think of me," Sophie said. "I had so much more I couldn't tell you. But now we can share something other than the dating blog."

The smile faded as they parted. Worry wound its way around Claire. "What happens if V doesn't want to see me anymore? Will my memories be taken? He told me that's what Guy does."

"You've kept their secret this long. I don't think they

would do anything. Besides, why do you think V wouldn't want to be with you?"

Claire shrugged, not wanting to put words to her feelings.

Sophie gave her a sad smile. "You can't compare everyone to your past relationships."

"Really?" Claire asked sarcastically. "You did."

"True, but I did it the wrong way. Take it from me, you can't compare a Dragon King to a mere man."

"This I'm *very* aware of."

Sophie held her gaze a long moment. "You haven't asked for this advice, but I'm giving it anyway. However long this lasts with V, enjoy it. Take each hour, each day at a time, and savor it, whether it's a week or an eternity."

"Eternity? Wait. I just realized that he's immortal. And I'm not." Claire's eyes widened. "Oh, no! Sophie. You're not immortal either."

If Claire expected her friend to look upset at the news, she was wrong. She took a good look at Sophie and finally shot her a look, waiting to get details.

Sophie rolled her eyes. "Obviously, V left out a few details."

"You can fill me in, though."

"A dragon mates for life. That's what you need to understand first and foremost."

Claire's stomach fluttered at the news. She could almost imagine being V's for eternity, always knowing that his love never wavered, never faded. How absolutely glorious.

"Are you listening?"

Claire jerked. "Yes. Sorry. Go on."

"There is a mating ceremony. Once it's done, each mate gets a dragon eye tattoo that symbolizes they're joined. It also means that the mate is granted immortality, to live as long as her Dragon King."

"You have this tat?"

Sophie laughed while nodding. "I do."

"So you'll live for . . . well, forever."

Sophie shrugged. "I guess. It doesn't matter to me as long as I get to spend it with Darius."

Claire could certainly understand wanting something as simple as that. She couldn't wait to see V again and see what else she might learn.

Their conversation was halted as they went back to seeing the last scheduled patient and two walk-ins. The next time Claire looked at her watch, it was time to wrap up for the day.

"No, no," Sophie said when Claire started to clean the rooms. "Get back to V. I've got this."

"I love you so much," Claire said as she grabbed her purse and ran to the door.

She nearly collided with Darius, who caught her before she could trip. Claire smiled up at him and said, "I'm not mad. Actually, I should thank you!"

"What?" he asked with a frown.

"Talk to Sophie. I've got to go."

Claire moved around him and jogged to her car. She had to make herself slow down and not speed on her way home. As soon as she pulled into the drive next to V's car, she unbuckled her seatbelt. Within seconds, she had the car in park and the engine off.

Her steps were quick and light as she made her way to the door. When she tried to open it, she found it locked. Since she thought V would have left it unlocked, it was a little disconcerting. Undeterred, Claire found her key and released the lock. She stepped inside the house, expecting to see V.

Instead, she found it empty.

Had he gone and for some reason left his car? Her disappointment was overwhelming. She walked slowly to the table and dropped her purse and keys on it. She didn't know why she'd thought he would be at her house. He hadn't said anything of the sort. But he'd been there when she left that morning.

"Bad day?"

At the sound of his voice behind her, she whirled around to find him leaning against the doorway watching her. "No."

"You looked upset," he said.

"Because I didn't think you were here."

He smiled and pushed away from the door to walk to her. "I always keep my word, lass. Now come here so I can kiss you."

As if she had to be told twice.

CHAPTER TWENTY-NINE

The taste of her lips was sublime. V had counted the hours until he could see Claire again. All he'd done was think of her throughout the day.

Her smile, the color of her eyes, the way her skin flushed when she was pleasured. She'd filled every corner of his mind and moment of the day. He'd helped in the distillery, did several loads of wash, and took Cassie's dog Duke for a walk in the Dragonwood.

The Great Dane had bounded through the trees with such joy that V wished Claire had been there to see it. V hadn't expected to come to love the dog so much, but he was a staple around Dreagan, and for some reason, Duke had taken an instant liking to him.

So much so that the dog scratched on V's door at night to come in and sleep with him. They had fought over the bed at first, and though V would never tell anyone, the dog won. Now when Duke chose to sleep with him, V only had a sliver of the large bed to call his own.

V smoothed back Claire's hair from her face as he cupped her head. "How was your day?"

"Long," she answered. "But much better now that you're here."

He liked the way happiness flowed through him at her words.

"How about yours?" she asked.

"Verra long. All I could think about was you."

Her eyes grew heavy-lidded as she pressed her breasts against him. "Hmm. Did you really?"

"Oh, aye."

She rose up on her tiptoes and briefly pressed her lips against his before looking into his eyes. "I told Sophie that I knew about the Dragon Kings."

"How did she take it?"

"With some shock, but it didn't last long. Sophie said she was glad that she could now talk to me about everything that she had been keeping from me."

V wondered what it felt like to have such a friend where there were no secrets. He didn't open up easily to anyone, which was part of the reason he'd never become really close with any Dragon Kings. It didn't help that he'd spent so much time in his mountain.

"What?" Claire asked, concern clouding her face.

He shook his head. "I was just thinking about how close you and Sophie are."

"She's my best friend. And while she might not say it, Darius is now her best friend. She's still pretty partial to me, though," Claire said with a grin.

"She's verra protective of you. So is Darius, for that matter."

Claire grinned from ear to ear. "That makes me happy because I love them both to pieces. What about you? Who is your closest friend?"

"I guess you could say it's Roman."

"You guess? You don't sound too sure."

V shrugged. "We went through quite a bit in Iceland. To be honest, I doona open up easily to others."

She tilted her head to the side, causing her blond hair to brush against his arm. "I would never have guessed that."

"It's different with you."

"You keep saying things like that, and I may never let you go."

"Maybe I doona want you to." V realized the statement was true the moment he voiced it.

Claire put her hand on his jaw and stared into his eyes. "I like how you say things like that."

He took her hand and brought it to his lips where he kissed the inside of her palm before flicking his tongue against her skin. The smile she gave him let him know she liked it.

"Want to go for a ride?" he asked.

Her eyes widened in excitement. "I'll go anywhere with you."

"Anywhere?"

She leaned her head back and laughed. "Yes."

He couldn't ignore the sight of her neck. V leaned in and placed his lips just below her ear and nuzzled the skin. She moaned then, and he went instantly hard.

"I want you," he whispered. "But no' yet."

It took a Herculean effort for him to step away. He slid his palm down Claire's arm and took her hand. When he tried to tug her after him, she pulled back.

"I like to be prepared," she told him. "Do I need to change? I don't want to be underdressed."

He looked her over, lingering on the swell of her breasts. "You're perfect."

Her smile was slow and utterly seductive as it pulled at her lips. "You sure know how to charm a woman."

V knew nothing of the sort. "I say what I mean."

"Then don't ever stop."

"I willna," he promised.

Her fingers tightened on his. Claire turned and grabbed her purse then faced him once more. "I'm ready."

They walked out of the house, pausing long enough for her to lock it. As she did, he sent his magic around the dwelling to protect it. He should have done it the night before, but he'd been preoccupied.

There were no Dark Fae anywhere near, but the Kings had other enemies. And V wanted to make sure that Claire was protected whether he was with her or not.

V walked her to the Rimac and opened the door for her. Once Claire was inside, he closed it and walked around to the driver's side. He slid behind the wheel and started the engine. With a glance in her direction, V backed out of the driveway and turned the vehicle in the direction of Dreagan.

"I should probably tell you what else Sophie shared."

He shot a quick look at Claire, but she was staring out the window. "All right."

"She and Darius set us up."

"I figured that out."

Claire's head whipped to him, surprise on her face. "You did?"

"Aye."

"You're not mad about it?"

He shrugged and slowed to take a curve before checking to see if another vehicle was approaching and then driving over the narrow stone bridge. "No' at all. Are you?"

"No, because this has turned out good."

V couldn't help but chuckle. "Good point."

He covertly watched her as they drew closer to the back

entrance to Dreagan—the one that was hidden so only those who knew about it could find it.

She looked at him, smiling. "We're going to Dreagan?"

"Unless you'd like to go somewhere else."

"I already told you. I'll go anywhere with you."

She had to stop saying things like that because he wanted to believe they were true. Mostly because he wanted her with him—everywhere he went.

He slowly turned the hypercar onto the drive and made his way down the long, curving lane with tall trees lining either side. Only when they drew closer to the manor did the space open and the mountain and house come into view.

"This place always takes my breath away," Claire said.

V knew exactly what she meant. The manor was stunning, the grounds immaculate, but it was the magic that sprang from the area that drew all—including mortals.

V pulled into one of the garages and opened the car door. By the time he got around to the other side, Claire was already out and waiting for him. He took her hand and walked her from the garage to look out over the mountains.

"Yours is out there, isn't it?" Claire asked in a soft voice.

"It is. I would take you there, but there isna much to see."

"It's your home. There is everything to see."

V turned his head to her. "You really want to see it?"

"If you want to show me."

"I do, but there is something else I'd rather you see first."

She faced him and said, "Then lead the way."

There was a real possibility that what he was about to do would backfire, but V had a sense about Claire. It wasn't just because she had kept the Kings' secret for so long. It wasn't even about sharing their bodies.

Everyone spoke of the light inside Rhi. Well, V saw that same light within Claire. She might not be Fae or have magic, but it glittered brighter than the sun. It proved Claire's decency, her honesty, and most importantly, her authenticity.

He didn't take her through the door to the house. Instead, he led her around the manor. Her gaze moved around slowly, taking it all in. She laughed when she spotted some calves playing in a pasture. The moment she saw Duke sunning in the grass, she went right to him.

V hung back, watching. Claire called out to the Great Dane, who lifted his massive head to see who it was. His tail thumped loudly on the ground as he waited for her to approach. When she was close enough, he lowered his head and rolled onto his back, waiting for his belly to be rubbed.

Claire didn't hesitate to give the dog what he wanted. And Duke closed his eyes, enjoying every second of it. Just as V enjoyed seeing the sun play upon Claire's blond hair while listening to her talk to Duke.

Seeing her at Dreagan did something to him. He couldn't explain what it was, or even why it happened there, but V knew there was no way he could ever walk away from Claire.

She looked over her shoulder at him, smiling brightly while waving him over. His feet began to move before he realized it. As soon as Duke saw him, the dog looked up and shook his head before letting out a loud bark.

"Hey, lad," V said as he squatted beside Claire to join in on the belly rub.

"He's beautiful. Is he yours?"

V laughed. "He actually belongs to Cassie and Hal, but he seems to have developed a bit of a crush on me."

"I can understand that," Claire said as she flashed him a quick smile.

"You'll have to fight with Duke to share my bed."

She quirked a brow. "Oh, I'll win that fight."

They grinned at each other before straightening. The dog jumped up and fell in step beside them as they continued walking.

V pointed out sections of land used for grazing by the sheep and cattle. He knew more about that part of Dreagan than the distillery, so he was glad when she didn't ask him any questions about whisky.

"The manor is so big it makes you forget how large the mountain really is," she said.

He nodded. "Only those who have been inside the manor know that it's connected to the mountain."

"I'm sure there's a reason for that."

"Aye," he said. "I'm about to show you once we reach the back."

V covertly watched her expression when they finally got to the back of the mountain, and she saw the enormous entrance. Her lips parted in shock, and her eyes grew round.

She looked at him then and grinned. "Another secret of Dreagan?"

"We have so many. This is where we fly in and out of most times."

Claire swallowed, nodding. The fact that she was silent worried him. A lot. She might know of the Kings but she hadn't seen one, and that could change everything.

"It's a really large opening," she said.

"We're really large."

She licked her lips as her gaze dropped to the ground.

Some of V's excitement dimmed. So maybe she wasn't as perfect as he had first thought. There was nothing wrong with that. "You know of us, but you've no' seen us."

"I have," she confessed without looking at him.

"The video?"

Claire nodded and finally slid her gaze to him. "But I also saw Darius and a couple of other Kings shift that night in Edinburgh."

"So you know what we look like."

"Yes. When can I see you?"

He wanted to shift right then, but he stopped himself. "Soon, lass."

CHAPTER THIRTY

Soon, lass.

The man was slowly killing her with his voice. But it would be a death Claire embraced happily.

"Do you remember the four Silvers I told you about?" he asked.

How could she ever forget them? "Of course."

"Do you want to see them?"

"Absolutely."

V chuckled. "That was a quick response."

"I can't believe you would even think I would pass up such an opportunity."

"You didna see your face when you saw this back entrance."

Claire inwardly grimaced. "It wasn't because I was scared. It made me remember how large Darius and the others were in dragon form. That made me think of that horrible night and the Dark."

"I asked Ulrik. Those Fae are dead. Otherwise, I'd find them and erase them from existence this verra minute."

She started to hug him for saying such a thing, but Duke decided that he wanted to stand between them.

V laughed, and they started toward the enormous opening. As Duke trotted beside Claire, she leaned close to the large dog and whispered, "Don't think I don't know what you're doing. It's called sharing. You might want to try it."

When Claire straightened, she caught V smiling at her. She rolled her eyes. "Let me guess, despite my whisper, you heard that."

"Aye. We have enhanced senses," V said with a shrug as if it were no big deal.

"Well, that would've been nice to know before I tried to speak privately to the dog with you next to me."

He squeezed her hand and nudged Duke ahead of them. Then he pulled Claire beside him. "Trying to keep secrets from me?" he teased.

"Everyone has them."

"That is true."

She looked up as they passed through the opening. The sheer size of it amazed her. Once inside with the sunlight behind her, they stopped so she could let her eyes adjust. Claire blinked several times, and slowly, she was able to see more of the cavern.

There was a huge carving of a dragon in the rocks. And that wasn't the only one. There were dragons of every size carved everywhere. There was no way anyone could walk into the cavern and not realize that it had something to do with dragons.

"Ulrik drew that one," V said as he pointed out the largest one. His arm dropped to his side. "I'm aware of Ulrik's part in what happened to you in Edinburgh. From what I understand from Darius, you never showed any ill will toward Ulrik afterward."

Claire shrugged. "He hasn't come around often, and Darius was there. I saw how he and Sophie acted with Ulrik and went with that."

"But you're angry with him."

Claire made a sound in the back of her throat. "It's difficult to explain. He was responsible for drugging and taking me. He did hand me over to the Fae. I know there are parts I don't recall because I was unconscious, but I know enough."

"The Dark might have had their hands on you, but they didna have their way with you."

"No," she said with a smile. "Sophie made sure of that. And when that nearly didn't work, Darius was there to make sure neither of us was touched."

V tucked a strand of hair behind her ear. "As I would have."

His words made her shiver because she knew he would protect her. It was there in his words, in his voice.

There was little light, so Claire wasn't able to see V as clearly as she wanted. But she didn't need to. She could feel the desire between them, the sexual tension that seemed to grow on its own anytime they were near each other.

He turned and tugged her after him. She was thankful that V had a hold of her hand because her knees were knocking together. Knowing what those at Dreagan really were was one thing. Learning their secrets and discovering a side of them reserved for only a select few was something altogether different.

Claire tried to look at everything as they walked deeper into the cavern, but there was so much to see that she missed the majority of it. Then she found herself following V through a tunnel. She looked around for Duke, but the dog must have walked off without her realizing it.

Her attention went back to the tunnel. It was wide and tall enough for two Dragon Kings to walk together, but what really amazed her were the lights she saw hanging on the stone walls. With no wires to be seen. She knew without asking that it was done with magic.

She thought of all the things she could do if she had magic. In her profession, she would use it to heal everyone who was sick. And it made her wonder why Sophie didn't have Darius do that. It was something she would have to ask her friend later.

They moved deeper into the tunnel. Claire saw others branch off, and there were also several smaller caverns, but V didn't stop at any of those.

He hadn't said anything since the last time he'd spoken, and she was beginning to worry a little. His pace was slow enough that she didn't have to run to keep up with him, thankfully.

Her thoughts halted when he suddenly stopped. Claire came up beside him and followed his line of sight into another cavern. This one wasn't nearly as large as the first, but it was still huge. Inside it was a gigantic cage that had a soft white light shining down upon it from overhead. Claire couldn't see where the light was coming from, but she followed it to look inside the cage.

There she saw the four silver dragons.

V released her hand and walked to the animals. He stopped beside one and put his hand upon it, softly stroking the scales. He whispered something that she couldn't make out, but it tugged at her heart. She couldn't imagine how he must feel knowing that the Kings and these four were the last of their kind on Earth.

She didn't move until V turned his head to her. Only then did she walk to him. She looked into his face, trying to see his eyes in the shadows.

"Do you trust me?" he asked.

She nodded in reply.

He took her wrist and pulled her closer to the cage before moving her arm through the bars and placing her palm upon the scales. Claire gasped when warmth—not cold—met her hand.

"They willna wake," V said near her ear as he molded his front to her back. "You can touch them all you want."

She found herself stroking the dragon as V had with Duke earlier. "Would they like this?"

"Aye," he whispered. "Verra much so."

"Why don't you wake them?"

His warm breath fanned her neck as he sighed. "It would be too harsh to do such a thing. The Kings are here, but the Silvers wouldna be able to fly and live as they had before. They would have to remain hidden. And alone."

"Yes. That would be cruel. I hadn't thought about that." She looked over her shoulder at him. "Do you think that you might be able to wake them one day?"

"That is no' something I believe I can answer. When we sent the dragons away, we never imagined so much time would pass without us calling them home. I fear they may never return."

"That's . . . sad," Claire said and looked back at the very large dragons sleeping twined together.

She didn't know how long she stood petting the dragon before she finally pulled her hand back through the bars.

"You're a rare find," V told her.

She turned to face him and frowned. "Why do you say that?"

"Do you know how many hunt us? How many search for any clues that dragons exist? You had that information and never sought to do anything with it."

Claire shrugged halfheartedly. "It would have hurt the Kings, those that saved me and Sophie. And it would have devastated my best friend. I would never do either."

"As I said. Rare."

V's compliment warmed Claire.

"Come," he said and took her hand again. "There is more I wish to show you."

Claire happily followed him. As they made their way through the tunnel again, she realized that she had yet to see anyone else. Frankly, she wasn't too keen on running into anyone. She wasn't sure how they would feel about her being there. For all she knew, they thought she was intruding.

V paused before a door, and as they walked through it, Claire found herself in the conservatory of the manor. "I've been here," she said.

Once V shut the door behind them, she looked at it, amazed to see that it perfectly blended with the wall and was hidden behind a plant.

V took her for a tour of the entire downstairs. Some of it she had seen, but she didn't care. Seeing it again with V beside her was fun.

She particularly liked finally being able to see the library. As a lover of books, being surrounded by so many was heartwarming. She could have stayed there for hours, but V pulled her out with a promise that she could return later.

He then took her to the kitchen, which, as she should have expected, was huge. The idea of the groceries that had to be purchased to feed so many nearly made her break out in hives. She was just thankful that she didn't have to buy any of it. Or cook.

It wasn't until they came out of the kitchen and were on their way to the stairs that Claire finally saw someone. And, of course, it had to be Con.

He bowed his head to her after he looked at V, but he didn't stop to talk. Claire was relieved. She wasn't sure what to say to him.

"You told him, didn't you?" she asked V.

He didn't pretend that he didn't know she was referring to the secret she'd kept. "I did."

"Is he upset?"

"On the contrary. Con likes you."

She was so shocked, she couldn't speak.

They continued to the stairs, and as she put her hand on the rail, she looked down at the large, wooden dragon that made up the banister and smiled.

V didn't stop at the second floor. He continued up to the third and then walked her down the hallway to a door on the left. He opened it and motioned her inside.

Claire poked her head in before walking through the entrance. The room was good-sized with a large bed, a fireplace, a table with two chairs, and a small sofa. There was nothing out of place, and the brown and other earthy tones were a good match for V.

"What do you think?" he asked.

She turned to face him. "It suits you."

He closed the door and slowly walked toward her. "I thought to show you more of Dreagan, but having you near me without tasting you is too much."

"You can show me the rest later," Claire said with a smile.

V paused in pulling her against him. "Are you sure?"

"Ummmhmmm."

"Lass, you're a woman after my own heart."

"Right now, I just want your body."

A moan fell from his lips. "It's yours. Take it."

"Do the clothes thing," she said as she rose up to kiss him.

He chuckled while kissing her but did as she asked. Cool air touched her skin, but it was soon forgotten as she felt the heat of V's body.

Her arms wrapped around his neck as he held her tightly against him. Their kiss deepened as he spun her and pushed her against the wall.

He pulled his head away, keeping his lips just out of reach of hers as he grasped the backs of her thighs and lifted her. The moment the blunt head of his cock touched her sex, she held her breath, waiting for him to sink into her.

CRAZY DATING WORLD

Have you ever had one of those days where you woke up with a smile and nothing could get you down? Well, I almost hate to admit it, but that has been me.

So . . . I had a second date. And a third. There will also be a fourth.

What does this mean? Actually, I have no idea. LOL. I've so rarely been in this part of dating that I feel like a baby just learning how to walk.

There is also the issue that I don't want to mess this up. I haven't figured out how things went right, so the last thing I want is to royally screw things. Which, as we all know from my numerous posts, happens.

Well. I take some of the blame. There is more than one person involved, so it's only fair that I share the burden of being a failure.

I honestly don't want to talk too much about this great feeling. I'm afraid of jinxing it. Yes, I actually said that. As many of you know, when we struggle through numerous dates to find someone we're compatible with, we really want things to work out.

And anyone who doesn't meet someone and hope it goes well or tells you they don't look ahead, imagining themselves with the person a month later, a year later, five years later, or forever, is lying.

We all do it.

We're human. We aren't meant to be alone. We're meant to find someone who shares—or at least understands—our quirks, someone who loves us, someone who will be there through the ups and downs of life. Someone we can count on.

Someone we love.

Who loves us in return.

For anyone who says all of that is BS, I tell them to look at the billion-dollar dating industry. Look through any magazine—women's or men's— and you'll see there is something inside about dating. In every issue.

So, call BS all you want. I know the truth. Millions of other men and women know the truth. For those who don't mind being alone, my hat's off to you.

For the rest of us, we're all hanging onto each other to stay afloat in this crazy world of dating!

CHAPTER THIRTY-ONE

The beams of moonlight coming through the windows broke the shadows of the room. V wasn't sure what had woken him.

His body was wrapped around Claire's, one hand resting on her hip while his other arm was beneath her pillow. A strange sensation went through him, starting from his head and moving downward.

He tried to close his eyes again, but whatever woke him wouldn't let him return to sleep. V slowly pulled his arm from under the pillow so as not to wake Claire. Then he carefully rose from the bed and stood next to it, looking around his room.

The . . . strange . . . sensation unsettled V. He couldn't name it, but it refused to be ignored. It was almost as if something were calling to him.

He walked to the window and looked outside, his gaze going to his mountain. In an instant, he knew what it was—his sword. He had to get to it.

V opened the window with his magic. Then he walked to it and jumped to the ground. The grass was damp with dew against his bare feet. He spotted the dragons on patrol in the distance. There was no way he could get to his mountain without being seen, so there was no use trying.

He ran toward a hill nearest him, pumping his arms faster. When he reached the peak, he jumped and shifted, letting his wings grasp the current and take him higher. He did his best to avoid others while making the quickest line to his mountain.

Finally, he was inside. He returned to mortal form and went to stand before the sword. Through rock and miles of land, it had called to him. He knew the sword like a part of himself, and yet, it felt strange. Too many years apart made him look at it like a stranger.

His fingers touched the cool metal. The moment his skin came in contact with it, something sizzled. V jerked in surprise.

He grasped the weapon between his hands to look at it from hilt to tip. It was still as beautiful as the first day he held it. He'd felt the power of it from their initial contact, which is why it devastated him to have it taken.

And why it was like a punch in the gut when it hadn't responded to him when he finally got it back.

His heart thumped wildly against his ribs. The sword had called him. Perhaps it was time he found out what the weapon wanted. V wrapped his hand around the pommel and let the blade drop.

The power he remembered rushed through him once more. It wasn't the spark of a day ago. It was a flood, surrounding him so that he knew he was whole again. The feeling was heady, and the joy was . . . exhilarating.

He couldn't help but think of Claire. A mortal shouldn't be able to cause any such happenings with his weapon, and yet there was no denying that's exactly what had happened. V didn't know how or why Claire was a part of it, but he would figure it out.

A part of him wanted to call the dragons home right then, but he knew it would be disastrous. Yet he feared to search for them. He was terrified that he would discover that they were all dead.

It was bad enough that the dragons were gone from their home. If V looked and discovered that the dragons had been wiped out, it would destroy him and every other Dragon King. Even Con.

Now that his control over the sword had returned, V still couldn't do what the others wanted. While he knew there was a chance the dragons were thriving somewhere, he also knew there was a very good possibility they weren't.

Kings had ruled the dragons for a reason. When the clans were sent away, no one knew what might happen to them. The Kings just wanted to make sure they lived.

And, in fact, the Kings might very well have sealed the dragons' fate.

V looked up, imagining the sky through the rock, one empty of his dragons. A world that no longer heard the magnificent roars of his kind. Instead, the realm was filled with loud noises from planes and other vehicles, war, and the incessant scream for more from the mortals.

For the first time in his life, V wasn't sure what to do. Did he continue lying to Con about being able to use his sword? What if the dragons were out there? He still couldn't bring them home.

What was worse?

Not knowing the fate of the dragons?

Knowing they were all dead?

Or knowing they were fine, but that the Kings couldn't bring them home?

Each scenario had its own pain, but the one the Kings had dealt with the longest was the first. With the Others attacking, this thing between Con, Usaeil, and Rhi, and whatever else might come at them, V knew the Kings didn't need anything else weighing them down right now.

He closed his eyes and thought of the night sky filled with stars, wondering which of them the dragons had been sent to. His heart clutched when he thought about his clan. In all the countless years, he hadn't allowed himself to think about them.

Now, he couldn't stop. Was the world they went to welcoming? Did it have magic? Was food plentiful? Were there other species on it? Who took over as the leader? Or was it a group of leaders?

Every question was like a knife to his heart. He could have answers. All he had to do was use his sword. All his fears could be wiped away in an instant.

Or, he could be doubled over with anguish.

V opened his eyes and took a step back from the weight of the decision. Though, if Con knew V could use the sword, the King of Kings would order him to do it. So, in fact, the decision would be Con's.

But that was unacceptable. V would be the one to see the outcome, not Con or any other King. Only V. Then, he would relay what he discovered.

He shifted, keeping hold of the sword. He shook his head and flapped his wings a few times. Then he made his way out of the large tunnel until he found the opening and leapt into the sky.

The moment he felt the wind whoosh over his scales, some of his anxiety faded. He glided over the tops of the trees before flying higher. This was the only freedom the Kings had. They could be themselves for a few hours a night, covered by darkness and the fact that few mortals cared about looking upward in the dark.

It was the only time V could say that he was glad the

humans were so self-absorbed. Otherwise, the Kings might not have even this little bit of freedom.

No doubt it would be taken away one day. V was sure that Con had already thought ahead to that. Constantine always seemed to have an answer for them, a way to continue on their realm.

But V suspected that, eventually, the Kings would have to leave Earth to find a new home. Would the mates go with them? V wasn't sure.

His thought immediately turned to Claire. He dipped a wing and swung around so that he flew toward the manor. His gaze went to his window, but she wasn't standing there.

Had he made a mistake in being with her? His concern was about his own feelings. His own . . . heart. Because he couldn't get enough of her.

He liked her in his bed at Dreagan. In fact, he liked her a lot. So much, that she constantly occupied his thoughts. All those weeks of watching her, he could have been with her, discovering her body, learning every facet of her life.

Normally, all V had to do to clear his thoughts was fly. But it wasn't helping tonight. There was too much clouding his mind. He flew into the back of Dreagan Mountain and shifted. He gripped his sword tighter and strode through the manor naked.

He walked into his room and pushed the sword under the bed, then he climbed beneath the covers and slid against Claire. She didn't wake even as she moved back to be closer to him. He wrapped his arms around her and held her close. Just where he wanted her.

The future was more uncertain than ever, but for just a moment, he basked in the happiness of the beautiful woman in his arms and the peace she gave him.

Tomorrow, he would face the rest.

CHAPTER THIRTY-TWO

Waking up at Dreagan was never something Claire thought she would do. Yet, that's exactly what happened. She opened her eyes to see that it was already morning. The light tapping of rain on the window made her want to snuggle under the covers and spend the day in bed.

She rolled over to look for V, and when she didn't find him, she clutched the sheet against her nakedness and sat up. Just a few seconds ago, she'd been feeling confident and secure. Now, only awkwardness and unease filled her.

Her head snapped toward the door when the knob turned, then it opened to reveal her lover carrying a large tray of food. He smiled when he saw her.

"Good morning, beautiful."

Damn. But a girl could get used to hearing that. She grinned while eying the tray. "I got a little worried when I woke to find you gone."

"Your stomach growled all night while you slept," he said after setting the tray on the table and facing her.

Claire closed her eyes while shaking her head and laughing. "Of course, it did. Because, apparently, it's too much to be sexy when I'm sleeping." She looked at him. "At least tell me I didn't drool."

"A wee bit." He held up two fingers barely apart.

"Lovely." She fell back on the bed and looked at the ceiling.

The next thing she knew, he was on his hands and knees over her. "Everything about you is sexy."

She reached up and wrapped her arms around his neck to tug him down atop her. "That is a perfect reply."

"If you doona let me up, the food is going to get cold," he warned.

Claire rolled him onto his back and smiled. "I just wanted to make sure I get to the food first."

She jumped off him and raced to the table while he laughed from the bed. Claire had only taken one bite of bacon before his strong arms slid around her from behind, and he kissed along the top of her shoulder.

"The food is all yours, lass."

She gaped at the tray then shifted to look at him. "I could never eat all of that. It would feed me for days."

He shrugged. "Eat what you want. I'll finish the rest."

Claire saw the way he looked at her, so she decided to remain nude as she sank into a chair and took a long drink of orange juice.

"I like this," V stated with a smile as he took the other chair.

"The whole time you were in the mountain sleeping, you didn't eat?"

He shook his head. "Immortal, remember?"

"Right," she said with a nod.

"I think I might have left a few things out with my stories."

Claire chose a waffle, slathering it with butter and then putting some syrup on the side of it to dip each bite into it before putting it into her mouth. She chewed and swallowed before she said, "You shared a lot that night."

"What did Sophie tell you?"

Claire licked the syrup from her lips. "That dragons mate for life."

"Aye. We do."

"I like that. I know that some people don't believe in monogamy, but I do."

V folded his hands over his stomach. "Did Sophie tell you anything else?"

"She might have mentioned the mating ceremony, a tattoo, and the fact that she's now immortal, as well."

V drew in a breath and released it. "It's all true."

"What's the longest a human has been, well, immortal?" She made a face. "That didn't come out right."

"I know what you mean," V said with a chuckle. "There are some that have been alive about a thousand years."

Claire lowered the fork with her next on it. "Here? At Dreagan?"

"Nay, lass. The Warriors and Druids from MacLeod Castle. We Kings only started to marry humans a few years ago."

She blinked. "Warriors and Druids?"

"I thought that might interest you. The Warriors are ancient Celts who have primeval gods inside them. They can be killed, but it isna easy to do. So, essentially, they're immortal. They have powers and are verra good allies in battle. And the Druids are mortals with magic."

"Here I thought all this time I had a leg up on so many others because I knew about the Dragon Kings," she mumbled, more to herself than him.

V jerked his chin to her food. "Eat. You need it since we skipped dinner last night."

That brought a smile to her face. They had been so

wrapped up in each other that they had forgotten about food. It was something Claire had always hoped to experience, and she had. And with the perfect man.

She took a bite of waffle before munching on another piece of bacon.

"Is there anything else you want to know?" V asked.

Claire started to shake her head, then she stopped and frowned. "You mentioned the fact there were no children between dragons and humans, that all the babies died."

"Aye." V looked out the window then. "It is a rare thing for a King to impregnate a human," he finally said after a bit of silence. "I suspect it's because our species are so different, despite the fact we can shift, but we really doona have an answer."

Claire finished her orange juice. "You said rare. So, it does happen."

"It's kinder if it doesna." He slid his ice blue eyes back to her. "Most women lose the babies within weeks of becoming pregnant. There have been a handful who brought the bairns to term, which is even harder because none of them was born alive."

"Oh." Claire wiped at her mouth with a napkin. "I guess that's good for some, like Sophie, who haven't really had time for children with her work. But then there are others. . . ."

V nodded. "Aye."

That one word said so very much. Without him going into detail, she knew that he wanted children. As if it weren't bad enough that the dragons were gone, the Kings were also fated to never have children. It just didn't seem fair.

Claire ate the rest of her waffle and half of another while V returned his attention to the window. It wasn't an uncomfortable silence. She worried what he was thinking, but she was also keenly aware that his troubles were magnified a million times over.

The simple fact that she was with him was enough. She didn't feel the need to bombard him with more questions or pry into his thoughts. If he wanted to share, he would.

After all, she had told him that everyone had secrets.

Suddenly, V looked at her. "Tell me something I doona know about you."

She laughed and sat back in the chair. "First, I'm done. So, have at the food. And second, really? I've lived a rather boring life."

"I doubt that."

"All right," she said with a nod when he sat up and began piling food onto his plate. "I've not had a serious relationship for nearly seven years. But not for lack of trying."

"Men are idiots," V said. "But before that? Was there someone?"

Claire cleared her throat and shifted in her chair.

"I've made you uncomfortable," V said. "Forget the question."

"No," she told him. "It's just not something I've spoken about in a long time. It's rather embarrassing, actually."

His gaze caught hers. "Doona fear telling me anything. I will never laugh at you."

She smiled, believing every word. "There was this guy. We dated for four years and lived together the last year. I was the type who didn't want to live with someone until I was married. He always had good reasons—or at least I believed they were good at the time—not to propose. And I felt wrong even bringing it up. But after so many years, it was like we'd come to a fork in the road."

"Aye. That's exactly it," V said and took a bite of an omelet.

"He strung me along for a long time. Then, one day, I

came back to the flat after work and all his things were gone. He left me a note taped to the bedroom that said it was over."

V slowly lowered his fork, anger churning in his ice blue eyes. "Tell me this man's name."

Claire reached over and took his hand while smiling. "I love that you say that in a tone that makes me think you would hurt him."

"Because I will."

"There's no need. It was a long time ago."

"He hurt you."

She lifted a shoulder and twisted her lips. "That's love and life. I've learned that the hard way."

V blew out a breath and went back to eating. "Did you love him?"

"Maybe. I don't know. If you go by the romance novels I read, then the answer is no. And, when I compare what I had to Sophie and Darius, then it's a definite no."

V finished off the omelet and picked up the last two slices of bacon. He handed her one. "So you'll settle only for true love? Is that it?"

"That's exactly it."

"Even if it means you spend your life alone?"

She nodded. "Even then. Isn't that what Dragon Kings do?"

"It is."

They stared into each other's eyes for a long moment. V then stood and walked around to her. She took the hand he offered and let him pull her to her feet.

"I know the clinic is closed on the weekend," he said. "I'd like to spend the day with you."

"There's no other place I'd rather be than with you."

His grin was slow and heart-stopping. "Verra good answer."

He then took off his boots and pulled off his shirt before tugging her toward the bathroom. She quite enjoyed watching him remove his clothes. When he was naked, she walked to him and slid her fingers into his long, dark hair.

"Shall I cut it?" he asked.

She shook her head. "I love it long. Just as I love this," she said and scraped a finger along the shadow of a beard that accentuated his strong jaw.

He quirked a brow. "Is that so?"

"It is."

"I like you like this," he said and lightly slapped her bottom.

Claire laughed. "I can't stay naked all the time. But I'll make a deal with you. When we're in your room or at my house, I'll keep my clothes off if you will."

"I'll gladly take that deal," he said and turned on the shower. "What do you want to do today?"

"I don't care. I just want to spend time with you."

"There is a place I want to show you."

She winced as she thought about her attire. "I might need to run home and grab some fresh clothes."

V grinned sheepishly. "I might have told Darius last night that Sophie would be doing you a huge favor if she gathered some clothes for you."

"Really?" Claire asked in surprise.

He frowned at her. "You're no' mad?"

"Why would I be? You solved my problem."

"No' when I want to keep you out of clothes," he grumbled.

Claire's laugh turned into a shriek when he picked her up and carried her into the large walk-in shower.

CHAPTER THIRTY-THREE

It was nearly an hour later before Claire and V emerged from the shower. They'd had to cut their morning short when V was called away.

She walked from the bathroom in just a towel after blow-drying her hair. On the bed, just as V had told her, was her overnight bag. Claire walked to it and unzipped the suitcase to see what Sophie had packed.

Claire pulled out a pair of jeans, two shirts, underwear and bras, socks, boots, and the two most important cases she never traveled anywhere without—her pre-packed toiletry and makeup bags. She and Sophie had traveled enough together that Sophie knew exactly where they were in her house.

Claire would really owe Sophie for getting everything together. She turned forward to grab the jeans she had tossed aside. As she did, her foot went under the bed and made contact with something.

"Bloody hell," she grimaced as pain shot up her pinky toe.

She grabbed the hurt appendage and rubbed it to try and diminish the pain. Then she dropped down and looked under the bed to see what she had hit. Her eyes widened in surprise when she spotted the sword.

Claire hurriedly stood up and dressed in everything but her boots. Then she kneeled back on the floor and bent to look at the sword again. This had to be the weapon that V had told her about. Why then was it under the bed?

Her fingers ached to touch it, but it wasn't hers. Obviously, V wanted it hidden. Whether to keep it out of sight or so she didn't find it, she didn't know, but she wasn't going to ruin their time together by poking her nose where it didn't belong.

V had been welcoming and open about who he was. She could destroy all of that by letting her curiosity rule her. V had said she could ask him anything, so instead of pulling the sword out and looking at it with fear that he would walk in on her, she decided to just ask him about it.

Claire straightened and sat back on her haunches. She was reaching for her toiletry and makeup bags when the door opened, and V entered. His gaze went from her to under the bed.

She swallowed nervously, feeling as if she had gotten caught. Which she pretty much had. V closed the door behind him but didn't say a word. And that only made things worse.

"I stubbed my toe," she told him. "I bent down to see what it was, but I didn't touch the sword."

V walked to the couch and sat on the far end. He rested his arm along the back of the sofa and jerked his chin to the weapon. "Take it out if you want."

Claire hesitated, not sure if V was angry or not. It wasn't always easy to tell with the Dragon Kings, and she was still getting to know V.

"Claire," he urged softly. "It's fine."

She blew out a breath and leaned forward once more.

Her cheek rested on the rug as she reached under the bed and wrapped her hand around the metal. At first, she didn't think she could move the sword, but then she felt it give a little. She tried to lift it, but she was shocked at its heft. But she didn't want to drag it on the floor, it didn't matter that it was a rug.

This was a Dragon King's sword, a weapon so powerful that a group had decided to steal it and keep it away from V. It deserved to be treated with care.

In the end, Claire had to use both hands to get it out. She didn't look at it, though. She rose to her feet and brought it to V.

He grinned at her and leaned forward so that his forearms rested on his knees. "There's no need to be nervous, lass."

"You hid it."

"I doona know why I put it under the bed, but it wasna to hide it. Touch it. Look at it. Tell me what you see."

Claire licked her lips and found her knees shaking. She wasn't sure what it was about holding the sword, but she felt lightheaded. Not wanting to make a fool of herself and fall, Claire sat cross-legged on the floor and rested the sword on her legs.

She rubbed her thumb along her fingertips since they felt as if they tingled. Surely, it was just her imagination. Or was it? The sword was made of magic and belonged to a powerful supernatural creature.

It took her a moment to become aware of the silence in the room. She looked up to find V watching her with such intensity that a shiver ran down her spine. Oddly enough, she drew courage from the determined look in his ice blue eyes.

A lock of his long hair fell forward, and he absently raked it back with his hand, never taking his gaze from her. That's when she realized that he was waiting to see what she would do.

Claire drew in a deep breath and then slowly released it. She looked down at the sword. She was awestruck by the beauty of it—if such a weapon could be called beautiful. But it was.

She ran the pad of a finger along the pommel, which had double dragon heads facing away from each other with their mouths open showing their long fangs.

The grip looked like dragon scales, some shaded darker than others. Claire couldn't help but think of the Silvers she had touched the day before. Every time V held his sword, it would be like touching a dragon.

Her inspection continued to the guard, which was dragon claws curved toward the blade. And the blade itself was as wide as V's large hand. At the top near the guard was a Celtic knotwork design in the metal.

She ran her eyes all the way down the weapon to the point at the end. Just by looking at it, she could see that it was razor-sharp.

Finally, Claire looked back at V. "I know very little about swords, but this one is exquisite. I think my favorite part is the scales on the grip."

"Aye," he said with a crooked smile. "I love that part, as well. Actually, I love everything about it."

"I can see why."

He glanced down. "You rubbed your fingers a moment ago. Why?"

She shrugged, "They tingled a bit."

"Did it feel as if something moved from the weapon into you?"

"Yes," she replied emphatically. "That's exactly what it felt like."

"Interesting. It has done that to me every time I've

touched it. Or it used to. Once I got it back in Iceland, I felt nothing for weeks."

She automatically reached over and put her hand on his arm. "Do you know why?"

"Nay."

"So you feel nothing when you hold it now?"

He swallowed but didn't answer. A full minute passed before he said, "I feel it now."

"That's great," she said. "Maybe you just needed some time with it."

"Maybe," he mumbled.

She cocked her head at him. "What do you mean?"

"It wasna until you that the sword responded to me."

Claire blinked, unsure that she'd heard him correctly. "Me?"

He nodded. "I doona know how, but you gave me back my connection to the sword."

"Me?" Claire said again, hating how loud her voice had become. "I'm no one. Just a mortal without any sort of special ability or magic."

V leaned forward and wrapped her hand around the grip of the sword. "You can tell yourself you are no' special, but the fact you feel the magic of the sword says otherwise. My weapon chose you. It's not something any other Kings' sword has done before."

"What?" she asked in shock.

"I doona know how, but you also have a connection to the sword, lass."

"Is that why you're with me?"

He gave her a look of confusion, but then his expression evened out. Without a word, he took the weapon from her and set it aside. Then he pulled her to her feet as he stood. His large hands cupped her face, cradling it as he stared into her eyes.

"I'm with you because every time I see you, I crave to touch you. I long to kiss you, and I hunger to claim your body. The many reasons I want you have nothing to do with the sword, and everything to do with how I feel when I'm with you."

All the words she wanted to say jumbled in her head and refused to fall easily from her tongue. So, she rose up and put her lips on his. It was the only way she could tell him that his words had not only been what she needed to hear, but they also touched her deeply.

He wrapped his arms around her and rested his chin atop her head as they both looked out the window. In a matter of days, they had shared many things. It brought them closer, holding them tightly as their bodies bonded.

"It's easy to believe we're the only two people here," she said. "Right up until you step out of this room."

"So we doona leave."

She smiled and leaned back to look at V. "I don't think we could get away with that for long."

"I disagree," he replied with a sexy grin.

Claire smoothed back V's dark locks. "You've shared so very much with me, but I still have a secret I haven't told you. Actually, it's one I'd rather show you."

"You doona need to."

"I do."

"Do you want to do it now?"

She nodded. "It's at my house."

"That doesna matter."

Making the decision to tell V was much different than actually doing it. Her nervousness grew on the way to his car, and it intensified as they drew ever closer to her house.

When they finally reached it, her hand shook so badly, she couldn't unlock the door. V finally had to take the keys and do it for her.

"It's all right, lass. This can wait."

She shook her head. "No. I really want to do this."

"Your words and actions doona fit."

"Please," she said and took his hand. "I'm just nervous because I've never told a single person."

V forehead furrowed. "No' even Sophie?"

"Not even her."

"Then show me," V urged.

Claire pushed open the door and walked into the house, still clinging to V's hand. She dropped her purse and keys next to the door and made her way to the kitchen table where she pulled out a chair and motioned for him to sit.

Then she went to her bedroom and retrieved her laptop. She set it up on the table before him and opened it. After a few seconds, the screen brightened to show him the page.

"I doona know what I'm looking at," he told her with a shrug.

Claire knew this was her chance to close the laptop and tell him to forget it. V would do it. He was that kind of man. Though he knew she had a secret, he wouldn't push her to share it until she was ready.

She'd thought she was. Now, she wasn't so sure.

Then she thought about everything he had shown and told her. He'd held nothing back. Not his sorrow, not his pain, not even his fears of the future. And especially not the fact that she was able to touch a weapon belonging to a Dragon King.

She wasn't used to anyone being so open and honest. Perhaps it was time she tried to do the same. Besides, she really did want V to know her deepest, darkest secret. The one she had kept to herself for years.

The one that she trusted him enough to share.

"Perhaps this will help," she said and moved the pointer over to click on another tab.

There, the blog *(Mis)Adventures of a Dating Failure* showed. V said nothing as he looked at it before going back to the other tab. He turned his head to her. "This is you? The blogger I've heard all the women at Dreagan talking about is you?"

Claire nodded.

His face split into a wide smile. "You chose to share this with me?"

"Yes," she replied.

"Ah, lass," he said as he pulled her onto his lap. "Give me a few months. I'll change your mind about men."

Her heart was near to bursting. "You already have, my Dragon King."

CHAPTER THIRTY-FOUR

Southern Ireland
Dark Palace

There was something in the air, a scent Balladyn recognized well.

Impending battle.

He stared out one of the many windows of his chambers on the top floor of the compound. The last time he'd fought alongside others, it had been during the Fae Wars when he was still in the Light Army and one of the strongest warriors Usaeil had.

Until the queen betrayed him to the Dark.

He should have died, but Taraeth spared him. The king had done so for his own reasons, but in the end, it was Balladyn who killed him and took over his position. For centuries, Balladyn had dreamed of ruling the Dark. Once he took the throne, he'd thought it was merely the fact that Rhi wasn't beside him that manifested his malcontent.

But he was beginning to think it was something else entirely.

Ever since his visit from the white-haired Reaper, Fintan, Balladyn's thoughts had been on the future. There were things in play that couldn't be undone.

Rhi clashing with Usaeil was one of them. Balladyn

knew firsthand how powerful Rhi was, but would it be enough to topple the queen?

At one time, Balladyn and Ulrik had made a pact to take out Usaeil themselves, but Ulrik was now part of Dreagan again. And Balladyn wasn't going to go there. He detested everything about the Dragon Kings.

Ulrik had been different because, while he was a King, he hadn't been part of Dreagan. That had changed. Which likely meant that any pact Ulrik made—especially one with the Dark King—meant nothing.

Then Balladyn thought of Rhi.

Whether she wanted to admit it or not, she was going to need all the help she could get while going after Usaeil. And Balladyn was no fool. The Dragon Kings would be right there with her.

Even *him*.

He was the true reason for Balladyn's animosity toward the Kings. The bastard had broken Rhi in a way Balladyn had never seen before. And all the while, Balladyn had held love inside that could have healed her. Except he hadn't had the nerve to tell Rhi.

Though he could admit now that he'd known deep inside that she would reject him. And he wouldn't have been able to handle that. So, he'd remained her friend, loving her from afar.

Just as he was now.

Again. Not even after briefly becoming her lover.

Rhi would never be his. It was a fact he was slowly coming to terms with. But that didn't mean he would stand by and watch Usaeil kill her. Because that's exactly what would happen.

The queen was more devious than Rhi knew. But Balladyn understood Usaeil. He knew how she thought, how she controlled others and made them do her bidding. It wouldn't be a fair fight between the two of them. Usaeil would use all of her considerable power to get the upper hand. Even with the Dragon Kings by Rhi's side, there was a very good chance she wouldn't win.

And Rhi, kind and honorable Rhi, would have her bright light extinguished well before her time.

Balladyn closed his eyes. While it was going to kill him to swallow his pride and fight alongside the Kings, he would do it. For her.

Everything was for Rhi.

If he were really lucky, he would die in battle beside the woman who had been his friend and lover—his everything. And if things went as he hoped, then Balladyn would be the one to take out Usaeil. The bitch deserved the worst pain imaginable, and he intended to give it to her.

It would do no good to try and talk to Rhi. After their last encounter, he'd let his temper get the best of him. No doubt she would continue ignoring his calls. Not that he could blame her. She had saved his life—albeit by using Con's magic—and Balladyn hadn't been able to handle taking anything from a Dragon King.

Yet he would have to do more than that soon. And he would. He would put aside his hatred and take whatever the Kings and Rhi had to say to him. He'd suffer whatever it took to be able to fight beside her.

But there was one more card Balladyn could play. It might turn out to be a bust, but he wouldn't know unless he tried.

"Fintan," he said as he opened his eyes.

Seconds ticked by as he waited for the Reaper to appear. Those seconds turned to minutes. Balladyn should have known that his call would be ignored. What had he expected? Just because the famed Fintan had paid him a visit and spoke candidly didn't mean they were friendly.

No one was friends with the Dark King, no matter who sat on the throne. Months ago, Balladyn could not have cared less about having allies. Now, it was all he could think about.

When he was still a Light Fae, he'd had numerous friends. There was always someone he could turn to if he needed. When Usaeil betrayed him, Balladyn had discovered that he could only count on himself. The court of the Dark was filled with treachery of every kind, and to trust was to give up your life.

But right now, he would trade his throne and all the power he wielded just to be a Light again. To have his position, his family, and friends once more.

Balladyn turned on his heel and drew up short when he found Fintan lounging in one of the overstuffed chairs. Fintan's red-rimmed white eyes were locked on him.

"How long have you been there?" Balladyn demanded.

It did no good to become angry that he hadn't realized anyone had entered his chambers since it was a Reaper he had called. The Fae didn't fear them for nothing. The Reapers had more power and magic than other Fae, which allowed them to go through any spells and wards that might keep others out.

Fintan lifted one shoulder half-heartedly. "Long enough to see that much weighs on your mind. Why did you call me?"

"I wondered if you could tell me if there is any way the Reapers might aid Rhi when she attacks Usaeil."

Fintan raised a brow as he sat forward and clasped his hands together as he rested his arms on his knees. "You think we would involve ourselves in a war between two Fae?"

"You know full well that this is about more than just Rhi and Usaeil. This has far-reaching consequences."

"Perhaps. What do you intend?"

While Balladyn's first response was one of irritation, he held himself in check. He tried to remember the composed Fae he'd once been. It wasn't easy, but that man was still inside him somewhere. Balladyn just needed to find him again.

He walked to the chair facing Fintan and sat. "I'll do whatever I need to in order to help Rhi and bring down Usaeil."

"Even if that means fighting alongside the Dragon Kings?"

"Yes," Balladyn said, trying to unclench his jaw.

Fintan's lips turned up in a slight grin. "Interesting."

"Which part? That I want to bring down the queen? Or that I'm willing to tolerate the Kings."

"The latter. I know well your hatred of them."

"And you also know why."

Fintan nodded slowly as he sat back. "That I do."

"You've not answered my original question," Balladyn said.

"Nay, I've not."

In other words, the Reaper wouldn't. Balladyn had expected as much, but he'd held out a little hope. He knew better than to do that. He and hope were well acquainted. Hope had a way of prolonging and sharpening pain when it did come.

"Usaeil deserves to die," Balladyn said. "You know that as well as I."

Fintan drew in a breath as he looked around. "Neither you nor I make that decision. Death does."

"And if I called to Death to ask the question I posed to you?"

"I wouldn't advise it."

Balladyn ran a hand down his face and leaned forward. "It's Rhi I'm more concerned with. She needs to live."

"That's out of my hands."

"Death had a Fae following her!" The moment the outburst left his lips, Balladyn regretted it. He rose and turned his back to Fintan.

There was a long bout of silence before the Reaper said, "As king, you control an army."

"We both know the Dark won't fight alongside the Dragon Kings."

"They don't have to know the Kings will be there. Give the order before the battle begins that the Kings are on your side to fight Usaeil."

There was a chance that could work. But Balladyn could also see it going very wrong.

Fintan walked to stand before him. The Reaper's long, white hair was in stark contrast to the all-black clothes he wore. "How long do you think it'll be before Usaeil comes for your throne?"

"I expect it any day."

"Then what are you waiting for?"

That was actually a really good question. "I don't know."

"Seems to me, the answers you seek are all around you. And you have all the power," Fintan said with a grin.

"Do the Reapers see the future?"

Fintan frowned as he jerked back. "Nay. Why do you ask?"

"You sometimes speak as if you see things I cannot."

"Because you're focused on one thing. I can see the whole picture. Gather your army, king. The battle we all know is coming will be here before we know it."

Balladyn grabbed Fintan's arm before he could teleport away. "And Rhi? Will the Reapers protect her?"

"I'm not sure she needs it. Besides, she will have you and your army as well as the Dragon Kings beside her. She doesn't need us."

"You can't know Rhi and not love her. You expect me to believe you don't want in on that fight?"

Fintan snorted. "What I want matters little. Death makes the decisions for the Reapers."

Balladyn released his hold on the former assassin. In the next second, Fintan was gone. While Balladyn hadn't gotten what he wanted, at least he had gained some insight.

He turned and stalked to the tall double doors. They opened as he neared. He paused and looked at two of the four guards stationed outside his chamber. "Get word to my generals. I'm calling the army."

The men bowed their heads and rushed off to do his bidding. Balladyn returned to his chamber and waited for the doors to close behind him.

There was one other individual Balladyn had an alliance with. There was much Balladyn wanted to learn about the Reapers, so he left Xaneth alone for the moment. If the time came and he called for the Light Fae, Balladyn hoped Xaneth would answer. Because if Balladyn found himself in that position, it meant that everything was going to hell.

He walked to the windows and snapped his fingers. A large table appeared. Balladyn held his hand about six inches over it and moved it from left to right. As he did, a map of Ireland appeared, covering the entire table.

On the map was a small fortress to the north—the Light Castle. In the south, an exact replica of the Dark Palace appeared.

Next, Balladyn touched the towns that he knew were controlled by the Dark, turning them red. When he finished, he did the same for those of the Light, turning them white.

It might have been years since Balladyn had been close to Usaeil, but he knew her, especially now that he'd seen the real face behind the beautiful mask she wore around others.

His next move was to mark the towns he knew and suspected Usaeil controlled, coloring them black. When he stepped back to look at the map, unease filtered through him when he saw just how much of Ireland Usaeil controlled—and that was only what he suspected.

It was time he did some digging into facts. And quickly. Time was of the essence.

CHAPTER THIRTY-FIVE

The more time V spent with Claire, the more he began to realize that he didn't want to be without her. No longer did he want to seek out his mountain. The mere thought of it made him want to grasp Claire tighter.

As he gazed into her beautiful brown eyes after she had told him her secret, there were feelings inside him that he wanted to share. But he didn't have the words. Then his chance was gone as a knock sounded on the door.

Claire frowned. "I wonder who that could be."

She rose from his lap and walked to the entrance and opened it. Darius stood in the doorway with a grim look upon his face. V rose to his feet as Claire looked over her shoulder at him.

If Darius had known V was there with Claire, why hadn't he used their mental link to communicate? V strode to the door, an uneasy feeling beginning at the base of his spine.

Darius shot Claire an apologetic look. "Sorry for the intrusion."

Claire's gaze slid to him as she gave him a soft smile. "I think our time is up."

"For now," V stated, wanting her to know that he wasn't leaving for good.

Darius licked his lips. "Claire, you need to return with V."

"What's going on?" V demanded, worry settling like a rock in his stomach. "Why did no one tell me to go back to Dreagan?"

"I was close. I saw your car, so I said I'd get the two of you."

V put his hand on Claire's back and said, "Come."

"Wait." She shifted away from him and grabbed her laptop, purse, and keys, then hurried back to his side.

Darius had already left by the time V led Claire to his car. He scanned the area, looking for danger. Just because he didn't see anything meant nothing. He, better than most, knew how an enemy could come from nowhere.

"It's bad, isn't it?" Claire asked.

He glanced her way. He wanted to allay her fears, but he didn't want to lie to her. "It isna good."

"Yeah." She climbed into the car.

V took another slow look around before he made his way to the driver's side and got behind the wheel. He didn't speed back to Dreagan, even if every fiber of his being told him to get there immediately.

"Can you tell me?" she asked.

V pressed his lips together. "I doona know more than you, really. Dragons are able to communicate telepathically, and we speak that way often."

"How convenient," Claire murmured. Her head snapped to him. "Oh. That's what you meant about why Darius was there."

"Exactly."

"Why wouldn't he or one of the other Kings use that ability to contact you? Have you ever been told not to do it before?"

"Never." And that's what concerned V.

Once he pulled up in the garage, he spotted Sophie waiting for them. He turned off the ignition and looked at Claire. "Go with her. I'll find you as soon as I can."

"Are you sure I should be here?"

"I am." He reached over and squeezed her fingers.

When she gave him a smile, he realized *she* was trying to alleviate *his* worry. V was so taken aback by it that he didn't have time to craft a response before Claire opened the door and got out.

V was slower to exit the vehicle. He watched Sophie and Claire enter the house. Right before the door shut behind them, Claire looked at him over her shoulder and shot him another smile.

He felt movement behind him and turned to find Darius and Roman. "What's going on?"

"Con and Rhi are getting ready to go to war," Roman said.

V had known this day would come. In fact, he'd expected it a lot sooner. Though now that it was here, he wished it would have waited a few more days.

"What changed?" V asked.

Darius shrugged. "We doona know much."

"And why no communication?" V questioned. "Who gave that command?"

Roman blew out a breath. "I think you better come with us."

V followed them into the house, but they diverted to the conservatory and entered the mountain. V was led to a cavern where Rhi, Con, and Ulrik stood, looking at a map of the world on the wall.

He knew this was the room Henry used to keep track of where the weapon might be, but those markers were now removed. Now, there were ones in Ireland, and it didn't take a genius to figure out those indicated the Fae.

Henry came in on the heels of V's entry. V hadn't spent much time with the mortal, but he knew how hard Henry worked to help the Kings. The fact that Henry was the JusticeBringer to his sister's TruthSeeker was something V hadn't delved into deeply. But anyone with magic was better as an ally than an enemy.

"What's going on?" V asked Con.

It was Rhi who flicked her long, black hair over her shoulder and said, "We're doing what should have been done months ago. We're taking out Usaeil."

V saw the way Con stared at the map. Some might take Con's silence for apathy, but V knew the King of Kings had already planned how to get to Usaeil. Right now, Con was going over each move he'd devised weeks ago. And he wasn't the only one.

Ulrik stood beside him, doing the same thing.

Rhi walked to V and looked up at him. "Usaeil is vengeful. I suggested to Con that the Kings get to Dreagan and bring anyone who might be used against them."

V nodded, liking the preemptive measure. "Good idea. What do you need from me?"

"Bait," Ulrik said.

V glanced behind him to see who Ulrik was talking about, but Darius and Roman were gone. Which left only him. V then focused on Con and Ulrik. "For Usaeil, I presume."

Con turned to him then. "This is when all the time you spent sleeping is going to come in handy. She doesna know your face."

"But she'll know I'm a King."

"Maybe," Ulrik interjected.

V crossed his arms over his chest. "What do you want me to do?"

It was Rhi who said, "Get her attention away from the Light Castle. The Captain of her Queen's Guard, Inen, has been in touch with me. I need to get to him and let him know what's about to happen."

V snorted and shook his head. "That's no' a good idea. Inen could be deceiving you."

"He's not," Rhi insisted.

V shared a look with Con. Obviously, he wasn't the only one trying to change Rhi's mind about this. She could be very stubborn, and she was showing just how much now.

"You do realize that you could be giving the upper hand to Usaeil if Inen betrays you, right?" V asked her.

Rhi looked away and put her hands in the back pockets of her black pants. "If Inen can get to the people and tell them the truth about Usaeil, then she will lose their support."

"She doesna care about them," Con said. "As I've told you repeatedly."

"But I do," Rhi stated.

V dropped his arms and looked at the map. "We'll be fighting Usaeil in her territory. It's going to be tricky regardless."

That wasn't the only thing that bothered V. Maybe it was because the Others had messed with his memories, or perhaps it was because he had seen firsthand in the mountain in Iceland what they could do, but it made him uneasy to attack in Ireland where the Fae held the upper hand.

Henry made a sound and then turned on his heel and left without telling anyone what caused him to react so.

Ulrik moved to lean back against one of the walls and ran a hand down his face. "We're all thinking it," he said. "One of us should say it."

Rhi looked at each of them. "Apparently, I'm not think-ing it. What are you talking about?"

"The Others," Con replied.

V shook his head slowly. "After all I've learned about the Queen of the Light, she needs to be stripped of her throne."

Rhi snorted loudly. "She needs more than that."

Con turned his head to V. "But?"

"We should fight here in Scotland," V said.

Rhi gave him a sassy look. "Scotland? Stud, I like you a lot. You buck the system, which I appreciate."

Con's expression grew tight at her words.

"But," Rhi continued, "this is Fae business. It has to be done on Irish soil."

"Fae business?" Con repeated in a soft voice.

Ulrik shot Rhi a look that said she should've known bet-ter than to say such a thing.

Rhi threw up her hands, palms out. "Whoa. Seriously? Con, you're the one who said you wanted to fight with me."

"The simple fact is that this will involve the Dragon Kings. All of us, most likely," Con said.

V could see the Fae's anger growing. He touched her shoulder to get her attention. "Look at the big picture. You want your revenge, and we want that for you. However, you have to look at everything."

"I. Am," she bit out. She looked at each of them. "Do all of you actually believe I'm not acutely aware of what it means that the Kings will be fighting her? Because I am. Painfully."

Ulrik pushed off the wall, a dark look coming over his face. "What does that mean?"

Rhi shook her head. "I need to calm down. I'll be back."

V watched her leave while Con turned back to the map.

V jerked his head toward Rhi, letting Ulrik know he was going after her.

It didn't take him long to catch up to the Fae. V fell into step beside her. "Slow down."

"Go back to Con," she told him.

"Rhi, stop."

She came to a halt so fast that he had taken two steps before he realized she'd stopped. "Why? What can you say to me that is going to help? Huh?"

"I don't know," he admitted. "I'm no' good at these things."

She rolled her eyes. "Then why are you here?"

"Because someone needed to talk to you."

"And you drew the short straw?" she asked sarcastically.

V drew in a deep breath. "You were in Iceland. You saw the extremes the Others have gone to. Can you stand here and tell me you are no' a little worried? And I doona need to remind you about New York."

"I don't care that Usaeil is part of the Others. I just want her dead and gone before she does something to my people that will destroy them."

"We agree that Usaeil needs to be dethroned but finding answers about the Others is important. We should be cautious."

Her gaze snapped back to V. "Cautious? That's the last thing we need to be. It's what she expects. And she will be anything but."

"You want a victory over her, right?"

Rhi gave him a flat look. "Obviously."

"Then set aside the vengeance that rides you. And I can tell you this because I was in your shoes no' too long ago. My rashness nearly ruined things. You're too smart to make the same mistakes. And, as you say, it's what Usaeil expects."

Silence met his words before Rhi licked her lips and turned her head away, all the ire gone from her countenance. "You're right."

"We'll win this. Just be a wee bit more patient. We have to take care of things here before we can set the battle in motion."

Rhi smiled, though it was a bit forced. Her gaze met his. "I heard about your woman. Claire, right? Tell her I said hello."

"She's here. Why no' go see her?"

"It's not really the time."

"Aye," V said with a nod. Then he grinned. "She is great."

This time, it was a genuine smile on Rhi's face. "I can see the difference in you since she's been around. Happiness looks good on you, V."

He let that sink in as Rhi went back to Con and Ulrik. V's thoughts turned to Claire. He was happy. Extremely so. And he never wanted it to end.

The smile faded as he thought of the Others. Going to Ireland was the wrong thing to do. He knew it in the pit of his soul. And yet, Usaeil needed to be dealt with in order to bring a blow not just to her, but also to the Others. Con might be able to lead Usaeil to some other location that could give them an advantage, but how much of one?

They couldn't chance underestimating Usaeil. And the queen had shown the lengths she was willing to go to in order to get what she wanted. Taking the battle to the Fae's land of choice would put the Kings at a disadvantage.

Or would it?

CHAPTER THIRTY-SIX

"It's no' a bad idea," Ulrik said a few hours later.

V inwardly patted himself on the back. After another heated exchange between Rhi and Con when they couldn't decide on who would go after Usaeil first, they had all decided on a little break. Except V and Ulrik stayed behind to keep planning.

"Of course, it isna," V said.

"I'm no' sure Con or Rhi will be happy about it."

"I'd rather be prepared than sorry. And both will realize it's a strategic move."

Ulrik ran a hand down his face. "I had a tenuous affiliation with Balladyn. I'll talk to him. But you're coming with me."

V didn't even have time to respond before Ulrik put a hand on his shoulder and touched the silver bracelet on his wrist that allowed him to teleport.

When V blinked, he stood in a hallway with soaring ceilings and giant columns. It wasn't overly decorated to show wealth, but anyone could see they were in a place of power.

"Welcome to the Dark Palace," Ulrik said.

V cut his eyes to him. "How much time did you spend here?"

"More than you'll ever know," Ulrik mumbled before he started walking.

The hallway was wide and deserted, but V kept on the lookout just the same. They turned a corner and spotted four tall Fae guarding a set of double wooden doors.

As soon as the Dark noticed them, one knocked on the door and opened one of them wide enough to enter. He was back out a moment later. The four then turned to allow V and Ulrik entry.

Ulrik never slowed his steps. Nor did he give the guards even a glance. V followed his example and soon found himself in an opulent chamber that stretched far in either direction.

He stopped beside Ulrik, and his gaze landed on a tall figure dressed all in black. Balladyn had the unmistakable good looks of a Fae, even with his red eyes and the silver streaks in his long, black hair.

The King of the Dark stood with his arms crossed over his chest and his feet braced apart. There was no welcoming smile as he stared at Ulrik. "After your return to Dreagan, I never expected to see you again," he said with a thick Irish accent.

"You know how quickly things change. I didna forget about our pact."

Balladyn snorted. "So, you think that means you can visit whenever you want? And bring another King into my domain?"

"It's about Rhi," V interjected.

Ulrik's lips flattened as he leaned sideways toward V and whispered, "I was about to say that."

Balladyn's red eyes shifted to V. "Who are you?"

"Vlad. But most call me V."

The king dropped his arms to his sides. "What about Rhi?"

"She's going after Usaeil."

"Tell me something I don't know," Balladyn snapped.

It was Ulrik who said, "It's happening soon."

"I knew it," Balladyn said to himself. He nodded and sucked in a breath. "If Rhi is planning with you, then I know she's in good hands."

It was obvious just how much Balladyn cared for Rhi, and V planned to use that to his advantage. "Rhi believes the battle should be here. In Ireland."

Balladyn raised a brow. "Where else would it be?"

"It's a big world," Ulrik stated.

V wanted to return to Claire so there was no use drawing out this conversation. "We want the Dark to join us in this fight."

Balladyn stared at him a moment before his lips curved into a smile. "I never thought I'd see the day a Dragon King would ask for my help."

"We only do it because of Rhi and your feelings for her," Ulrik said.

That wiped the grin from Balladyn's face.

V lifted one shoulder in a shrug. "The move is yours. You know Usaeil and her tricks. Rhi is powerful. Will it be enough against Usaeil, though?"

"The Kings will be fighting with Rhi," Balladyn said.

Ulrik nodded. "Aye. We will."

"Then why are you concerned?" Balladyn looked between the two of them. "Because you are. I can see it."

Ulrik sighed and glanced in V's direction. "There's a new enemy out there."

Balladyn quirked a brow, his interest piqued. "Is that so? Who is it that can cause the Kings to show such worry?"

"We call them the Others," V said.

By the muscle jumping in Ulrik's jaw, he wasn't happy that V had shared such information. But as he stood there, V realized there was a possibility that Balladyn might know something about this secretive group.

And since the Dark's face had gone slack, V had been right.

Ulrik took a step forward and quickly said, "What do you know?"

Balladyn gave a quick shake of his head. "Not much. Very little actually. Just something written in one of my books," he said and motioned behind him.

V looked beyond Balladyn to the shelves filled with books and scrolls that he hadn't paid attention to before. "What did you find out?"

"Just the mention of them. The Others," Balladyn said. "It was only once, written in the margin of a book."

Ulrik walked past him to the bookcases. "Which one? Let us see."

"Perhaps you've forgotten who rules here," Balladyn said as he turned to stare at Ulrik.

V moved to the King of the Dark. "I apologize for our brashness, but this group is extremely powerful."

"Don't play that card with me. I know the Kings are the most powerful beings on this realm."

Ulrik fisted his hands by his sides and turned his head to Balladyn. "The Others consist of *mie* and *drough* Druids, as well as Dark and Light Fae. They combined their magic."

"Fek me," Balladyn murmured, apprehension filling his continence.

"Precisely," V said. "And while you may no' understand how powerful their magic is, let me say that it was enough to get into my head and repress certain memories."

Balladyn didn't say another word. He walked to a book-case and reached high above him to pull a small, green book from the shelf and set it on the table.

Ulrik moved to Balladyn's right and V to the King of the Dark's left as they watched him thumb through the pages until he came to it. Balladyn pointed to the script in a Fae dialect.

"There," the Dark said.

Ulrik jerked his chin to it. "What does it say exactly?"

"The Others. Nothing more, nothing less," Balladyn explained.

V looked over the pages, waiting for his magic to translate the words. He looked back at the margin and then, a moment later, he made out the two words.

When his gaze returned to the pages, he was also able to read them, but he didn't want to take time to do it. "What is the passage about?"

"Nothing really," Balladyn said with a shrug. "It talks about allies the Fae once had before we split into Dark and Light."

"That couldn't be the Others," Ulrik said.

V nodded in agreement. "Because the Others have Dark and Light Fae. But there's a connection here. We're just not finding it."

"Do you believe the Others might show up at the battle?" Balladyn asked.

Ulrik wrinkled his face as he shook his head. "I doona think so. Their focus is us, but we believe Usaeil is part of the Others."

"I wouldn't put that past her," the Dark stated. He stepped back to look at both of them. "You know there are Dark involved in this group. Why would you take the chance that I'm not part of it?"

"Because of Rhi. You'd never do anything to harm her," Ulrik said.

V leaned a hand on the table. "All we ask is that you have your army ready in case we need you."

"I've already done it," Balladyn told them. "But I won't tell my men why I've called them. I've no doubt that Usaeil has spies here."

"Just as you have in her court?" Ulrik asked.

Balladyn shook his head. "If I did have spies, I'd know what she plans. Trust me, I've sent countless Dark, and every one of them is caught."

Ulrik raised a brow. "Can you no' do the same?"

"I'm working on it," Balladyn said tightly.

"Rhi says she can trust Inen. Is she right?" V hoped Rhi was right, because if she weren't, then one of them would have to tell her.

Balladyn ran a hand over his jaw. "Inen coveted the position of Captain of the Queen's Guard for centuries until he finally got it. He and Rhi butted heads often, but Rhi is usually right about people. Trust her."

V held out his arm to Balladyn. "Thank you."

The Dark looked down at it a moment before they clasped forearms, their grips tight. "This doesn't mean we're friends."

"It means we're allies. For now," V said.

They shared a smile before Balladyn turned to Ulrik, and they repeated the gesture. V pivoted to leave when Con suddenly appeared.

The King of Kings stood as silent as stone, staring at them, unblinking.

"Con?" Ulrik called.

The King of Kings looked straight at Balladyn. While Con kept his face impassive, the anger rolling off him was palpable. V exchanged a look with Ulrik, who moved to stand between Con and Balladyn.

"Con," Ulrik said again, louder this time.

Balladyn moved so he could see Con. "The only reason you're not being swarmed by a thousand Dark is because you saved me."

"You think I fear any Fae?" Con said in that soft voice that belied the fury inside him.

V had had enough. "Con! What is going on?"

Black eyes shifted to him. "Rhi is gone."

Ulrik shrugged. "She probably went to calm down again. She did get a little riled when we were discussing how to attack Usaeil."

Without a word, Con tossed a small piece of paper into the air. V caught it and read it before his gaze jerked to Ulrik and then swung to Balladyn.

"What?" the Dark asked.

V licked his lips before he read aloud. "This is my fight. As it always has been. Stay out of it. Rhi."

"For fuck's sake," Ulrik said as he turned away, raking a hand through his black hair.

Balladyn held Con's gaze. "And you think I talked her into that decision?"

"I came here to make sure you have her back. Whether she wants the help or no'. She may listen to you," Con said.

Balladyn's nostrils flared, and his red eyes briefly lowered to the floor. "I doubt it. But I'll be there."

"So will we," Con stated.

V fought not to roll his eyes. "That's great. We're all going to be fighting alongside Rhi, just as we planned from the beginning."

"We just need to know when she plans to make her move," Ulrik said.

V squeezed his eyes closed a moment. "I might have

told her no' to do what she normally would because Usaeil would be planning on that."

"With Rhi, she could do anything," Balladyn said.

"Con," Ulrik called and pointed to the green book. "You might want to see this."

Several tense seconds passed before Con walked to one side of the table and reached for the book so he didn't have to stand near Balladyn. His gaze lowered to the pages as his magic translated the words.

His head snapped up to look between V and Ulrik. "This is more than anyone else has found."

"It's all I've seen," Balladyn said. "And I've read every book in here at least a dozen times."

A muscle worked in Con's jaw. Then, with great effort, he said, "Thank you."

Balladyn bowed his head briefly. "I owed you."

"You owe me nothing. That favor was for Rhi. No' you," Con replied and then disappeared.

V still hadn't gotten used to knowing that Con could teleport just as Ulrik and the Fae could.

"We'll be in touch," Ulrik told the Dark.

Balladyn nodded. "Same here."

V met the king's red eyes right before Ulrik transported them back to Dreagan.

CHAPTER THIRTY-SEVEN

She really didn't belong. That thought kept going through Claire's mind while she sat beside Sophie and the other mates inside Dreagan.

Claire wasn't even sure what room they were in. It was large enough to easily accommodate them, but she couldn't remember if V had shown it to her or not. After all, she had been so wrapped up in him and the excitement of being shown Dreagan, that everything was a little hazy. Plus, there were a lot of rooms. Surely, she wasn't expected to remember them all.

"I tell you, I'm going to figure it out," Kinsey stated confidently, breaking into Claire's thoughts.

Sammie shoved aside her long, sandy blond bangs that hung in her eyes. "You keep saying that, but we've yet to find out who it is."

"I think Kinsey will do it," Faith stated in her Texas accent and swung her sherry-colored eyes to the computer guru.

Kinsey laughed. "I've not found anything to stop me yet. But I admit, this is more difficult than I thought it would be."

Claire leaned close to Sophie on the sofa and asked, "What are they talking about?"

"I know what your mind is on," Sophie said with a chuckle. "The *(Mis)Adventures of a Dating Failure* blog. We have an ongoing bet of where this woman lives. Kinsey and Ryder will figure it out soon enough."

Claire sat back and tried to sink as far into the cushions as she could. She actually thought about telling the others she was the author, but she had gone to such extremes to hide her location that it seemed wrong to tell them now.

When she'd first put up the blog, it had been a way for her to work out her frustrations and fears while talking about an issue she knew many people dealt with. It had never entered her mind that her posts would go viral—and in a big way.

She had companies contacting her wanting to advertise on her blog, and while the added income would've been nice, it would have made keeping her identity a secret even harder. So, she declined every offer that came in.

It wasn't long after that she realized that people were actively trying to track her down. Thankfully, she had some friends from University that specialized in computers, so she had gone to them for help. The two guys and one girl were so wrapped up in their online gaming that they were happy to take her money, give her what she wanted, and never ask what it was for.

Though, with everything she'd heard about Ryder, she expected him to have found her already. Kinsey, as well. And yet, everyone—including Kinsey—acted as if they didn't know that she was the creator of the blog.

"Have you read it?" Gianna asked her.

Claire looked into the American's emerald eyes and

found the lie falling from her lips before she could stop herself. "Of course."

Sophie laughed. "Of course, Claire has read it. We have discussions each time there's a new post." Sophie's gaze then turned to her. "Where do you think this woman lives?"

Claire shrugged. "She could be anywhere."

As the debate went on around her, Claire wondered what would happen if she told them that she owned the blog. She bit her lip and looked around the room at the array of women. Some were already mated to Kings, while others were about to be. She was the only one who was neither, which made her keenly aware that she had no business being with them.

Her gaze met Kinsey's violet eyes. She stared a long moment at Claire before giving her a slight bow of her head.

It was a good thing that Claire was sitting because she would have fallen over otherwise. Kinsey knew.

Kinsey *knew*!

Claire's heart raced, and her palms grew clammy. She couldn't catch her breath, which made the room spin.

And all the while, she couldn't imagine why Kinsey hadn't said anything to anyone—even her. Well, she just had, but not before then.

The conversation about the whereabouts of the writer for the blog halted as Eilish, Shara, and Esther came into the room. They had done a sweep of the manor, or so Claire had been told. She wasn't sure why just those three, but maybe she'd find out if she could get a hold of herself.

"Claire, I could use your help," Kinsey called as she got to her feet and started toward the doorway.

She had no other option but to go with Kinsey. When Claire stood, her legs shook. She waited a couple of seconds to steady herself, then followed Kinsey into the kitchen.

The tall beauty stopped by the large sink and leaned a

hip against it while smiling at Claire. "As you can see, I'm not going to tell anyone."

Claire licked her lips. "How long have you known?"

"Months. Ryder and I decided it was best if we kept your secret since you had gone to so much trouble to hide it. Though I can't figure out why."

Claire shrugged and glanced over her shoulder to make sure no one was behind her as she walked closer to Kinsey. "It just seemed easier to be anonymous, and when everyone tried to find me, I liked that they couldn't."

Kinsey winked at her. "You don't need to worry. Ryder added some security to your site so that no hacker will ever be able to locate your identity."

"Thank you."

"You're Sophie's friend, which in turn means you're our friend, as well. And now with you and V together, you're well and truly one of us."

"I'm not sure what V and I are," Claire hastily said.

Kinsey flashed her a smile. "I saw the two of you together earlier. He can't take his eyes off you."

"Really?" That made Claire giddy.

Kinsey nodded her head of dark brown hair. "Really. It also says a lot that you're here."

"It's new, though. And, honestly, I don't even know what it is. It's not like we've talked about it."

"You will. Sometimes, it's better to let things flow, but if you really need to know, ask him. I don't know V as well as some of the others. He's quiet and keeps to himself from what I've seen. But from what Ryder told me, you've brought about a good change for V."

Claire thought about how V had shared his story with her and how he'd so readily opened up to her. And if she brought about a change in him, she knew for a fact that he'd brought a change in her. It was more than the desire that heated her veins each time she thought of him. Without a doubt, she knew that V was the other half of her soul, the piece she'd been looking for. "He's been alone for so long."

"And now he doesn't have to be." Kinsey pushed away from the counter. "If you ever want to tell the others about you writing the blog, they'll keep your secret."

"I know. Each of you keeps a bigger, more important secret. I've only told one person."

Kinsey's eyes widened, and she lowered her voice as she guessed, "You told V."

Claire nodded, a smile pulling at her lips. "It felt good to tell him. That's where we were before Darius came to find us. Do you know what's going on?"

"Not really," she said, the corners of her lips turning down as she glanced out the door. "When the Kings get this secretive, it means it's something pretty bad."

At the sound of approaching footsteps, Claire turned to find Sophie walking toward them. "What are you two talking about?"

"I wanted to see if Claire was handling things all right," Kinsey said.

Claire cleared her throat. "Actually, I was about to ask a question."

"Sure," Sophie said.

Both women stared at Claire, waiting. "Why was it only Eilish, Esther, and Shara who went to check the grounds? Shouldn't we all have gone?"

Sophie bit her lip and wrinkled her nose. "I'm guessing V didn't tell you that part."

"We've been . . . well," Claire said, thinking of their time making love, which made her smile at the memories.

Kinsey laughed. "Oh, girl, we know. So, what do you know about us?"

"She knows the basics," Sophie said.

Claire added, "V also told me about not being able to have children. And he mentioned the Druids and Warriors at . . . oh, what was the name?"

"MacLeod Castle," Kinsey supplied.

Claire nodded, pointing. "Yes. That's the one."

Sophie made a sound in the back of her throat. "I'm glad he told you about the Druids. So, Eilish is one of the most powerful Druids around."

"But she's not the only one here," Kinsey said.

Sophie twisted her lips. "Well, Esther and Henry can't do magic like Eilish, but they do have a connection. Darcy used to be able to do magic, but she lost her power. Long story that we'll tell you later," Sophie said before Claire could ask what had happened.

"There's a chance she's getting some of it back," Kinsey interjected.

Sophie nodded. "Then there's Faith, who seems to have a link to the Druids as well, but we haven't connected those dots yet."

"Oh, and Shara is a Fae. She used to be Dark, but she turned Light," Kinsey said.

Claire looked between them. "Wow. That's . . . wow."

The two shared a laugh. It was Sophie who said, "I'm pretty sure my face looked just like yours when I learned all of this. Soon, it'll be second nature."

Everyone assumed that Claire and V would stay together, but she wasn't as confident as the others. All she had to do was look at her past to see one failed relationship after another.

She knew V was The One for her, but that didn't mean things would work out. V was an immortal with a very powerful position. She was a nobody that had nothing to offer.

Though if she had the opportunity, she'd take a chance with V. He was . . . well, everything. She'd tasted what it was to be his, and no one else could ever compare. And yet, she couldn't keep a relationship. That meant she was obviously doing something wrong. If only she knew what it was, so she could fix it and give her and V a chance.

"I can't wait for you to meet Rhi," Sophie said, breaking into Claire's thoughts.

Claire blinked and looked at her friend. That was quite an odd name. Was it coincidence that Sophie knew someone named Rhi, and that Claire had just met someone with the same name?

"Rhi is a Light Fae," Kinsey said. "She's stunning, of course. As all Fae are. She's also a riot. She and one of the Dragon Kings once had a thing."

"Once?" Claire said.

Sophie shrugged. "None of the guys like to talk about it. I do know Darius was the one sent by Rhi's King to break it off with her. Darius doesn't talk about it often, but he hates that he was involved."

"I met a Rhi the other day."

Sophie and Kinsey exchanged a look. It was Sophie who said, "That's not a very common name. Rhi is around here sometimes, though."

"What does she look like?" Claire asked.

Kinsey laughed and crossed her arms over her face. "Long, black hair. Gorgeous, silver eyes. And a body that can wear anything and look good doing it. She has a taste for fashion and really high heels."

"I met her." Claire was sure of it. The description was dead-on to the woman at the spa. "We talked while we got our nails done. She actually picked out these colors," she said and held up her hands.

Sophie peered closer at Claire's nails. "That doesn't surprise me. Rhi always has a different color on her nails."

"And designs," Kinsey added.

"That's right. Designs, too," Sophie said.

Claire took in a steadying breath. "She's the one who gave me the advice that led me to show up at the pub the other night."

Kinsey grinned from ear to ear. "That's absolutely something Rhi would do. Despite her affair going wrong, she's very close to several Kings. She's risked her life for many of us."

"I adore her. I just wish I knew who the King was so I could give him a good flick on the ear," Sophie said, her ire showing in her voice and the set of her face.

Kinsey nodded in agreement.

But Claire was still stuck on Rhi. "Why didn't she tell me who she was?"

"You'd have to ask her," Kinsey replied.

Sophie touched Claire on the shoulder. "Come on, you two. Jane has pulled up the blog. Apparently, a post went up recently that we missed."

Claire glanced at Kinsey, who gave her a little nod as if nudging her to tell the others. Perhaps she should. "Hey. It's me," she told Sophie.

Sophie frowned. "What is?"

"The blogger. It's me."

Sophie laughed and lightly slapped her on the arm. "Nice try. There's no way you could do something like that and not tell me."

Claire almost mentioned how she'd kept her knowledge of the Dragon Kings a secret, but she just smiled as Sophie walked away.

Kinsey came up beside her. "Well, you tried. Looks like

you're going to have to prove it to her. If you want Sophie to know, that is. It's your life. That's why Ryder and I kept it to ourselves." She took a couple of steps then stopped and turned around. "I have to admit, I love the blog. You say everything I used to think when I was dating. It's good that others know they aren't alone. I always thought I just didn't know how to date. You're doing a really good thing. Don't forget that."

Claire smiled her thanks as Kinsey returned to the others. It had been easy to pretend ignorance about the blog when it was just Sophie. But if there were any chance that she would be at Dreagan more, perhaps Claire did need to tell the others.

Or maybe just Sophie.

CHAPTER THIRTY-EIGHT

Once back at Dreagan, V remained in the cavern with Con and Ulrik. Con said nothing as he stared at the map. Though V hadn't been at the Dark Palace long, he learned much by what he had seen and heard.

Just as Ulrik predicted, Balladyn would do anything for Rhi. V had to wonder how far the Dark Fae would go for Rhi, and V suspected that Balladyn would give up his life if it meant saving her.

"Balladyn really loves her," V said.

Ulrik nodded. "If Rhi returned that love, they could be happy, I think."

"With Rhi as a Dark?" Con asked without looking at them.

V's gaze shifted to Con. "You believe she would turn?"

"The darkness within her grows every day," Ulrik said. "She holds it off, but with someone like Balladyn—"

"A Dark," V interjected.

"She would give in," Ulrik finished.

V blew out a breath. "Maybe that's her destiny."

For a long moment, no one said anything. Then, Ulrik said, "I disagree. I believe Rhi is meant for something important, and it isna to rule the Dark with Balladyn. I think she should be Queen of the Light."

"She would be a good choice," Con said.

V couldn't refute that. "What now? Do we wait for Rhi to make her move?"

"No." Ulrik ran a hand over his chin. "We strike first to give Rhi a chance to get to the Light Castle and talk to Inen."

"You think he can be trusted?" Con asked as he turned to look at them.

V threw up his hands. "I barely know Rhi. I know nothing about Balladyn or Inen, but Balladyn believes we should trust Rhi's judgment."

"Perhaps we shouldna trust what the King of the Dark says."

Ulrik crossed his arms over his chest and leaned back against the wall. "Rhi needs him, and Balladyn loves her. That means he would never do anything to harm her."

"Just because you love someone doesna preclude you from hurting them."

There was something about Con's words that unsettled V. His thoughts turned to Claire once more. The last thing he wanted to do was hurt her in any way, but that might be out of his hands now that they'd been seen together. Her association with the Kings put her on the radar for any of their enemies. At least he could watch over her. And he would. He wouldn't let anyone hurt her.

"You would know," Ulrik replied to Con.

A look passed between Con and Ulrik, and V wisely remained out of it. Having slept for so long, there was much about the goings-on at Dreagan that V had yet to learn. This was one of those things where he knew just enough to understand the underlying current.

He was aware that Con had loved someone. If V hadn't been so wrapped up in finding his sword each time he woke, he might have learned more about his brethren. Now, he had to piece things together until someone told him all the details.

But it wasn't difficult to conclude that whoever Con had loved was long-gone. And it had ended because of Con. By the look Ulrik shot the King of Kings, Ulrik wasn't going to let this go anytime soon.

V wanted to get back to Claire, but he couldn't walk out of the cavern until this was sorted. "I agree with Ulrik. Balladyn willna hurt Rhi or put her in a position to be harmed. He will be there with the entire Dark Army to fight with her."

"Usaeil will expect that," Con stated. "She knows how Balladyn feels about Rhi. Why do you think Usaeil betrayed her best warrior to the Dark? She wanted Balladyn gone so Rhi would have one less person to turn to."

V made a face. "That backfired on Usaeil. I hope Balladyn is prepared because the queen will go after him."

"He's no fool. He'll be ready," Ulrik said.

V hoped so. "I doona understand how Usaeil can hate Rhi so."

"Jealousy," Ulrik offered.

Con's black eyes pinned V. "Anything you need to tell me?"

V knew Con was asking about the sword. He shook his head, still believing it was better to keep what he knew to himself. For the moment, at least.

"The first move is tonight. It starts with me meeting Usaeil," Con said as he walked past them.

"Wait. What? You can no' meet that bitch alone," Ulrik hollered after Con. When Con didn't return, Ulrik raked a hand through his hair in agitation. "Wonderful."

V glanced at the archway that Con had walked through. "This is Con we're talking about. If anyone can handle Usaeil, he can."

"But at what cost?" Ulrik asked.

That made V frown. "What are you no' telling me?"

"Con willna say it, but he feels responsible for some of what Usaeil has done to Rhi."

"I know many of the Kings are no' pleased that Con took Usaeil to his bed, but when does he ever do anything for himself?"

Ulrik cocked his head to the side as he looked at V. "Never. This was a first."

"Are you sure it was about him?"

"No," Ulrik admitted after a brief hesitation.

V raised his brows. "Con has always been about the Kings. In every decision he's made. Including letting the woman he loved go."

"Aye."

"Did anyone ask why he bedded Usaeil?"

Ulrik jerked back as if offended. "Of course. He said it was because he couldna take just anyone as a lover. Con made it clear to Usaeil that it was just about the sex."

V snorted at that. "And everyone believed that?"

"Aye," Ulrik said irritably. "It made sense. And Usaeil ended up being like the woman from *Fatal Attraction*."

"What?" V asked in confusion.

"It's a movie. The title should speak for itself."

V squeezed his eyes closed for a moment. He hated how much he'd missed with the others. Not just the references to human things, but the interaction with the Kings themselves, and being involved with daily life. All because he couldn't contain his need to find his sword.

"I missed a lot, too, you know."

V's slid his eyes to Ulrik.

His friend shrugged. "It's there on your face sometimes, though you never mention it. I see how you subtly gain information about whatever you missed. I may no longer be banished, but I wasna here for the camaraderie and the closeness. It's . . . hard to come back after so long and see the things I wasna part of. It's all around me. In everything. Every word, every action."

"Aye," V murmured.

Ulrik's description was exactly how V felt. It had never entered his mind that Ulrik might be going through something similar.

The King of Silvers shot V a half-smile. "You were never hated like I was."

"I didna make things easy on the others by leaving each time I woke. Look at the destruction I caused."

"Unknowingly," Ulrik stated. "There's also a case to say it was the Others' doing. I, however, did things on purpose."

V drew in a breath, letting his chest expand. "Do you think we will ever feel as if we truly belong here again?"

"With time, aye."

"Having Eilish makes it easier, I suppose."

Ulrik's grin was quick and wide. "I'll no' deny that. That woman is everything to me. I loved her far longer than I knew. She is my match in every way. But then I suspect you know a little something about that."

"Claire." V didn't even pretend not to know what or who Ulrik was speaking about.

"Listen to the way you say her name," Ulrik said. "It's almost like a prayer. It's obvious you care for her."

V nodded, not denying it. "I blamed my restlessness all those millions of years on being without my sword, but the truth is, I've always felt as if my life was missing something."

"As if you were no' complete."

V swallowed and nodded. "I thought there was something wrong with me. That perhaps I could never be satisfied with what I had. Claire eases the restless parts of me. She has removed the blinders I didna know I wore, allowing me to see everything differently."

"You're in love with her. Doona do as I did and waste a single moment. Take whatever time you have with Claire. If she's your mate, you'll know it. The certainty is there, undeniably."

It was there. V just hadn't told anyone.

Ulrik's brows rose on his forehead as he smiled. "Ah. I see. Have you told Claire?"

"Nay."

"Do you want her as your mate?" Ulrik cut his hand through the air. "Of course, you do. A King can no' fall in love and recognize his mate and no' want her." Ulrik studied V. "Perhaps my question should be: are you going to take her as your mate?"

"I'm no' sure I have the strength to let her go."

"Then tell her how you feel."

V's brows drew together. "It's too soon. It's only been a few days."

"Only you can decide when you share your feelings with her. I kept mine to myself, and Eilish nearly died. After I had her back in my arms, I wanted to tell her everything. But I still couldna. No' until she saved me. Claire is mortal, V. She can die from a disease, in a car wreck, or because of any number of things. If she's your mate and you want her, then doona wait to make her yours."

"And what if she doesna want to be my mate?"

Ulrik lifted one shoulder. "Then she isna meant to be yours. We have a wee bit of time before tonight and this war with Usaeil is full-blown. Go to Claire. Make love to her, hold her, talk to her, but *be* with her."

As Ulrik passed him, he slapped V on the arm and shot him a smile. V didn't remain in the cavern long. He turned on his heel and went looking for Claire. He found her in the library up on the second floor, standing next to a book-shelf, reading.

He simply looked at her. The sky was filled with dark clouds that promised rain. The lamps and chandelier bathed the large room in soft light. Her long hair fell over one shoulder as she tilted her head. V longed to twist the length around his hand and kiss her.

Suddenly, Claire's head lifted, and her brown eyes landed on him. Her lips immediately curved into a wel-coming smile. "Hi."

"Hi," he replied, returning her grin.

She replaced the book and made her way to the spiral staircase. As she descended the steps, he walked toward her, meeting her at the bottom. He pulled her in and simply held her, savoring how she felt against him.

"Is everything okay? Or do I need to be worried?" she asked.

V pulled back and took her hand as he led her to one of the large Chesterfield sofas. He sat and tugged her onto his lap. Once she was settled, she raised a brow and waited for him to talk.

"I'd like for you to remain at Dreagan," V told her.

She licked her lips. "I don't see a problem with that. However, I'd like to know why."

"We're about to go to war with the Queen of the Light, Usaeil. She and Rhi are no' on good terms. Usaeil has also set her sights on Con as her mate, and she willna take no for an answer."

Claire gave a quick nod of her head. "Earlier today, I learned some of what has happened to Rhi. I met her, actually."

"Really? Today?"

"A few days ago."

Alarm shot through V. When he'd spoken with Rhi today, she'd said nothing about meeting Claire, and Rhi would have. That's not something she would've kept to herself. "Are you sure it's the same Rhi?"

Claire frowned at him. "Kinsey and Sophie described her, and it sounded just like the woman I met at the spa. Besides, how many women look like that with the name of Rhi? I like her. I'm glad you and the others are helping her."

"But it puts you at risk." V said nothing of his worries to Claire. He wanted to talk to Rhi first. If she would come when he called after the note she'd left Con.

Claire shrugged. "I'll be fine. Do what you need to do. I'll stick with Sophie."

V pulled her to him until Claire's head rested on his shoulder. She linked one of her hands with his, and he used the other to stroke the back of her hair.

"What is this that we're doing?" she asked.

He kissed her head and placed his cheek against it. "A verra good question, lass. I want to keep seeing you. I want you as mine."

"Good," she replied, a smile in her voice. "Because I very much want you as mine."

V tightened his hold on her. "This might get rough."

"You're a Dragon King who has powerful enemies. Of course, things will be rough. In case you missed it, I'm a pretty durable, resilient woman. I can take a lot."

"I know. Why do you think I was drawn to you?"

"I thought it was because of my hot body." She was silent for a heartbeat before she giggled.

V leaned back to look down at her and smiled. She was definitely his mate. But it wasn't time to tell her. Soon. Soon, he would tell her everything.

"Oh, your body had a lot to do with it," he replied. "Shall I prove it to you?"

Her eyes lit up. "Yes, please."

She let out a yelp as he lifted her, putting her on her back on the thick rug of the library. The screech turned into a moan as he captured her lips in a scorching kiss.

CHAPTER THIRTY-NINE

Claire's body still hummed from the intense orgasm V had given her. She didn't care that she was naked in the middle of the library, or that anyone at Dreagan could walk in and find them.

With his weight atop her, she wrapped her arms around V and lazily stroked his back and the dragon tattoo while imagining she caressed V in dragon form. She really hoped that she got to see him soon.

He lifted his head and looked at her. His long hair fell forward to frame his face and tickle her cheek. She smiled and slid her fingers through the cool strands.

"What are you thinking when you look at me like that?" he asked.

She was taken aback for a moment. At one time, she would have come up with some witty remark, but V wasn't just any man, and he deserved more than what she gave to others.

"I think how handsome you are. I wonder what you ever saw in me, and then I'm glad about whatever it was so I got to know you. I think about the fact that this isn't your real form. Yet I'm grateful for it so I can touch, lick, and kiss you."

His ice blue eyes darkened before he murmured, "Ah, lass."

She leaned her face against his hand that cupped her cheek. After all the dates she'd been on, she'd come to recognize when a man was playing her. V had been honest from the beginning. It was a refreshing change that affected her deeply.

"I love your voice," she told him.

One side of his lips lifted in a sexy grin. "Just my voice?"

"I enjoy everything about you."

His smile vanished as he grew serious. "I doona know what is to come over the next few days or weeks."

"I'll be here."

"I left our bed last night."

She looked up at him, waiting for him to continue. When he didn't, she asked, "Where did you go?"

"To my mountain. My sword called to me. It's why I brought it to the manor."

Now, she was intrigued. "Oh?"

"Do you remember when I said I couldna feel the power of my sword when I finally got it back?"

She nodded.

He rose up on his hands. "After you and I had that lunch together, I felt something when I picked up the weapon. Last night, I tried again. The power is back. I can once more control the sword."

"That's good news," Claire exclaimed.

"I've said it before, but I'll say it again. Somehow, you're involved," he insisted. V pushed up onto his knees and placed his hands on his legs. "I know you doona believe me, but it's the truth."

Claire pushed herself into a seated position. "It's not that I don't believe you. It's just that I can't understand how I would have anything to do with it."

She got the feeling that he was about to tell her how she could be a part of it, but he must have changed his mind because he briefly lowered his gaze.

Claire decided to change the subject. "What happened with the sword? You said you could control the power now. Did you use it?"

"I couldna." He reached back and shifted to sit on the edge of the couch. "All I could think about was no' finding the dragons. With everything the Kings have been through, I didna want to be the one to tell the others that."

She moved to her knees and put her hands on his legs. "You mean what all of you have gone through? You're part of things here. I think you've forgotten that."

V shrugged apathetically. "I doona know why I can locate the dragons and call them home."

"You said the magic chooses who will be King. I think it also knew you would be the right person to have such power."

His gaze shifted from doubt to contemplation. "I suppose."

"I know it," Claire told him. "You didn't look for the dragons because you were concerned about what you might find. You didn't think about yourself. You thought about the others and the consequences of whatever you found. Much as Con always does."

V shot her a knowing look. "I doona have the same responsibilities as Con."

"In some ways, you have more. Only you can look for the dragons. Only you can call them home. Only you. Not the King of Dragon Kings. *You*." Claire lifted one shoulder in a shrug. "I bet you wanted to know if the dragons were all right. I also bet that you didn't look because you knew you'd feel obligated to tell Con whatever you discovered."

"Am I that predictable?"

"No," she assured him with a grin. "I just know you."

He pulled her to her feet. "I've kept the others out, but we need to join them soon."

Claire laughed. "I should have known you made sure we weren't disturbed."

"No one sees my woman naked but me."

His woman. She really liked the sound of that.

Claire dressed, exchanging frequent looks with V as he pulled on his clothes. Now that she had an answer to her question about what they were, she also realized that he came as a package deal. It would never just be the two of them. It would always be Dreagan and the rest of the Dragon Kings as well as their mates.

Some might not like the idea of it, but after spending a few hours with the other women, Claire realized it was much more than just a large group. They were a family. They leaned on each other, supported each other, and like any family unit, they bickered. But at the end of the day, they stood together.

Just like the Dragon Kings.

She and V walked hand-in-hand to the door. When he opened it, V paused and looked down at her. That's when she knew he had to leave.

Claire placed her hands on his chest and smiled up at him. "I don't need to tell you to be careful, do I?"

He chuckled softly. "I'll do my best."

"Make sure you kick some ass."

"That I can promise."

She found it difficult to keep the smile in place. Fortunately, V leaned down and kissed her. It was a long, slow kiss full of promise.

Claire hated when he ended the kiss and pulled back. She kept her arms around his neck and looked into his handsome face. "Don't worry about things here. You know we'll be fine. It would take a really dumb person to attack Dreagan."

Instead of alleviating V's worries, he frowned instead. "That is exactly something Usaeil would do."

"What? I'm confused."

V's attention shifted over her shoulder. "Con."

Claire tried not to fidget as the King of Kings altered his course and headed toward them. It was Con, after all. To her surprise and enjoyment, V took her hand in his. She calmed in an instant. V had let her know with that small action that he would stand beside her.

Con's black eyes landed on Claire. He bowed his head, and for a moment, she wondered if she should curtsey. In the end, she opted for a smile.

"How are you settling in?" Con asked her.

She nodded quickly. "Very well. Everyone has been wonderful."

"It helps that you already know some here."

What he didn't say—and what she was very aware of— was that she'd known their secret for some time. Claire lifted her chin. "That does help, yes."

Con's gaze moved to V. "You look concerned. You know Claire will be safe here."

"That's just it," V said. "I'm no' sure any of them will."

Claire jerked her head to V. She hadn't been worried before, but now she was.

V's statement got Con's attention. "What do you mean?"

"Your plan is to go somewhere and call to Usaeil, right?"

Con nodded. "It is."

"Then what? You think Usaeil will have a run-in with you and no' retaliate?"

"I expect her to."

Claire looked between them, trying to navigate what was going on without asking. Because she wasn't going to ask. But she really, *really* wanted to know what all this was about with Con going to the Queen of the Light—who wasn't all that she seemed.

V grunted. "How many of us are you taking with you?"

"I go alone," Con stated.

"Why? Usaeil willna be. And you know it."

Con folded his arms over his chest and studied V for a long, silent minute. Claire hoped that Con never looked at her in such a way. "You think she can harm me?"

"I think we shouldna underestimate the Others," V replied.

Just the mention of them made Claire nervous. And she hadn't had any interaction with the group. But after what they had done to V, everyone needed to be wary.

Con dropped his arms. "What are you thinking?"

"I'm thinking exactly what I told Rhi. I warned her no' to be predictable and do something that Usaeil would expect."

Con drew in a breath and shook his head as he smiled ruefully. "I'll be damned. We were about to make that same mistake. Decide where you want to be, V. With me or here."

"Here," V stated.

With a brief nod, Con turned on his heel and walked away.

Claire waited until he was out of sight before she looked at V. "What just happened?"

"Usaeil isna stupid. I hate to say it, but she's actually verra smart. It's gotten her all that she's acquired over the centuries. The fact that she's been able to hide her true nature all these eons without us knowing says just how good she is."

Claire rushed to keep up with V as he headed toward the stairs. "I still don't understand."

V slowed his steps. "She has long suspected that Con and Rhi are together."

"Are they?"

"Nay, but Usaeil doesna believe that. She will guess that Con and Rhi will work together to attack her."

Claire parted her lips as she nodded. "Oh, I see. In Usaeil's eyes, a man and a woman can't be friends. They're either lovers or not."

"I wouldna call Rhi and Con friends. Friend*ly* is more accurate." They reached the third level and made their way to V's bedroom. "Since Usaeil will rightly guess that Rhi has joined forces with us, the queen will also predict that Con will use some ruse to get Usaeil out of the castle so Rhi can get in."

Claire tripped over her own feet as the meaning of what V was saying hit her. "It's a trap. Usaeil is setting a trap for Rhi."

"Aye, she is." V opened his door and waited for Claire to enter. He closed it behind them and leaned against it. "It's also a trap for Con. Usaeil intends to hold both of them."

"Can she?"

V shrugged. "I honestly doona know. Rhi, definitely. Con? We'll find out soon enough. This is where Usaeil has to plan on the possibility that Con willna come alone. Matter of fact, she's hoping he'll bring most of the Kings."

Claire frowned as she searched her brain for a reason, but she couldn't come up with anything. "Why?"

"So Usaeil can send her army here."

Claire laughed, thinking it was a joke. By the look on V's face, it was anything but. "Can she get here?"

"Con stopped her from coming to Dreagan months ago. The boundary is set to keep others out, but it'll also alert us if anyone crosses the barrier."

"But that won't do much good if she sends an army."

"All the Kings were originally supposed to go with Con and Rhi."

"Leaving Dreagan to be protected by Druids and Shara."

V's lips flattened. "If you hadna said something, I might no' have pieced it together."

This was the second time he had given her credit for something that she didn't feel as if she'd had anything to do with. But now wasn't the time to think on that.

She squeezed his hand. "You're staying here, aren't you?"

"Aye."

Claire smiled and released V's hand. "Don't worry about me. Go do whatever needs to be done. I'm not leaving Dreagan."

For the second time, V looked as if he wanted to tell her something. Instead, he gave her a quick, hard kiss, and then he was gone. When the door shut behind him, Claire looked around the room and wondered if she was prepared for what was coming.

I KNOW HOW TO DATE.
I KNOW NOTHING
ABOUT RELATIONSHIPS

How many of you read the title and inwardly nodded in agreement? Well, I'm right there with you.

I recently spoke about being happy, about finding someone but not wanting to jinx it in any way. I know I said I didn't want to talk about him, but I can't help myself. He's that amazing.

Because it has been a while since I've been in a relationship, I felt as if I were trying to walk on a frozen lake where the ice was breaking up all around me. I couldn't find my way, and I had no idea which direction to turn.

I realized that the only one who could help me was him. It was up to me to ask him what exactly we were to each other . . . together. Were we just having a little fling? Or was it more?

I like to think I can face any problem head-on. That I don't shy away from embarrassing or uneasy situations. But I had a hard time getting the words out. It was because I really like this guy.

I mean REALLY like him.

As in, I think he just might be . . . The One.
There. I said it.

*My heart is racing just typing the words. I have
written and deleted them a hundred times because,
in the back of my mind, I wonder if I've doomed
this budding relationship and myself by writing
what's in my head.*

Yet I'm going to leave the words.

*I've always laid it all out for everyone reading
this blog. Why should this time be any different?*

*Each of you has seen my struggles with dating,
of being alone, of being rejected, and me learning
how to navigate the online dating landscape. It's
been far from easy, but I hope the mistakes I've
made have helped some of you take a different
path.*

*I've actually learned from you. Yes, you! The
private messages and the posts on the blog have
taught me a thing or two, as well. I love the
exchange of information. I love how we—men and
women—have banded together to help each other
out.*

*Let me give you an example. A couple of
months ago, a woman replied to my post with an
issue about a guy who was hot and cold. She
didn't know what to do. Fortunately, one of the
male readers jumped in and gave her some sound
advice, which enabled her to end it with the
indecisive guy. Many of you read the dozen or so
exchanges by these two below my post.*

*What few know is that they took their conversa-
tion off the internet and discovered that they lived
in the same city. They decided to meet up for
coffee to discuss their various dating disasters and*

found they got along well. So well, in fact, that they went on their first date a week later.

I'm happy to report that both have contacted me independently. They have been inseparable since. I sincerely wish them the best. And maybe, just maybe, we'll get a wedding out of it!

CHAPTER FORTY

For the third night, V stared up at the stars from the Dragonwood. Each day that Usaeil didn't go to Con and no Fae showed up at Dreagan, the more apprehensive he became.

He'd been so sure of what Usaeil planned. It had seemed so simple in its complexity—and exactly something Usaeil would do. Why then had no action been taken?

No matter how many times the Kings urged Con to call an end to his attempt and return to Dreagan, he remained in Venice. He'd chosen the city, hoping that being away from Scotland would tempt Usaeil.

"Something isna right," Darius said as he came up beside V.

"I've said that for days now."

Darius looked around them. "We all agree with you."

"Con really needs to return."

"Ulrik is trying to talk him into that now. I'm glad that Ulrik went to Venice, too, because if anyone can convince Con of something, it's the King of Silvers."

V lowered his gaze and looked at Darius. "What is Con waiting for? Obviously, Usaeil knew this was a trap. That means she realized we figured out her trap, as well."

Darius hesitated a moment. "Con thinks if he waits a little longer, he can make her think that it isna a trap, and she'll come."

"She willna. She's going another route."

"Neither Rhys nor Ulrik can get Rhi to answer them. They've even contacted Phelan for help."

V knew it wasn't a good sign when they had to turn to the Warrior for help. Luckily, Phelan was like a brother to Rhi, so she should answer him. "How long has it been since Phelan called to her?"

"Eight hours."

"She's no' going to go to him then," V stated. "She knows we would go to Phelan."

Darius shifted and leaned his back against a tree. "With neither Usaeil's or Rhi's whereabouts known, our plans are for shite."

"Maybe," V said, nodding slowly as he gazed into the night. "Or maybe no'."

"Meaning?"

"From what both Con and Rhi told us, Usaeil is furious with Con for no' going along with her plans for them to be together."

Darius shrugged. "So?"

V shot him a flat look. "I might have been asleep for several millennia, but even I know a woman like Usaeil will retaliate when scorned. And instead of going after Con himself—"

"She'll come at what he cares about most," Darius said as he pushed away from the tree.

V nodded in agreement. "Dreagan, and us."

"She'll never win against us. It would be sheer folly."

"Usaeil knows she can no' kill us, but she can hurt us and Con in other ways. She either wants Con angry, or she wants him to turn to her for help."

Darius ran a hand down his face and sighed loudly. "Shite. She could go either way."

"I've been thinking of that dream or whatever you want to call it that Dorian had when he was in New York. He said he saw the Kings and mates dead, scattered all around Dreagan. And that it was Usaeil who had done it, though she told him her name was Rhi."

"Usaeil can no' kill us," Darius replied.

V raised a brow. "But you're no' thinking of just what the Others can do. I felt it. I lived it. I broke through their magic. It's strong, Darius. Verra strong."

"Fuck," Darius mumbled and turned away.

V understood Darius's anger. The Others didn't outright attack. They set traps and scenarios where they somehow knew exactly when and where the Kings would be. On top of that, the Others' magic was unknown.

For all the Kings knew, they had finally met their magical match. It was a distinct possibility that the Others could kill them.

Dmitri, Rhys, Kiril, and Con were the only other Kings besides V and Roman to feel the strength of the Others. The rest of the Kings had no idea what awaited them.

Because V knew the Others were far from done with them.

Both V and Darius turned their heads at the sound of someone approaching. Roman walked from the trees, an uneasy look on his face.

"I've got a bad feeling," he told them.

Darius grunted. "We all do."

"It's worse for Dorian."

V spun to the manor. "Does he think this is like his dream?"

Roman shrugged and shook his head. "Dorian is adamant that the mates leave Dreagan."

"That's the last thing that needs to happen," Darius stated.

"None of us saw what Dorian dreamed, what he believes to be real," Roman replied.

V looked between the two of them. "We shouldna discount Dorian's vision. It was magic used by the Others when Dorian touched that black dagger, a weapon that was given to the mortal by none other than Usaeil."

"Con needs to get back now," Darius said worriedly. "I'm telling Ulrik."

Though V felt better that Ulrik would tell Con their worries and that it might get Con and the other Kings back to Dreagan, his worry still wouldn't lessen.

As one, the three of them headed back to the manor. Those on patrol were so high up in the sky that no one would be able to spot them—not even the Fae. V had already taken his shift, but he knew he'd be back up there later.

V headed straight to find Claire. She was in the kitchen with Denae and Grace, washing dishes. She turned her head to him without him even saying her name. They hadn't had any time alone since the library, but each time he saw Claire, she gave him a bright smile.

Now was no exception. V wanted to go to her, hold her, but he knew if he did, he wouldn't want to let go. And there was work to be done.

She nodded to him and mouthed, "I'm good."

He fisted his hands, needing to feel her warmth, her soft curves. V winked at her before turning on his heel and making his way into the mountain.

When he reached the cavern, he spotted Ulrik. His excitement that his brethren were back dimmed when he saw Ulrik pacing. V glanced at the map on the wall. Henry talked to Ryder via an earpiece, while Ryder worked up in his computer room. Together, the mortal and Ryder were tracking any mention of Rhi or Usaeil. Rhi's pins were bright pink, while Usaeil's were green.

What stuck out the most to V was that not a single pin was actually on the map. Anywhere. It was as if both Fae had disappeared from existence.

"Where's Con?" V asked, looking around for the King of Kings.

Ulrik looked up, his face a mask of anger and unease. He halted in his pacing. "He used that damn watch Death gave him. I saw him. He was on his way here."

Henry whirled around at the news. "Was?"

V frowned, hoping he hadn't heard Ulrik correctly. "Are you telling me that Con isna here?"

Ulrik pivoted and slammed his fist into the wall of rock. The punch sent his hand deep into the stone as more of the slab crumbled and fell to the floor.

"Bloody hell," Henry murmured.

V pointed at Henry. "Tell Ryder. Every King needs to search for Con right now."

Ulrik pulled his hand free of the wall and dropped his chin to his chest. "We willna find him. I'm no' sure how, but Usaeil has Con."

"Con wanted to trap her, but Usaeil set a trap for him," Henry said.

V shook his head. "Con would have expected that. There's no way he would be taken so easily."

Henry wrinkled his nose. "Unless Usaeil was patient enough to wait until everyone returned to Dreagan."

A muscle twitched in Ulrik's jaw. "I made three trips with Kings. Con was there each time I returned. He reached for his pocket watch to come back to Dreagan the same time I brought the last Kings."

"He wouldna go somewhere without telling you or any of us," V said.

Ulrik tugged up the sleeve of his shirt to touch the silver cuff he wore. V grabbed his arm before he could teleport.

"Where do you think you're going?"

A muscle ticked in Ulrik's jaw. "Balladyn."

"He hates Con. Do you really believe he'll help us find him?"

Ulrik jerked his arm free. "I'm not going to just sit around waiting and speculating."

"I think you're going to come up with a plan. It's what you do best. You know Con, Rhi, and Usaeil."

Henry folded his arms over his chest. "And you, V, know the Others."

Ulrik glanced at Henry and nodded. "I need everyone who has had any contact with the magic of the Others down here. I might know Rhi, but there are others who know her better. Get Phelan here. And Rhys."

"Everyone else?" V asked.

Ulrik looked up, his gold eyes steady, his expression even. "Everyone else needs to be on patrol."

CHAPTER FORTY-ONE

The joyful, cheery atmosphere of the house was gone. Snuffed out as easily and clearly as a candle flame. Claire noticed it bit by bit as the days passed into a week, and then a week and a half.

No matter where the Kings looked, no matter how skilled Ryder was with electronics and accessing data, there had been no sign of Con anywhere.

The same with Rhi and Usaeil.

Claire and Sophie kept their hours at the clinic, but they were never alone. Darius, V, and at least one more King was with them at all times.

For his part, V tried to keep his worries in check. But when Claire woke last night to find him staring out the window, she had gone to him and wrapped her arms around him. It had taken some convincing, but she finally talked him into sharing with her all that he felt.

He wasn't the only one. The other Kings were all tightly wound. Every last one of them.

Ulrik had essentially stepped into Con's role, but he wasn't alone. Kellan stood with him. There were many

Kings that Claire hadn't met personally, but she was surprised to learn that the Kings had a Keeper of History.

It was Kellan's job to record all that happened with each Dragon King. He didn't remember it all. Just saw what occurred and wrote it down, removing it from his memory.

Even with his ability, Kellan didn't have specifics to where Con was. However, he had seen that the moment Con grabbed the pocket watch, Usaeil appeared behind him. In the next instant, both were gone.

Claire hated not being in the know. She got parts of information from Sophie and the other mates, and then a little more with V. Yet she felt left out.

She didn't blame anyone. She wasn't really a part of Dreagan. She wasn't a mate, and it wasn't as if V had professed his love for her or she for him. The only reason she was there was that she shared V's bed.

Not that Claire was upset by it. She was content to be a part of Dreagan in any way she could. Her problem was that she wanted to do more. But how could she? It wasn't as if she could stand against the Fae or even a Druid.

She walked down the stairs and heard voices. When her gaze landed on Eilish, Esther, Shara, and Darcy talking low as if planning something, she was reminded again that she had nothing to offer anyone at the estate.

"It's hard, isn't it?"

Claire's head whipped around at the sound of an American accent. She found Jane watching the foursome as they walked away.

"Yeah," Claire replied.

Jane tucked a strand of auburn hair behind her ear as her amber eyes slid to Claire. "I sometimes lie in Banan's arms and dream about having magic so I can fight alongside him. Then I remember that even a Fae and Druid can't last long beside a Dragon King."

"I feel so helpless."

"Each of us who doesn't have magic feels that way. It's our burden to bear. Our mates," she paused and smiled, "or the King we're with, carry the weight of keeping their world and all of us at Dreagan safe."

Claire walked past Jane to the double glass doors that led to the manicured area at the side of the house. "Because the Kings' enemies know they can't kill them. But they can hurt them through us."

"Exactly. It's been done time and again. The mates with magic feel the responsibility just like the Kings, so they do what they can."

"While we sit and wait. Powerless and vulnerable."

Jane came to stand beside her. She cut her eyes to Claire. "Powerless maybe. Vulnerable? Never."

Claire shifted to give her a troubled look. "And how do you propose to fight against a Fae or anyone with magic?"

"With my wits and whatever else I have at my disposal. I'm not alone. And neither are you. We have each other. The Kings who stayed behind might be preoccupied, but we stand together. Always."

Claire grinned at Jane. "Thanks for the reminder. It's easy to wallow in self-doubt."

"I have to give myself that talk often, so don't feel bad. I saw you watching Eilish and the others and realized that you might very well feel the worries each of us gets from time to time. You've just kept a smile on your face, which has fooled most of us."

"I don't want V to worry."

"He does. And he will. Just as you will. Be there for him. Even if he doesn't talk."

Jane gave Claire another smile before she walked off. Claire returned her gaze to the window. V was out there somewhere. No matter how many times she tried, she had yet to see him in his true form.

Frantic voices came from upstairs. Claire turned and looked, waiting to see who it was.

"How in the world did we run out? Between all of us?" a Scottish brogue asked.

Claire recognized the voice as Iona's.

Then came a British accent. "As if I have the answer."

A moment later, both Iona and Devon appeared. They spotted Claire at the same time and rushed to her when they reached the bottom.

"Claire," Devon said. "We're asking everyone if they have any pads, tampons, and the like."

Iona rolled her eyes. "Can you believe with all of us, we're still running low?"

"Sophie and I can grab some when we come back from the clinic tomorrow," Claire offered.

Devon wrinkled her nose. "I heard Anson say that might not happen."

"Oh." Once again, Claire felt left out. She shrugged. "I think I have a few with me."

Iona smiled gratefully. "That's great. When do you think you'll need them?"

"I should start on the fifteenth. I'm very regular," Claire told the women.

Devon frowned and shared a glance with Iona. "Today is the eighteenth."

Claire's mind went blank.

"What's going on?" Eilish asked as she came toward them.

Iona said, "We're running out of feminine products."

The Druid grinned and clicked the silver finger rings

on her hand together. Boxes of products appeared behind Devon and Iona. The two quickly grabbed up armfuls and went to dispense them.

It took Claire a minute to realize that Eilish was still there. Claire looked at the Irish beauty with her dark hair and green-gold eyes.

"You look troubled," Eilish commented.

Claire tried to shrug, but suddenly, the room was spinning, and her knees grew weak. Eilish was by her side immediately, holding her up.

"It's okay. You're okay. Let's sit you down."

Claire didn't know where the chair had come from, and she didn't care. She knew she was close to hyperventilating. "Wh-what day is it?"

"The eighteenth."

From the date of her first period, Claire had been as regular as clockwork. She always started on the fifteenth. Not once had she even been a day late.

"Claire? Look at me," Eilish called as she squatted before her. "Tell me what's going on. I can help."

"I think . . . I think I need a pregnancy test," she finally managed to get out.

Eilish grasped her hand. In the next breath, she and the Druid stood in V's bedroom.

"You need privacy," Eilish said by way of explanation. Then she held something out.

Claire saw the box but hesitated to take it. "I can't be pregnant. V told me that it's rare for a mortal to get pregnant."

"Rare, but not impossible," Eilish said in a soft voice and held out the box again. "You won't know until you take the test."

With shaking hands, Claire took the box and, with legs that felt wooden, walked into the bathroom. She took out the stick and did a quick read-through of the instructions. It was the first time in her life that she had ever taken a pregnancy test.

As she lowered her pants and sat on the toilet, Claire kept hearing V's words about how rare it was for a King to get a mortal with child. And how those who did lost the babe, or carried to term, only to birth a stillborn.

There was a knock on the door before Eilish said, "Claire? You've been in there for over five minutes. Is everything all right?"

Five minutes? She put the cap on the end of the stick and set it on the sink before she cleaned herself and stood to pull up her pants. Then she washed her hands, careful not to look at the stick to get any sort of answer to the question running through her head.

When she finished, she opened the door to Eilish. "It's there," she said, pointing behind her.

Eilish looked around her before green-gold eyes focused on Claire once more. "You didn't look?"

"I can't."

The Druid nodded and moved aside for Claire to walk out. Claire tried to sit on the sofa. Then she moved to the chairs. Finally, she gave up and paced. The longer Eilish remained silent, the more worried Claire became.

"Tell me I'm just late for the first time in my life," she begged Eilish.

The Druid walked out of the bathroom, holding the pregnancy test in her hand. "I can't do that."

Claire's legs gave out, and she crumpled to the floor. "Oh, God."

Eilish was beside her in an instant. "You're living in a magical place. Anything can happen. Forget what V told you."

Claire wished she could do that, but she couldn't. She

met the Druid's gaze. "How many others have lived here for much longer than I have? How many have become pregnant?"

"A lot. And none that I know of."

Emotion welled up, choking Claire. "I can't be pregnant. I-I can't!"

"You're going to be all right," Eilish said as she wrapped her arms around Claire.

"I'm going to fall in love with the baby just as I am with V. Then I'm going to lose it." The truth of it was like a knife right through Claire's heart.

Tears poured from her eyes before she could stop them. All she wanted was V, but she knew he had other duties at the moment. And she wouldn't tell him even if he were there. He didn't need her fears and anxieties on top of everything else he was dealing with.

Claire clung to Eilish as she gave in to the overwhelming tsunami of dread and panic within her. She didn't know when someone else came into her room or how long Sophie held her.

It was Eilish who told her the news, and it was Sophie who began to calm Claire down. It took some time, but the tears lessened, and Claire was finally able to breathe easier.

Sophie smiled as she wiped the tears from Claire's cheeks. "Do you want me to get V?"

"No," Claire said so loudly it was nearly a shout.

Eilish rubbed a hand along Claire's back. "No one is going to tell him but you. That's your decision."

Claire sniffed and looked between the two women. "Could the test be wrong?"

"No," Sophie replied. She cocked her head to Claire. "I've got my bag. Do you want me to give you a checkup and tell you how far along you are?"

Claire looked at the rug she sat on, the same one she and V had made love on. "I'm just a few weeks," she replied.

"Let Sophie have a look," Eilish said.

Claire let them help her to her feet. She removed her pants and lay on the bed while Sophie got her bag. As Claire looked at the ceiling, all she could think about was holding V's baby.

A bairn with ice blue eyes and dark hair.

Her thoughts skidded to a halt when V's words about them being different species came back to her. How were dragons born? She'd never thought to ask. That's when the tears came again.

CHAPTER FORTY-TWO

Not even a flight around Dreagan helped V anymore. After his patrol, he'd made his way into the mountain in search of Henry. He found the mortal in the cavern, looking at the map once more.

With still no sight of Rhi or Usaeil, Henry had made use of the map by returning to his original search for the Dark Fae. Then he incorporated the places where Usaeil might be in control. It was a good thought.

For as long as the Kings had been worried about what the Dark controlled, they hadn't realized how much power Usaeil was quietly gaining.

There were black pins all over Ireland now, denoting the towns that Henry and Ryder believed Usaeil controlled. The sheer number of them in relation to the red ones for the Dark Fae was staggering.

Henry turned his head to V. "Con could be anywhere. And I've not looked outside of Ireland yet."

With lines of strain on his unshaven face, the mortal looked as distressed and troubled about Con's disappearance as the rest of them.

"He isn't my king," Henry said, "but I consider Con a

friend. If you don't think I'm doing everything I can to help, you're wrong."

V briefly lowered his eyes to the ground. That's exactly what had been going through his mind. In reality, V just wanted someone to blame, and it was easy to point a finger at the human.

The Englishman snorted loudly, his face full of mocking anger. "I still haven't truly accepted my role as Justice-Bringer, but I even tried to use that power last night. That's when my sister reminded me that it only works on Druids. The one time I want it to work, it won't."

"You're doing a good job," V told Henry. Then he raked a gaze over Henry's haggard appearance. "When was the last time you slept?"

"I don't know. I lose track of time down here."

Ulrik walked in then. "It's been nearly forty-eight hours since you've taken a break, Henry. You're due."

V could tell it infuriated the mortal that he had to rest and sleep. Henry wanted to soldier on like the Kings, but the simple fact was that he couldn't.

"I'll rest for a couple of hours," Henry conceded indignantly as he strode out of the cavern.

V shook his head as he walked closer to the map. "I'm having a hard time believing that Usaeil is able to hold Con."

"Maybe he isna trying to get free."

V jerked his head to Ulrik, frowning. "I hadna considered that."

"I've fought Con. Twice. There is much about him no one knows. Especially the part where he doesna let all of his power loose."

Now that was a surprise. "Why no'?"

Ulrik shrugged. "You'd have to ask Con. I suspect it's because, in the back of his mind, he's always worried an enemy might come one day. Someone that can actually defeat him. Anyone who has studied us will believe that Con's power has a max. They'll learn differently at the right time."

"Like when Usaeil attacks."

"Just like that," Ulrik replied with a grin.

V drew in a deep breath and released it. "I still doona like it. And while I like your idea on things, I can no' help but wonder if Con is trapped."

"You mean like Roman was in Iceland."

V briefly closed his eyes and turned so his back was to the map and he could look directly at Ulrik. "You saw what the Others' magic did to him."

"We saved him."

"Barely."

Ulrik's lips flattened. "The Others are strong. I've never denied that. They tried to get to the Kings by using that wooden dragon. While it was brought to Dreagan, it didna have the consequences they wanted."

"We assume," V interjected.

"Then there is you. The Others altered your memories. You broke through their magic."

V couldn't take all the credit for that. "If it hadna been for Sabina and her brother, I wouldna have been able to do that."

"It doesna matter what began it. You're the one who discovered what to look for in order to rip through their magic. You did that."

"How is that going to help Con?"

Ulrik grinned. "No matter how cunning you think he is, he's much more. He's more astute, and defter than anyone realizes."

"Oh, I'm verra aware of all of that," V said with a snort.

Ulrik shook his head, his smile widening. "It's more

than you think. Con hides more than his feelings. He shows what he needs to those around him to secure his position. The rest, he keeps inside, waiting for the day he needs it."

V had thought he knew Con. It looked like there was much more to the King of Kings than he realized.

"Con told me his plan after he'd been King of Kings for a decade," Ulrik shared. "I laughed then because I honestly couldna imagine us having an enemy greater than our magic."

V shook his head. "Con could have taken all of us down during the war with the humans."

"Easily," Ulrik agreed. "But he didna. He knew there wasna a need. If there was ever a doubt that he's the right one to lead us, the answers have been there through the eons."

Which meant that they needed Con back at Dreagan. Soon. No matter what Ulrik said, V still wasn't convinced that Con allowed himself to be held.

"We need to talk to Rhi," V said.

Ulrik's lips twisted. "I'm still trying. She willna answer."

An idea ran through V's mind, one that made his stomach turn. "You said the darkness wanted Rhi. Could her association with Balladyn have brought it closer to her?"

"Maybe," Ulrik said with a shrug. "What are you thinking?"

"What if Rhi fell to it. What if she's working with Usaeil?"

Ulrik's head jerked back as if he'd been punched. "Never."

"Rhi has helped us time and again. Why would she turn away from us right when we are about to go after Usaeil? Why will she no' answer our calls?"

For long moments, Ulrik stared at him. Then, the King of Silvers ran a hand down his face and murmured, "Fuck."

The sound of boot heels clicking on stone announced someone's approach. V looked toward the entrance and spotted Eilish. She immediately smiled at him, but it was forced. And when she looked at Ulrik, V saw the fear and urgency in her gaze that she tried to keep hidden.

Ulrik held out his hand, and Eilish walked to him. They embraced. It made V think about Claire. He needed her touch. Needed to hold her and feel her heartbeat.

"You should take a break, as well," Ulrik told him. "Go see Claire."

It was the quick glance that Eilish shot him that made V feel as if something were wrong with Claire. V didn't say anything as he strode away in search of his woman.

He found her in their bedroom. V had stopped thinking of it as his after only a few days. Claire sat in the corner of the sofa, her legs tucked under her as she stared into the dark fireplace.

She looked as if she were lost deep in thought, her mind far from Dreagan. Concerned, V walked to the couch and sat beside her. As soon as he took her hand in his, he felt how cold it was.

"Vlad," she said when she turned her face to him.

"You're like ice." He started to rub her hands and arms to bring some warmth.

She watched him for a few moments. "I have something to tell you."

"What is it?" The words came easily, but he could tell by the tone of her voice and the way she wouldn't meet his gaze that what she had to say wouldn't be good.

All he could think of was that she wanted to leave Dreagan, that she could no longer handle the stress and fear.

And he couldn't blame her. He didn't want her to go, but he wouldn't stop her either.

Minutes went by without her saying anything.

"Claire?"

"I am cold," she suddenly said. "Will you hold me?"

He scooted back on the sofa and wrapped an arm around her. When she leaned against him, he brought his other arm up and held her securely. "Doona be afraid to say whatever it is you need."

"I've thought of a million different ways to tell you, but none of them seem right."

"Take your time. I'm no' going anywhere."

He closed his eyes when she gripped his shirt tightly. She was deeply upset, and he didn't like that. V wanted to know what bothered her so he could fix it and put a smile back on her face.

"I thought I could keep it to myself. I thought it would be the right thing to do so you could concentrate on everything else that's going on."

He kissed the top of her head. "I can handle whatever is on your mind."

Silence met his words. It lengthened until there was no doubt that she had changed her mind about telling him. He didn't push her to speak, though his mind raced with ideas of the kinds of things it could be—and none of them were good.

"I'm pregnant."

For a moment, his mind went blank. Then he thought of all the times he'd longed for children of his own. Desired to teach his hatchlings how to fly and fight and use magic.

V's thoughts came to a screeching halt when he remembered that Claire was human. She wasn't a dragon who laid eggs. Then he recalled the success rate of a dragon and mortal coupling.

V squeezed Claire tighter. He wasn't sure what to say. Would it be better for everyone if she lost the bairn sooner rather than later? He wasn't sure he could survive seeing his child stillborn.

They had only been together for a short time, which meant Claire wasn't that far along. How could he rejoice in the life growing inside her when he knew it wouldn't survive?

"Your silence is what I feared," Claire said.

V grasped her arms and shifted her away so he could look at her face. "I'm quiet because I'm no' sure what to say. I know this isna going to be easy for you."

"Or you." She put her hand on his cheek. "You wanted children, didn't you?"

"I've had other things to worry about."

"I'm sorry I'm not strong enough to give them to you."

At her words, he frowned. "Listen to me carefully. This has nothing to do with you. You are strong and brave enough to do anything. This is about two species who are incompatible. That's all."

"Maybe I'll be the one who changes things."

He smiled and pulled her back against him so she didn't see the remorse in his eyes. "Aye, sweetheart. You might verra well be."

They remained just as they were, silent and lost in their thoughts. V hated that it was Claire who would have to go through this. It had been a blessing so far that none of the other mates had gotten pregnant.

Losing a bairn—wanted or not—was a traumatizing experience. Every King and their women had each been through so much. It seemed unfair that this was piled on top of it all.

V rubbed his hand up and down Claire's back. "I will be here for you."

"I never doubted that." She swallowed. "I thought it might be better not to love this child since the odds are that I'll lose it. But . . . I'm not sure I can do that."

He squeezed his eyes closed to hold back the emotion. "Love our child with everything you have, as I will. We can do no less since it was love that created it."

Claire sat up. When he opened his eyes, he saw the tear streaks down her face. She dashed the droplets away and sniffed as she studied him.

"What did you just say?"

He inwardly grimaced. "Something I've wanted to tell you for some time. I'm in love with you, Claire. Surely, you know that."

The tears came again, dropping quickly to roll down her cheeks. V struggled to figure out how to take back his words or say something that would fix whatever he had messed up.

Then a smile pulled at her lips, causing his heart to skip a beat. There was no denying the joy that erupted on her face as she looked at him.

"You love me?"

"Verra much, lass."

She threw her arms around him and squeezed his neck. Then, she whispered in his ear, "I love you, too."

V sighed as peace once more filled him. That's when he knew that as long as he had Claire, he could do anything. Face any hardship.

Because of her love.

CHAPTER FORTY-THREE

He was going to have a child.

V halted his thoughts as he aimlessly walked the grounds the next morning. He couldn't allow himself to think that. There was little hope that the babe would survive the first few weeks. And if it did, the odds favored the baby being born dead.

Still, Claire was pregnant. With his child. A life grew inside her, made up of the two of them. No matter if the bairn survived or not, this moment was one of joy.

At least that was how V was going to look at it.

Because to think the worst would only bring pain to both himself and Claire. He would stay positive for her. Regardless of the outcome, he would never forget the moment she'd told him, never forget the absolute euphoria he felt.

If there were pain later, he would cross that bridge when he came to it. And carry Claire over it if that's what it took. He would shoulder any pain or torment for her.

He and Claire had spent a quiet night together. They didn't speak of what might or might not happen with the baby. Instead, they focused on their love. They laughed, they held each other, and they made love throughout the night.

But with the dawn came the realization that he had to be prepared for whatever happened next. Not just with the baby, but also with the upcoming encounter with Usaeil. Because it was just a matter of time before the queen came. Everyone knew it. And they were ready.

V's gaze moved to the sky. If a bairn were born that was half-human and half-dragon, would it be able to shift? Would it look human? Or would it be a mixture of both, forever unable to move in the mortal world?

He spotted Hal letting a dog loose to herd the sheep into another pasture. V made his way over to the black-haired King of Greens.

Hal glanced over and saw him, welcoming V with a smile. "The dog needed some exercise."

Besides Duke the Great Dane, Dreagan had two herding dogs for use with the sheep and cattle. There were also some cats wandering the grounds and the Dragonwood.

Hal's moonlight blue eyes glanced V's way. "I'd hoped that after finding your sword, you might have some quiet time to acclimate to this world we now live in. Having Con tell you about the advances every ten years is one thing. Experiencing it is another."

"Verra true," V agreed.

If it weren't for Con's trips to the Kings who slept, they would wake not knowing the world they had to become a part of. V hadn't always wanted Con's visits, but they were necessary.

Hal put his hand on the wood of the fence and watched the black and white Border Collie round up the sheep and move them into a nearby pasture. "It doesna feel right no' having Con here."

"It's the no' knowing what's going to happen that I doona like."

"The stillness before the battle. I always hated it."

V grinned as the dog finished with the sheep and then nosed the gate closed before he leapt over the fence and came running back to Hal with his tongue hanging out of his mouth.

"Good lad," Hal said as he bent over to pet the dog. Hal glanced up at V. "I saw Duke head into your room this morn."

"Just about every morning." V chuckled. "He jumps into the bed beside Claire as soon as I let him, and there's no use in me even trying to reclaim my spot."

Hal chuckled. "Duke has his favorites. I thought it was you for a while."

"So did I. Looks like Claire took my spot."

"Well?" Hal asked as he straightened.

V frowned at Hal's stare. When he looked down, the dog sat beside Hal, staring at V as well. "Well, what?"

"Is Claire your mate?"

V grinned. "Aye."

"It didna take you long to find her once you woke."

Of that, V was grateful. He cleared his throat. "Have any of the mates become pregnant?"

Hal thought about that for a moment before he shook his head. "None. At least that I know of. It's a blessing. I know I wouldna want to go through the loss."

"Aye. Too true."

"Doona get me wrong. I've often thought about creating a child with Cassie. She would be an amazing mother. But I've no' thought about any of them becoming pregnant in a long while. I used to worry about it a lot, though I never told Cassie. Why do you ask?"

V tried to come up with a response when Hal's eyes widened in shock.

"Ah, shite," Hal murmured. "Claire's with child, aye? I shouldna have said all those things. I'm sorry."

V lifted a shoulder and forced the bit of smile he could muster. "You didna say anything that I hadna already thought."

"Still, I should know better. What are you going to do?"

"What can we do? We sit and wait. And hope."

Hal ran a hand through his long, black hair. "Maybe things will be different now. Times have changed."

"Maybe." It was the same thing V had told himself.

But he knew it for the lie that it was.

Hal turned and looked at the manor. "I wonder if we should wait for Usaeil to make the first move. Perhaps we should go to the Light Castle."

"I like that idea," V said, a real smile pulling at his lips. "A lot, actually. Come on. Let's talk to Ulrik."

The two made their way into the mountain and found Ulrik right where V knew he would be—the cavern with the map. Ulrik turned his head from the diagram when they entered.

"We should go to the Light Castle," Hal said.

Ulrik frowned. V could see an argument forming, but then Ulrik paused. He chuckled softly and shook his head.

V grinned. "Exactly."

"The two of you go," Ulrik said. "See what you can find out."

V shared a grin with Hal. "We might get lucky and talk to Usaeil."

Hal nodded, his smile one of anticipation.

Ulrik removed his silver cuff and tossed it to V. "Take this. Just put your finger on it and think about where you want to go. You and Hal have to be touching for you to bring him with you."

V caught the bracelet and slipped it onto his wrist. "Doona come for us if we doona return."

"The hell we willna."

Hal shook his head. "V's right. You'll have your answer if we're detained."

Ulrik walked to stand before them, looking from one to the other with his steadfast gold gaze. "Let me make this perfectly clear. We're brothers. I'm no' going to leave Con, and I sure as hell willna leave the two of you."

"Aye," Hal murmured.

V nodded. "Doona tell Claire where I've gone. I doona want her to worry."

"In case you didna already know, that's a constant thing," Ulrik said with a laugh. When neither V nor Hal joined in, Ulrik's frown returned.

V licked his lips and sighed. "I suppose everyone will know soon, so I might as well tell you. Claire is carrying my child."

"I'll watch over her," Ulrik promised. "We all will. And Cassie, too. Now, go."

V held out his elbow to Hal. As soon as his friend had a hold of it, V thought of the Light Castle and touched the cuff. In the blink of an eye, they were outside in the middle of a thunderstorm.

Before them stood the tall, opulent white stone of the Light Castle. Even in the rain, it appeared as if nothing could dim it.

"Shall we go in?" Hal asked as he jerked his chin to the unmistakable giant double door entry that stood three hundred feet away.

V shook his head. "We willna have to wait long before we're paid a visit."

"You doona want to go in?"

"I do. But if I step foot inside the castle, I'll tear apart every room looking for Con."

Hal grunted. "Good point. I doona suppose we'll be lucky enough to have Usaeil pay us a visit."

No sooner had the words left his mouth than the doors to the castle opened, and a man walked out.

"Luck doesna favor us this day," V said.

Hal made a sound in the back of his throat. "It will when it matters."

The Light Fae ignored the rain that drenched his longish black hair as his silver eyes looked from Hal to V. "Dragon Kings don't visit us often."

Hal frowned, but V knew there was a chance that Con had come to the castle to see Usaeil. "And you are?" V asked.

"Inen. Captain of the Queen's Guard," the Fae pronounced in his Irish accent.

"And friend to Rhi," Hal added.

The Fae jerked his gaze to Hal, studying him for a long moment. "Rhi has been banished from the Light."

V crossed his arms over his chest while lightning flashed around them. "We know. We'd like to talk to Usaeil."

"That won't be possible."

"Because she willna see us?" Hal asked. "Or because she isna here?"

Inen's nostrils flared. "Pick one. You can't get into the castle."

V took a step closer to the Fae. "Rhi said you can be trusted. Even Balladyn agrees with that."

"Balladyn?" Inen asked, his black brows snapping together.

Hal nodded. "We worried that Rhi might no' be able to

put her faith in you, but the King of the Dark said that Rhi is good at determining someone's character."

Inen blew out a breath, spraying water as he did. He glanced to the side. "What do you want?"

"We want to know the last time you saw Usaeil," Hal demanded.

Inen shook his head. "A few weeks ago. She was here for a little while, and then she left again. I've not seen her since."

"And Con?" V pressed.

"The King of Dragon Kings?" Inen asked. "No, I've not seen him in many months."

V blinked the rain from his lashes. "What do you know of the Others?"

Inen lifted his shoulders in a shrug. "I've never heard of them."

"Are you sure?" Hal asked.

Inen nodded. "I am. Who are they?"

V hesitated for a moment, wondering how much to tell Inen. "That's what we're trying to figure out. The Fae are involved."

"The Dark are always involved with evil," Inen said, derision dripping from his words.

Hal grinned. "Interesting since we know that the Light are also a part of the Others."

Inen shook his head in denial. "That can't be possible."

"It is," V assured him. "Is there any way Usaeil could be mixed up with something like that?"

Inen's gaze fell to the ground as he shook his head. "There is much I'm discovering that shouldn't be possible but is. I wish I could tell you that Usaeil would never do something like that, but I can't. The simple truth is that I don't know."

"Which is answer enough," Hal said.

V dropped his arms as he caught Inen's gaze. "We know Usaeil is involved. You should hear it from Rhi, however. Watch yourself, Inen. Usaeil has plans that won't be in the best interest of the Light."

"Rhi told me to call the army," the Fae said. "She warned me to have them on my side to turn against Usaeil. I didn't listen to her."

Hal twisted his lips. "There's still time."

Inen let out a bark of laughter then. As V watched, the man vanished, replaced by none other than Usaeil herself.

The queen waved her hand, halting the rain. She stood dry beneath the sunlight as water dripped from V and Hal. This was a scenario that V should have been prepared for.

What he couldn't figure out was how he and Hal hadn't spotted that Usaeil was using glamour. It was a gift the Kings had, though somehow it hadn't worked this time.

"Oh, I do so love tricking you," Usaeil said as her silver eyes moved from one King to the other. "It's just so easy."

Hal glared at her, refusing to speak. V decided that was the best approach, as well. It was time they left. V shifted his arm, ready to grab Hal and teleport back to Dreagan, but then the queen's words stopped him.

"How does it feel to know a child grows in your woman's womb?"

V's heart dropped to his feet, and blood rushed loudly in his ears, drowning out everything for several moments. He didn't bother asking the Fae how she knew. The answer was all too obvious.

Usaeil smiled triumphantly, the glee in her eyes shining brightly. "I figured that to get near anyone at Dreagan, I just needed to pretend to be Rhi. I spoke with Claire at length. I was the one who urged her to go after you. And, I might have cast a spell to make sure your seed took root.

There's nothing like reminding the Kings what they're missing by mating with humans."

"I'm going to kill you," V stated.

Usaeil's smile vanished, and her eyes shifted and glittered red. "Better men than you have tried. If you want Claire to live, you'll make sure no Dragon King attacks this castle. And if you want to see Con again, you'll bring Rhi to me."

Fury consumed V. He shifted and readied to devour Usaeil in dragon fire. Except, in the next second, he was in a mountain—his mountain.

CHAPTER FORTY-FOUR

Claire stilled on the stairs when she heard the roar. There was no mistaking what it was. Without understanding how, she knew it was V.

The sound reverberated through her. She heard the fury and the hatred. Claire turned in a circle on the stairs, trying to determine where the roar had come from. It sounded distant.

V's mountain.

Claire rushed down the remaining steps and ran out the side entrance of the manor. Her gaze took in the range all around her. She knew the direction of V's mountain, but not which one.

All she knew was that she needed to get to him. No matter how long it took, even if she had to search every peak herself.

"I can take you to him."

She whirled around at the sound of the Irish accent to find Shara behind her. The beautiful Fae stood solemnly. Claire took in the thick stripe of white hair next to Shara's face. She didn't hide it but left the ribbon visible as a reminder of what she had once been. Of what she had willingly left behind.

Shara moved closer. "You knew it was V."

"I did, but I don't know how."

The Fae's smile was a little sad. "Being a mate to a Dragon King can be difficult at times."

Mate? Surely, Shara wasn't comparing Claire to herself? Claire wasn't a mate. Was she?

Her knees grew weak. Bloody hell. Maybe she was. V had said he loved her. A King didn't say those words lightly. Why hadn't Claire realized what it meant? Was it because she was so wrapped up in the fact that she was carrying his child? One that she might lose any day? Or was it one of a million other things?

Shara touched Claire's arm to get her attention. "Take a deep breath. You need to pull yourself together if you want to see him. The Kings brought V to his mountain instead of here for a reason. If V sees that you're upset, it will make things worse."

"Of course." Claire wished she could breathe evenly. Where was Sophie? She really wanted her best friend with her.

"There is much the Kings do and try to keep from us," Shara said as she dropped her arm to her side. "They think they're protecting us. I call it the horseshit that it is. But when something bad happens, like Con disappearing, they do what the Kings do best—close ranks and go in all-out protection mode."

Claire nodded in understanding. "Protection for us because we're here."

"Precisely." Shara's silver gaze briefly slid away. "At one time, some of the mates thought it might be better to leave for a bit, but we realized how futile that is. By loving a

Dragon King, we accept the good and the bad—and the bad is a hundred times worse than you expect."

Claire raised a brow as she looked Shara over. "Are you trying to talk me out of being with V? Do you believe I'm not up to the task of loving him?"

"I wasn't sure anyone had told you the risks involved with being here."

"Oh, I can handle the risks," Claire stated, resolve settling in her bones. She didn't like anyone questioning if she could manage things. "I've been in the thick of it with the Dark Fae, thank you very much. I've seen the Kings shift. I know exactly how deadly their enemies are, and that has never swayed me from befriending any of them. And as far as V is concerned, nothing will stop me from being with him. I love him."

Shara suddenly smiled. "I knew you were a fighter."

"What?" Claire blinked, taken aback.

The Fae chuckled softly. "I wasn't kidding earlier. You need to pull yourself together, and you weren't getting there quickly enough. I just gave you the nudge you needed."

Claire's mouth fell open.

"I'm sorry for that," Shara said with remorse. "I know the need that goes through you wanting to get to your mate, but I'm also very aware of how a King thinks and feels when he sees the woman he loves upset."

Claire shook her head as she licked her lips. "Don't apologize. I should be thanking you. I've not been thinking straight since I found out about the baby."

"Baby?"

The disbelief on Shara's face made Claire wince. "Bloody hell. I'm usually better at not blurting such things out."

"Claire . . . you're pregnant?"

Claire nodded. "Just found out."

A smile lit Shara's face. "That's amaz—" Her voice trailed off as the smile fell away.

"Yeah," Claire said. "You don't have to say it. V and I spoke at length."

Shara held out her hand. "Then you really need to get to V. Just remember, hold it together."

"What if he doesn't want me there?"

"A King always wants his mate. Trust me on that."

Claire nodded and grasped Shara's hand. She wasn't expecting the slight rush that moved through her from teleporting. It caused her to cringe, but she soon forgot about the sudden nausea when she found herself surrounded by darkness.

A moment later, a dozen or so small lights were shining from high above to shed soft light on the area. That's when she realized that she stood in a large cavern with beautiful formations of stalactites and stalagmites.

As soon as her gaze landed on the gigantic dragon standing in the center of the space, she forgot to breathe. She gasped in delight at the sight of the copper scales. The metallic sheen of them was as stunning as how the deep color faded to lighter on his belly.

Claire moved away from Shara and looked up. V stood still as stone, his ruby-colored eyes fastened on her. His large head dipped slightly, allowing her to get a better view of the horns that protruded from his temples and curled inward.

His nostrils flared as he drew in a breath. The sound was loud. Claire leaned to the side to see wings folded against his sides. Claire also caught the tip of his tail curled near him.

She returned her gaze to his face and smiled. "I feel like I've waited a lifetime to see you. I can't find the words to tell you how utterly magnificent you are."

Claire took a step back when V shifted into his human form. He stood naked, uncaring who was in the mountain with them. V's face was lined with anguish.

"What is it?" she asked.

He said nothing as he stalked to her and yanked her against him. Being enfolded in his arms was just what she needed. She closed her eyes and clung to him.

When he didn't answer, only held her tighter, Claire didn't push. Her mind raced with all sorts of possibilities for V's reaction, and they all came back to one thing—her.

Claire opened her eyes and looked around as best she could without moving her head. Out of the corner of her eye, she saw Shara standing to her right. On the left, Claire caught movement, but she didn't know who was there.

"I'm sorry, love," V whispered.

"Tell me you're all right," she told him. "I heard you. I heard the roar."

"I'm better now that you're in my arms."

V leaned back to look at her. He shook his head and then turned away, raking a hand through his long, dark locks. Claire didn't move as he stopped after a few steps with his back to her. She let her gaze run over the tattoo that covered his back and the backs of his arms.

Something flew through the air at him. V caught it without looking. That's when Claire realized it was a pair of jeans. He tugged them on, but it still took him a few moments before he faced her once more. He was deeply troubled, and that was nearly overshadowed by the fury he barely kept in check.

Claire looked to where the jeans had come from. She spotted Hal and Ulrik standing in silence. This only made her more anxious. The unknown churned in her stomach, and for a moment, she thought she might be sick.

Hal quickly looked away from her gaze. Ulrik, on the

other hand, gave her a nod as if silently telling her to get V to share whatever he was keeping locked inside him.

"V, you said last night that I could tell you anything. Now, I'm the one stating that," she told him.

He leaned his head back to look at the ceiling of the cavern. "I've spent the majority of my life right here in this part of my mountain. It was easy no' to think about the things I missed, like sharing moments with my brethren or just seeing the world, when I could focus on finding my sword. When I had my weapon, I once again pushed everything else aside to try and reclaim the power I had with it."

V turned his head to Ulrik and Hal. "I didna want to tell anyone that no' only could I no' call the dragons home, I couldna even use my sword to find them."

Claire's heart ached for V because he was admitting to those in the cavern what he had kept inside himself. She started to go to him but hesitated.

He pivoted to face her. "You caught my attention no' long after I returned to Dreagan. I saw you one day in the village. It was raining, but you didna care that you got wet. You jumped into a puddle with a toddler, and your laugh went right through me. After that, I searched for you every time I went into the village. Soon, I was there every day, hoping for a glimpse of you."

If she didn't already love him, she would after such a confession.

V blew out a breath. "Then we spent that day together. It was the best time I could remember having. I didna want it to end."

"Neither did I," she told him.

One side of his lips lifted in a smile. "You surprised me at the loch. I didna think you would get into the water."

Claire laughed softly. "I surprised myself."

"I knew then that I wanted you, needed you." His smile dropped. "I couldna resist the pull you had over me. If I had known. . . ."

She lifted her brows, waiting for him to continue. But he didn't. Claire took a step toward him. "If you had known what?"

V closed his eyes for a heartbeat. "If I had known what Usaeil planned, I never would have spoken to you."

"What did she plan?"

A muscle worked in V's jaw, but he didn't reply.

Claire moved to stand directly before him. "What did she plan?"

"She disguised herself as Rhi to talk with you at the spa."

Her heart began to pound erratically, unease racing down her spine. "For what purpose?"

"To get you and me together."

Claire's blood turned to ice. She knew she shouldn't ask, and yet, the words fell from her lips. "Why?"

"Because she put a spell on you to ensure that you would become pregnant."

Even though Claire had known the answer, hearing it made it real. She put her hand on her stomach and met V's ice blue gaze. Claire didn't know if the Fae's spell would ensure that the babe survived or died, but she couldn't think of that right now. She had to focus on her man.

She put her hands on V's bare chest. "I don't care who is responsible. We were meant to be together. I wouldn't change that for anything. No matter what happiness or sorrow comes our way, we will face it together."

"Och, lass," V murmured as he wrapped his arms around her. "I didna think it was possible to love you more than I already did, but I do."

"Does that mean I can help you kick Usaeil's ass?"

There was a chuckle behind her from one of the Kings, but there was no smile on V's face when he looked down at her. She put a hand on his cheek.

"I know," she told him. "Just make sure she pays for her crimes."

"Oh, she will." His eyes glittered with the promise of retribution.

CHAPTER FORTY-FIVE

V nodded at Claire to reassure her that he was fine before Shara returned the two of them to the manor. Once Claire was gone, V gave in to the rage once more. He clenched his fists, imagining wrapping his fingers around Usaeil's throat before he engulfed her in dragon fire. Her screams would be music to his ears.

She deserved it for all of her atrocities, but especially for putting Claire in the position to possibly lose a child.

"You know Usaeil could be lying," Ulrik stated.

Hal shook his head. "I disagree. The only way she could know about the pregnancy was if she put the spell in place."

V knew the heartbreak that most likely awaited him and Claire, and it was all because of Usaeil. If he hadn't hated the queen already, he certainly would now.

"Usaeil did exactly as she said," V replied. "She also has Con."

Ulrik's eyes narrowed. "She wants the Kings and the Fae to join together. How does she believe this fits into that plan? It's in direct opposition to it. All this will do is cause us to go to war."

"No' to mention her part with the Others," V pointed out.

"She has a plan. Of that I'm sure," Hal replied.

V nodded as he looked from Hal to Ulrik. "I agree. Usaeil does have a plan. Somehow in that twisted brain of hers, this is going to work in her favor."

"It shows how little she knows Con," Ulrik replied with a smug grin.

Hal's brows shot up on his forehead. "Con is likely to kill Usaeil before Rhi can even get close enough."

Ulrik's lips twisted. "Aye. That's verra true."

"The Light need to know who Usaeil really is."

Hal blew out a loud breath. "I'd hoped Inen would be the one to fill his people in. For all we know, he's dead."

"That means Rhi can no' trust that it was actually him she spoke to," V added.

Ulrik immediately shouted, "Rhi, I need you here immediately. It's about Usaeil and Inen!"

The three Kings looked at each other, waiting to see if the Fae would respond. She had been ignoring them for weeks now. Would this be the one thing that got her attention? V sincerely hoped so because if Usaeil managed to kill Rhi, whatever hope there was for the Light would die with her.

"This better fekking be good," came an Irish voice from behind V.

He whirled around and saw the Light standing with a hand on one hip, and her head cocked to the side.

"Well?" she pressed.

Ulrik sighed. "Where the hell have you been?"

"I came because you said this was about Inen. Tell me now, or I leave," Rhi threatened.

V glanced at his friends. "Hal and I went to the Light Castle."

Rhi gave him a look of utter disbelief. "Why in the world would you do that?"

"Because Con is missing," Hal told her. "We think Usaeil has him."

The Fae merely blinked at the news.

V tried not to let her silence or lack of outrage upset him. "Hal and I believed we were talking to Inen."

"Who I trust," Rhi added.

Ulrik made a sound in the back of his throat. "That might no' be wise."

Rhi's silver gaze swung to V. "Why?"

"Because Ulrik, Con, and I spoke to Balladyn."

At this news, Rhi's eyes widened. She dropped her arm to her side but said nothing.

"Balladyn said that you were good at picking your friends. He told us that if you trust Inen, so should we." V paused a moment to let that sink in. "Unfortunately, we told Inen this."

Rhi shrugged. "So? You can trust him."

"That's the thing. We can no'," Hal said.

V waited until Rhi's gaze was on him once more. Then he continued. "Before our eyes, Inen's shape disappeared to reveal Usaeil."

Rhi's nostrils flared. "The Kings can sense when a Fae uses glamour."

"No' this time," Hal replied.

Ulrik said, "There's more. V."

V wished with all his might that things had ended there with the queen. But they hadn't, and he wasn't going to let Usaeil win.

"A few weeks ago, Claire went to a spa. She ran across a woman with long, black hair and silver eyes. One who had a certain love for getting her nails done."

Rhi slowly shook her head, shock contorting her face.

V didn't stop. "She told Claire that her name was Rhi. She then urged Claire to go after what she wanted—me. It worked. I took Claire as my own that night. Now, Claire is with child."

"No," Rhi murmured.

V paused and drew in a deep breath. "Usaeil knew about the bairn when Hal and I spoke to her. She admitted to masquerading as you in the village to get close to Claire so she could put a spell on her to ensure that she got pregnant."

Rhi spun around, her hair whirling with her. Her fists were clenched, her shoulders tight with indignation, while resentment and anger rolled off her in waves. The Fae began to glow.

Ulrik hesitantly took a step toward Rhi. "We told you all of this knowing you might very well have such a reaction. But the truth is, we need you, Rhi. Your people need you."

"I should have gone after Ubitch months ago," Rhi said furiously. "Con talked me into waiting. I listened to him, and look what that has gotten everyone."

V winced when her glow got brighter. If Rhi didn't calm down, she could blow up the entire realm. V probably should have worded things better. Then again, there wasn't an easy way to sugarcoat anything when it involved Usaeil.

Suddenly, the glowing stopped. Rhi turned to face them. V wasn't the only one who saw the flash of red in her eyes before it disappeared. This was the darkness that had been mentioned.

"Rhi," Ulrik said. "It would be easy to give in to the darkness that calls to you right now. Your fury all but welcomes it."

"What would you have me do?" she asked. "Continue shopping and partying like none of this has happened?

Shall I get my nails done again? Or leave the realm and try to make a new life? Tell me how you dealt with the anger all those years, Ulrik, because I know the answer better than others."

V slid his gaze to Ulrik to find the King of Silvers flatten his lips and actually wince a little at Rhi's words. V was well aware that the only one who knew what Ulrik had gone through after being banished and unable to shift was Ulrik himself, but there were things Rhi might have seen that no one else had.

"Aye," Ulrik said with a nod. "You know I plotted Con's downfall. I wanted all the Kings to suffer as I had. I doona deny that. But this is different."

Rhi barked with laughter, but there was no mirth in the sound. "How is this different? Because you're on the other side?"

"Because this is no' just about the Dragon Kings. This is about the Fae—all Fae," Ulrik pointed out.

V then said, "For whatever reason, we believe Con is allowing himself to be held by Usaeil. He's waiting for the opportune time to strike."

"So you believe." Rhi lifted her chin. "I've tried to tell Con for a while now that Usaeil is more devious than he could ever imagine. He underestimated her. And all of you are doing the same."

"The Light will listen to you," Hal said.

Rhi snorted loudly and swung her head to him. "I know Usaeil well enough to know that she's told them all kinds of lies so they will turn on me. And there's no point in even thinking of using Balladyn or his army. The queen will be on to him."

"There's no keeping Balladyn from helping you," Ulrik told her.

Rhi walked to a smaller boulder and sat on it. "The

smart thing to do would be to call in allies so we can join forces. The Warriors, Druids, and even the Reapers, if they will help. Maybe the Dark will join in. But all of it will end in death. For everyone."

Hal started to talk, but Rhi spoke over him.

"How can any of you forget what happened with Dorian in New York? The black blade that put him in a state that he nearly couldn't come back from. Remember that? The Con you all know and have come to count on could be gone if Usaeil has found another such weapon."

V shook his head. "I doona believe that. It will take a lot more to bring Con to his knees."

"Really?" Rhi asked, a thin, black brow quirked. "And what do you think he would do for all of you?"

Ulrik turned on his heel and raked a hand through his hair. "Fuck."

Even Hal's gaze dropped to the ground.

V hated that he'd missed so many important things by sleeping through all those years. He knew that both Ulrik and Hal were thinking about how Con had let the love of his life go all those years ago. V might not have been there to witness Con with someone, but the fact that the King of Kings had let his love go was something V couldn't fathom.

And yet Con had done just that.

"He would die for each and every one of you," Rhi said into the silence that followed. "He would do it again and again and again if he knew it would save you."

V understood then. "This isna about Usaeil or the Fae. This is about the Others."

Rhi briefly met his gaze and swallowed loudly. "Yes."

"We know Usaeil is part of the group," Ulrik said. "We figured that out after Dorian's encounter in New York."

Hal asked, "What are we missing?"

Rhi held out her hand, palm up. A moment later, a tattered scroll appeared. She looked at them, waiting for someone to take it.

Finally, V walked to it. His touch was light as he took it from the Fae and returned to stand between Hal and Ulrik. He carefully unrolled it. Another moment passed as his magic worked to make sure he could translate the writing he didn't recognize.

It was one short page. A confession of sorts by a Light Fae. The name had been torn away at the bottom, but the Fae spoke about the group that Usaeil—who wasn't yet queen—put together on the Fae Realm after a visit from a group from another realm.

V rolled up the scroll and lowered it. "Where did you find this?"

Rhi glanced at the ground. "On the Fae Realm. I went back to the Light Castle there and searched the library. It's where I've been. I just found that."

"What other group is this person talking about?" V asked.

"It has to be the Druids who joined the Others," Hal said.

Ulrik shook his head. "Maybe. Maybe no'. What this does give us is definitive proof that Usaeil is responsible for putting the group together. It also lets us know that there are outside forces involved. For all we know, they're still involved."

"It also tells us that Usaeil has targeted the Kings from day one," V said. "Even before the Fae came to this realm."

Hal shrugged, his lips twisting. "For all we know, that's why the Fae came. For us."

Ulrik shook his head. "Wait. If Usaeil was part of those wanting to hurt us, why would she want Con as her own?"

"That's simple," Rhi said.

They all turned their gazes to the Light.

Rhi lifted one shoulder. "Usaeil has to be wanted. Con didn't want her. Then, he did. Usaeil thought she'd gotten what she desired."

"Only Con ended it," Hal said with a nod.

Rhi shot him a smile. "Bingo. Usaeil might have had one objective at the beginning, but make no mistake, she has changed that."

"I'm no' so sure," Ulrik said and looked at V.

V grunted. "There are things in place, as you well know, Rhi. Iceland."

"True," Rhi said as she crossed one leg over the other. "Usaeil could have forgotten about those, but I don't think so. I think it's more likely that she could not care less about any of you. She has her sights set on what she wants. And it's threefold."

Hal frowned. "Threefold?"

"She wants Rhi dead," Ulrik said.

V crossed his arms over his chest. "And she wants to be Con's mate."

"But, most of all," Rhi added, "she wants to reign over everyone and every*thing*."

Hal raised a brow. "That means she'll have to get rid of Balladyn, as well."

They all looked at one another.

It was Rhi who said, "That can't happen."

V cleared his throat. "There's something else you should know, Rhi. Usaeil has demanded you in exchange for Con."

The Fae laughed. "Well. Isn't that interesting. And not at all surprising."

V exchanged a look with Ulrik and Hal. He'd thought that would upset Rhi, but apparently, he'd been wrong.

Rhi got to her feet. "We don't have a lot of time to put a plan into action. It needs to start now. Usaeil won't wait long for you to bring me to her, and the longer Con is with her, the worse it'll be for him."

"Do you have any suggestions?" Hal asked.

She smiled. "I'm coming up with a plan. I'll be back."

CHAPTER FORTY-SIX

Claire wasn't all right. She was so far from all right that she didn't know which direction to turn. But she trusted V. She knew that he was doing everything he could.

But would it be enough?

She blew out a breath, thankful that Shara had left her alone. Claire needed some time to digest the new information, and she hadn't wanted to do it with an audience. By now, the entire manor most likely knew about her pregnancy. She knew there would be those who schooled their features not to look too happy or concerned—which only made the entire ordeal even worse.

However, knowing that it hadn't just been happenstance that Claire had become pregnant, that the Queen of the Light had instigated it, was just too much. The pitying looks everyone held back would surely be on full display.

Claire hadn't asked, but she wondered if the queen's involvement meant even more doom for her unborn babe. Or was there hope? Having magic involved with creating a child couldn't be good.

If it were that easy, the Kings would have done it long

ago. The fact that they hadn't pretty much answered most of the questions running through Claire's head.

She didn't know how long she stood in the bedroom alone, staring out the window, before V's arms wrapped around her. Neither of them said anything—because there wasn't anything to say. All they could do was wait and see what happened with the baby.

"I'm sorry," V murmured in her ear.

She turned in his arms and smiled up at him. It wasn't forced either. "There are ups and downs in any relationship. So ours might be a wee bit more complicated than that."

One side of his mouth lifted in a smile. "Just a wee bit?"

"Well, it is the Queen of the Light," Claire said. "I suppose I must give her a little more."

V searched Claire's gaze as he became serious. "This might be happening to us, but everyone at Dreagan is involved. Everyone stands with us."

"I know. And that does help." She wound her arms around his neck. "What happens now? War?"

"That has been inevitable for some time, unfortunately. There are mixed feelings about Con no' returning. Some think he's biding his time. Others think he might be in a position where he can no' get free."

With everything that Claire had learned of the Kings, it seemed impossible that Con was in a position he couldn't extract himself from to return to Dreagan. "What do you think?"

"I think he's waiting for the opportune time to strike at Usaeil. What better way to do it than by making her believe he is trapped? Then, when the attack happens, he'll strike from inside."

Claire had to admit, it sounded like a good plan. "Is there a chance that he truly is imprisoned?"

"Aye," V said and walked away to plop down on one of the chairs. "I hate to say it, but there is."

"And there's no way he would choose her over Dreagan?"

V shot her a look of disbelief. "Nay, lass. Never. He gave up the love of his life."

"Why did he do that?"

"I doona know the particulars, but knowing Con as I do, it had something to do with the rest of us. He's sacrificed everything for the Dragon Kings and Dreagan. There is nothing that Usaeil has that would make him choose her."

Claire raised an eyebrow and asked, "Nothing? Are you absolutely sure?"

V's face lined with worry. "I know that Con would do anything to protect us. If there is a chance that Usaeil has something planned against Dreagan that Con feels might fall in her favor, then aye, he would choose her. For us."

"That's what I thought. There could be any number of reasons that Con isn't back."

"Aye," V murmured worriedly.

She steadied herself. "So, what's the next move?"

"I doona know," he said with a shrug.

"You don't know?" Surely, that couldn't be what he'd said. Claire kneeled before him, leaning back on her haunches to put her hands on his knees as she looked into his blue gaze. "You're Dragon Kings. Didn't you tell me that no one on this realm has magic more powerful than you?"

V gave her an odd look. "I did, but there are the Oth—"

"I didn't ask about them. I'm talking about you. I'm talking about the Dragon Kings. This is your home. Someone has taken your leader. Would Con wait around for something to happen?"

V narrowed his gaze on her. "Woman, are you trying to get me to go to war?"

"I want you to do whatever it is you would do if I wasn't here. Don't think about me or the child within me."

"You ask the impossible."

She rose up on her knees. "V, you have to. This is bigger than the baby, me, or even us. This is about everything you and the other Kings have built. This is about a woman, a Fae, who has tricked and manipulated everyone to get what she wants. She has to be stopped. I'm going to be fine." She took his hand and put it on her stomach. "We're going to be fine. You go do what has to be done."

V's frown deepened. "Are you sure?"

"I'm not going to tell you that I won't be frightened or worry, but I am telling you that I came into this with my eyes wide open. You didn't become King of Coppers because you sat and waited for it. You became a Dragon King because you're the strongest of your clan."

He skimmed his knuckles down her face. "Damn, lass. I doona know whether to kiss you or throw you onto the bed."

"You can ravage me when you return victorious," Claire stated.

V cupped her face and gave her a slow kiss. She wanted to cling to him, to beg him to stay behind, but she wouldn't. She was enamored with the Dragon Kings because of their power and strength. It was what had first drawn her to V, and she wouldn't change him for anything.

"I'll be back after I talk to the others," he promised.

Claire kept her smile in place until the door closed behind him.

V strode into Dreagan Mountain and found Ulrik in the cavern just as he thought he would. Except Ulrik wasn't alone. Eilish was with him.

"Apologies," V said and started to leave.

Eilish hurriedly said, "Please, stay. I was just leaving."

V moved to the side as the Druid passed. Then he turned to Ulrik. "What's wrong?"

"Our mating ceremony is on hold until Con returns."

"Shite." V had forgotten all about that. Only the King of Kings could do the ritual. "I'm sorry."

Ulrik shrugged. "We both want Con returned and Usaeil out of the way. The fact that we know Usaeil is part of the Others will go a long way to bringing them down."

"We think. For all we know, there is more than one Light and Dark Fae involved."

"You have a point, but Usaeil will be a big one to remove."

"Without a doubt."

Ulrik drew in a deep breath. "You walked in here with a purpose. What's up?"

"Claire reminded me that I am a Dragon King."

"And?"

V grinned. "I think Rhi's been right all these months. We shouldna wait to go after Usaeil."

Ulrik paused before he said, "The queen will be expecting an attack."

"No' what I have planned."

Ulrik's face split into a smile. "I've been hoping someone else felt this way. I'm dying to go after that bitch. So is Rhi."

"Do you think we can get Rhi on board with us?"

"She's still no' happy with us, but I think our last conversation helped. It's too bad we didna come to this decision earlier. Hopefully, Rhi will respond when we call to her."

V looked toward the map, his gaze moving to Ireland. "Someone needs to tell Balladyn what has happened."

"I agree. He's dealt with us before. I think we should both go."

"When?"

"Soon," Ulrik said. He blew out a breath. "We need to update those at MacLeod Castle."

V hadn't spent much time with the Warriors and Druids, though he knew all about them. "Maybe Rhi will do it for us."

"I'm no' counting on Rhi doing anything right now other than showing up to kick Usaeil's ass."

A chuckle escaped before V could stop it. "We need to remind Rhi and anyone who gets close enough to the queen that we need to find out where Con is. She could have put him anywhere."

"You agree with Rhi, then? You think Usaeil might have used some kind of weapon on him?"

"That dagger is the root of evil, Ulrik. Who knows what else Usaeil has. And, right now, I think it would be wise to hedge all of our bets until Con has returned home."

Ulrik nodded and quickly shook his head. "I didna think I'd return to Dreagan only to step into Con's shoes. Regardless of what I wanted all those eons. In the back of my mind, I always knew that Con would win if we battled."

"I'm glad it never came to that."

The King of Silvers grunted in response. "Let's gather the others. Everyone—including the mates—need to be filled in on everything."

V nodded and turned on his heel to make his way to the manor. Between him and Ulrik, within thirty minutes, they had everyone in the main cavern of the mountain.

The atmosphere was subdued. Worry clouded the women's faces. V didn't miss how everyone shot covert looks at Claire, but his woman kept her head high and confidence in her step. He alone knew the fear that gripped her, but she hid it well.

Claire winked at V and tightened her fingers on his. Every moment, she proved that she was his match in every way. Her strength of will and character shouldn't surprise him, but it did. Lesser women would have crumbled under the weight of it all. Yet, she stood tall.

Claire bent, but she didn't break. It was a trait of the Kings, and one that all the mates had.

The whispered words drew to a hush when Ulrik climbed atop a boulder and looked out over the crowd. He looked down to his right where Eilish stood, smiling up at him with encouragement.

"I doona want to be up here," Ulrik said as he looked at them. "I'd much rather Con stand here and have this conversation. The fact that he's no' here is felt throughout Dreagan. Each of us is dealing with his absence in our own way.

"Some of you may have already heard that V and Hal took a quick trip to Ireland today. They went to see if they could get information on Usaeil and perhaps learn if Con was at the Light Castle. It didna quite go as planned.

"Some are hesitant to have the Dark Fae as allies. I understand since you have been fighting them for centuries. But this isna about the Kings and the Fae. The only reason the Dark are involved is because of Rhi. Balladyn, as King of the Dark, decides when and where his army fights. Everyone here knows of Balladyn's love for Rhi. He's going to stand with her against Usaeil for many reasons, but mostly because he cares for Rhi. I'm no' sayin̶ ̶̶ ̶̶ ̶̶the Dark. But we need them. More so now than ̶̶ ̶̶̶

Ulrik's chest expanded as he took a brea̶ Captain of the Queen's Guard, is someon̶ Balladyn agreed with her assessment. So, y̶ how thrilled Hal and V were when none other than Inen walked out of the Light Castle to meet them. They spoke of Rhi and how Balladyn had said that Rhi was good at picking those she could trust. Then they asked about Con."

V glanced at Claire, knowing what was coming, but she was holding strong.

Ulrik licked his lips. "We've known since Dorian was in New York that Usaeil is part of the Others. Sadly, we underestimated her. Because she used glamour to look like Inen in order to speak to V and Hal and was able to do it so that neither of them detected it. And that wasna the first time she has used such glamour. She recently did it in the village, as well, disguising herself as Rhi to speak to Claire. I wish I could say that Usaeil's plan ended there, but it didna. She spelled Claire to ensure that she would become pregnant with V's child."

The gasp that went through the room was like a shot in the night. V wanted to wrap his arm around Claire for protection. Then he looked at her. She didn't need it. At least not from those at Dreagan. She met his gaze and gave him a small smile.

The tightness in his chest lifted.

Then he recalled the part of Usaeil's talk that he hadn't shared with Claire.

"Usaeil has demanded that no King attack her castle in exchange for Claire's life," Ulrik said. "She's also insisted that Rhi be brought to her if we want to see Con again."

Rhys snorted loudly from the left side. "It's a great way for Rhi to attack."

"That's our thought, as well," Ulrik said. "I'm just waiting on Rhi to answer my call."

There was a shimmer in the air before Rhi appeared on left. "As if I'd miss such an opportunity."

"You've no' heard the plan," Ulrik said.

Rhi shrugged and glanced at V and Claire. "No one uses my face to deceive those I care about. I've made it known for some time that I am ready to go after Usaeil."

"We all are," Warrick said.

A cheer erupted in the cavern.

Ulrik held up his hand for quiet and looked at Rhi. "You understand that we have to make it appear that we're going to betray you."

Rhi smiled. "That'll be what makes this so much fun. I can't wait to see Usaeil's face when she thinks she's won, only to realize she's lost everything."

"How do we know this is Rhi?" Claire asked.

It was a fair question, one that should have been addressed the moment Rhi appeared.

"Con ensured that the queen can no' enter the manor," V explained. "Usaeil can no' enter any part of Dreagan."

Claire nodded as he spoke. "And what about the fact that she can use glamour without you knowing? Wouldn't that mean she can get past Con's magic?"

"Never," Ulrik said with a smile.

Rhi jumped from the boulder and walked to Claire. "I'm very sorry about what Usaeil did to you. It's beyond cruel. If it makes you feel better, someone here can ask me something that only I would know."

Roman's voice was the first to speak. "Who retrieved V's sword in Iceland?"

"Sabina," Rhi replied as she looked at the gypsy. "She was also the one who had to use it on you so that the Others' prophecy of V plunging it into you and thereby killing you wouldn't come to pass."

V met Claire's gaze. "It's Rhi. Only someone there to see all of that would know."

Claire's smile wasn't as easy as V had hoped

still bothered her. But he would wait to ask her about it since Ulrik wasn't finished.

"I called everyone together because this has to be a mutual decision," Ulrik said. "We're no' just going to find Con. We're taking down the Queen of the Light. We'll be fighting beside the Dark. I doona know yet if the Warriors and Druids will join us, but any allies will be welcome. If anyone objects to this, now is the time to speak up."

The silence was deafening and left all the Kings smiling in anticipation of what was to come. While others began asking specific questions, V maneuvered Claire so that they were off to the side by themselves.

"What is it?" he asked her.

She shrugged, her face crinkling with worry. "I'm sorry. Maybe it's because I was duped before, but I'm worried that isn't Rhi. What if it's been Usaeil all along?"

V was taken aback by the suggestion, mostly because it was a valid one. He looked toward Rhi, who spoke with Rhys and Thorn. Since V hadn't been around like some of the other Kings, he motioned for Roman to join him.

"What's wrong?" Roman asked.

V glanced at Claire. "Is there a possibility that Usaeil could have been masquerading as Rhi for weeks or months?"

Roman frowned, his gaze also going to Rhi. Then he shook his head as he returned his gaze to V. "Never. I've seen Rhi and Con interact too many times. It would've been obvious had Usaeil tried to be Rhi. The queen might pretend to be an actress, but she's no' that good."

Claire smiled then. "That's good to know."

Once Roman returned to Sabina, V raised his brows at Claire. "Are you truly convinced?"

"I probably won't be until Usaeil is gone for good."

"I doona blame you. Everyone will be keeping a close eye on Rhi just in case."

Claire gave him a quick kiss. "Watch your back, babe."

"Always," he promised.

But it was the fact that she'd used an endearment that had him grinning like a fool.

CHAPTER FORTY-SEVEN

It was weird how life could shift so drastically in such a short period. It had happened once before when Claire was unwillingly sucked into a world of dragons and Fae.

This time she had gone voluntarily, enthusiastically even. It was easy when Vlad looked at her with his ice blue eyes. She had seen them turn frosty for some, but when he gazed at her, they were always heated and full of desire.

They walked hand-in-hand from the cavern out of the large entrance he had taken her through the first time he brought her to Dreagan.

The future might be bleak, but Claire chose to look at it a different way. After years of searching for The One, of believing that she would never find the love she craved, of thinking that she would spend her life alone—V had walked into her life.

She'd not only found the man of her dreams, she'd also found love. The kind she had never given up on. The kind she knew she deserved.

There would be times of strain. She expected that being with a Dragon King. V had duties that would always come before her. She accepted that. And yet she knew without a doubt that he would always protect her.

She had a family at Dreagan. So many brothers and sisters that it boggled the mind. But at the same time, it seemed perfect and right.

Claire wasn't sure what she would tell her parents. She wasn't the only one at Dreagan who had living family, so she knew it was just a matter of deciding how to handle things for the short time her parents were still alive.

"You're smiling."

Claire looked at V and shrugged. "Of course I am. I have you."

"I come with a lot of baggage."

"Everyone does."

"Aye, lass, but mine isna the kind that stays in the past," he cautioned.

She stopped walking and faced him. "I know what it means to be with you. I know full well the dangers and the worry. But with it comes so much more. Your love and having each day with you. I'll take those and whatever comes with it willingly."

"Everything?" he asked and put his palm on her stomach.

She covered his hand with hers. "Everything. Usaeil claims this is her doing, but who's to say that it wasn't just Fate? Regardless of the how or why, we created life. I'm going to hold onto that—whatever may come."

"You continue to surprise me," V murmured with a seductive grin.

Claire bit her lip and looked up at him through her lashes. "I have a favor to ask."

"Name it."

"You don't even know what it is yet," she said with a laugh.

He shrugged, still smiling. "I'll give you anything you want."

"I want to see you again."

V blinked at her. "Is that all?"

"Can I see you fly? What about doing some magic? I don't care. I just want to see you."

"Gladly, love."

She could hardly contain her excitement when he took several steps back, never breaking eye contact with her. When he stood there without shifting, Claire started to worry.

It was the dark clouds gathering overhead that caught her attention. She looked over her shoulder and spotted Arian. The King winked at her before nodding to V.

"He needs cover," Arian explained.

Claire hadn't even thought of that. She noticed that others were watching them from the cavern. It had begun as a private moment, but she realized that the Kings and mates stood with her and V as family.

"You want to see magic?" V asked her. "I'll show you my power."

In the next blink, his body shifted into dozens of bats. Claire gasped in delight as they flew around her. She held out her arms, smiling in utter astonishment.

Then the bats came together again, and V stood before her in his dragon form. His ruby eyes studied her for a moment before he lay down.

Roman walked to Claire. "V's power is the ability to shield himself when he shifts. Humans see bats."

"Giving rise to the legend of Dracula," Claire said with a nod of understanding.

"He's waiting for you," Roman said.

Claire looked from Roman to V and back to Roman. "Waiting for what?"

"To take you flying."

Claire's gaze jerked to V. He wore the same look he had the night he'd taken her to the loch. She hadn't hesitated then, and she wouldn't now. She rushed to him as Roman instructed her on how to climb upon V's back.

Once seated, she realized that she didn't have anything to hold on to. Maybe this wasn't such a good idea. She could fall off and plummet to the ground. Then she realized how silly that was. V would never put her in a position where he couldn't protect her.

"I'm ready," she told him.

Claire glanced into the opening of the mountain. She spotted Sophie and Darius watching. Sophie waved, a bright smile on her face. It seemed like a lifetime ago that Claire was the one who'd watched her friend fall in love. Now, it was Sophie's turn. It was perfect that they had each found their own Dragon King.

V got to his feet and spread his wings. The gust of wind from that movement caused Claire's hair to fly into her face. She laughed, eager to be in the air. As if reading her mind, V leapt.

She clung to his scales, leaning low as her heart jumped to her throat. When she was brave enough to look down, she saw that the ground was moving farther away.

Claire raised her face and looked out before her as V glided over a mountain. Every movement he made was smooth. It didn't take her long to sit up and take in the full experience of riding atop a dragon.

The wind whipped around them, but V never took her too high. She gazed down at the many mountains and valleys. She'd known the Dragonwood was expansive, but she didn't fully comprehend it all until V flew over it.

The lochs, rivers, and waterfalls from this vantage point were spectacular. Claire tried to remember where each was to go back and visit them on foot, but there was just so much she wanted to see.

Soon, she realized that V had slowly begun to descend. He flew between two mountains, following a stream through a valley. Sheep scattered at the sight of them, bleating loudly—not that she could blame the poor animals.

Then, to her surprise, V flew upwards and landed upon the top of a mountain. As soon as he tucked in his wings, she climbed down from his back. She'd barely faced him before he returned to his human form. His very fine naked form.

"That was amazing," she told him, letting her gaze run over his gorgeous body. "All of it. From the bats to seeing you again to the ride."

He walked to her. "You can have that every day for eternity."

Claire's heart missed a beat. He'd spoken of his love, but he'd never said anything about forever before.

"I've known for a while that you are my mate," V said as he tucked a strand of her hair behind her ear. "I wanted to give you some time with us as a couple before I brought this up, but when I tried to come up with the perfect time, I couldna. This isna about the upcoming battle, Con missing, or the bairn. This is about my love for you, about wanting you by my side for eternity. If you need time to consi—"

She put her finger on his lips to silence him and shook her head. "Don't finish that thought. That was . . . perfect. I love you so much that I wonder how I went through life without you. My soul knew you instantly. I don't need time to consider anything. I've been yours from the moment I walked into the loch with you."

V pulled her against him and lowered his head to claim

her lips. The kiss began slow and sensual, but it quickly turned fiery.

"Can we go to your mountain?" Claire asked between kisses.

He chuckled. "Lass, you're standing on it."

"Take me inside," she urged him. "And make love to me."

His gaze heated with hunger as he held out his hand to her. "This is no longer my mountain. This is ours."

She didn't get a chance to respond before she found herself surrounded by darkness. A moment later, soft candlelight filled the area. Claire looked around at the cavern where V had spent countless millennia. There was a pile of blankets spread out, numerous pillows situated to the side, and so many candles that it boggled her mind.

Her gaze met V's. "We're going to have a fabulous life."

"We certainly are."

He walked her to the blankets and drew her into his arms. "Doona ever be afraid to tell me what you're feeling. I can no' help if I doona know what's going on in your mind."

"I promise to tell you everything. Don't ever keep me in the dark about what's going on with the Kings or if you leave on some special mission."

"I promise," he told her.

Claire grinned up at him. The smile stayed in place until his lips met hers, and he lowered her to the blankets.

EPILOGUE

The next day ...

Claire didn't hide her smile as she looked at the large clock over the mantel. Many of the women were in there with her, but it didn't matter where everyone was on Dreagan. Thanks to Kinsey, every mate and Dragon King was about to get a surprise.

"It's been a couple of days," Elena said with a frown. "I've gotten so used to having almost daily posts from the blog that it's odd not to have one. I love reading about her dates."

Claire caught Kinsey's gaze as the hour struck. She nodded at Kinsey. With one press of a button on Kinsey's mobile, everyone's phone, computer, and tablet at Dreagan switched to a hidden page on Claire's website.

She and Kinsey watched everyone reading. When Claire had written the words, she hadn't known how freeing it would feel to share such a secret with so many who had become friends and family.

It was a short message stating that she was the owner of the *(Mis)Adventures of a Dating Failure*, and that she wanted the others to know the truth.

One by one, the women looked at her, but Claire's gaze

was on Sophie. It felt like forever before Sophie looked up, shock covering her face.

"I should have told you," Claire said to her best friend. "I knew you would keep the secret, but it snowballed so quickly. And it was just so easy to pretend that it wasn't me."

Sophie tossed down her phone and rose to hurry to Claire. She enfolded Claire in a tight hug. "You don't owe me an explanation. And you did try to tell me it was you. I didn't believe you."

There was a moment of shared laughter through their tears. The others joined in, and soon, Claire was surrounded. Everyone wanted to know her worst date and if everything she wrote was true.

Claire looked between the wall of bodies to the doorway and spotted V leaning against it. They shared a smile. She'd thought that she had a good life before, but she hadn't realized how great things could be with the right man.

There was so much up in the air, most importantly what would happen to the life growing inside her. But she was going to take it one day at a time. Some days would be good, some bad. Today was a good one.

Who knew what tomorrow held. War was on their doorstep. Anything could happen, but she had faith in the Dragon Kings. Claire had faith in her man.

Magic had chosen every King at Dreagan. That power had seen the goodness in their hearts. It accounted for something. Especially when they stood against someone as evil as Usaeil.

They would win. Because there was no other option.

Rhi stood on the rocky bank and watched the ripples in the river as it drifted past her. She went through everything she remembered about her parents. They had been above reproach. There was nothing about her father that ever made Rhi think he was involved in anything nefarious.

And yet he had been.

His name had been on the stone wall in the mountain on Iceland. She wanted to deny it, to erase it from her thoughts, but she couldn't.

No doubt Usaeil would use that knowledge against her. Or try to. It was something that would have shocked Rhi and thrown her off her game. But she was prepared now. At least, she hoped she was.

Rhi thought about her visit from Death. For some reason, the Mistress of War believed that Rhi had what it took to take down Usaeil. She wasn't so sure, but if she let doubt take up residence within her, then Usaeil had already won.

Was it because of her father that Usaeil had made Rhi feel like a sister? Had her father known what the queen wanted? Rhi couldn't remember ever seeing the two of them alone, but that didn't mean it didn't happen.

She thought of her house on the Fae Realm. There was nothing left. If there were, she would go and search for something that linked her father to Usaeil and the Others.

His name on that wall had sealed his fate.

And hers.

Rhi would have to tell the Kings. Death already knew, which meant that the Reapers most likely did, as well.

"Rhi."

She sighed when she heard Balladyn call to her. She knew she would have to face him soon, but she wasn't quite ready. There was too much crowding her mind at present.

Usaeil had threatened the Kings with Claire's death if any of them attacked the Light Castle. Was it a bluff? Usaeil didn't care about the castle or those within it. So why use that threat?

And where did Ubitch have Con? More importantly, how had the imbecile allowed himself to be taken?

Rhi started laughing as the pieces fit together. "You wanker, Con," she said. "You knew Usaeil would come for you. You didn't know when or how, but you knew it would happen."

Based on the description of what Kellan had seen, Usaeil had surprised Con, coming up behind him just as he grabbed the pocket watch to return to Dreagan. Somehow, the queen had prevented Kellan from seeing anything more to do with Con, which was something that had never happened to the Keeper of History before.

It let Rhi know just how powerful Usaeil was. To be able to fool the Kings with glamour and keep Kellan from seeing Con took incredible amounts of magic.

Something Usaeil wouldn't be able to do on her own. She had help. And Rhi suspected that she knew exactly who was helping the queen—the Others. Or what was left of them.

"It won't be long now, Usaeil. I'm coming for you."

The Fae Realm

No one returned anymore. It was a reminder of what they'd once had.

And what had been lost.

Usaeil stared at the ruins of her once glorious castle. The one on Earth didn't compare. The Fae Realm might be uninhabitable, but there were plenty of others out there to establish another planet to reign from. It had to be some-place strategic if she were going to rule the universe.

"Always plotting."

Usaeil lifted her chin at the voice. She turned and met

the green eyes of the Empress of Druids. "Moreann. I don't like to be kept waiting."

The *mie* smiled smugly in reply. "Whatever you have to say had better be good. I don't like coming to this place."

Usaeil watched as the Druid looked around what was left of her realm with disdain. "Careful. You need me as much as I need you."

"So I do," Moreann said as she clasped her hands before her.

They stared at each other for a full minute before Usaeil said, "I have Con."

"You still want what you can't have."

"I can have him. And I will."

"He will be your downfall."

Usaeil barked a laugh. "You underestimate me. Just as he did."

"He's a Dragon King, Usaeil. He's part of those we want to be rid of."

"Oh, they will be dealt with. But I have plans for him. Imagine having someone as powerful as Constantine to do my bidding."

"*Our* bidding, you mean," Moreann corrected.

Usaeil smiled and nodded. "Of course."

"Is that all you've brought me here to say? What about Rhi? Have you brought her into the fold? We need her."

"I'm very close. I need a little more time," Usaeil lied.

It didn't matter what any of the Druids told her, Rhi would never be a part of the Others—or anything else. The Fae had caused enough trouble, and she would die a very painful death at Usaeil's hands.

Moreann's eyes narrowed on Usaeil. "Be quick, or I'll contact Rhiannon myself."

Usaeil waited until the Druid was gone before she said, "It's never going to happen. And soon, you'll bow to me. Just like everyone else.